Praise for *The Tourists*

"[An] ambitious and darkly contemporary first novel. . . . You don't need to draw the parallels with *The Great Gatsby*'s rootless socialites to hear the slither of snakes in the grass."

—Ariel Swartley, *Los Angeles Magazine*

"What Hobbs has really picked up from [Bret Easton] Ellis is his talent for authentic dialogue that has the crackle and rhythm of conversations at gallery openings and happy hours, boozy lunches and takeout dinners—the ambitious poses, casual undermining, not-so-casual chest puffing. . . . He captures the restlessness and ridiculousness of the sushi set's adult-onset angst with note-perfect acuity and a wry sense of humor."

—David Daley, *USA Today*

"*The Tourists* sketches, with a light touch, characters who are almost chillingly familiar. . . . They'll either make readers smile or bring back awful memories of the people they learned to put up with in college. Part of what's catching reviewers' eyes is a narrator who in the wrong hands would have been flat or dull but whose plight makes the book irresistible after the first few pages . . . [he] is appealingly quiet, reserved and observant."

—Scott Timberg, *Los Angeles Times*

"An impressive debut in which keen insights are often strewn amid the narrative like shiny pennies on a dirty sidewalk. . . . *The Tourists* strongly calls to mind the 'brat pack' novels of Ellis and Jay McInerney, with an undercurrent of *The Great Gatsby* as well, as updated to here and now, and sure to make sensitive readers worry about the future of this generation."

—Karen Campbell, *The Boston Globe*

"Watch your back, Dana Vachon. Two weeks after being crowned the literary darling of the moment . . . the *Mergers & Acquisitions* author is already in danger of being dethroned by the next big thing. Jeff Hobbs, author of *The Tourists,* has become L.A.'s latest lit darling."

—John Clarke, Jr., *Variety*

"At once witty and sincere, tender and brutal—and funny funny funny—Jeff Hobbs's *The Tourists* is an irresistible love story and marks the debut of a major new talent."

—Adam Davies, author of *The Frog King*

"In *The Tourists,* Jeff Hobbs introduces us to a world where educated and ambitious young Manhattanites compete for the ultimate souvenirs. It's a world where sexual power trumps intimacy, status counts for more than self-awareness—and achievement takes the place of accountability. This is an intriguing, unnerving novel, embedded with devastating secrets gradually revealed."

—Amanda Filipacchi, author of *Love Creeps*

"With a deft hand, Jeff Hobbs goes deep into the core of young New York, gracefully detailing the longings, hunger, and achingly realistic heartbreaks of a generation at loose ends. *The Tourists* is a captivating debut."

—Allison Lynn, author of *Now You See It*

"As they struggle through life in the city, these characters orbit success—and each other—dangerously. In *The Tourists,* Jeff Hobbs makes an auspicious debut, showing himself to be a smart and surprisingly seasoned hand."

—Ron Carlson, author of *A Kind of Flying*

THE
TOURISTS

JEFF HOBBS

SIMON & SCHUSTER PAPERBACKS

New York   London   Toronto   Sydney

SIMON & SCHUSTER PAPERBACKS
A Division of Simon & Schuster, Inc.
1230 Avenue of the Americas
New York, NY 10020

First Simon & Schuster trade paperback edition August 2008

SIMON & SCHUSTER PAPERBACKS and colophon
are registered trademarks of Simon & Schuster, Inc.

For information about special discounts for bulk purchases,
please contact Simon & Schuster Special Sales at
1-800-456-6798 or business@simonandschuster.com.

Designed by Dana Sloan

Manufactured in the United States of America

10   9   8   7   6   5   4   3   2   1

The Library of Congress has cataloged the hardcover edition as follows:

Hobbs, Jeff.
    The tourists / Jeff Hobbs.
        p. cm.
        1. Couples—Fiction. 2. Bisexual men—Fiction. 3. Manhattan
    (New York, N.Y.)—Fiction. 4. Domestic fiction. I. Title.
PS3608.O234T68 2007
813'.6—dc22   2006052269

ISBN-13: 978-0-7432-9095-1
ISBN-10:   0-7432-9095-X
ISBN-13: 978-0-7432-9096-8 (pbk)
ISBN-10:   0-7432-9096-8 (pbk)

To Bret Easton Ellis, for reading this more times than anyone should have to read anything, and for teaching me, with extraordinary patience, how to write—or at least how to try. I am and will remain in awe.

To be a tourist is to escape accountability. Errors and failings don't cling to you the way they do back home. You're able to drift across continents and languages, suspending the operations of sound thought.

—DON DELILLO
The Names

I

1

A MEMORY from eight years ago:

It's late spring, our junior year at Yale—a time when classes are getting easier and one lazy day starts following another until it seems as if winter never really existed—and about a hundred of us are sitting on a quad lawn where the drama division is performing scenes from *Love's Labour's Lost*. I'm with Ethan Hoevel and the girl who introduced us earlier this year, and we're all just hanging there taking in the calm, cool night before the parties start and things get out of hand.

The show drags on and the night air grows colder and we're wanting the thing to end so we can go on to the next thing, which is really all we ever want these days no matter where we are. And while an actor is crumpling under his heavy robes, his voice muffled by a white cotton beard, Ethan stops watching the play entirely and instead looks across the stage circle where David Taylor is sitting with Samona Ashley. We both know they're the new couple still in their beginning—that dreamlike space where they aren't yet daring each other to say the words that might actually have a consequence and instead can just laugh while touching each other's face or steal a kiss in public that still feels intimate and exciting—which is why it doesn't register with either of them that I've followed Ethan's gaze to David wrapping his arm behind her, his hand on the small of her back, or that I'm studying her face as she leans into his hand and rests her head on his shoulder and props her knee gently over his thigh.

My feelings for Samona Ashley don't penetrate the world they're in.

But still, as David takes her chin in his hand to kiss her, I can't help wondering how—on this night, in this moment—the dim light from a hundred dorm-room windows can give such an ethereal quality to their being together, and how it can illuminate so clearly their ignorance of all the awful things to come.

When Samona prolongs the kiss by clasping her hands on the back of his neck—her dark skin standing out sharply against his pale skin; her curly black hair intermingling with his straight auburn hair; her soft curves pressing his lean, angular limbs—I force myself to turn to Ethan and murmur something vague and meaningless about the incompetent stage direction.

But Ethan's not listening—he's still watching them with an unsettled gaze.

And even though I'm already aware that for Ethan Hoevel, just like for David Taylor and Samona Ashley, it's the beginning of something—Ethan will announce that he's gay two weeks after this night in the spring of our junior year—it will only be much later, after everything ends, when I'll be able to look back and imagine him visiting this moment often in his mind, always remembering this glimpse of David Taylor and Samona Ashley—two people he doesn't even know—as the beginning of something that he, Ethan, has ended.

Eight mostly uneventful years passed after the night on the quad, punctuated by four or five address changes, professional stasis, the beginnings and requisite endings of a few minor relationships, and—near the end—the onset of that lonely, latent kind of panic which accompanies the realization that you can no longer afford not to know where your life is heading.

And then it was mid-May in New York City: that fleeting window made up of no more than two or three weeks when everyone sheds their black coats in favor of bare skin, still winter-pale. The parks, cafés, boutiques, bars—all of them were humming with skin seeing its first true daylight in months. It was a good time to teach yourself to live again, to learn all over what it's like to walk on the street with your head up.

Which was why, when Ethan called around nine o'clock, I left my apartment on Tenth Street to go meet him.

The guy who lived one floor below mine was sitting on the stoop, smoking a cigarette, his Doberman pulling on a choke chain as I slipped by, hugging the railing. I headed west past the Second Avenue Deli and St. Mark's Church, where the benches composed the usual gathering of homeless people staking their claim for the night alongside yuppie couples sharing Starbucks fruit salad out of clear plastic containers. A massive woman with hair down to her waist, knotted and dusty, stood in the center of the triangle of benches on grotesquely swollen bare feet. She called out in a honeyed voice: "One man suckin' another man's dick and no one *knows* what's right," saying it over and over before I hurried out of earshot, crossing diagonally down Stuyvesant to Ninth Street and Third Avenue.

I stopped in a bookstore to browse new hardbacks I wanted but couldn't afford, and then on to Astor Place, trying not to stare as I walked around a cluster of spike-haired kids smoking cigarettes and dope, lounging around the big steel cube that sat in the center of the island, wearing T-shirts stained with crude-ironic slogans that I didn't understand. I turned down Lafayette, where the girls were already lining up behind a velvet rope for Wednesday-night karaoke at Pangea in hopes they looked enough like models to make it inside. I took Lafayette all the way down to Grand Street, where I turned west into SoHo, choosing my route more carefully now that I had to weave through couples window-shopping. I went south on West Broadway, hurrying past the chaos of Canal and into Tribeca with its way-past-their-prime rock clubs and new bistros that were never going to last. It was quieter down that way and I slowed my pace. The river was close and it was in the air: spring drifting fresh into the city from way up the Hudson where it was always cool.

I smoked half a cigarette outside Ethan's loft on Warren and Greenwich because I was still feeling a little tense since he called—he had that effect on me. Even the somber, folksy music coming down from the roof didn't help ease that tension.

The doorman got up from his *New York Post* (cover: BROOKLYN MAN DROWNS IN PROSPECT PARK TRAGEDY) to punch in the elevator code. Ethan had never given it to me; his way of keeping me at arm's length. The elevator took a full two minutes to reach the ninth floor while I watched the slanting shafts of light crawl down the wall inside the cage. Then the door creaked open into Ethan's loft, which tonight was lit red by a Japanese crepe-paper lamp that sat near a window.

It was the apartment that people in the city aspired to their whole lives: the entire ninth floor, long and wide, whitewashed hardwood, floor-to-ceiling windows looking down onto Warren Street, and filled with sleek furniture Ethan had designed himself. A faux-marble round pod—half bedroom, half design studio—occupied the center of the loft. Narrow walkways curved around either side of it past bookshelves and into a stainless-steel kitchen with a glass door refrigerator, inside of which a six-pack of Budweiser was waiting for me. I snatched two, moving around the stacks of cast-iron cookware from all over the world—mementos of his frequent traveling—and the exotic spice jars lined up behind the counter. Bay windows looked out over the river and beyond to Jersey City. In the far corner, a spiral staircase led to the roof. The door at the top was open and the music drifted toward me: Ani DiFranco in one of her less angry moods, which seemed okay for this kind of night.

Ethan had his feet up on the wall facing west over the river where the Hoboken ferry was making its way toward the Jersey City lights. A half-full bottle of Domaines Ott sat in his lap next to an empty wineglass, which he filled as I settled in the lounge chair beside him. Ethan was tall, dark, wire-thin, recalling a handsome and much less freakish incarnation of Joey Ramone. It was chilly but there was no wind, so he was only wearing an undershirt and shredded vintage Wranglers.

I pointed to five spotlights interweaving in the black sky above us. "What do you think those are?"

He gazed at the lights and feigned deep concentration before answering, "Either a movie premiere or the warning of another terrorist threat?"

"Moving in patterns . . . says . . . premiere?"

He shrugged and sipped his wine and took the cigarette I was offering. I lit it for him casually.

"Haven't heard from you in a while, Ethan."

"I've been busy." He stopped to pour another glass of rosé. He seemed to consider something before adding, "Very busy, in fact."

Then there was more silence until he started humming along with the Ani DiFranco song, which I recognized but couldn't name.

"Busy with work?" I finally asked.

"Not really—no more than usual."

"Traveling, then?"

He shook his head. "Haven't been wanting to go away for a while. Maybe sometime soon."

"Any . . . good parties, then?" I was flailing a bit.

"Parties." He sighed. "I'm over it." He started humming again until the song ended. "But you first. What's really going on with you?"

I took a drag to relax before telling him work was slow but steady and the apartment was a mess and I was really looking forward to summer—the usual—and I added that the last girl I'd allowed myself to get excited about, Amy, had found someone better—actually her ex-boyfriend named "Brian something"—and she'd said good-bye to me over the cell phone about two weeks before.

He nodded and gazed out over the water while I talked. And after I finished—without turning to me—he asked, "So how'd she say it?"

"Say what?"

"Good-bye."

"I think it was something like: 'I hope to catch up—take care.'" Ethan put his smoke out and lit another as I added, "It's one of the last things you hear from a person who never wants to see you again, right?"

"Definitely," he agreed, wincing. *"Take care."*

"It's so fucking despairing."

The word lingered as the disc changed to U2 and we just drank and took drags as "Where the Streets Have No Name" pulsed across the rooftop, and then we were nodding our heads to the music and didn't need to talk for a while because we'd both been in this place before—some random night, the two of us sitting alone, letting the music amplify the moment until all its small details seemed far-reaching.

Ethan tapped out the bass line on the armrest of my lounge, and I was studying his face in the dim cigarette glow while "I Still Haven't Found What I'm Looking For" faded in slowly. A light breeze swept through his hair, briefly lifting it away from his eyes. I realized that he hadn't looked at me tonight—not directly—and that his voice had been sounding so much softer and more distant than it usually did. I wondered why he'd called.

Leaning forward to open the other beer, I tried to hide the hesitancy in my voice as I asked, "So what's . . . going on . . . with you?"

"I'm sleeping with someone new," he said, seemingly offhand as he turned the music down and put out the half-finished cigarette. "Wait, is that what you're asking?"

"Anyone I know?"

"Actually, yeah. She is."

I took a swallow of beer. "She?"

He nodded. "A gorgeous girl. Just . . . really sort of . . . I don't know: she's gorgeous."

"*Gorgeous,*" I finally said. "That's so very poetic of you, Ethan."

"I guess you would know since you're the writer," he replied evenly, ignoring my sarcasm. "But what else can I say? She's gotten to me."

"Well, well, Ethan Hoevel's finally been had—and by a woman, no less." I forced a laugh. "How do I know her?"

"It's someone we went to college with."

He chose this moment to turn toward me, and I leaned away—that strange smirk etched onto his face made me anxious.

He locked his arms over his head. His spine cracked.

And a dull ache rose in my chest even before he said, "It's Samona."

I was remembering dark and flawless skin. I was flashing on deep brown eyes, almost black. I was hearing the echo of that alluring, sultry voice. It still haunted me.

"Samona Ashley," Ethan said.

"You mean Samona *Taylor,* right?" The words streamed out with an unintended urgency. "Because you're . . . you're aware that she's . . . married, right? And that you still have a boyfriend. Right, Ethan? You're aware of these facts?" I shook my head slowly.

He rolled his eyes, mocking me with his calmness. "How did I know you'd go there?"

"It just seems like . . . like there's a certain gravity here and—"

"Yes, but does the gravity have anything to do with the reasons you just stated?" He smiled suggestively while waiting for me to answer, but I could only keep shaking my head and sit deeper in the lounge chair. "Yeah, she's married," he went on quietly. "Yeah, I'm with Stanton. Yeah, it's wrong. But"—he turned away again—"only if you choose to see it that way."

"Is there any other way to see it?"

He sighed and opened another bottle of wine that was hidden in the corner by his feet. "Not for you, I guess."

The intro to "With or Without You" drifted into the background, and we both became quiet. I sipped my beer and gazed around us. To the north the Credit Suisse, Chrysler, and Empire State buildings stood in an evenly spaced trifecta. And though the roof used to be nestled in the shadow of the World Trade Center before it fell, Wall Street was still a sharp skyline. East was the Brooklyn Bridge and the dim neighborhoods beyond.

Then my beer was gone, and I took a deep breath.

"And does Samona know, Ethan, that you're—"

"A fag?" He cut me off.

"Well, I was going to say queer but . . . yeah." I paused. "Does she?"

He didn't answer.

I walked up the river toward Jane Street that night, and as I passed the Holland Tunnel, the roar of cars moving in and out of the city shook me with the realization that maybe by now—as I walked along the water alone—Samona was already in the lounge chair where I'd been sitting, and maybe she was whispering into Ethan's ear with that deep and sultry voice and maybe he was whispering things back to her, and maybe this whole thing had begun with that—a whisper.

There were so many questions that all of the answers seemed impossibly distant, and I didn't want to confront any of them.

Because Samona Ashley had shown me once that the ultimate rejection resided in the silence of watching her walk away.

Because even eight years of noise in New York City wasn't enough to purge that silence.

Because jealousy was as undeniable as it was destructive.

Back in my apartment, a deadline for an article was waiting: a vague, uninteresting piece I was writing up for *The Observer* about the redevelopment of a street on the Lower East Side, things everyone who read the *Times* or even the *Post* already knew. Meaning: I spent the following five days on hold with city officials or talking to Chinatown business owners in a language I didn't understand or having my computer crash on government Web sites. And since there was nothing to write anyway, I let myself be distracted by Ethan's far-flung eyes and the way he'd held his wineglass tight with all five fingers and the grating sound of his laughter and the moment he'd said her name so allusively.

When Ethan Hoevel screened me on his cell a week later, I stammered something like, "Hey, it's me . . . uh, I don't know, just calling . . . I'm . . . around . . . "

He didn't return the call, of course—all I got from Ethan was silence.

2

ETHAN DISAPPEARS after we graduate college. School has been hard for him. After coming out near the end of our junior year at a traditional Ivy League university complete with the Gothic architecture that hides exclusive secret societies (which is only to say that it isn't an easy place for anyone to come out—despite the large gay populace on campus and the generally liberal attitude), Ethan finds it especially stressful and needs to escape. So he graduates with honors—the only Spanish-language and mechanical-engineering double major our school has ever produced—and spends a year and a half teaching gym class to kids in small mountain villages in Peru.

The rest of us take the more conventional route. I bring my belongings home to the suburbs outside Baltimore and spend two weeks explaining to my father (a mid-level accountant) why I "lack the necessary programming for business school" while assuring my mother (fourth-grade teacher) that I "will give serious thought to the kind of girls I have relationships with." And while I'm being strategically bombarded by these two people (who got married in 1964, and who never left the suburbs) I can't help but feel wholly indifferent to the basic assumptions they cling to regarding my life experiences thus far; I've outgrown any feelings of guilt associated with all the things they don't know about me.

And while my father ruffles through the *Baltimore Sun* and my mother tries to misplace all my ripped jeans and black T-shirts, I streamline everything I have into a duffel bag and a backpack and board a train to Penn Station in Manhattan.

"You want to be a what?" my father asks as I purchase my ticket. "You want to be a *writer*?"

"No, not a *writer*," I reply brazenly. "A *journalist*. I just want to sit down with a pen and paper somewhere and figure out what intrigues me in this world."

I stay a few weeks with a girlfriend on the Upper East Side and very soon she isn't a girlfriend anymore and I find new places to live because that's what young people do in the city—that and find work. My first employment is as an associate editor three days a week for a duck-calling catalog. My career—if you can call it that—limps forward from there.

I don't think about Ethan. I push him out of my thoughts until he doesn't exist. And when you're twenty-three and twenty-four and making your way in New York, you don't think about anyone, really, except yourself, so forgetting people is an easy game. I also do not want any memories of him because they are too painful and I cannot afford the distraction.

In the end it isn't hard to do. His name is mentioned by various college friends, but as time goes on those friends become fewer. Meanwhile, moderate professional successes come and go: small bits in *The Observer, The Sun,* middling human-interest Web sites, a left-wing newsletter. I cover restaurant openings and book parties to pay the rent and do well enough to live in Brooklyn for a while ("Only six stops on the L!" I remind friends) and then—after graduating to movie premieres and celebrity charity events—a studio sublet in the East Village (sixth floor of a six-story walk-up, the stairs keeping me from the post-college weight all my friends are gaining).

Ultimately, as I drift through these motions, the defiant idealism that appalled my father so deeply at the train station morphs into a jadedly self-aware fading of ambition.

This happens in less than two years.

Nothing intrigues me.

*   *   *

When Ethan Hoevel and I finally cross paths again in November, two and a half years after graduation, it's one of those encounters that seem preordained.

An editor at *The Observer* who has a long-standing crush on me and has thrown a significant amount of paying work my way because of that crush, invites me to a Chelsea gallery opening filled with young and pretentious New Yorkers, and I know it will be painful and hard to endure—the usual—but because of the way the city works, I find myself in the position of not being able to say no to the editor at *The Observer* who is burdened with the crush.

Ethan sees me first. I am waiting at the bar for my fifth glass of wine.

"Things fall apart." The voice is behind me.

"The center cannot . . . hold?" I reply haltingly.

"Mere anarchy is loosed upon the world."

It is the preface to the one class we ever took together—Literature of Imperialism, fall semester, junior year. The first book we read was Achebe's *Things Fall Apart*. And since the class was filled with irritating students who liked listening to themselves talk, Ethan and I would sit alone in the back of the room, where he scribbled unflattering caricatures of our classmates. That was also the semester Ethan played bass in a rock band called the Amber Blues and wrote a song (which became a hit at campus parties) about a guy missing an arm and a leg, pining for the woman he would never get. *"It only takes one arm to hold you/but we have two hearts between you and me."* (I have no idea why I remember those lyrics as clearly as I do.)

I turn around. "Ethan Hoevel," I say, weaving a little from all the wine.

"I wasn't going to say hi," he says. "I was going to let you enjoy getting on with your life while I got on with mine."

"But you didn't."

"Only because I'm bored and alone."

"That sounds like a line of a pretty sad song, Ethan."

Automatically we're back to the gentle sarcasm that couched all our conversations at Yale.

"Don't you want to ask me what I do? Where I live? Why I'm at this ridiculous place?" he asks, staring straight at me.

"Not really."

He takes my arm and leads me to a small plastic cube on a pedestal in a corner. DRUGS, SEX, ROCK 'N' ROLL is its boldfaced title, *Ethan Hoevel Designs* in italics underneath. Inside the cube are three objects: a piece of plastic the shape and size of a credit card, one condom, and a pair of mini-headphones that looks like something a Secret Service agent would wear. I point to the plastic thing.

"It's a bowl," he says flatly.

"Like . . . for . . . ?"

"Pot."

"Oh."

"It fits in your wallet." Ethan shows me the small bulge running down the center that ends in a little concavity. "Somewhat clever." He shrugs. "Nothing brilliant."

"I guess the real question is: Will it sell?" I ask.

"Already has."

"How much?"

"I don't want to embarrass you."

I don't know it now (I don't know anything, really, during this time) but since Ethan returned from Peru he's been quickly gaining a name for himself in the design world. New York is always in search of the next big thing in any field and somehow Ethan has become one of the select few in his. The speed with which he attained this notoriety is impossible. He has lived in different villages in the Andes Mountains for two years and then—only six months later—he's making a down payment on a dream loft in Tribeca. People I knew didn't do that.

We leave the opening together. I tell the editor I'm feeling sick and don't think I can handle dinner but maybe sometime soon.

Ethan and I go to a bar in the meatpacking district and he buys. He savors a martini (he hasn't yet acquired his taste for wine) as he tells me that in Peru all he did was snort too much coke, which—it took him two years to realize—he could have been doing here.

"The moonshine snake brandy was kind of interesting, though."

"Moonshine what?"

"Actually, viper, to be more specific."

"Well, that sounds like it would be intriguing until you drink it."

"There's an actual dead viper fermenting inside the bottle. It's coiled up."

"Aren't vipers poisonous?"

"One bite can kill you." He shrugs. "Depends on the viper."

And then I can't help myself. A rush of feeling courses through me. I have not seen Ethan for two and a half years and I grip his forearm.

"Peru must have been so amazing, Ethan." Now that I'm fawning all over him, he stops talking about Peru but doesn't push my hand away. He lets it linger. Because of Ethan I get very drunk that night, even though he does not—he chooses not to. When he decides to stop buying drinks that means it's time to leave. He mutters something about wanting to take a walk. The only thing I'm feeling as we put our coats on (it's winter now) is a flood of admiration existing just on the fringes of envy, which I have yet to realize is what most people feel in the presence of Ethan Hoevel. He has these deeply probing eyes that seem to absorb and admire everything about a person, and I can't help feeling special and wanted. Yet through the haze of feeling special and wanted, it strikes me that he must treat everyone this way, and that, really, in the end, I am not that special, I am not so wanted. It becomes apparent how little I have to say.

My disappointment sobers me up slightly as we leave Pastis. Ethan says he's going to take a walk through the West Village to his new place in Tribeca. And then he asks me if I want to come. I pause briefly—thinking about things, sorting them out—and then say I do.

"What do you remember about me?" he asks as we start walking.

"Ethan," I warn.

"No. Seriously. What do you really remember about me?"

"You were in a band."

"What else?" he asks. "I'm curious."

"Now?"

"You remember about us? Right?"

"Yeah, Ethan, I remember about us." I say this with fake-heavy sarcasm but it comes out sounding wrong since I am so drunk. "Why are you asking me about that? It's in the past."

He studies me curiously for a moment before saying, "Forget it."

That he's just messing with me is obvious even through the haze.

He's having fun trying to make certain memories—the memories that seem dreamlike—all too real again.

The mood shifts and Ethan tells me I'm drunk and that it would be best for both of us if he sends me on my way. As he hails a cab I walk up to him, slurring my words. "Maybe I can help you, Ethan."

"How?"

"I mean with your work . . . maybe with my connections . . . I have a lot of them . . . I've been in the city awhile—I know how it all goes down."

"I'm sure you do," he murmurs, his arm raised, concentrating on the cabs coming down Ninth Avenue.

"I've had a lot of success with this, Ethan."

"That's really great," he says in a monotone.

A cab cuts across three lanes and pulls up to where we're standing.

"I think it's something you should consider . . . I'd be happy to help you . . ." Now I don't know where I am and I reach out to Ethan to steady myself. When I touch his arm I say genuinely, "And, yes, I do remember . . ."

Ethan opens the door for me. I climb in, mumbling my address. Ethan gives the driver a twenty and watches from the curb as we drive away, and a few minutes later I'm passed out in my bed.

When I wake up the next morning I start looking in my pocket for matches to light a cigarette. By the time I pull my hand out and his number is in it (when had he done that?), I've already figured it out. The one thing Ethan doesn't want or need is my help.

Which brings me inevitably to a second conclusion: Ethan wants something more.

Senior year at Yale Ethan becomes a myth. He locks himself in the mechanical-engineering lab up on a hill a mile away from campus to work on his senior project. Every month or so people glimpse him at meals and at the more notorious parties, dancing with guys, grinding it out to the hip-hop blasting from the wall of speakers before disappearing again, back to the lab. There are only rumors because no one knows what he is doing.

Except me.

I only see his senior project once: a single wing suspended in a glass vacuum, a confluence of art and physics. He calls me to come and visit him after he finishes it that April and I reluctantly agree to see him again after a year of barely seeing him at all. That walk up Science Hill is not easy—the steep incline, the icy spring weather, and the fear of being alone with Ethan in a contained space far away from the quads and dining halls filled with people. I linger in the cold outside the building for ten minutes, seriously thinking about turning around. He doesn't say anything when I walk in. He just switches on the machine.

Air flows through the vacuum at various speeds and angles, and the wing begins to oscillate according to predetermined graphs stacked on a table beside it, and it becomes clear that what Ethan has done—what he has spent almost a year of his life doing—is isolate one of the most beautiful and magical of worldly phenomena—flight—and strip away the beauty and the magic until there's nothing left but a form—black and smooth and shapeless—that he controls. A year of his life is inside this glass box, that dubious and uncertain final year of college. He has put himself in his claustrophobic lab surrounded by stacks of thick books about airplanes and birds and wind. The walls are covered with posters of jets and rockets, the Wright brothers, eagles, clouds, a map of the planets. He has created another world for himself.

I glance around the room, then back at the box. I don't know what to say.

When he sees my reaction he shoots me a disapproving look.

I am in the lab at the top of Science Hill for less than ten minutes.

Three months later Ethan Hoevel disappears into Peru.

When Ethan comes back to New York two years later—when he's just on the cusp of his wealth, his notoriety, his face in the magazines— what I know of him still lingers in that little room on Science Hill.

He is now a products designer—mostly chairs and living-room settings. It is something he has done in his "abundant free time in Peru"— creating forms in his mind that people could sit on—where he has been inspired by "the simplicity of the chairs and benches" (this is a quote from a feature on Ethan in *Dwell*). But there is nothing simple about Ethan's designs, which are embodied in the type of chairs you see in SoHo (*Interiority, Interiology, Format, King's Road Home*) and which you never think of buying because they're all so ungainly and abrasive and expensive.

The first piece I see of Ethan's—coincidentally in a Tribeca store window a few days after our encounter—is his most popular and lucrative: a gleaming silver aluminum sheet, maybe a few fingernails thick, that loops up and down like a breaking wave (which actually served as his inspiration; Ethan is from California and loves the ocean). It resembles an *h* in graceful script. My instinct is to consider it an eyesore—sci-fi pretentious, obtrusive even in the darkest corner, outrageously other. And yet, over the next year, almost every engineering design firm and computer tech company in the country (this is all happening at the height of the Internet boom) will fill their conference rooms with full sets. Spurred on by this success, he'll begin designing tables and lamps and sometimes entire rooms to match them. His more earthy designs—oranges and reds, plush cushions—will find their way into boutique clothing stores in Nolita and yuppie bars in midtown, in Madison Avenue salons and West Village restaurants and lounges in the Flatiron district.

He returns from the other side of the equator in the spring of 1999, and by the summer of 2000, it will be *Ethan Hoevel Designs* everywhere.

But to me, when I meet him at the gallery in November—where he's just part of a group show before his fame truly blossoms—and he gets me drunk and he puts me in that cab on Ninth Avenue, Ethan is still the guy I was afraid to visit on Science Hill.

The morning after, I'm staring at his phone number in my hand and realizing that for all his coolness the night before, Ethan Hoevel does, in fact, want something from me. The question he's asking me by slipping his number in my pocket is: Do I want something from him?

Later, still severely hungover, and leaning toward the dusty floor to pick up a spoon I dropped while stirring my instant coffee, I make a decision to call Ethan. He doesn't answer. A few weeks later, when he jokingly informs me that he was standing there listening to my halting, fumbling message—that he knew it was me and simply didn't pick up, that he was still keeping me at arm's length—I am once again outside that lab at the top of Science Hill in my navy blue winter coat, wondering if I should go in.

I try staying in touch but only sporadically. We are almost friends again but not quite. There is a new separation between us now. From various distances over the next few years I glimpse him walking into a bar or a nightclub or I pass him sitting with some hot guy in the corner booth of a new restaurant that I have to write up for *New York*. I find myself following the trajectory of his career in obscure magazines: the products' design that leads quickly to interiors, and then sets for music videos, and finally to art-directing a film for Miramax. His life flows on like someone's dream. He is seen and adored and he never has to look for work or invitations to parties or publicity or sex—it all finds him, which is an anomaly in a city where the vast majority of people spend the vast majority of their time hopelessly seeking all of those things. But this dream is not necessarily Ethan's. From my vantage point—that of a freelance writer who spends his days composing pitch letters to editors and arguing for bylines and jockeying for story space and waiting on hold for fact checks and hoping that I'll find someone, sometime—I know he's dreaming of something else, and that for Ethan everything that is so effortlessly offered to him is just the busy surface of pseudo celebrity (which is why he travels so often—to Costa Rica, to Mexico, to Iceland, to Japan, to all kinds of places, everywhere).

Ethan Hoevel has a deeper need, and I will come to know (and I still believe I am the only one who will ever truly know) that it is a need for something darker.

I know that what he really wants exists beyond the fame he's already promising himself that night at the gallery opening.

My favorite chair of Ethan's is the most simple: two identical sunset-red circles, one for the seat and one for the back, connected with a single L-shaped aluminum tube that turns down into a sleek spider-leg swivel. It is one of the few things Ethan designs that don't sell very well, and on my twenty-sixth birthday he gives me a pair for my writing desk and breakfast table—with the exception of a mattress, the only furniture I own.

3

AFTER THAT SPRING night on the rooftop where Ethan Hoevel mentioned Samona, it occurred to me on the long walk home that I had seen David Taylor, her husband of four years, back in the dead cold of January during one of our Yale track reunions—a sports bar in midtown, cheeseburgers, the Knicks losing on an overhead TV screen. Things were tough for me that winter. I hadn't been able to pay more than the minimum on my credit-card bill for the third month in a row and there was a widening gap between me and everyone surrounding me—and this disparity became especially noticeable sitting at a hardwood table with a group of ex-athletes in expensive suits concealing beer bellies, and scalps that were starting to shed hair but still managed to maintain a youthful color via $150 highlighting treatments at the Avon Salon in Trump Tower. I didn't hate them, or even dislike them, and it was easy to talk and laugh over shared memories. But hovering above all that was my particular insight that manifested itself like a hallucination:

It's seven years earlier and we're all running around an oval loop in our matching blue-and-white school-issued gear, and then—without us realizing it—this enclosed loop opens and people like David Taylor stay in one lane, and people like me wander.

And while I could barely afford a burger and a Corona at our reunion seven years later, David took care of the entire table by passing his credit card to our waitress on the way to the restroom.

*   *   *

In college David Taylor and I are both English majors who run the same event on the track team, so we find ourselves taking most of our classes together (in fact he's in that same Imperial Literature class with me and Ethan Hoevel) before jogging out to the track a mile from campus each afternoon. He is clean-cut and handsome, and when he first arrives on campus he automatically—amiably—goes out with Yale's best-looking girls. He's the kind of guy who calls you "pal" but in a way that isn't annoying. He's the kind of guy who shaves his pubic hair and tells his "buddies" how it makes him look "bigger" and everyone laughs, but he's also the kind of guy who then complains to me during our jogs that it really just itches a lot and scares potential hotties off.

In lit classes, he's never much of a writer, always opting to carelessly crank out his papers the night before they're due in his room on the top floor of the Sigma Alpha Epsilon house (junior year he's treasurer). "Ninety percent of what you learn in college happens *outside* the classroom" is an axiom that David Taylor likes to repeat often.

On the track, he's legendary throughout the Ivy League for winning the indoor eight-hundred-meter championship as a freshman, coming from behind in the final fifty meters to overtake the reigning senior champion from Princeton. But that victory becomes a weight on his shoulders: even though David Taylor is always in the top three, he will never win another championship. He doesn't have the body of a power runner—he's too lean and not particularly tall—but still, he's able to run like a steady and enduring machine. And since his speed and strength don't come from muscle, I always think they come from some intense and basic desire located deep inside of him to just *beat* the other guy—David Taylor seems to have that particular ambition. He leads every workout, and over hundreds of thousands of meters through four years of practice I lag behind him, watching his legs churn on and on and wishing mine could do the same.

Though David and I are always more than just casual acquaintances, we never approach true friendship. He's too pleasant, too mellow; success comes too easily to him.

When he starts dating Samona Ashley near the end of junior year, I push him away even more.

Then we graduate and take vastly different paths: while I drift into the poverty of the wandering, he signs on with Merrill Lynch directly in May of 1997 (the conception being that banks think highly of champion athletes, and he has that eight-hundred-meter victory very near the top of his résumé) and remains there for two years before moving on to a start-up hedge fund called The Leonard Company. He puts in ninety-hour workweeks, performs very well, and soon becomes the boring person we all knew he always was. At the track reunions he stops amusing us with mildly crude one-liners and instead starts talking about interest rates and the market and all the costs and benefits and risks that compose his life, which only serves to invite the question: What risks could there be for a guy who already has a six-figure salary, a luxury high-rise apartment, and Samona?

His answer to that question—and the only real risk he ever seems to take—is marrying Samona Ashley at the age of twenty-six. I read their announcement on the Weddings/Celebrations page in the *New York Times* Sunday Styles section and after thinking about it for a long time finally find the nerve to call David and offer my congratulations, but he never returns that call and I only hear about the ceremony from old teammates who'd been invited—a medium-size event in Darien, Connecticut, the sole memorable detail being that Samona engaged in a screaming fight with her mother at the garden reception, which then ended early. When the topic turns to how much David paid for Samona's Vera Wang dress ("not less than ten-five," a voice mutters), I tune out—it's still too painful for me to dwell there.

Later, whenever I mention the unreturned call, David Taylor will mime scratching his head and say it must have gotten lost in his voicemail box. We stop hanging out beyond the biannual track-team reunions, our excuses including his work schedule and marital obligations, and because I am broke most of the time:

I never admit the real reason to him, and it never becomes clear whether or not he knows.

Samona only comes up in our conversations unintentionally, and I invent ways to avoid the topic.

Whenever a mutual acquaintance asks me to describe David Taylor, I always answer in a noncommittal way: "He's a likable guy," and I can only say this because in a city like New York—where everyone has an angle, where everyone wants something from you or else they don't give a fuck—there's comfort in a guy like David Taylor. His lack of mysteriousness goes a long way.

Near the end of that dinner last January someone asked David Taylor how Samona was doing—like someone always did in order to segue into the obligatory "marrying too young" jabs—and David said that she was "really great"—like he always did in order to avoid them—and as I chugged my beer to ignore the conversation, he changed the subject by turning to me and asking how my writing career was going. After I told him that it had been a struggle lately finding work, David—in a graceful, offhand manner—threw out that The Leonard Company was issuing a new prospectus on their Web site for the next quarter and needed someone to write it, and that it wouldn't be much work but would pay well—probably better than any magazine. If I wanted the job, David would recommend me. It was pretty much a sure thing, he suggested.

A few days later, I almost called on his offer. I was in the middle of dialing the seven digits when I hung up—something stopped me from making the call to ask David Taylor for help.

And I never had to figure exactly what it was because of an unexpected windfall that came through in the form of covering February Fashion Week for *Maxim*. Ethan Hoevel had set it up with a single phone call. It was a week of running around to all the top shows, cataloging models and outfits, drinking too much, sleeping too little—and I felt uplifted by the silly distraction of it all. It was like coming back into the world after an exile—money in my pocket, the phone ringing, messages demanding my appearance, actual deadlines to meet. I even made out with a Tommy Hilfiger model at Spa (though when my hands reached for her pants, she mentioned something about a boyfriend). And I forgot about The Leonard Company and the morning I had almost called David Taylor.

But Ethan Hoevel's admission about Samona Ashley three months later changed that, because if the admission was in fact true, then I wanted to know more.

(Part of me assumed that this infatuation—the way I couldn't expunge certain images from my head—was all just journalistic impulse.)

(The rest of me, of course, knew better.)

And since I couldn't ask Ethan—for my own reasons, I couldn't trust him—and I couldn't ask Samona—I was afraid of what she'd make me feel—the only person left I could talk to was David Taylor.

And at the end of May, finally, I picked up the phone.

It was 4:45 in the afternoon, right after the market closed on a Thursday.

"Leonard Co," was how he answered. There were a multitude of phones ringing and throngs of people yelling in the background.

"Hey, David? It's—"

"Hey, pal." He cut me off sharply. I couldn't believe he recognized my voice.

"Did I catch you at a bad time?"

"Busy, just real busy," he said, sighing, distracted.

"It's really loud there," I said. "Thought you had your own office."

"Yeah, the door's open. Something tweaked in the ventilation system." He shouted out a garbled sentence at someone and then returned to me. "They're doing all these renovations on my floor and something got tweaked. What's up?"

I hadn't thought this out—he caught me. "I guess you need to get a fan." I could hear him typing and he sort of said "hmm" but not necessarily to me. "Would it be better if I called a little later?"

"No, it's okay," he said, and then added, "Just make it fast. What's up?"

"Well," I began hesitantly. "I was thinking back to January and how you might have been needing someone to write that prospectus for the Web site?"

"Oh . . . yeah. I mentioned that, didn't I?" Static interrupted him. "Wait—hold on a sec." He was still typing. "Okay. Sorry about that. Right, the prospectus. Yeah, wasn't that a while ago?"

"I never called. I got totally sidetracked but—"

"Hey, it's cool. I'm not sure what's going on with that now. Not exactly my thing." A pause, and it suddenly seemed quieter on the other end. "So . . . you're still interested? You want me to ask around again?"

Everything slowed down for me. This was why I hadn't called the last time—the tone of voice that seemed specifically engineered to remind me that David Taylor worked in a skyscraper in midtown while I barely worked at all. And it didn't even matter that I knew him well enough to assume it wasn't intentional—his condescension still translated so thickly through the phone that I almost told him his wife was having an affair.

"I'd really appreciate it, David," I said. "I really could use the work."

"It's not a problem," he said.

There was an awkward silence before I asked, "Is everything cool over there?"

"Fine," he replied. "I mean, work's a bitch, but I'm used to it."

"And . . . how are things on the . . . home front?"

The typing stopped.

"Fine," he said, deadpan. And then, "Do you need anything else?"

"Maybe we should grab lunch one of these days."

"Look, it's too busy here to talk now," he finally said. "No rest for the weary."

"Well, can we catch up?" I asked a little too fast. He breathed in—taken aback by my insistence—so I added, "You know how we can't really talk at the reunions and I just want to hear about how things are going with you, and how Samona's doing."

Someone, a woman, was talking to him. I could hear her voice sounding urgent in the background. But I could also tell that David had held up a finger, which was meant to quiet her, and then he said flatly, "Samona's great." There was another silence that we were both carefully attuned to, and then just as quickly snapped ourselves out of.

"Good. I'm really glad to hear it."

After a brief hesitation, David said, "Look, I've gotta run, pal. Someone's here."

"Okay. Sure." I was shaking.

"I can do lunch," David said. "But can you come up to midtown?"

"I don't know if I can afford it," I half joked.

A week later—a nice afternoon at the end of May—I put on an old linen suit and sandals and walked up Third Avenue through Murray Hill, past Grand Central up to Fifty-second Street. The restaurant was called Corotta, and though I had read about it I'd never been there because it was the kind of place where a tiny entrée cost forty dollars and afterward, when you had to find something to actually *eat*, you went to the nearest Wendy's and scarfed down a burger. I had walked fast and arrived early. The hostess led me to "Mr. Taylor's table" and a bottle of San Pellegrino materialized. The place was packed.

David was fifteen minutes late, but I didn't care until I saw another guy tagging along behind him. I was disappointed that a third person was joining us and I kept a fixed smile on my face as David introduced James Gutterson as a former all-Ivy hockey player from Cornell who, after a two-year MBA program at Hunter, was striding through the analyst sector at The Leonard Company. "Understand you were an athlete, too," was the first thing James Gutterson said to me, eyeing the sandals I then tucked out of sight beneath the table. He had a Canadian accent.

"Just track," I said.

James thought about it for a moment, then conceded, "Track's tough."

"Yeah," David snorted. "All. That. Running."

I stared at him, a little mystified. "I miss it, though, sometimes," I said.

"What's there to miss?"

The waiter came and David ordered a bottle of shiraz, which James tasted and approved. James stopped his pour at half a glass.

"I have to take it easy," he muttered. "Fucking busy up there."

David agreed. He only had a half glass as well. The rest of the bottle was apparently for me. And why not? Where was I going after lunch?

I was about to ask James if Cornell had ever won the Ivys but he just missed cutting me off by saying, "So David tells me you're interested in working for Leonard." His voice carried the heavy air of commitment, and then I understood why David had brought him.

"Maybe, like, freelance."

"We do that sometimes. But just for the Web site."

I tried paring things down to their most basic essentials: I'd spent the last seven years writing almost exclusively about parties with the occasional low-level city election or local opinion piece tossed in a few times a year. So: benefits, gallery shows, restaurant openings, and Fashion Week had sustained my career—I mean, right?—and by extension this little thing known as "my life." And if the feebleness of my accomplishments hadn't started to bother me until quite recently, then what was so shameful about a quick freelance job regarding leveraged buyouts and the market turning? When I compartmentalized my thoughts this way

(and ignored the fact that a big reason I'd chosen my particular career path in the first place was that I never wanted to set foot in a bank for fear of ending up like David Taylor and James Gutterson)

(and buried my certain ulterior motives to which David seemed oblivious)

then the job at Leonard didn't seem so bad.

I realized I had daydreamed off course and was awakened by James Gutterson clearing his throat.

"Mind if I peek at your résumé?"

It took me a second to realize he wasn't joking.

"I know, I know—bad manners during a meal but time is really tight and I just want to help figure out where you might fit in." James reached for the bread basket but scowled and changed his mind. "Corporate communications is kind of a big deal."

David was zoning out on the menu and I realized he wasn't going to help.

"Could I maybe give you an oral one?"

James sighed and offered a tight smile. He glanced over at David, who didn't look up from the menu. "Sure."

I started talking. It didn't really matter to any of us. We just surrendered to the reality of the moment. It was all so dull. The pieces on rent control seemed like they should have been impressive but they weren't and I knew it. I thought I had covered a few "important" events—the unveiling of the *Intrepid,* the tearing down of Columbus Circle for the new AOL Time Warner Center—but no one cared. We ordered lunch (no appetizers—no time). I kept talking. James's interest was waning while David was glancing around the room, recognizing a few people with a nod of the head. With no reluctance I threw out that I had also covered Fashion Week for *Maxim* and suddenly their interest in me was reactivated.

"Did you meet any models?" James asked.

"Sometimes. Yeah."

"You tap any ass?" he asked flatly.

"Actually, yeah," I lied.

I noticed David was frowning. I remembered that Samona Ashley had modeled for about a year after graduation, and his silence brought me back to the real reason I had asked David Taylor to have lunch with me: Ethan Hoevel was tapping Samona's ass. That thought came back in a rush and I poured myself another glass of wine while James went on about models for a while—suggesting he had slept with many though I could tell from the contempt in his voice he had slept with exactly none—and then the food came. I had forgotten that David never had anything particularly insightful to say and when he did say something it was obvious that he had thought about it too much—nothing ever just slipped out, which drained every sentence of spontaneity and guarded every observation with thinly veiled conde-scension. He spoke like a computer trading program.

"Are you married?" I asked James.

He shook his head and answered back with his mouth full and I couldn't understand what he said. He saw my quizzical expression and wiped his lips with a napkin, swallowing. "Nope—I still like to hate-fuck."

He winked at me. David was taking small bites of his little block of salmon.

There was nothing to say after that.

I had almost finished the wine and we all realized there was no rea-son for any of us to still be at Corotta—except, of course, for the secret one. And as I watched David take his careful bites while focusing on the afternoon ahead, even that started to seem like a shameless and cruel experiment. But I went with it anyway.

"How's Samona?" I finally asked him.

"She's great." He was staring at his food while he ate.

"I haven't seen her in a long time."

"We ought to get together," he said, but it sounded noncommittal.

James had finished his duck ravioli and was chugging water. He stared indifferently at the ass of a waitress who walked by. "Samona's hot," he said.

David put his fork down gently, making a statement but not too much noise. "Come on, James."

"You're too sensitive, Davey." James raised his eyebrows at me. "Don't you think Davey's too sensitive?"

Before I could answer David told me, "She opened a fashion print studio in SoHo a few months ago."

"That David Taylor funded," James pointed out.

David ignored the remark. "So she's running that now."

"Fashion printing, like . . ."

"Printing colors on fabrics for designers." David thought about it. "Basically. Yeah."

"Don't get too excited," James warned David. Then to me: "Davey made his wife write him a business proposal before he forked over the"— he turned his fingers into quotation marks—"necessary start capital."

David thought about something and slowly turned to James. "'Forked over'?" he asked, eliciting a groan. "You think it's bad practice for someone to write a business proposal? Especially a woman who has never run a business before?"

Before James Gutterson could tack on the words *But she's your wife,* I asked, "And how's it going?"

David paused thoughtfully again. "Well, it's not in the black yet. Maybe sometime late next quarter?"

"Economy's shit for small businesses," James said.

"Fashion's not exactly small business," I lamely argued.

"Samona's piece is," James said. "You know how many fashion print studios there are in this city?"

"A lot?"

"Three hundred and fifty-seven," David answered very quietly.

"And how many modeling agencies?" James pressed.

"Forty-two." David sighed. "We've been over this, Jimmy."

"It's called a niche market." This was directed at me, again with fingers as quotations.

I had finished the bottle of Shiraz. I was going to have to take a subway home. I was still hungry.

"Look, she's having a good time with it," David said. "She's doing fine."

That last part was the answer to my initial question. But when David felt like he had to add, *"We're* doing fine," in a voice that suggested the opposite, so many new questions arose. Then he turned back to James to address his earlier comment. "The proposal was just to get her thinking about it clearly. It was a road map."

"Well, she must know the turf pretty well." I offered this as a rebuke to Gutterson's lack of faith. "I mean she used to be a model, right? They know how the business works."

"She only modeled for a little bit." David was defensive and looking at me strangely now. "Not even a year." Then he put his fork down and regarded me very seriously before asking, "Did you know Samona well?"

And then I was mindlessly wiping my mouth and reeling to come up with some sort of nonanswer that would direct the conversation elsewhere, but Gutterson suddenly looked up from the dessert menu and blurted out, "David needed her back home for him. Davey needed someone to cook dinner or at least nuke leftovers." James put the dessert menu down and announced he wasn't going to get anything because he was watching his weight.

David sighed and agreed. I wanted another drink.

"How'd you hang on to her?" James asked while we waited for the bill. "I mean when you were working trading-floor hours and she was running around town with all those good-looking young guys?"

David was pulling out his credit card, motioning for me to put my wallet away. "What? I'm a senior citizen suddenly?"

"You know what I mean."

"Look, there was no competition. Most male models can't read let alone form a sentence. What did I have to be jealous of?"

There was a long pause. "Read? Who the hell *reads*?" James finally asked.

"People read books," I said. "People read the paper."

James ignored me. "You're so full of shit, Davey. You read the fucking *Wall Street Journal*. What did you talk about that was so interest-ing?" Even though James was just fooling around, there were under-currents of cruelty to his bland, baby-faced facade. "What made you so much more captivating than these male models that Samona of course had absolutely no interest in? Please, tell us."

David pondered this, leaning back in the chair, tipping the front two legs an inch off the ground. Dear God, I thought. You could roll a boulder through this place while waiting for a reply from David.

"We were in love," he said.

I couldn't help but add significance to his use of the past tense.

I stopped a waiter and asked for a Peroni. I hadn't eaten anything that day and the chicken breast I ordered had been about the size of my thumb and after a bottle of wine I was feeling light-headed.

"Most male models are gay anyway," I threw out.

"Yeah." David glanced at me as if we had a mutual understanding. "It's a . . . gay culture."

"Really gay," I stressed.

"Right," James said, smirking. "Not what I've heard, guys, but *whatever*." The waiter put a plate of biscotti on the table with my beer and the check, with instructions to pay for the beer at the bar. Both James and David were looking at me expectantly wondering why I had ordered it. As I finished the beer—and thought about ordering another—it occurred to me that David Taylor was simply not the kind of guy who would even consider his wife might be cheating on him, and as James cleaned up the biscotti plate and went on and on about how most male models are straight (he was right, of course) and ice hockey and how easy and simple everything had been back at Cor-nell, all I could do was stare across the table at David and think: He's a good guy with the slight flaw of being boring. David Taylor—com-placent as he was—did not deserve to be fucked over by Ethan Hoevel—a talented little fag who could get anybody he wanted. Suddenly I was overwhelmed by sadness and I was sorry I had called David and I was ashamed by it all: the expensive meal and the useless banter about the Web site and my measly résumé and hate-fucking and models—because beneath everything was the fact that David Taylor's wife was cheating on him with a former classmate of ours, and I felt as if I were the only person in the world who knew how sad and cruel Ethan Hoevel could really be.

When the bill came and David said he could expense it, James looked over his shoulder as he filled out the receipt.

"You gotta tip more than that, Dave."

"Pardon?"

"That's fifteen percent," James said. "You should leave at least eighteen."

"I come here all the time."

"In that case you should leave twenty. It's not your money. Plus it's good karma," James said grimly. "And God knows we need it."

David harshly scribbled an amount. "Eighteen percent. That's reasonable." And then, as he stood up from the table, "Karma my ass."

As we left the hostess called out, "Have a nice day."

I walked them to their office at the corner of Fifty-first Street and Seventh Avenue.

"Take care, buddy." James hit me lightly on the shoulder. "E-mail me that résumé. It's James-dot-Gutterson at Leonardco—one word—dot-com." And then, because we both knew the offer was probably no good, he simply walked away.

David stood with me as I lit a cigarette.

"You shouldn't smoke." David said this after I had already taken three drags.

"You're right." I didn't want the cigarette anyway—lighting it had been an automatic response to being drunk. I stubbed it out in the ash can next to us.

He looked at me in a curious way that was becoming increasingly familiar and said, "I'll tell Samona you said hi."

When David walked into the building on Fifty-first and Seventh Avenue, he turned back with a puzzled expression, like he had one more question, but then he changed his mind and navigated a series of revolving doors. I watched as he buzzed through security with his automatic employee key card. He turned back once more—again with puzzlement—before disappearing in the direction of the elevators. Then I walked toward Times Square looking for a McDonald's.

4

AFTER THAT LUNCH I pursued editors with rare diligence. I called contacts to bully my way into some bigger magazines—my noble and lofty ambitions including *Esquire* and *The New Yorker* and *Rolling Stone*. The Fashion Week piece in *Maxim* last February might have paid two months' rent but it failed to jump-start my career since it had ultimately been cut to shreds (it was all pseudo eye candy, cluttered and cheap-looking bullshit), and I blamed Ethan Hoevel for trying to salvage my little life by plunging me into that world for seven days. I had to force myself to believe that I had amassed an impressive collection of articles; I had to force myself to believe that they were worth sending out.

And I suppose the motivating factor for all this was the feeling of uselessness that gripped me as I awoke from my nap after that lunch at Corotta with David Taylor and James Gutterson, lying on my mattress staring up at the water-stained ceiling and asking myself what in the hell led me to set up a lunch with an old friend just to try to decipher whether he knew the same awful secret I did. I came up with an answer immediately: I didn't work enough.

(But that wasn't the real reason. The real reason I had set up that dull lunch in midtown was more complicated because it was tied to Ethan Hoevel and Samona Ashley. Their presence had hovered over that meal—in fact it had been more distinct than any of the men sitting at the table.)

I tried to push them all from my mind by latching onto a new article pitch that seemed to carry some weight: the pollution problems at the Gowanus Canal in Brooklyn. I had read a brief article about this in the *Times* that morning and it stayed with me: the situation was supposedly "dire" and the local population was "suffering" and kingdoms of rats were appearing "everywhere" and contaminated water seeped through the earth and was flooding the basements of housing projects along the northern rim of Brooklyn.

That same afternoon, in a rare and impulsive burst of activity, I took the L train out to the Gowanus Canal, but I couldn't concentrate. The rotting dock pilings, the pair of orange sneakers abandoned on the muddy banks, a broken fishing rod, a used condom—useless details were all I noticed, and they drew me back into the realization I'd been dodging all day: nothing I could write would change anything in Brooklyn. In fact, nothing I could do would ever change anything—it was that simple. And as I stared out over a large putrid stream of water flowing slowly past me, I knew that this included the tiny soap opera involving three people I knew in college.

As a writer, by nature, I was supposed to be attuned to people's lives. I was supposed to observe from the fringes, figure out what intrigued me (as I'd naively lectured my father once), then pull back in order to translate their little stories, find what was funny or hopeful or romantic or pathetic or sad, make them ring true enough to mean something, and then give them a title.

But the flaw that incapacitated me—it hit me now as a revelation, while I stood in a puddle of algae pulling the condom off my shoe with the fishing rod—was that New York hadn't taught me yet how to be alone. This was what kept me corralled in the purgatory of club openings and fashion shows: I spent all my time trying to get past the velvet rope and through the door, always angling closer—but closer to what?

What did it matter if I was concerned with David Taylor and Samona Ashley?

What did it matter if I'd been in love with a girl once, and the girl had walked away from me and forged her life with a guy I'd run track with in college?

What did it matter if that girl was now having an affair with Ethan Hoevel?

I couldn't change people—not the core of them. I could only listen. I could only watch. I was just another East Village burnout who drank too much and was approaching thirty and who just wanted to forget about everything and uphold a semblance of moving on in a jaded, hectic city.

After walking up and down the Gowanus Canal muttering to myself and lighting cigarettes in this state of mild self-loathing, I went back to Tenth Street.

I stared into my blank computer screen before deciding to clean my studio. This ended up taking only fifteen minutes. There were things under the bed—clumps of hair, a stack of change sticky with something—that I simply couldn't deal with. Disgusted, I went back to the computer and spent half an hour deleting old files: articles I had written years ago for defunct periodicals like *Golf-Pro* and *New York P.M.* I promised myself I'd start eating three meals a day. I promised myself I'd start working out again. I promised myself I'd drink less. I promised myself I would avoid three former classmates from Yale.

But then a voice announced, *"You've got mail!"*

```
From: David.Taylor@Leonardco.com
To: readyandwaiting@hotmail.com
Sent: Tuesday, May 27, 8:57 PM
Subject: Fwd: 15 Monkeys


hey pal, today was fun. sorry about james. i
thought he might be able to help. anyway here's
an invo for a cocktail party—you might want to
come. samona will be there. it would be good for
us all to catch up. regards, d.


6 PM Wednesday, June 2, at 988 Fifth Avenue,
Apartment 12D. Cocktails to celebrate the
purchase of N.W. Reinhardt's "Fifteen Monkeys."
RSVP to: rtor77@aol.com
====================================================
This message is for the sole use of the intended
recipient. If you received this message in error
```

please delete it and notify us. If this message
was misdirected, The Leonard Company does not
waive any confidentiality or privilege. The
Leonard Company retains and monitors electronic
communications sent through its network.
Instructions transmitted over this system are
not binding on The Leonard Company until they
are confirmed by us. Message transmission is not
guaranteed to be secure.

===

I wrote back the next day.

Thanks. Appreciate it. Maybe will see you there.

A reply came just a minute later.

you need to rsvp if you're gonna come. d.

I didn't write back.
People who wrote e-mails without capital letters irritated me.
Who was too busy to hit the shift button?

The following Tuesday afternoon—the day before the *Fifteen Monkeys*
party—Ethan returned my call from three weeks earlier. I'd been
waiting to hear from the Events Page editor at *New York* magazine
in response to the pitch letter I'd halfheartedly sent on the
Gowanus Canal, so I picked up the phone fast. I kept a landline
just for these calls because a 212 area code seemed more respect-
able and less desperate than the mobile alternative 917—a minor
illusion.

"Hey."

I recognized the voice immediately. "Ethan."

"You called?" he said and didn't wait for me to answer. "Want to
come to a gallery opening tomorrow night?"

"What's it for?" I asked tersely.

"Some interior design thing. I have to go for clients. I don't really want to go but it shouldn't be bad. Plus we should catch up. It's been too long."

"You didn't call me, Ethan. That's why it's been too long."

"Oh, stop it. You know I don't always call back right away."

"But that doesn't make it nice."

"Nice? Who has time for *nice*? I'm busy. Christ, I don't know why I even bother with you sometimes." He breathed in, then exhaled. "Look, you wanna come or not? We can meet after my class."

(For almost a year, Ethan had been teaching an industrial design class at the New School.)

"Will Stanton be there?" I regretted asking this right away.

Ethan paused. I could actually hear him smiling. "He might have something else going on that night."

"I guess you two aren't as attached as you were before," I said. "I mean, a few months ago you were giving each other—what? Three? Four nights a week? But I guess it's hard with the new girlfriend and all."

"Stanton might actually give you a call today," Ethan said, letting my comment fly into nothingness. "That was the other thing I wanted to tell you."

"I don't want a call from Stanton." I sighed. "Jesus, Ethan—"

"Do you want to hurt Stanton's feelings?" Ethan asked, genuinely interested.

"I didn't know he had feelings." I stopped, relented. "Look, I barely know him, Ethan. Why in the hell would Stanton be calling me?"

"His clothing line is starting a run in that new Urban Outfitters near you. He wants to check out the displays and I told him you'd probably be around."

"There's an Urban Outfitters in the East Village?" I muttered.

"I think you two should get to know each other better."

"I'm busy today."

Dead air floated across the wires.

"What are you doing, Ethan?" I suddenly asked. "You're trying to pawn your so-called boyfriend off on me because of Samona?"

The dead air kept coming but I could hear Ethan breathing and I couldn't tell whether he was amused or pissed off and then everything was interrupted by a beep. Someone was calling me.

"Look, Ethan, I've gotta go," I said in a rush. "I'm not hanging out with Stanton and I've got to take this call. Bye."

"I'm just saying it'd be nice if you went—"

I hung up before Ethan could say any more.

I screened the call thinking it actually might be Stanton, but it was the Events Page editor's assistant at *New York* magazine. She said they "enjoyed" the Gowanus pitch but "probably" wouldn't be able to "find space" for it in any of the fall issues, yet they were looking forward to "discussing" it next year. Meanwhile, I was thinking that if they'd even read the pitch letter, they'd know it would be entirely outdated by next month.

I decided after the message was left that screening calls was bad karma, and since Stanton wouldn't be calling my landline anyway, I answered the next call a half hour later, uselessly hoping it was the editor calling back because they had suddenly found space.

It was Stanton on his cell coming down Tenth Street.

"Ethan gave me your landline. Can I come up?" he asked. "You know I've never actually seen your place."

"I haven't cleaned it in a long time and it's pretty nasty."

"I like pretty nasty."

"I'll meet you on the street." I sighed, knowing that Stanton was the type who'd wait outside my building until I came out.

When I got outside, Stanton was up against the railing on the stoop. The Doberman from downstairs had its head buried in his crotch and was growling, and Stanton, of course, was laughing. The Doberman's owner was pulling on the leash as he said "Down boy" until Stanton started flirting with my neighbor, which caused my neighbor to yank the dog away. Expressions like the one on Stanton Vaughn's face were not the reason the guy from downstairs sat on the stoop with his dog all day—he liked people to lose their cool and suffer. And then it happened: the dog relented, wagging its stump of a tail and pawing at Stanton, who had, as usual, won the round— something else tamed.

*   *   *

Stanton Vaughn is his own cliché: the southern farm boy cut from the football team, the aspiring actor who becomes the successful model who drops out. Stanton Vaughn is the guy who finally hooks up with the right connection one night on a rooftop on Little West Twelfth Street.

That night occurs in the summer of 2002. By this time, Ethan has established himself as a set designer and he's now doing the set for a low-key fashion show on a rooftop in the meatpacking district. Stanton—just out of a brief modeling career—is freelancing as a stylist. Stanton knows who Ethan Hoevel is, as does most everyone in the industry at this point, and Stanton is not shy about seeking Ethan out and mentioning to him that he wants to "get into design." Stanton name-drops a few investors who have said they'd be interested in his work, and Ethan, who is bored and pissed off at the fashion show because this isn't the kind of work he does anymore—he's doing it as a favor for an ex-lover—just keeps nodding.

So it seems strange at first that Stanton ends up staying the night in Ethan's loft on Warren Street after this show.

And it seems even stranger when they soon commit themselves to a relationship.

Ethan will only confide in me later (after Stanton has essentially moved into the Warren Street loft) how it happens, how beneath all of Stanton Vaughn's self-absorption, Ethan Hoevel starts to see something that entertains him. For instance, Stanton Vaughn has spent time in China. Depressed about his failed acting career, Stanton headed back south, and through a chain of events too routine to recount here ended up singing backup vocals for Peggy Randall, a country-and-western singer on the northern leg of an ill-fated tour. Her big song— "Lookin' for a Woman to Love"—was the first country single about lesbianism and had become a cult hit with liberal college kids and fans of novelty songs. But among her intended audience, which is the audience that bought records, it only registered in one way: Peggy Randall was passionately loathed, then ignored. An executive at her record company decided to send Peggy Randall to China, where country labels were trying to break into that billion-plus market. Peggy Randall (and Stanton Vaughn) toured there for three weeks before being brought home, China proving to be as disinterested in her as Alabama and West Virginia and Tennessee and Kentucky had been.

And Ethan Hoevel has been wanting to go to China for a long time, but the logistics of going—embassies, tour groups, transportation—have always seemed too complicated for someone who prefers to travel on a whim.

When Stanton Vaughn tells Ethan this story the night they meet, the bored and pissed-off Ethan decides to take Stanton back to the loft in Tribeca overlooking the Hudson River, where, after a bottle of Domaines Ott, Ethan starts asking questions relating to China and then moves to obscure alt-country bands and British fashion designers from the sixties—all the right questions even though Stanton can answer none of them. But this lack of worldliness appeals to Ethan Hoevel, because he's so tired of all the fey, jaded fags he meets who only want to talk about their gym routine and the supplements they take and which movie star is in the closet and which club draws the hottest guys and how young is too young? Stanton Vaughn does not seem to be part of that circle Ethan has grown exhausted by, so things get serious very fast. The next week Ethan takes Stanton to Mexico with him. In late June of 2002, Stanton starts living in the loft and leaves traces of himself there in the slight touches of Japanese decor, the gold-leafed banana tree near the bay window, the coatrack laden with leather jackets. Ethan admits that he's officially "seeing" Stanton only after I keep pressing him about it. But Ethan, as he's telling me about his new "boy," is noticing how "uncomfortable" I am about "the situation" (even though I have never met Stanton) and my discomfort "bothers" him, so Ethan's resolution is as follows: Stanton and I will spend a day together, just the two of us—without Ethan.

So on a humid, wet afternoon in early August of that year, Stanton and I meet at the Second Avenue Deli, where he buys me a pastrami sandwich with money Ethan gave him for the occasion. I do not eat. We walk silently all the way west to the river, and he matches my pace while his hand keeps brushing my hip—that's how close he is—and then we stop for a soda at Chelsea Piers (Diet Coke for him, Dr Pepper for

me) and watch some boys play street hockey, and then back through
Chelsea (predictably, an unnerving array of guys on the street seem to
know him), where we end up seeing a Sean Penn movie at the
Clearview on Twenty-third, and where Stanton Vaughn keeps trying to
grip my thigh with a hand that I continually brush away until I have to
move to another row in the near empty theater. I am not sure if Stanton is genuinely interested in me or if it is a test Ethan wants to see me
pass—though I can't wrap my head around what the desired results are.
Either way—it isn't going to happen. After the movie Stanton tells me
he has his own place in the West Village and invites me over for a glass
of wine, but it's all so boring and prefab: the "wicked" grin, the distinctive "gleam" in his eyes, the alarming combination of hope and
desire he isn't trying to hide. I don't want Stanton, so we part ways. I
am too frazzled to even pick up the phone and call Ethan when I get
back to the apartment on Tenth Street.

When that afternoon has finally (thankfully) ended, I know the
following things: I know how Stanton Vaughn was cut as a sophomore
from the Clarksdale High School football team in the fall of 1993 (the
same season that Ethan and I enrolled at Yale). I know how he moved
toward his interest in hooking up with guys by entering the drama
division, where he ended up starring in the school's spring production
that year. I know that Stanton Vaughn played Lennie in *Of Mice and Men*
(a piece of casting that causes my mind to reel) and, emboldened by
the response, I know that Stanton moved forward: out of Clarksdale
and toward Little Rock and then Cleveland and then Chicago—acting
small parts in dinner theaters—and finally all the way to New York
City, where he hoped for the big break that would never come. I know
that his Mississippi drawl (which he had buried) manifested itself
whenever he cursed. I know how Stanton Vaughn fell into modeling—
he slept with the "right" connection. I know that, ultimately, Stanton
couldn't handle being a model because Stanton can't handle rejection.

The one thing I don't know: What does Ethan Hoevel see in him?

"You might have heard this already," Stanton says to me that
afternoon as we walk out of the movie theater. "But most male models don't do well. At least not for very long. It's a tough business."

Stanton's defending himself, trying to make me see that he isn't the user I think he is. He wants to make himself sympathetic. He wants me to buy Stanton Vaughn. I let him make the pitch:

Near the end of the modeling, Stanton was spending his days lugging a leather portfolio around on subways where all those fucking kids from the Bronx were screaming and fat women hogged up the available seats reading romance paperbacks and he'd wait in the lobbies of agencies with a bunch of other guys—all of them identical-looking—and there was always some kind of soft-core hip-hop shit playing in the background, Usher or Janet Jackson *everywhere,* and Stanton would give his portfolio to a girl just out of F.I.T. because her parents told her she had to vacate the Park Avenue apartment and *do* something with her life and the girl just out of F.I.T. would look at Stanton and (with a cute little squint) say, "I don't think you're right for this shoot," and Stanton would want to strangle the fuck out of her because he had just ridden all the way across town on the fucking subway and everything about the business was horrendous.

"Do you want to see my portfolio?" he asks me coyly, turning toward the Village. "It's in my apartment."

I vow silently that I am never moving through the doorway of Stanton Vaughn's apartment (even though, later, at one point, I will).

So I try to change the focus. I find that it's easy as long as it remains centered on him.

"But weren't you in the shows?"

Stanton liked the shows but after a month or two passed—and that's *if* you're doing well—there's always some scrawny stylist yelling at you because your shoulders are getting too big or you're eating too much sushi (carbs! carbs!) instead of sashimi and you've gotta stop lifting weights (Pilates! Pilates!) because you need to be leaner, but Stanton *had* to lift weights or else he felt soft and useless, and the money from shows really wasn't that good and it definitely didn't make up for all the hassle.

"Aren't you a stylist, too?" I ask once the tirade ends.

"I'm a designer."

(Which reminds me how after Ethan decided to get involved with Stanton Vaughn that June, he then launched Stanton's career as a designer almost instantaneously, setting him up with a publicist and a few key investors and getting the word of mouth rolling, which is all a moderately talented, sporadically inspired person like Stanton Vaughn needs to get started.)

"But you were styling, right? When Ethan found you?" I mention his name for the first time that day.

"When we found each *other*." He winces.

"I don't want to get into semantics with you but Ethan got it all started, right?" I haven't learned yet that the only way to deal with Stanton Vaughn is to retreat.

He stops dead on the corner of Twenty-first Street and Eighth Avenue. He points a finger at me. His eyes frighten me.

"I'm a designer, okay? Ethan was there because he's my partner. But I am the source. AKA: the creative drive? Get it?"

I put up my hands. "Got it."

It hit Stanton one day that the money was never going to be that good for him walking the ramps in shows (the real money was in catalogs, and Stanton Vaughn didn't have that "paternal vibe" that the catalogs liked) and that even if he did pursue it, all of it would soon be gone anyway because there were armies of other guys—younger, fresher, better-looking—waiting to replace him and it hit Stanton (he was filling in at the last moment for a no-show at Calvin Klein) that it wasn't the guy walking the runway that was making the real money (a few hundred bucks upped to a measly thousand during Fashion Week—*come on*) but it was the guy who designed the clothes who made a killing. Stanton had been looking in the wrong direction. Stanton decided then—for longevity's sake—he needed to design.

He doesn't have Ethan's talent. But he has something almost as powerful—an intimidating and forceful rage. In fact it underlines every word he speaks. Maybe it comes from growing up in the rural South with the ubiquitous cheating and abusive failure of a father and the mother addicted to forgiveness, both of whom Stanton left behind all those years ago. Or maybe this rage materialized when he arrived in Manhattan, with all its concrete surfaces and sharp corners that were so tough to navigate. But it is the rage of Stanton Vaughn that will fuel his success, enabling him to bully his way into advertisements, investors, showcases. He pours rage into his designs. He pours it into his relationship with Ethan (who reveals to me a few nights later that Stanton Vaughn is the best sex he's ever had with a man; "Don't underestimate the power of hate-fucking," Ethan says in the same awful and hypnotized drawl that James Gutterson will use at the lunch at Corotta).

To his credit—as much as I don't want to go here—Stanton is beautiful. He has all the prerequisites: tall and big-shouldered with a boyish waist and thick shaggy hair that sweeps across a nicely chiseled all-American face. He insists on blaming his failure in modeling on the fact that his shoulders are too big. But he persists in admitting that, in the end, it all worked out. "Without these shoulders I'd still be on the L train with my portfolio." I try to decipher this sentence—knowing that in Stanton's head it makes perfect sense—as we pass the restaurant where Ethan got me drunk the night I met him after he returned from Peru.

"You want to see my portfolio?" he asks again.

My afternoon alone with Stanton Vaughn ends with the dripping suggestion of those words. And as I try to erase it from my mind on the way home, I never once consider the possibility that he will still be in Ethan's life—let alone calling me on the telephone to hang out at Urban Outfitters—two years later in the summer of 2004.

In front of Urban Outfitters Stanton was staring unhappily at the display window. There were three racks—shirts, pants, and sport coats (Stanton designed what he liked to call "Boi-Wear," which was reflected in his logo: a lean muscled chest with conspicuous nipples). The shirts were the most distinctive—a weird blend of retro-punk with a smattering of Egyptian symbols, what Stanton referred to as urban-*sheik*. This line sold far better than the more upscale one he designed—suits in monochromatic blacks and browns and grays, and generally not much different from what you would find at Club Monaco or Banana Republic, just more expensive. Stanton had already shouted at a teenage cashier to "fetch" the manager and another tirade began once the boy scampered away. Oh fuck—Stanton should have known that a fucking Urban Outfitters in the fucking East Village—of all fucking places—wasn't going to do it right. How fucking hard is it to display clothes on a fucking rack? All it takes is a little fucking common sense. Urban Outfitters was so fucked up (as were Barneys and Bloomingdale's apparently) and Stanton should have never agreed to distribute there. He had let his sponsors talk him into getting the momentum going for Fall Fashion Week. But that's why he wanted me: I was the witness to this catastrophe. And it *was* a catastrophe since Stanton was a perfectionist, y'know? Like Ethan. That's why Ethan and Stanton got along so well—they were both perfectionists. They always understood the *perfectedness* of each other. And Stanton had to be a fucking perfectionist because he was a fucking *designer*.

It went on and on until the manager was walking toward us. He was our age (as was everybody we knew in Manhattan during that time) and he enjoyed arguing with Stanton, and was actually smiling when he forced Stanton to show him his business card and then Stanton had to call the distributor on his cell phone before the manager would even discuss changing the display. Because the fucking shirts go in the fucking front and *they're* the ones that catch the eye—it's the fucking shirts that draw the buyer in and didn't anyone understand that? Didn't anyone understand anything?

When it was all conscientiously prolonged and all the necessary calls had been made, the manager had the teenage boy switch the pants and the jackets and move the shirts up to the front of the display window. Stanton wouldn't leave until this was finished, and he didn't offer to help. He was too preoccupied with closely analyzing the stitching on a pant leg and shaking his head as if someone had just fucked up something else. And then he just continued glaring at the manager and the teenage boy, his arms crossed, tapping his left boot impatiently. He ignored the small group of people who had gathered on the sidewalk outside, captivated by Stanton's flailing arms throughout the dispute. Stanton was wearing a vintage leather jacket with yellow racing stripes on the sleeves and silver zippers everywhere, and ripped jeans with patches; as much as it bothered me, it was hard not to notice that he looked good, like he usually did—the tight red T-shirt complimenting his taut abdomen, the jacket making his broad shoulders look even bigger. I turned my mind away. It was strangely cold out for June.

"You need any clothes?" Stanton asked when we were walking away from the store an hour later.

"No. I'm fine."

He looked me over and fingered the collar of my clearance-sale T-shirt. "Really? I don't think so."

"What's that supposed to mean?"

"I need a drink," Stanton said. "I'm thinking sangria."

"A little early in the day, isn't it?"

He looked at his watch—a silver Timex implanted in a thick leather band. "It's almost cocktail hour," Stanton said. "Jesus, when did the casually employed get so soft?"

"Stanton, I have work," I said tiredly. "I'm busy."

"You don't have shit to do. You know it and I know it. We need sangria."

"I'm going home and you're not following me this time."

"Look, I have to talk to you." Stanton stopped walking and suddenly his face crinkled in an expression that was meant to denote concern but failed. "It's . . . about Ethan."

I stopped walking, too.

Stanton glanced around to make sure no one was listening. "I'm worried about him," he said. "About Ethan."

"What about Ethan?"

We went to Xunta, a tapas bar on Eleventh which had just opened for the evening—Latin music, red Christmas-tree lights intertwined with fishnets hanging from the ceiling—and we were the only ones in the place. We sat at the bar, where the first carafe of sangria went straight to my head and I was so starving that I started pounding the empty jam jar against my mouth to dislodge the orange and lemon sections from the bottom of the glass. Stanton ordered calamari and blood sausage, but the plates were so small that the food didn't do anything to kill my hunger or soak up the carafes of jug wine and rum, and meanwhile the smell of the sausages bubbling with juice was only making me nauseated.

I was waiting for Stanton to tell me why he was so concerned about Ethan (the only reason I was sitting with him in Xunta) but I was soon darkly drunk and starting to spin. Instead of Ethan, the first carafe revolved around Stanton's new one-man show entitled *Stanton's Revenge,* and I just stared at him, slack-jawed, while he went on and on about this long monologue he had written and wanted to perform off-Broadway, and how it would start with Stanton being cut from the football team back in Clarksdale, and it would ascend through the trials of his acting career before peaking with his first sexual experience with a man. The ending would be his debut as a serious up-and-coming designer on the New York scene, and the fame that followed.

"Is China going to fit in somewhere?" I asked. "I mean, like, the whole Peggy Randall thing?"

"You're drunk and adorable." He motioned for a second carafe.

I didn't think I could listen to this anymore. But Stanton didn't care because he was, like, going through this renaissance, y'know, and maybe it was the weather, this gorgeous, rejuvenating early summer weather even though it was cold out today, but maybe it was something else, too, but Stanton had been thinking all this time about acting because he missed it so much and even though he had promised himself to never think about acting he couldn't help looking back on his life—y'know?—and there was something that was just churning inside of him and that something was—ta da!—his life and all the things he had to bury along the way: football, his dad, small-town hypocrisy, coming out, and all this time he was carrying around index cards so he could jot down the random memories that were churning inside of him.

We finished the second carafe in a matter of minutes, and Stanton ordered a third.

I envisioned with pleasure Ethan breaking up with Stanton the moment this thing went into rehearsal.

And then there was the screenplay Stanton had finished and it was really good and it, too, was sort of a memoir, another return to his roots in Clarksdale and the plan was to direct it but not star in it since he was new to the scene and all—y'know?—but once he got some investor interest he would get going on the casting of this piece of drivel and again he would delve into the football scene and the quarterback he blew and all the coke he snorted while modeling. I was seriously wasted by this time and trying hard to sit up straight and concentrate while Stanton told me how his character—the character of Stanton Vaughn—was remolded in a series of dream sequences throughout the movie into a "trannie-slut" which was really so taboo in places like Clarksdale but "interesting taboo" everywhere else, and her name was Lucy but her nickname was "Luce" and then Stanton was asking *do ya get it? do ya get it?* and elbowing my ribs as I was trying to knock the last orange wedge off the bottom of my jam jar.

And then he shut up, considering something, and turned to me.

"And this is where you come in," he said.

"What?" The orange rind wasn't coming off.

"Well, I want to ask you something."

I paused and returned his gaze. "Yes?"

"Since I don't want to star in this thing—I mean, shit, I'll be too busy directing the fucker—I wanted to know something."

"What is it, Stanton?" I asked, teeth gritted, lifting the jam jar back to my mouth.

He breathed in and smiled widely, as if granting me a favor. "I wanted to know if you'll play my first lover in the movie of my life."

He winked and elbowed me again, harder this time, which caused the glass to crack against my tooth and the last orange rind to fall into my lap. It only took a second to understand that the tooth was broken—there was a hard fragment under my tongue. I cried out—a reaction delayed by the gleam in Stanton's eyes—which caused the waiter mopping the floor behind us to rush over. Stanton finally stopped talking, and as the pain set in moments later—waves of it pulsing through my mouth—Stanton put his hand on my back and caressed it in widening circles.

"What happened?" he asked. "Does that mean no? I'm just asking you to *consider*."

We took a taxi to Stanton's dentist, and because I was so drunk the pain settled into a dull ache. Stanton had wrapped the broken half of my tooth in a napkin and carried it in one of the myriad pockets of his leather jacket, and as I leaned forward in the lurching cab, he started rubbing my back and I couldn't sober up enough to tell him to stop. In the waiting room of Stanton's dentist, whom he had called on his cell while we were stuck in rush-hour traffic on Sixth Avenue ("It *is* an emergency, Dr. Nadler"), I watched a little boy playing in the "children's corner." He was running a plastic yellow school bus across bookshelves and walls and his mother's leg and it was driving me crazy, but it was the only thing I could concentrate on. Stanton was still rubbing my back with one hand and turning the pages in *Town & Country* with the other. I just kept nodding my head, wondering why I wasn't a little boy in the children's corner anymore. Why was I in this place aching with pain? And did the pain really have anything to do with a broken tooth? How did I get to be twenty-nine?

Stanton went on about the screenplay while reading the magazine.

"Then—in the dream sequence—Luce meets the right man and learns how to love him. But it's sad because her family is all screwed up. But she changes. That's the point. It's really a story about how one person can change another person."

"No, they can't, Stanton." These were muffled, broken, slurred syllables.

"My, my—what a cute little pessimist you are."

"People don't change." I was on the verge of tears.

"Look." Stanton pointed to a page in the magazine and rolled his eyes. Ethan's picture was there—the same picture that had been reproduced in so many periodicals, with the deep sad eyes and the half smile. "A *superstar*, right?" Stanton sighed before flipping the page.

As if inspired by Ethan's picture, Stanton rubbed my back more firmly and his hand moved lower until the receptionist announced my name. Stanton made arrangements for Ethan to pay for the cap, and then he told me he had to go shower and change for a distributor's meeting at Arqua.

"Dr. Nadler will take care of you," he said, nudging me along gingerly.

"What about Ethan?" I asked. "You wanted to talk about Ethan."

Stanton crinkled his brow as if he were trying hard to remember something. He was also targeting the sangria stain splattered across the crotch of my pants.

"Nothing," he finally said. "Or I forgot."

"What did you want to tell me about Ethan, goddammit?" I needed to know.

Stanton looked around the waiting room and then, whispering loud enough for the hygienist to overhear, "It was the only way to get your cute little ass sloppy drunk."

With a theatrical flourish he turned away. But then he remembered something. He unzipped one of the pockets in his leather jacket and pulled out the napkin with the broken tooth.

"We almost forgot this."

He took my hand and pressed the yellowed ivory into it.

5

_____

THE NOVOCAIN WORE off quickly and even with the Vicodin the dentist prescribed my tooth still felt sensitive—it throbbed when I tried to say anything, but I couldn't talk anyway because my tongue wouldn't touch the roof of my mouth and I experienced an explosion of pain if anything went in that wasn't room temperature. I had expected Ethan to call and check up on me since I was sure Stanton would have told him about the incident at Xunta—with a grin to insinuate that maybe it was something more, the grin that would stir the pangs of jealousy—but he never did. I drank a cup of unheated rice soup and two warm beers and popped three of the white tablets, and then—thinking it couldn't hurt—an old Percocet from my medicine cabinet. And suddenly it was night and I was lying in bed murmuring out loud how much I loved everyone and how much I wanted to tell everyone this and I finally decided to look up David Taylor's invitation to the cocktail party. Soon it was glowing on the computer screen, but when I was about to switch it off—since there was no way I was going—I noticed a new message waiting for me.

From: samona.taylor@printingdivine.com
To: readyandwaiting@hotmail.com
Sent: Wednesday, June 2, 4:18 PM
Subject: Party Tonight

How r u?! David mentioned your name the othr day
and it brought back all these memories. Do u
believe we're almost 30? Do u believe we graduated
7 years ago? Wow. Its all happening! Anyway,
don't know if you'll get this note in time but D
told me u got an invitation for 2night and I hpe
you can come—it's been a long time since I've
seen u.
Thinking of U,
SAT

And a blurry confidence grew inside me as I read her words over
and over.

Her voice whispered *Thinking of U* through a haze as I put on a brown
corduroy suit.

The scent of her hair, ingrained in my mind years ago, was pun-
gent as I splurged on a cab up to 988 Fifth Avenue (I was so out of it,
the subway didn't even present itself as an alternative).

The image of her lithe body stood specterlike beside me, beckon-
ing, as the doorman asked if I was here for the Randolph Torrance
party and had me sign a register, and since the Vicodin was impairing
my speech—I felt great but couldn't say anything—he finally shrugged.
"The party's almost over anyway."

The first thing I saw when I entered 12D was the light screaming
from a high-wattage bulb over the subject of tonight's celebration: a
wall-size canvas of fifteen monkeys sitting around a table in formal
attire, their simian faces expressionless. I spaced out on the painting as
the mumble of conversation from another room drifted toward me. A
dull pain brought everything back into focus and I shuffled into the
room the voices were coming from. There were about twenty-five people standing around while seventies rock (*"Brandy, you're a fine girl . . . what
a good wife you would be . . ."*) was coming from somewhere hidden and it
took longer than I liked for my presence to become known. There was
a subtle lull in the conversation and a few people turned my way.

I immediately noticed the woman standing next to James Gutterson.
She was the only caramel-skinned person in 12D.

Samona Ashley had always been so exotic and graceful that whenever I was in close proximity to her the room would bend in her direction—like it was doing now. *Thinking of U* flashed through my mind.

With heels she was an inch or two taller than James, and she was smiling at something he was saying and the smile drew me in and yet was so enigmatic that it showed me absolutely nothing—I couldn't tell if she was sincere or humoring James Gutterson or mocking him. This vantage point—trying to decipher what Samona Ashley was thinking and being hopelessly incapable—brought me back to all those nights in college. Meanwhile Gutterson's hand kept moving to Samona's back and she kept brushing it aside with increasing annoyance until she muttered something and turned away and James gruesomely mouthed the word *bitch*.

She glanced over at me briefly—but there was no recognition—and a Vicodin-fueled sigh streamed through my lips coupled with a low, insuppressible moan. Because the effect of Samona Ashley hadn't diminished in the eight years since I'd last seen her on graduation day. A meaningless glance—the flash of those black eyes, the way her coiled strands of glossy hair swept gently over her shoulder, her skin a smooth shadow in the dim light—and I was instilled with a dazed but overwhelming urge to possess her.

The fact that she didn't recognize me did nothing to quell this urge.

When she turned away, the urge remained and became more severe.

Which was when an image broke through the Vicodin cloud: Ethan Hoevel fucking her.

And as she joined another group of people it seemed as if the rest of the room lost interest in me as well, which drove me to the bar for a double Scotch—the only thing that was going to move me farther into the party. A hand lightly touched my shoulder—David Taylor's hand—which reminded me of Stanton's hand before it had moved down to the small of my back in Dr. Nadler's office. David squeezed my shoulder muscle like he used to do before we raced and asked, "What are you drinking?"

I held up my Scotch.

"Scotch? Jesus, what are you? Seventy-six?" David grabbed an Amstel.

"I have this toothache and—"

"Let me introduce you to our host."

David guided me toward a group of guys standing in a darkened corner. I finished the Scotch in about ten steps and noticed that David had put his hand on my back while leading me to his friends. I was quickly introduced as an old classmate, a writer who might be able to help the lit department with his downtown flair. The Leonard Company guys—young and tall and blandly handsome, sucking on Heineken bottles, sipping martinis—all nodded uninterestedly, and then David introduced me to our host standing in their midst, Randolph Torrance, a flamboyant man in his late fifties who was one of David's biggest clients (which was why so many Leonard Company guys were at the cocktail party) and who took an immediate interest in me, shaking my hand with an irritatingly firm grip. His eyes gleamed with intent, but the Scotch and Vicodin obliterated my unease. I was floating with a smile plastered on my face, able to field questions from Randolph Torrance like "And whom do you write for?" with answers like "I casually employ myself," which amused the old queen, causing him to lean into me until I stepped back and gestured at the room where the painting of the monkeys was hanging, and asked, "So you bought that, huh?"

"That's why we're all here." How Randolph Torrance managed to make that sound like a come-on was a mystery to me.

He moved closer as I backed away—it was a dance—when suddenly a glass broke somewhere in the darkness. The sound of it shattering caused Randolph to flinch and excuse himself.

The moment Randolph Torrance left, a conversation ensued about the painting, but the corner was too dark to tell who was saying what.

"Jesus, two-point-five for that piece of shit? And he's celebrating?"

"It's an investment."

"It's retarded."

"Fuck you—he's eccentric."

"He's a crazy old faggot with too much money."

"Yeah, like you wouldn't suck his dick to get the commissions—"

"Wait, is *that* what Taylor had to do?"

Raucous laughter.

"Come on, pal." This was David, deadpan.

The talk reminded me of why I'd never joined a fraternity, and smugly resented the friends of mine who had (including David Taylor)—the backslapping, the rough embraces, the constant cock-talking, the intense drinking that led to tears and hugs and "I love ya, dude's," and the sitting around the common room in boxer shorts, legs intertwined—it all seemed more homoerotic than anything you'd see in an Abercrombie & Fitch catalog and with a thicker veneer of hypocrisy. The Leonard Company guys continued talking about the horrible painting.

"I mean, in ten years what's that thing gonna go for?"

"Depends on the market for monkey art." This was said soberly and no one laughed. "Who's the artist?"

"A German. Reinhardt. He paints monkeys, I guess." This was a British accent.

"That is the creepiest shit, man."

"Doesn't he get it? The more monkeys he paints, the less this thing is gonna be worth. Didn't anyone take Econ 115?"

"Torrance could still turn a profit. Take a little boy down to the Caribbean in his Gulfstream and party for the weekend."

"No leverage potential. High risk. Doesn't merit." This was the British accent again.

The Vicodin was moved to speak.

"Merit what?" I asked in the direction of his silhouette.

"Investment," he answered back flatly.

"What if it's not?" I said.

"What if it's not what?" He seemed confused, but he was sincerely trying to stay with me.

"An investment."

I felt the stunned silence. And then one of the shadows ended it with: "Well, then it's a positively shitty painting to hang on your fucking wall."

I was floating in the kind of space where I could just turn away from people and move back to the bar without saying anything. I grabbed another Scotch and glanced over at Samona, and when I did the slow burn of pain in my tooth returned. I started walking toward her. James Gutterson had been replaced by Randolph Torrance, and he seemed very uninterested in Samona even though there was a kind of longing in her voice as she told him things, and through the space in which I was floating I could see that although she was working for her husband, trying to charm the host-client, she was also failing at it. She couldn't break through because Randolph Torrance had his eyes on me.

When she started following his gaze to see what was distracting him, I quickly walked to the opposite side of the room and stared at a wall.

There were photos of a recent skiing vacation Randolph Torrance had taken with a short, portly man, and there was a painting of a chapel at Williams College, presumably his alma mater, and a large watercolor of a Hamptons beach house with the title *Water Mill, 1978*. I started humming to myself and couldn't stop.

When I turned around again, David had replaced Randolph Torrance at Samona's side and they were now alone, staring at each other. High heels made her exactly his height, and from my vantage point across the vast and ornate room, I saw him put his hand against the small of her back—where there was a break in the dress, an opening, skin—and as he leaned toward her, she leaned into his hand, and it was another kind of dance. He said something, and there was tension. She turned away from him. He tried to pull her back with his hand, which had moved to her hip, and he said something else. She shook her head tersely. And then she laughed. I couldn't hear it—there was too much going on—but from the expression on her face it was bitter, presumably because David Taylor had never said an intentionally funny thing in his entire craven life. Then she recoiled and started walking toward the bar. David did not follow.

I was going to talk to her. I was going to see if she remembered me.

Her back was facing me from the bar, that diamond of dark skin gazing out through the opening of her dress where David Taylor had placed his hand.

Another surge went through me, but I fought it because jealousy was useless, destructive (but undeniable, right?) and then the image appeared once again like a flashback—in color and very clear—of Samona in Ethan's bed in the round pod in the middle of his loft, and she was naked with Ethan kneeling behind her, moaning, and Ethan was staring down at where the curve of her back became her ass. I had to finish the Scotch in a gulp.

And I had to shut my eyes tightly—they were watering—but I had to do it without clenching my teeth.

When I opened them Samona was walking toward me.

I heard a woman's voice—*her* voice—say my name.

I breathed in. She looked firmly at me with her black eyes and extended her hand, which just hung there, limply, waiting for mine.

I couldn't hear anything as I finally shook it.

She was shimmering and I was still floating and I was being penetrated by something—a memory, a song, a kiss, her walking away.

So how was lunch with David and James? I can't believe you're a writer—how's that going? Has the East Village really become so expensive? Are you still running?

I was hearing her words and her voice as if they were separate things. My answers were more like deflections because I did not want Samona Taylor to know anything about me and the aimless failures that defined my life, and I did not want her to know the reason I was here at the party.

"David told me you started your own business." I finally cleared my throat.

"Did he tell you that?" The smile on her face faltered slightly. "Yeah."

It was the wrong thing to ask because we both fell silent.

I tried again: "This sort of reminds me of the Zeta Psi formals but without the kegs and the random hookups."

She laughed politely and touched my hand that held the empty Scotch glass, and then she brushed against my jacket and I watched as her arm fell back to her side, and it wasn't until my hand was almost to hers that I realized this was happening—I was reaching for her—and pulled back roughly. The empty glass fell to the floor but didn't break. We watched it roll in slow motion until it settled against the wall beneath the painting. She smiled politely, emptily.

I was shaking again. It was a mistake being this close to her.

"I think the random hookups are still here," she murmured while looking across the room at different people. It was an innocent sentence but it jolted me enough to stop trembling.

"Like who?"

She sighed and craned her neck. "Well, there's the lush alcoholic wife who always embarrasses her stiff husband." She was staring at a couple I couldn't see. "She's not actually hooking up yet. She's just stuck at this party and dreaming about the affair."

David was staring at us from across the room where he was locked in a conversation with Randolph Torrance, who saw who David was looking at and started leering for me to join them. Samona and I were standing near a corner where James Gutterson was motioning toward the monstrous canvas, making giant curves in the air with his arms and spilling wine with each overemphatic gesture.

"It must be hard running a fashion print studio in this city."

This was me.

"Yes. I know. David keeps reminding me of that fact. On a daily basis."

This was her.

Some facts from eight years ago—some minor, some not:

David Taylor is the track star who scores whatever points the team needs, and he's admired by thousands across campus who have never met him.

Samona Ashley is, at a glance, the beautiful party girl with a taste for amaretto sours, the arm candy for dumb handsome guys at dances, the dark-skinned exotic one who wears sexy dresses even to Student Activities Committee meetings, the girl who wins the campus model search (after entering it as a joke), the girl who wreaks havoc on the emotions of a huge swath of disbelieving Yale men because she seems so otherworldly but at the same time, because of that enigmatic smile, maybe—just maybe—attainable.

So it is inevitable—at least natural—that two integral members of Yale royalty will, at some point, sleep together.

What is less inevitable: that a drunken fuck will become something sustained—the propagation of shallow attraction and collective expectation conspiring into what is thereafter commonly referred to as a relationship.

And though David Taylor and Samona Ashley are soon seen as a perfect couple in Yale's tightly enclosed universe, those of us who are close enough to be aware of their problems constantly ask one another a basic question: whether this will—or more important, whether this *ought to*—last.

There are the drinking binges that cause David Taylor to urinate in his sleep while in bed with Samona Ashley.

There are the crabs that David "inherits" on an overnight trip from "unwashed" motel sheets.

There is Samona's intimate—what David Taylor calls a "creepshow"—relationship with her blue-blooded Episcopalian father, Keith Ashley, which consists of daily phone calls that often end in tears, and which leads to David's suspicion as to why Samona dates only white guys. He ultimately shrugs it off as simply a "daddy" fixation, but this is tricky for David to do since Keith Ashley also has crew-cut brown hair, pale skin, a high-pitched voice to go with his wiry stature, and was the SAE treasurer at Yale thirty years earlier. The eeriness of all their similarities is something David will never address out loud.

There is the rage that this father-daughter relationship invites from Tana Ashley, Samona's "crazy" Ghanaian mother whom Keith met while doing Peace Corps work in the seventies and whom Samona apathetically refers to as "Tana from Ghana," and who has a talent for telling Samona she's too fat during her daughter's most vulnerable moments. The fact that Tana Ashley explains her harshness away by claiming to possess "unimaginable childhood secrets" does nothing to help Samona shrug off her onslaughts.

There is Samona being diagnosed with bulimia, and the counseling sessions at the Mental Health Center that David sometimes accompanies her to, and sometimes does not.

There's the student body that wants to believe in the serene and perfect sphere that David Taylor and Samona Ashley inhabit, because it gives the girls something to aspire to and it lets the boys off the hook when it comes to the prospect of scoring a girl like Samona Ashley—there is a huge, collective sigh of relief when it becomes apparent that Samona is off the market. And even though rumors about them are constantly drifting around campus, they are ultimately ignored because no one wants to believe them. Besides, other people's longings and fantasies have nothing to do with why David and Samona will stay together.

There is the perfect timing: David is tired of chasing tail (or being chased) through the bars and clubs and frat houses of New Haven, and he's tired of the semi-limp fucks and the morning-afters that end with the inevitable walk of shame back to his room in Sigma Alpha Epsilon.

And Samona, after a string of relationships with selfish men who only want to nail the princess and be able to say they'd slept with a black girl, responds to something in David: he's sweet, he's possessive, he comes from a modest background but has a clearly defined and sincere dream of what he desires his life to be that involves more than moving to a city to make a shitload of money. Samona Ashley has never been with a man who maintains this earnest kind of focus and drive.

There's my last image of David and Samona together: the two of them at graduation, sharing a joint during the commencement address.

And there is the element that completes that image, which at the time seems innocuous, but soon—as I tell this story looking back over everything that has fallen apart—will unveil itself as prophetic: Ethan Hoevel sitting in the row directly behind them with his sad-faced Irish mother and his scowling, bearded older brother.

Ethan Hoevel is glaring at Yale's perfect couple with an intensity I don't understand.

I know this to be an accurate representation of the events.

Because before the ceremony begins, Ethan and I merge randomly on intersecting stone walkways in the sea of black gowns, and I look into his green eyes, and they're saturated with unease, and I know that one thing I can do for him before our lives diverge again is sit beside him, silently, during the ceremony.

And on that June day so many years ago, in the space between the two foldout chairs we're sitting on, hidden out of sight beneath our graduation gowns, Ethan Hoevel has forgiven me and is holding my hand.

As usual, I had been at the party too long, and my reasons for coming had gotten lost somewhere along the way. I was getting very wasted and listening to James Gutterson talk about the market and how tanked out it was and how everything was going to fall apart soon, how it already *was* falling apart, blaming it on greedy day traders and corrupt accountants and first-years just getting their sales license who were always clicking the *sell* box when they were supposed to be clicking the *buy* box for Christ's sake, and don't even get him *started* on young women in what they call business casual (which resembled what Heather Locklear used to wear on *Melrose Place*) who hadn't learned yet that it took *balls* to be a trader.

"It's just a shit world," the British guy was saying drunkenly, spilling his gin martini onto Randolph Torrance's floor. "And it's all going to collapse into shit and rubbish some night while we are all asleep and . . . would anyone care to do some blow?"

I was so pumped full of Vicodin and Scotch that I was trying to stop myself from drooling. I was vaguely aware that Van Morrison's *Greatest Hits* was playing. My tooth was full-out throbbing and soaking it in alcohol wasn't helping anymore. And I was so hungry—there were no hors d'oeuvres anywhere, just some bowls of mixed nuts I couldn't eat because of the tooth—and then predictably the hunger became anger: anger at Stanton taking me to the tapas bar in hopes of—what? And anger at Ethan for being involved with a guy like Stanton, and for lying to me about Samona (where was she? I'd lost her somehow), and I was angry at David Taylor for inviting me to this party as some sort of charitable outreach, or was it a failed attempt to recapture what we had all (*no, wait, what* you *had*) lost on graduation day?

And then I was floating toward the door when I noticed someone standing there in the dark, surveying the room.

This person was wearing ripped jeans and a black Gucci shirt that fit well over his thin, muscled frame, and a cashmere peacoat that fell just above the knees.

The entire room paused as the women (even the married ones) scanned him suggestively and the men rolled their eyes and exchanged grimaces—futile attempts to dismiss the stylish elegance of this party crasher which had, the moment he'd entered the room, toppled their cool facades.

It was Ethan Hoevel.

"Moondance" was playing and I felt in danger just being there.

I moved back into the darkness and watched as Ethan finally picked Samona and David out of the crowd and sauntered toward them.

The British guy had found me and was saying, "People are doing blow in the bedroom, and our host would like *you* to join them." But he was blocking my view and I just tilted my head and said nothing until he left, making a frustrated sound and clearing his nose.

I watched as Ethan Hoevel shook David Taylor's hand.

I watched as David Taylor put that hand on Ethan's shoulder.

David was squinting, trying to remember this oddly familiar face, and then I saw the moment in which he did.

Because of where Samona now found herself in this world, her smile did something it had never done before. Her smile showed exactly what she was thinking.

David Taylor was looking around the room, and I slowly started backing away when I realized he was looking for me.

But he didn't find me because I was pressed against a wall in the darkness and moving out the door, knowing exactly why it was that the smile Samona Ashley Taylor had been perfecting her entire life—the smile that haunted you by hiding her every thought and feeling under the slightly curled lip, the smile that had lingered in my mind for eight years—was now failing her.

6

THE NIGHT IN the spring of 1996 starts in a dorm room in Trumbull Hall with a "pregame party" consisting of Cuervo shots and cans of Busch while a group of us listens to Bob Marley's *Greatest Hits,* and we talk about how Meyerson's cold-war class is a total bitch because all the junior girls are just there to mess up the curve, and how Nick has been sleeping with Karen even though he's dating Jessica but everyone thinks Nick is gay anyway and it's a pretty twisted situation.

And then some of us move to an eighties-themed dance party in a quad which is mostly groups of girls jumping up and down every time they hear a song they recognize. Since the DJ is taking requests, this is happening pretty much with every song. The dance party is sponsored by the college which means: no booze.

So a few of us relocate to the Purple Cow party at Zeta Psi which is supposed to have cases of champagne but it's all gone and punch and keg beer is what we're looking at, and there are some girls with mud on their faces dressed up in football pads—initiation for the women's ice-hockey team which most of us don't know exists. There's a big confrontation at the door because someone's talking to someone else's girlfriend and one of them is a drama guy and the other is a football guy and you know that's not going to be fair so people have to get in the middle since the drama guy (Adam?) has just been *talking* to her, nothing more, and the football guy (Daryl?) is piss drunk, though after the situation gets resolved and Daryl's passed out somewhere, it is circulated that Adam has, in fact, fucked his girlfriend.

Dancing at Kavanaugh's Pub: a decent jukebox and specials on margaritas, but pretty boring and consisting mostly of freshmen since they don't card.

Somehow it gets to be 2:30 in the morning.

Then we're at Sigma Alpha Epsilon—Late Night—and it's MGD in oversize red plastic cups, and I can't find anyone that I've been hanging out with that night and don't really know who I'm looking for anyway since I can't remember who's been where, so I'm thinking that the night will be over soon and when was the last time a night had ended any differently?

And then Samona Ashley is sitting next to me on the armrest of a tattered sofa and I can't help noticing that our hips are touching, actually pressing together while "Sweet Child o' Mine" grates through blown-out speakers, and I flash across all the moments I've been this close to her without being drunk enough to say something. There was the "safe-sex tutorial" during freshman orientation, where I thought the way she was smiling at everything new around her was the most beautiful thing I'd ever seen, and I managed only to offer a strained grin during the "condom on the banana" illustration before she looked away. There was the Introduction to Art History class we shared first semester sophomore year, where for two hours twice a week I'd gaze toward wherever she was sitting, glancing over her shoulder at the crooked doodles she'd draw, trying to tune out whatever athlete or frat boy happened to be flirting with her. There was the early evening during exam week when I'd been jogging on the New Haven Green and seen her on a bench, alone, highlighting a textbook, and I'd just kept running past her, noticing how she'd looked up at me courteously but choosing not to return the look. And through all these moments I was only wishing that I could be the kind of guy who just sits casually on a bench next to someone like Samona Ashley and effortlessly makes her laugh—it always starts with making someone laugh; the kind of guy who could then get to know her better, make her fall in love with me, structure each day around her, bring her into my world while becoming absorbed into hers; the guy who could make his life serene that way and erase all the bullshit striving and angling and confusion and pining that saturate this time.

But since I'm not that guy—since I never move closer than a few desk chairs away—I don't get to know Samona Ashley through the first three years of college, and she never becomes anything more than the center of a hollow dream.

And yet, now as she's nodding off beside me at the SAE party—she has sat down next to me, alone—and she's saying, "So where else have you been tonight?" and this seems focused in my general direction and I reel off the list of places that I remember in no particular order and mumble, "Most of the night sucked but this is kind of cool," and her eyes meet mine for the first time—she's drunk and stoned; I understand this but don't care—and though it is obviously a struggle to hold her head up and her eyes are glazed, she looks at me long enough so I can see how deeply black and beautiful her eyes are up close, which is when I realize that Samona Ashley, a girl I've only seen before across crowded rooms with her arms around other guys, is talking to me right now and her face is just a few inches away and I am smelling her hair for the first time.

She's sliding off the armrest when I catch her, and she says my name and smiles—what could be a suggestive smile, what could be anything—then murmurs *thank you* and then somehow her lips are touching mine and this is a kiss—Samona Ashley kissing me, and I'm kissing her back and tasting beer and some kind of lip gloss, and five seconds later we're still kissing and my hand is on her hip and hers is on my chest and I'm hoping that since it's late and it looks like this party's winding down, she will go home with me, and the only other semblance of thought occurring over and over is: this is so simple, this is so easy . . .

But one of the SAE brothers bores through the room saying something about police and the guys living in the house gather together near the front door (David Taylor is among them) and then Samona isn't kissing me anymore. One of her girlfriends is motioning for her to drop the cup and leave with her and then the party officially ends and we're all out on the street without our red plastic cups.

And the last thing I see that night—the thing that ultimately sends me home—is Samona Ashley talking to David Taylor on the stoop out-side the house.

I hear a few weeks later that the night at Sigma Alpha Epsilon was the first night they slept together.

After that, I will see her at random places and I will not be able to keep myself from thinking that my most memorable experience dur-ing four years at Yale took place in five seconds on the night she fucked David Taylor.

7

I WOKE UP the morning after Randolph Torrance's party with no remembrance of how I got home. French fries were scattered all over the bed and a half-eaten cheeseburger sat on the nightstand. The only reason I even considered getting out of bed was that my tooth still throbbed and it was 6:30 and I was never going to fall back asleep. I took the last of the Vicodin and listened to the message on my phone from sometime during the night:

"It's me, Ethan. Listen, I know you were at that fucking depressing monkey party last night, and it made me sad you didn't tell me you were going. You should have . . . Samona told me you might be there and that's one of the reasons I went—to see you . . ." He sighed. "Maybe avoiding rudeness would be a first step toward moving along with that little thing you call a life? Let's just leave it at that for now . . . Maybe some other time we can talk about all the things you don't really know . . . I can't help thinking that you're . . ." He trailed off and I thought my phone had cut out. Then his voice returned. "Well . . . call if you're compelled."

I certainly wasn't compelled, and instead I went out and bought the *Post* and a fruit smoothie, which shocked my tooth but the Vicodin was washing away the pain. Bleary-eyed, I read every word in the *Post,* starting with sports in the back and working my way toward the front: the Yankees were on a winning streak but traded their best lefty, handbags from Juicy Couture were a must-have, two actresses from *Friends* were vacationing in Hawaii, photos of the Hilton sisters curtsying with Ashton Kutcher at a club opening on Twenty-second Street were laid out next to a fireman who had died in a building collapse on the edge of Harlem.

By the time I finished it was after nine. I logged onto the Internet and saw that David had e-mailed.

```
From: David.Taylor@Leonardco.com
To: readyandwaiting@hotmail.com
Sent: Thursday, June 3, 5:52 AM
Subject: last night

glad you came by last night. sorry you disappeared.
a yale guy Ethan Hoevel came by sometime right
after. think you knew him. good guy—is he gay?
might end up doing some work for us. how random
is that? ok, stay in touch. regards, d
```

I noticed two uppercase letters.
I replied.

```
Thanks for throwing me the invite. Great to see
you and your wife (old lady, ball & chain, other
half, lifelong love, etc). I'm very jealous—and I
woke up this morning in bed with a half-eaten bag
of french fries. Do not ask.
```

And just as I hit send, a new message popped up.

```
From: samona.taylor@printingdivine.com
To: readyandwaiting@hotmail.com
Sent: Thursday, June 3, 9:02 AM
Subject: (no subject)

Hello there. I very much enjoyed seeing u last
night. It brought back lots of nice memories.
```

Will u come by the studio sometime? Maybe tomorrow?
Fondly, SAT

I read it a few times and always came back to "nice memories."
I wrote back.

Samona. Yes, it was a good time. You looked
great. I'm pretty swamped though—want to say next
week instead?

Then I closed my e-mail, turned my cell phone off, and set the
landline to go straight to the machine, like Ethan did when he traveled, and I began three days of quiet, solid work.

They went by fast. I didn't drink at all except for the occasional
beer with take-out sushi (a risk but an inexpensive one). My tooth
started feeling better. My apartment looked clean. My computer was
streamlined and running smoothly. The editor at *New York* magazine
called back and I pitched my Gowanus idea very lucidly and she
promised to try her best to clear up some space. On Sunday I went
back to Brooklyn and interviewed random residents about pollution.
I also covered a bar opening in the meatpacking district as well as a
fund-raiser in a mausoleum-like apartment on Central Park West for
the New York City Council speaker who was running for mayor next
year.

And on Monday, soothed by the recent activity, I was finally ready
to see Samona Taylor.

I wore dark jeans and a blue polo shirt and headed west to University Place, then down through NYU and SoHo. It was muggy and
gray, with sprinkles of warm rain. People sat around Washington
Square sweating in the heat. And I prepared myself for a short meeting with a girl I hadn't seen (soberly) since college. It was just a formality, I told myself. I would compliment her on how she looked and
send my best regards to her husband and say encouraging things about
her studio based on my limited experience in the fashion industry,
and I would throw out a few ideas about getting more publicity and
suppress the inevitable pangs of desire for her and ignore the jealousy

I felt toward David and Ethan, and I would keep my fantasies of various combinations of the three of them in a large bed to a minimum. I walked across the slippery cobblestones of Greene Street with a clear head.

There was no one in Printing Divine when I opened the door and entered the reception area. The studio inhabited a narrow space— maybe seventeen feet across—that stretched deep into the block, and the twenty-foot-high ceiling with skylights helped ease the claustro- phobia I caught while I waited. The floors and walls were all white-on- white, and two chairs and a small sofa made up a waiting area along with a wooden table layered with magazines. Vintage movie posters hung everywhere (*Last Tango in Paris, Rear Window, An Affair to Remember*) alongside the occasional framed promo from recent events (Betsey Johnson at Lotus, the Tommy Hilfiger party at Lot 61). Unrecogniz- able New Age music played softly from speakers. Lying on top of the reception desk was a guest register and a "comments" book. Beyond the desk were two glass-walled offices, both deserted.

I opened the "comments" book—all blank pages with dates on top of each one. I went for the guest register but there was a creak overhead.

A woman nearing forty was descending a staircase that was tucked against the wall to my right. The first thing I noticed was how dispro- portionately long her arms seemed next to her short body. She scanned me up and down, just like I was doing to her (just like everyone was always doing to everyone else in this city) and then she asked in a very high voice, "May I help you?"

"I'm here to see Samona."

"She's upstairs. Do you have an appointment?"

"I'm just an old friend." I told her my name.

"Nice to meet you," she said with too much enthusiasm. "I'm Martha. Her colleague."

As we shook hands, heavy footsteps sounded throughout the canyonlike studio and Samona's voice came from somewhere above us.

"Hello down there."

I looked up too fast and a cramp shot through my neck.

Samona was leaning over a railing and she was wearing a red silk blouse that accentuated her breasts and revealed a small, dark freckle that I'd never noticed before.

"I'll be right down."

"Take your time. I should have called. I'm sorry."

"No problem," she said, smiling at me. "Take a seat in my office and I'll be right there. Martha, would you take over for me up here?"

Martha grumbled under her breath and rolled her eyes. "Sure. No problem."

A few minutes later the two of us were sitting across from each other at a small conference table, drinking lukewarm green tea while talking vaguely about business. The room was cramped and Samona was scrolling through a very thin portfolio, talking about things like organic dye distributors, ink settings, gloss, thread counts. I just went along with the fact that she didn't seem to know very much about any of it.

"And we usually use a quarter-inch bleed around the fringes." Samona paused. "Or wait—it depends. We use a full bleed with darker fabrics so the colors won't run. Right. That's right."

I gazed at her while she went on, talking as if I were a client of some kind. I asked a few polite questions—"Who would be your dream client?" "How amazing is it that you started your own company?" "Didn't you major in art history?"—and she gave basic answers while squinting at the portfolio, absently rubbing at a smudge.

"So, what were you working on?" I finally asked, clearing my head. "Before I barged in here."

"Well, I was upstairs where all the real work gets done. Down here's just, like, bookkeeping and phone calls."

"Right," I said. "Right."

She seemed distracted—there was something she wasn't saying yet—but she grew slowly more animated as she went on. "But upstairs, upstairs it's all state-of-the-art presses. And right now we're basically working on two jobs. One's pretty big—Betsey Johnson and—"

"How'd you land her so early in the game?" I asked, trying to sound impressed.

"Martha's husband," Samona said. "He's a stylist. He does wardrobes." She paused, and then assured me, "Betsey is totally happy with the work we've done."

"Who's the other client?" I asked.

"Not as big," Samona said. "A designer you probably haven't heard of yet—Stanton Vaughn."

She glanced away.

Somehow, I wasn't surprised.

"I just saw some of his stuff at the Urban Outfitters around the corner from where I live," I finally said in the most casual voice I could muster.

Suddenly she looked back at me and laughed. "You shop at Urban Outfitters?"

Stuck, I managed to say, "Just for, like, underwear and . . . scarves."

It was "scarves" that caused a silence to envelop the room while Samona stared at me intently, as if I were a riddle that needed solving.

"Anyway"—her rolling voice started up again—"we have our sights set a little higher than Stanton Vaughn. I mean"—and now she leaned in conspiratorially—"we've been hearing that he imports his material from Indonesia."

At first I didn't know what this meant.

And then I made a guess and jumped in for the save. "Ten thousand little kids with infected blisters working for seventeen cents a day?"

Samona nodded grimly. "That's really not something we want to be connected with."

This exchange caused her to stand up. "It's boring down here—why don't I show you the presses?"

She led me upstairs into a claustrophobic space where the printing machinery was packed too tightly between the narrow walls, the racks of clothes, and a low ceiling. There were three printing presses, and spaced between them were cutting boards and a measuring table scattered with small magnifying glasses, dye trays, slicing tools, and an iMac connected to a scanner and a large photo printer. The smallest press was pushing out a set of retro-black shirts marked with the logo of a muscled chest while Martha stood behind it monitoring the output.

I recognized the clothing.

So: Ethan was going to save Samona and her little business.

The same way he had saved Stanton.

The same way he had tried to save me.

Just because we all needed him to—and because he could.

I wondered aloud how they'd managed to arrange the machines and racks to actually fit in this space.

"We hired an interior space consultant," Martha called from across the room in her little-girl voice.

"Was that in the proposal you wrote for David?" I asked.

Samona stopped. "He told you about that?"

"I wrote most of it," Martha added.

"He's a businessman, and he was investing his money," Samona said defensively. "Of course we wrote a proposal."

I changed the subject by gesturing toward Martha. "Is that how you two met?" I said loudly over the hum of the machines.

Samona seemed relieved to be asked a question she could easily answer. "Oh, I've known Martha since my modeling days."

"I was a stylist then," Martha said. "And Samona's a Pisces, and I'm a Taurus and—you know—Neptune and Venus, parallel orbits." She squinted at me. "What's your sign?"

"I don't really believe in horoscopes." I tried to smile.

Martha leaned forward over the machine. "When were you born?" I told her.

"You're a Virgo." She leaned back again, satisfied. This information seemed to explain exactly what I was doing there.

"What does that mean?" I asked her while trying not to stare at Samona.

"You're ruled by Mercury. That means communication." Martha studied me. "It also means you're practical, adaptable, but generally you're indirect—among other things."

"Should I be writing this down?" I asked.

"It's a weather report. You don't have to write it down. Just be aware."

"The weatherman is only right about a third of the time."

Martha shrugged like it was my loss.

Samona rolled her eyes. "Martha is an evangelist of the zodiac."

Then Martha turned back to the machine and said to me, "So what do *you* do exactly?"

"I'm, kind of, a writer. I guess. Journalism, mostly—I do a lot of fashion reviews."

"Oh?" Martha looked up, intrigued, scanning me up and down again as if trying to gauge whether or not this was actually true.

Samona chimed in. "Hey, maybe you could write up a little story about a boutique textile printing company started by two friends with an eye for fashion and a taste for adventure!"

"I could . . . try," I replied, distracted by the way Samona was looking at me, her dark eyes wide and expectant and impressed.

I had to pull away by focusing on Martha, who had already lost interest in me—she'd seen the way I was staring at Samona, I quickly realized, and she knew that the reason I'd come here had nothing to do with fashion journalism—and she murmured, "So, you two were friends in college?"

Samona and I exchanged half smiles.

"Yeah," I said. "We knew each other."

"Not well," Samona corrected. "More like we knew *of* each other."

"You knew about me?" I blurted out. Then I picked up the sleeve of one of Stanton's shirts. The fabric was warm.

"Careful," Martha warned, moving to take it from me but then, for some reason, retreating. "Dye's still wet."

"Is this Betsey or Stanton?" I asked. The entire situation seemed to call for me to pretend like I didn't know anything.

"That's Stanton," Samona said. "Wait, this machine is too loud—let me pause it."

She hit a few buttons before Martha exclaimed "Don't!" and there was a grinding noise from deep inside the machine. The press stopped rolling. There was another sound: the rending of fabric. And then the shirts stopped coming out.

Martha went to the keyboard and started hitting buttons but all that did was cause another grinding sound.

The computer across the room beeped and said "ERR-OR."

Martha turned the power off. The loft was silent except for the New Age music.

"Sorry," Samona said. "I've done that before."

"I know." Martha just stared at the machine, her hands on her hips. "Shit."

I cleared my throat and said, "Maybe I should go . . ."

"No. No." Samona put her hand on mine just like she had done in Randolph Torrance's apartment. "Stay," she said. "Please. Don't you want to have lunch?"

"ERR-OR."

"I was just going to get some noodles at this little place in China-town—"

"No, no—we'll order something." Samona's voice sounded desperate.

"You must be busy, though, and now you've gotta take care of this." I waved my hand around the machine, where Martha had pulled the console off and was staring inside.

"How about paninis? There's a great place around the corner." I had turned toward the stairs but Samona grabbed the back of my shirt.

Martha turned around. "Samona, we're going to need this press this afternoon."

"ERR-OR."

"Look, I'll fix it, Martha. Why don't you just go pick up something from Angeli and it'll be all fixed by the time you get back."

Martha was focused on me now, and I sheepishly looked away and pretended to inspect the wounded machine.

"Just pick up a bunch of the mozzarella and tomato, okay?" Samona was almost pleading as two twenties materialized in her hand and found their way into Martha's pocket.

"ERR—" Martha hit the return button on the way to the stairs. She didn't say anything as she left. The electronic bell over the door rang when it opened and rang again when it closed.

The two of us stood very still. And then Samona, who seemed to be calming down slightly, let go of my shirt, and in the quiet I could hear her subtle exhale. She began following instructions on a side panel and opened the top of the press and leaned inside.

"This should only take a second," she said apologetically. "It's just stuck, I think."

"Do you . . . need any help?" I offered, but was cut off by a deep grinding of plastic and metal. Samona cried out and leaped away from the machine, clutching her hand. She shook it limply from the wrist. There was a black dye stain across her blouse, just below her breasts.

I had to force myself to avert my gaze and concentrate on the skin of her hand, which was already swelling.

I took her hand in mine. Her fingers were incredibly soft and uncallused.

"It doesn't look too bad," I said. "Do you have any ice?"

"It's fine," she muttered. "It's okay."

"It's starting to swell."

"I'll get some ice in back."

And then, after an uncomfortable silence gave her no choice, she pulled her hand away, and it left a deep black ink stain on mine.

"You know what," I said. "I think I can probably fix this."

"The fashion print business: man's work." She sighed and attempted a smile.

When she went downstairs for the ice, I leaned into the machine. The mat and roller were steaming hot, and a tattered shirt collar was jammed in the teeth. I started easing out fabric, gently at first, trying to preserve what was left of the shirt.

Samona came back upstairs while I was still inside the machine.

"Normally, when this happens, we just take the roller out, but it's probably too hot still, right?" Her voice came from behind me.

"Personally, I blame Stanton Vaughn," I said as a joke, handing her a clump of mangled sleeve. "How'd you get him, anyway?"

There was another kind of pause behind me.

I couldn't see her but I knew she was there and I started thinking about a horror movie where half a man's body was in one room and the other half was protruding from the wall in another, where an animal was waiting to choose the most vulnerable moment to strike, but it was so dark you couldn't see what the animal was—the yellow gleam of its eyes the only reason you knew it was watching.

"Samona?" I asked.

"You know how I got him."

I tried to keep my voice steady, and even though I had finished the job, I stayed leaning inside the machine. "No. I don't. How?"

"Ethan."

A long pause.

"That was thoughtful of him." I came up out of the machine. She was holding a blue ice pack against her hand.

Another long pause.

She made a small gesture toward me. "You've got dye on your shirt."

I shrugged. "I'll buy another one at Urban Outfitters."

A flash of a sad smile. She wanted to say something else. She lowered her head.

"I wasn't sure what you knew." She moved toward the machine and turned on the power. It clanked and grinded for a few seconds before it began running again with a clean, smooth hum. The remains of the mangled shirt rolled onto a tray. "Even though you're the only one who . . . knows anything, I think."

"That's a dubious honor. But I guess . . ." I trailed off and studied the ceiling.

"You guess what?"

"I guess it brought me here. I mean, I barely knew you in college, and now it's eight years later and all this stuff is going on . . . and I'm here. How weird is that?"

"Eight years." She just stood there looking guilty. "Yeah."

I took a deep breath. "Samona?"

She looked up at me.

"Does this whole thing make you nervous?" I said this gently, without accusation, but her sad smile hardened.

"What do I have to be nervous about?" she snapped.

I couldn't reply because it would have come out desperate. She was standing next to me and I didn't care if she noticed that I was staring at the stain that slashed across the blouse beneath her breasts. I wanted her to notice. I didn't know where this confidence was coming from.

"Will you tell me something about Ethan?" she said in a distant voice. "Something I don't know yet."

"I'm not sure what you do know."

"Not very much," she said. "Hardly anything."

"And is that . . . why you asked me here?" I tried to sound casual. I tried to stay calm. I tried to pretend that I didn't care what her answer was. I looked away.

"Kind of," she answered, hesitant. "But not totally."

"He travels," was all I could come up with. "He's traveling all the time. It's like his thing."

"And where does he go?"

"Why don't you ask him, Samona?"

"I'm not sure he'd tell me."

"Where do you think he goes?" I asked.

She paused and then, in a sad whisper, "Everywhere." She shook her head. "Nowhere. I don't know—I wasn't close to Ethan at Yale like you were. I didn't even know he went to our school." She paused. "I guess I was too busy."

"Doing what?"

"I don't know. Hanging out. Not studying. Student Activities Committee. Intramural volleyball. Getting wasted on a nightly basis. Going to the art museum." She stopped to laugh, spiteful at how pointless it all sounded. "Whatever other shit I did while you and David were running around in circles every day."

The machine's humming made it easier for the conversation to take on a more intimate tone.

"So . . . how much did he tell you?" she asked. "About . . . us?"

"Nothing."

We were motionless. She gazed past me and sighed.

"Seriously," I went on in order to end this. "Ethan doesn't tell me very much. I don't know him as well as you think I do—"

"I get it, I know. But if you want . . ." She paused and seemed to weigh something in her mind before adding, "I can tell you—I'll tell you how it happened." She lowered her face, glancing up at me with a seductive meekness as she added, "I wouldn't mind telling you."

I didn't answer—I was reeling at her proposition and wondering what could possibly be motivating it—and she interpreted my silence as her cue to begin.

"I was at a gallery on Mercer Street right after this place opened. He was there, too. He recognized me from school and started talking to me . . ." She closed her eyes and trailed off, and I assumed she would end there—a few simple sentences, tinged with enough innuendo to satiate whatever curiosity had brought me to her but still vague enough to be set aside and, ultimately, ignored.

Then I would leave her shop and move on; I would screen Ethan if he called again; I wouldn't reply to e-mails from Samona or David; I'd pull away and focus on work and pretty soon the summer would be over.

Except that she didn't stop—she only paused to take a breath.

Then she told me exactly what happened that night.

And through it all I stood there, listening soberly, frozen, because:

(and the following awareness became fully and painfully clear only then, while she spoke)

I had built my world in such a way that the only thing I could offer Samona Taylor—my only significance to her—was that I happened to share small histories with both her husband and her lover, these histories rendering me the most appropriate person to hear her confession and, just by allowing her to tell it to me, absolve her. But what Samona Taylor didn't know was that hearing her story threw me back into an alternate reality I'd spent the last eight years trying to forget, and

(this was the most crippling part)

in that reality, I could have had her—I could have had Samona Ashley—and we could have moved through the city together, sealed off from everyone else, and I wouldn't have had to be alone.

Then the way Samona finished forced me out of my regret.

"And now I need a promise from you." Finally I looked at her face.

"Does . . . it matter that I've never made a promise I've been able to keep?"

She smiled. "I have to ask you not to say anything. Not that you would, but . . . okay?"

"Samona . . ." I started.

And then the bell above the door rang and Martha was back. She heard the press running again and called up, "Fantastic!"

Samona brushed a tear from her face and composed her expression.

She said, "I hope to catch up with you soon," and made me take a sandwich home.

I left without saying good-bye.

8

I WAS HALFWAY home that afternoon, and Samona's words would not leave my head; they played and replayed, over and over and over. There was something about their echo—the persistence of it—that was more than just a painful annoyance.

Part of me wanted to be involved. Part of me wanted to be a character in the story of Samona Taylor and Ethan Hoevel. Part of me wanted to be standing beside them.

And then I stopped on the corner of Mercer and West Fourth Street, and this turned out to be the moment in which certain events coalesced vividly in my mind; events which I couldn't help myself from reimagining; events that hurt me as I filled in details that she'd left out; events that Samona Taylor had chosen to recount to a guy she assumed was too inconsequential not to listen and too uncomplicated not to keep the secret.

In early May during the summer before she turns thirty, Samona Taylor goes to a certain gallery opening in SoHo where she's supposed to meet Olivia (Olivia knows the artist) and then the two of them will have dinner at Balthazar. But Olivia has to cancel because her husband isn't feeling well, and Samona is sitting alone in Printing Divine shutting down the computer and turning off the stereo, and she is dreading the empty night waiting in front of her, and since the gallery is only a few blocks away on Mercer, she decides to walk to the gallery anyway, have one or two glasses of wine, and then take a cab back to The Riverview. But the third glass of wine (she did not intend on having) goes straight to her head, and then David calls her cell phone because he won't be home until after midnight and it's just so typical and frustrating that she simply says, "See you later," and clicks off. Samona has never been comfortable at parties without someone she can cling to, but that third glass of wine pushes her over the hump and she starts feeling, well, sophisticated. Having just opened Printing Divine (made official by the small piece about it in the Sunday Styles section of the *Times* and a photo of her on Page Six at the party celebrating the opening and the mention in "BizBash"), Samona thinks she might be recognized, but this hope fades, and after thirty minutes of overhearing conversations between Park Avenue socialites and Tribeca hipsters with trust funds ("But the artist hasn't found his *identity* yet . . .") she starts feeling lonely and sad, and she's waiting for someone she can reject, some asshole dressed in Prada with whom she can flirt before ridiculing, which will then give her the excuse she needs to leave the gallery on Mercer Street and head up to the boring comfort of the apartment in The Riverview, where she might talk to her father for a few minutes on the phone before falling asleep in an empty bed. But no one comes and she can only float through the gallery for so long before sadness completely overwhelms her.

Someone catches Samona near the door just as she is leaving.

(Ethan Hoevel would inform me later that summer how he'd been at the same gallery on Mercer Street that night because he'd known that one of Stanton Vaughn's investors would be attending the opening, and since the problem of Indonesia was being associated with Stanton Vaughn's name with an alarming frequency, this particular investor had been having "serious doubts" about Stanton's future and hadn't returned any of Stanton's calls. So Ethan Hoevel deemed it a good idea to casually—accidentally—bump into the investor at the opening, with Stanton, of course, since Stanton always had more credibility when Ethan was with him. But Stanton never showed up that night—Stanton was actually screwing a young sculptor in Williamsburg—and so Ethan Hoevel was at the gallery alone, and he finally found the investor and flattered him by gushing about how great the art was and how it was such a wise move to invest in this artist at the very moment he was finding his *identity*, then used that to segue into Stanton and how "Boi-Wear" still had serious potential even though, yes, it was true, the industry had been losing interest because of a particular allegation regarding the labor situation in Indonesia, but the sweatshops were just harsh rumors in a harsh business—even though, as he thought about it, Ethan didn't actually know where Stanton got his materials and that was because, it just hit him, he had never seen the receipts—and the investor was buying it because it was coming straight from Ethan Hoevel. Then, at the end of his speech, as Ethan extended his arm for a handshake, he trailed off, because across the room he saw Samona Ashley floating alone in a corner next to two panels dotted with planetary bodies, and she was studying each panel separately even though they were meant to be taken in together from a distance. He saw her over the shoulder of Stanton's investor, who was in the midst of telling Ethan that he would keep his stake in "Boi-Wear," and then Ethan didn't have to stay at the gallery anymore. But he didn't leave because he was staring at Samona, who looked sort of lost and maybe a little sad, a woman who—if she left the brightly lit gallery on Mercer Street and walked through cool, dark, presummer SoHo, alone— would only become more lost and sad.)

The first thing Samona notices about this man is the way his eyes are so intensely, achingly green. And she immediately likes what he's wearing: a vintage pair of 517 Levi's (she can't remember the last time David wore a pair of jeans), authentic cowboy boots, a black Calvin Klein T-shirt, and a gray sport coat from Barneys. Those two things (the eyes and the clothes) are the reasons Samona Taylor lets this tall, thin man stop her at the door of the gallery on Mercer Street rather than dismissing him with a flash of her wedding band and the well-practiced turn of her shoulder, like she has dismissed so many others.

"Have we met before?" he asks.

"I don't think so," she says. "Should I recognize you?"

"Jeez, I was hoping you would," he says. "Because I recognize you."

Samona studies the face in front of her. She doesn't know who it is. She hasn't seen him anywhere recently. But then a time and place she has nearly forgotten comes back to her and she smiles, embarrassed.

"I remember you now. You went to Yale."

"That's it." His relief touches her.

She barely remembers him, and for some reason, on that night, she's glad about that fact. She wants them to remain strangers at first. She wants to move through the process of getting to know this man.

They go back into the gallery, reintroducing each other, and when she hears his name she recognizes it right away from the trade magazines, and she tells him about her new business and then Ethan Hoevel starts advising her on how to get Printing Divine more press— he has seen the piece in the *Times* and the mention on Page Six but has she ever thought about hiring a PR firm because he knows some good ones, and soon Samona Taylor isn't listening anymore because she has lost herself in Ethan's sadly entrancing eyes. It happens that easily.

When he asks her if she wants to grab a bite to eat, she decides to keep the reservation that Olivia made at Balthazar and the two of them leave the gallery together and walk to Spring Street. Even though she has a table reserved, the maître d' knows Ethan and seats them in one of the three coveted booths saved for celebrity walk-ins that overlook the teeming restaurant.

"I'm not trying to impress you," Ethan says, a little sheepishly.

"Well, maybe that's why I'm so impressed," Samona says, her head swimming with the four glasses of Yellow Tail she drank at the gallery.

Ethan consults with the sommelier and orders an expensive Burgundy she's never heard of, and then he concentrates solely on her in a way that makes her particularly aware that right now there's no droning on about market quotes or arguments concerning the print shop and the possibility of moving to the suburbs. She notices that even though the booth is oversize with just the two of them in it, they're sitting more closely than they were when they first slid in, and Samona wonders when this happened.

"So I know what you're doing now," Ethan says. "But I don't know where you've been all these years."

"Well, I'm—" Samona is trying to decide what to tell him, what she wants him to know, and then she sees him glance at the wedding band.

"Married?" he asks.

"Yes. I'm married."

"To that guy we went to school with? The runner?"

"Yeah." She laughs. "Do you know him?"

"If it's the same guy you were dating in college, yeah, I think I do. He was someone very . . ." Ethan searches for the right word and comes up with ". . . prominent."

"David Taylor." She says the name flatly.

"That's right," Ethan says. "David Taylor."

Samona wants to change the subject.

"And what about you?" she asks. "Were you—one of those prominent guys?"

"If I had been, wouldn't you have remembered me?"

"I guess so." She feels as if the balance between them keeps tilting.

Ethan registers this. "Forget it. It was a big school. I guess I was prominent in my own piece of it."

"That's a little evasive. Don't you want me to know?"

A curious expression creases her face, like she's just remembered something.

And Samona asks if Ethan Hoevel knew a guy who ran track with David Taylor. Because she recalls that the two of them—Ethan and this guy—seemed to hang out a lot during junior year, and she'd been aware of this only because David Taylor had intimated to her—without getting into the specifics that he did not have—that this guy had become "a serious part" of Ethan Hoevel's world.

Ethan's face hardens as he sips his wine, and after he sips the wine again, he says, "Yes."

But Samona is still lost in her memory and murmurs, "So what does it mean to be in 'Ethan Hoevel's World'?" And then she shakes her head as if to clear it, and says, "I'm a little drunk."

From then on, Ethan Hoevel does not take his eyes off her, even when she wants him to while she's savoring every bite of her risotto. The food sobers her up and she starts feeling relaxed again and expansive and Ethan has such immense confidence in himself, which Samona finds extremely (she does not want to go to this place—she's been fighting it all night) arousing. She has met a thousand men in this city who exuded confidence, but only in reaction to the demands the city placed on them. It never felt genuine to her—and not one of them ever managed to turn her on. Ethan's confidence is darker—she discerns a torrent of conflicting thoughts buried beneath his cool exterior—and yet seems to manifest itself so effortlessly. This complicated and sexy—yes, sexy, definitely sexy—confidence is something she has never seen in David Taylor. But sitting in the large red booth at Balthazar (they have moved even closer to each other) she understands that she's never been looking for it. David glazed over with fatigue and routine a long time ago; David's eyes are bloodshot from the stagnant glow of the computer screen; David has been fading away from her.

And now, his leg pressing against hers, she's sitting with a successful artist—lucid, gorgeous, alive—who's staring at her as if he wants to know everything.

Before the meal ends she is telling Ethan about the marriage and her discontent, the sadness and hopelessness, how he made her beg for the money to start Printing Divine, and what rendered the begging even more pathetic was that it wasn't just about a print shop—what David really wanted her to beg for was the chance to *do* something with her life, and then she's telling Ethan how they argue almost daily about her desire to find a loft in Tribeca instead of staying in their cookie-cutter one-bedroom in Hell's Kitchen, and how she dreads the inevitable moment at every dinner when David, after two tumblers of Grey Goose, brings up the subject of having children and moving to Connecticut or, worse, New Jersey, and—after Ethan and Samona have put another bottle of Burgundy away—how their lovemaking never lasts long enough, and Ethan just keeps staring at her through those tortured eyes, and she slowly decides that it isn't his confidence that is so attractive, but his pain.

For the first time in two years she feels real desire.

When she hears him invite her to his loft in Tribeca, she hears herself answering "Yes."

When she enters the loft nine floors up on Warren Street, her eyes are tearing because it is the loft she's always dreamed of, and it is almost too painful to stand in its center because it's a reminder of all the things she wants and doesn't have.

And after Ethan opens a bottle of Domaines Ott on his moonlit roof, she feels his hand nestle gently against the small of her back, and another hand caressing the nape of her neck. And she lets him.

An hour later she feels him thrusting up into her and they're both moaning softly, in tandem, and as her orgasm nears she's almost whimpering, and then Ethan stares into her eyes—shocked open by pleasure—for the duration of her release, and there's something about the way he's looking into her so steadily, as if he's studying her, that makes her believe he doesn't do this often, that she's special.

The awful fear that she will regret this night never finds her.

She weeps with relief.

And afterward as she dresses, tingling, he watches her from the bed, and she loves that he doesn't feel the need to say anything.

David is asleep when she returns to The Riverview that night.

And instead of getting into bed with him, she takes a long shower, and even after all the wine she can't sleep—she's too excited—and so she finds her old yearbook and stares at the black-and-white photo of Ethan Hoevel, his expressionless face brought to life by those piercing eyes, and only then can she peacefully fall asleep.

As I continued walking up Mercer Street and then east on Eighth, and the images unfolded, I understood that maybe with the wine and the sex but most likely with her opening of that yearbook, a relationship was set in motion.

What I also knew (and what Samona couldn't have known, because if she had, this relationship would have concluded before it was ever conceived) was that she and Ethan were already gravitating toward an unforeseen ending that was, in fact, embedded in another beginning that took place years ago, in a dormitory basement, in Trumbull College, on a crumpled couch, in a darkened corner.

9

I MEET ETHAN Hoevel during the first few weeks of our junior year in the fall of 1995, when an ex-girlfriend of mine, Debbie Wranger, who now lives across the hall from Ethan, introduces us, deciding that we will get along "quite well." When I press her for further explanation, she just answers that Ethan and I are both "deep" and leaves it at that. The first night I meet Ethan the three of us go out to dinner at a sushi bar near campus and Ethan Hoevel doesn't make that much of an impression on me at first. (I don't even know he's in my Literature of Imperialism class until he casually mentions it.) What I first assume is that Debbie wants me to meet a new boyfriend of hers; that the introduction of Ethan Hoevel is a slight dig at me for breaking off what, I thought at the time, was a fun one-night stand unfortunately stretched out over an entire sophomore term. In a way it works because I start thinking that Debbie Wranger is cuter than I've ever noticed before, and then the jealousy starts flaring since Ethan Hoevel is clearly much better looking than I—and he seems a lot more interesting, already beyond all the college bullshit but not in a pretentious way. It's just that he has already begun focusing on grander things. Gradually, and over a lot of sake, Debbie Wranger and her motivations disappear from the conversation while Ethan and I talk about books and classes and the social scene. I like how he seems to choose his words carefully yet say them enthusiastically, like they're off-the-cuff, and that, no matter what the topic is, he always says the thing you're waiting to hear. As an insecure junior, I admire this right away.

At the party at Woolsey Hall later that night, "Roam" is blasting out on the dance floor and the three of us—wasted not only on all the sake we have consumed but large cups of grain-alcohol punch as well—make a sandwich with Debbie in the middle, and then it gets turned inside out so that I'm in the middle, and Ethan is behind me, pressing into my back—but it's cool, it's in the moment—and we keep grinding away through "Like a Prayer" and "Stand!" and it's a drunken threesome that's getting a little out of control, but that's what is fun about it—the night is so unexpected—and then at some point it ceases to be a threesome, because Debbie has stepped back to watch us before she slowly moves off the packed dance floor and disappears into the maze of the party, which leaves Ethan and me rocking out wildly to "Sweet Child o' Mine" (the same song that will play later that year when I will kiss Samona Ashley at Sigma Alpha Epsilon). Then we take a break and squeeze ourselves onto a crowded sofa and talk so intimately about humdrum stuff—girls, classes, The Future—that everything boring suddenly seems revelatory, and the party ends sometime before dawn. As I walk back to my dorm I happily realize that I have met a genuinely interesting guy who finds me genuinely interesting, too. This has never happened before. There has always been a distance—that strange lack of intimacy I encounter with men. I pass out thinking that Ethan Hoevel has broken through that distance and in doing so has activated something in me.

How many good male friends do I have? Except for David Taylor there is really no one—and even David is a victim of his own tact. Men in my world never feel the need to get to know one another. When you grow up in the suburbs with parents so straight they both wear pajamas to bed and don't kiss in public, being "good friends" with a guy doesn't necessarily constitute closeness. There's no confiding, no tears, no feeling of emptiness when someone's not around, and instead we have sports, part-time jobs, nights spent hanging out in local burger joints—all essentially meant to waste time until we're old enough to move somewhere else. There's no attachment because, in the end, the relationships are as much based on what we don't know about each other as on what we do know. Then I leave Baltimore for college and it's the same thing except with different people and the added element of being half-drunk most of the time. So I never stop to consider these distances as problematic until I meet Ethan Hoevel and get my first glimpse of real sadness. Because Ethan—even on the first night I meet him—embodies a supreme sorrow (which he doesn't try to conceal) that I respond to. I am the one who always tries to keep things light. I am the one who always moves on to the less controversial topic. That's all I know how to do—I am the optimistic person who has never been wrecked by pain or doubt or suffering; these sensations have never been a presence in my small, stable life. The feelings I have for Samona and my meek way of dealing with them are the closest I've come to genuine torment, and at the end of the day those don't add up to anything, really.

But Ethan has this way of bending our conversation toward the world's greater darkness—often in unflinching detail, ruminating about fate and luck and death and the cruelty of the universe—and of forcing this unfamiliar sensibility to resonate with me. Ethan Hoevel knows—it seems he has experienced directly—that things don't always work out for the best, that life travels over a very jagged arc, and this is a different attitude from the privileged classmates surrounding us whose lives are blossoming with an infantile optimism (including me up to this point). There is pain coursing through Ethan Hoevel, and I soon feel an overwhelming urge to console him.

In the beginning all I can tell him is, "You usually get through the hard times by realizing that everything will work itself out for the best in the end."

"But what if it doesn't?"

Ethan sees how shocked I am and then softens. "I guess they would for someone like you."

This is another blow because, at this time, Ethan is pretty much right.

I stay calm, my voice remaining low. "Why do you say something like that? How are we any different?"

(He doesn't answer then. But we are different. I just don't know it yet.)

Because Ethan Hoevel knows—somehow—that all the years of one's life can lead easily up to a single defining moment which will be—most likely—a disappointment. And since, once that moment passes, there will presumably be plenty of time left to live, it will take so much strength not to let that disappointment define the rest of it. In the rarefied world of our university, so many of our peers don't really give a shit about anything except the next dance, the next party, the next hookup, the way they look. The disappointments that occur here are so mundane—a kiss turned away, a glass of wine spilled, a keg sputtering out, a term paper failed—that even if things don't go as expected, there is only a vague complaining before moving on to the next thing. But Ethan's complaints are so pointed, so filled with something close to heartbreak, so crushingly honest, that I become angry at myself and Debbie Wranger and everyone else around us who are so naive and deceitful and ignorant. The pain in Ethan's gleaming eyes is honest, and it is his honesty that will shape me.

"I'm going to tell you something and I'm not sure how you'll take it."

I am not surprised. I don't care. It registers quickly. By this time I am already aware.

"I know what you're going to tell me, Ethan, and it's cool."

He glances at me and thinks things through.

We are in my room, drinking beer, listening to a mixed CD Ethan burned for me, mostly U2 and Jeff Buckley. We're pregaming before the parties start. I am propped up against two pillows on my bed, back against the wall, and Ethan is cross-legged on the floor, leaning forward, ripping the label off his bottle.

"I thought you must have known from the first night."

"I didn't really think about it."

"I don't know if I believe that."

"Well, I guess when we were dancing . . ."

He grins and looks away. "You never said anything."

I shrug. "There was nothing to say."

"Or maybe you weren't paying attention."

"What was I supposed to do? Guess? I barely knew you."

"You're the first person I've ever told."

"Why weren't you sure how I'd take it? I mean, you're making this more about me than it is about you." I sip my beer.

"Maybe it's easier that way."

Ethan always knew, he tells me then. He knew when he made the eighth-grade soccer team, and he knew while he lost his virginity to the hottest girl in high school when he was only a freshman. He knew in tenth grade when he bought beers for the straight friends he found attractive, hoping to win their approval with the purchase of a six-pack (Ethan Hoevel never got carded), and he knew when he was dancing between three girls on a kitchen table at a high school graduation party. He knew when he was joking around in locker rooms after practice when he tried to keep his gaze at eye level with other teammates (despite his slim frame Ethan Hoevel was strong—he had muscle—and fast and was on the football team, where a litany of internalized torture presented itself, the most prominent being the unrequited love for the gorgeous quarterback), and Ethan knew when his sculpture teacher would talk about how the ancient Greeks relished capturing the beauty of the male form and he was involuntarily paying closer attention.

But he never acted on it until the beginning of his third year at Yale (just before he met me) when he found himself getting a blow job in the bathroom at a popular pizzeria off campus, leaning against a wall under a naked lightbulb, a beautiful drunken girl's head bobbing up and down a few feet below the line of graffiti scrawled across the wall that he was staring at: DARREN BROADBENT IS A FAG! Instantly Ethan reached down to the girl and told her she could stop. The epiphany was that simple, but what was it exactly? Who was Darren Broadbent? Was Darren Broadbent actually gay or was it a random slur? Or had someone written this happily, made ecstatic by the thought that Darren Broadbent was, in fact, gay and they could not control their joy over the news? Ethan read a lot into that one slashing line of graffiti— he gave it an ambiguity that it certainly did not deserve. But that was, for whatever reason, the catalyst. And the next night Ethan agreed to go back to the room of a senior who had been cruising him all term and at four in the morning he was sitting on the bed and the senior's hand was on Ethan's thigh, and then in a rush, their lips met and a warm, strong tongue pushed itself into Ethan's mouth and Ethan knew there was no way he would ever stop this because once you were liberated you could never go back to the way things were.

He waits for me to say something else—a very specific thing that I know he wants to hear—but he's going to have to ask.

"I wasn't sure if you were—"

"What?" I cut him off.

"If maybe—"

"Maybe what?" I do it again. This is my way of not letting the moment occur.

"If you were . . . too?"

I just stare at him and don't answer, watching his expression gradually shift from confusion to expectance to desire.

"What would it matter if I was?" I finally say. "We're friends. Right?"

He frowns. "I didn't expect such a cool reaction from you."

I'm shrugging again. "I'm a cool guy."

Ethan's coming out doesn't seem to change anything between us for a while. I try to pretend that what I said to him ("I'm a cool guy") is true and I then become loosely involved with a girl because we're both willing and there's no reason not to—I don't care about her enough to get hurt in the end, and when I'm with her, I usually picture Samona. Ethan spends a few more nights with the senior and manages to keep it hushed even as he becomes bolder about his new self. There are always parties, and classes become more important, and another track season starts, and at the end of the tunnel is graduation.

The night it begins is in November. Almost eight weeks have passed since we shared our first dinner with Debbie Wranger, and the two of us are in Trumbull College and bored and drunk and it's a sorority party that we don't want to stay at, but it's too cold outside to go anywhere else and so we're just standing in the corner figuring out what to do, trying to form a plan. He tells me to follow him to the basement.

"What for?" I ask.

"Privacy," he says in the dim blue light of the common room.

"Ethan, I don't want to hang out in the basement."

(But I am just saying this—at this point, I simply need the extra push.)

"Follow me."

I hesitate only because that's what I always do. I know what is going to happen—Ethan has been subtly pushing for it ever since we first met—but I am not sure if I'm ready. When I hesitate in the common room of Trumbull College, Ethan gazes at me with an expression I have never seen on him before. He has become empowered by something because this new expression says, basically: *I dare you.*

He leads us downstairs. The basement is a concrete room illuminated by a lone fluorescent bulb. It is just a kitchen: sink, microwave, refrigerator, a table with a row of empty beer bottles lined up along the edge, and a long, clumpy sofa pushed into a darkened corner. I will remember how the wooden rafters lining the ceiling creak under the weight of the party. I will remember Ethan locking the door. I will remember him turning around and saying, "So they don't catch us." I will remember him pulling two beers out of the fridge. I will remember him flopping down on the couch and motioning for me to join him. I will remember waiting but not sitting on the couch next to him. I will remember him leaning over and kissing me. I will remember thinking I can do this, and then I am kissing him back harder. And then the two of us fall onto the couch, and the rafters keep creaking loudly above us. In the basement of Trumbull College I am totally aware of the present—the locked door, the solidity of the room and the heaviness of what is happening in it, the beer bottles that suddenly seem so fragile I almost want to rearrange them, the two of us searching for different things in the same embrace. We finish quickly and almost on cue there's a pounding on the door that Ethan locked. We stare at each other for a moment, dazed by what just happened.

I am not going to be the one who looks away first because I feel that I still have to prove that I am the liberal guy, that I am not uptight, that everything is cool.

Still locked onto me, Ethan gets up from the couch, and before unlocking the door, before turning away, he hesitates for another moment. When I see what that hesitation means, I look away.

That junior year it isn't kept hidden but what is there to hide? I am a jock on the track team who has about eight conquests to his credit, and Ethan isn't out of the closet and identified by his sexuality yet, so no one's going to guess anything anyway. The surface we present is one of two friends who simply hang out together. He has his life and I have mine. Junior year is a busy world, and I am half-stunned with work, and track practice takes up every afternoon, and I'm trying to move through everything with an easy smile. In other words: we aren't holding hands while walking across the quad. When my mother asks over the phone if I'm "seeing anyone," I give her vague details without using any pronouns and am amused by the way she draws her own conclusions. When my father forwards an e-mail from his accounting office with a stupid gay joke (*Question: What do you call a fart in the men's room of a gay bar? Answer: A love call*), I e-mail back one of my own (*Question: Why did the gay man take a job at the loading dock? Answer: He loved taking deliveries in the rear*).

And since Ethan is something I didn't expect, I can view our time together as simply another interesting thing that has happened to me— the "writer" I want to become pushes for it, the "artist" feels the need to cross borders, to taste everything, and so I can take comfort in the fact that I am using Ethan as much as he is using me.

And that's my mistake: I don't see it as an affair; I'm content to think, okay, I'll see what happens; I never take it as seriously as Ethan does. It's just an unexpected development that I've really never fantasized about and consequently am unprepared for—Ethan presents himself to me from out of nowhere. None of it seems particularly weird or profound. It isn't earthshaking. It doesn't scare me after that first time. I simply find it ironic and experience it with a shrug. (Though if you told me a year before that I would be lying naked on Ethan Hoevel's bed as if it is the most normal thing in the world, I would not have believed you. I would have walked away from you. I would have ignored you.)

And, ultimately, there is a factor that was always going to end it.

I simply never found boys beautiful, and there has always been a girl on campus—exotic, graceful, dark-skinned—who means something to me.

Remnants of maybe our last conversation in May before the end of junior year. Eight months have passed since that night in the basement of Woolsey Hall.

We are lying in Ethan's bed in the darkness, afterward, sober, naked, our legs intertwined, talking about nothing and staring at the ceiling.

"What will you miss?" he asks. "After we leave here?"

I hesitate. "The strange moments." I sigh, stretching my arms over my head. "The ones I didn't expect."

"Like right now?" he asks.

"Well, this whole year was sort of a surprise." My weight shifts on the bed as I remove my leg from between his.

"You were a surprise," he says softly, resisting the movement of my leg.

He thinks I am being playful but then sees that I'm not.

"Well, becoming friends with you was a surprise as well," I say. "And it was a really nice one. It's kind of dumb to have to say this to each other."

He finally lets go of my leg. I am relieved.

"What do you mean?"

"I mean—do we need to be talking about this?"

He becomes silent, considering something.

I reach over to the nightstand and finish a beer we opened before we fell into each other. I notice how intensely he's watching me as I drink from the bottle.

"What?" I ask, startled.

"Where are we gonna be in five years?" he asks.

Something in me tightens—a tiny cluster of fear. I try to brush it off by laughing. "Shit—I don't even know where I'm gonna be five *hours* from now."

"You'll be in your room passed out." He pauses, turns away. "Or someone else's room."

I am silent. He's right. There is a girl who casually interests me. Ethan knows about her even though I've never brought her name up in front of him. What he doesn't know is that—as usual—this girl is basically a defense mechanism against my feelings for Samona. But so what?

"Well, it's not looking that way now, is it?" I'm comfortable enough with Ethan that I can reach over and stroke his cheek, very briefly, just to calm him. "I mean, I'm here with you now."

"But I asked you about the future." He turns over so his pale, narrow back faces me.

The dreaded words. I don't want to get defensive. I don't want things to get out of hand. This is a phase of our friendship and not the friendship itself. This is not going to last forever. But, hopefully, we are. I say none of these things.

"I don't know what you're talking about. We're good friends, Ethan."

He protests. "We're more than that."

"What's more than good friends?"

And so it continues until Ethan officially comes out and—since there's really nothing for me to come out of—we fight. I want to keep the friendship going but Ethan wants so much more than I will ever give him. I explain that he means more than that—I am longing to hold on to a friend who's important to me—I dread the day that Ethan wants a commitment. When I finally tell him that I "probably" (it is such a careful speech I prepare) am not gay, that I, in fact, "do" love him but that our friendship needs to "move to another level," that it is something I "don't" regret, that I let it happen, that maybe I "even wanted it" to happen, and that "honestly" it has "not been a big deal for me" (that is the phrase that hurts Ethan the most) Ethan shuts down completely. It is the last time we speak, and it is what drives Ethan to the mechanical engineering lab up on Science Hill a mile away from campus where he will spend his entire senior year. In the end it is Ethan who leaves me.

During that final year I occasionally bump into Ethan and he has nothing to say to me, but I'm busy with track meets and overwhelmed with three English classes and even though I miss hanging out (more than I ever imagined I would) I try hard to forget about him. I tell myself that no matter what you do or how you act people will always just drift in and out of your life and you really won't be able stop them (unless you truly want to, Ethan would have argued) and most of the time you'll just have to wipe the tear from your eye, and the ache in your chest will fade, and over time you will forget, and you will travel on, like Ethan Hoevel did.

II

10

_____

*(The following text is an incomplete history, presented in installments, and based on infor-
mation the author compiled beginning in the spring of 1996 and continuing until the
present day. The sources of the information include but are not limited to conversations
at biannual track reunions, the occasional drinks party with mutual acquaintances, circulated rumors, and the author's own more directed research. Certain details reflect the
author's projections that he imagined to be true.)*

THE STORY OF DAVID AND SAMONA

Part 1: The Dream

AFTER GRADUATING in May of 1997, David Taylor began his job at
Merrill Lynch as an "intermediary salesman" in the international
market sector. He shared a two-bedroom sublet in Battery Park City
with another Yale graduate who had a similar job at a different company. David took the apartment because it was within walking distance of the World Financial Center on Vesey Street.

Each day started at 3:45 A.M. David Taylor woke up, showered,
dressed, and walked through the predawn streetlight of downtown
Manhattan. It was a fifteen-minute walk, and he made a point to do
it every morning. These were fifteen minutes that he gave to himself
before giving up the next sixteen hours to everyone else. These were
the fifteen minutes when David Taylor would think about college and
how he had often scheduled his classes so he wouldn't have to be out

of bed until noon. By 4:30 A.M. David Taylor was sitting at his desk in time for the opening of the overseas markets. His desk was in a large room on the twenty-first floor of building four, where David and eighteen other men his age sat under fluorescent lights, the borders of their workstations defined not by the walls of a cubicle but by computers and power cords. Investors would call David and tell him what to buy and what to sell. He plugged their numbers into his Excel spreadsheets and then passed the requests along to the floor traders.

David Taylor had signed a two-year contract ($55,000 annually) at the end of which he would have to decide whether or not to leave Merrill Lynch.

Some days he would spread twenty minutes of work over fourteen hours with the goal of being the first one in the office to leave. Since everyone else was doing the same thing, they usually coordinated their departures with one another via Yahoo! and Hotmail accounts, avoiding the screening of company e-mail. And everyone who had escaped would make his way to a bar in the Millenium Hilton for a few drinks (usually more than a few) where they would talk about the market—where it had been, where it was going, how someday they would reap the benefits—before making weak efforts to pair up with any available girls and move on to the next place, or else go home. But David Taylor—who more often than not would forgo the routine girl chasing since he knew that if and when he went home with some oversexed young stranger, he'd then somehow have to wake himself up before dawn in an unfamiliar part of town and be even more tired and depressed than he already was—would usually just come back to the Battery Park City apartment by seven (he rarely saw his roommate, who worked domestic market hours) and he would eat Thai or Chinese takeout and watch back-to-back reruns of *The Simpsons* and maybe call Samona before going to bed no later than 8:30, and while falling asleep he would remember watching *The Simpsons* with his fraternity brothers and how he missed that camaraderie and the simple human contact of it all and its lack of desperation. That was really the only thing he noticed about his coworkers as the millennium approached—how desperate they all were to stay late, to get ahead, to make their millions young, to get laid, to get high on something more exciting than coke (which was "so eighties and early nineties"), to establish themselves as the plucky new wave of prodigies who were going to take over this antiquated world of finance before their window closed.

David Taylor didn't want to be a part of that.

He never had the ambition to change anything bigger than himself. He just wanted to lay low, float under the radar, and get through "being a kid" fast so he could move on to the next segment of his life as quickly as possible.

David Taylor was also aware of how lonely he was.

Through all this, he spent a not insignificant portion of his time wondering how he arrived on the twenty-first floor at Four World Financial Center, staring into the green luminescence of his computer screen. What had happened to that dream he'd had, which had once seemed so conceivable? That dream which had been spawned during Thanksgiving break junior year, lying on his bed in the attic of a house outside Chicago reading *Heart of Darkness* for his Literature of Imperialism class, marveling at how he could be listening to the murmurs of his parents, who were sitting in the dining room downstairs drinking whiskey and arguing about the new brick patio—how this could be happening after three known affairs (his father, Patrick, who ran a small chain of hardware stores, had a short fling with David's nanny and then another one-night stand with the widow who lived six houses away; his mother, Judy, had been fucking the squash coach at Northwestern University, where she was secretary to the dean of the English department, for years) and one second mortgage and ten thousand arguments over trivialities like the heating bill and how much rum to stir into the eggnog and what angle to set the grand piano and why did Patrick want to stop at one child when Judy still needed a daughter? What could they be talking about now, a day before Thanksgiving? How could they still be talking at all? How could they have allowed their lives to reach this point? Why hadn't they just surrendered to each other at some stage along the way and then moved on to something at least mildly more fulfilling?

The dream that David contrived in response to his parents' late night of drinking—what he considered the antithesis to the way they simply settled for each other and a life of mild discontent—began with him getting a master's degree in education, preferably in New York or Boston or D.C. (those cities that drew stampedes of recent college grads seemed interchangeable). And while he was doing this, he'd substitute-teach part-time in local high schools and be that cool young person who gets high fives from all the male students and unrequited crushes from all the girls. He'd learn how to be tough and earn people's attention, and at night he'd do something cool for spending money (his family in Chicago had none) like bartend in a neighborhood dive. And then very soon David would have his degree and take a salaried position as an English teacher in the public school system, where he'd get through the rigorous days by knowing he was doing something important and challenging and also by looking forward to the summer, which he would spend relaxing in the Hamptons or Cape Cod or the Jersey Shore (depending on what city he ended up in) with old fraternity brothers and whatever girl he happened to be dating. After a few years of this—having paid the necessary dues and rid himself of debt through city financial aid programs—David Taylor would move on to a private school that had an opening, preferably an exclusive boarding school in Massachusetts within driving distance of Boston and New York, where he'd live in a modest house with a yard, and coach track—working out alongside his runners, whipping the rich kids into shape—and teach Shakespearean romances to people who were too young to understand the subversiveness, but who wanted the class anyway because Mr. Taylor was leading it and Mr. Taylor kicked ass ("please, call me Dave," he would say offhand, in the dream). Meanwhile his office window would overlook a set of rolling hills blanketed with the red-and-yellow leaves of autumn or purple with snow in the winter, and before long (he never harped on the particulars of this, but simply believed it would happen naturally) he would have a loving wife and two children and on the weekends he would play soccer with his sons on the football field inside of the track where he coached. And it never mattered—in the dream—that it was all just a glorified extension of the environment he was most accustomed to, and that David Taylor's plans, someday, might be confronted by a reality which challenged the ease he so craved.

What had happened to that dream?

That dream had died—been murdered, actually, without David even knowing it—in the final weeks of his junior year at Yale, when David Taylor was just getting serious with Samona Ashley. And since she would be living in NYU housing that summer with two girlfriends while interning at the Gagosian Gallery in Chelsea, David decided that he wanted to be in New York with Samona. He was going to live with two of his fraternity brothers (who were also interning in the city) on the Upper East Side and drink the summer away and spend most nights with Samona and on weekends they would go out to the Hamptons, where the Sigma Alpha Epsilon vice president's parents had a house in Amagansett. That was the plan, and it seemed like a damned good one. So he posted his "résumé" on Jobtrak.com and did a keyword search on *Manhattan* and applied to basically anything that was available (which did not include much at the end of April): a psych research program at Sloan-Kettering which involved running CAT scans on paranoid schizophrenics, tutoring low-income children at Mentorship USA, assisting at an executive head-hunting firm, and a summer internship at Merrill Lynch.

Merrill Lynch was at the bottom of David Taylor's list.

But they were the only one who requested an interview.

David Taylor was interviewed by a guy only two years older than he who also ran track in college, and so David—who had been nervous about the interview—was put at ease almost immediately when his eight-hundred-meter championship became the main topic of their conversation. Within minutes, he was offered the internship, which he accepted because it meant he could drink with his friends and have sex with Samona and not worry about money and it would all be great. So he would have to wake up early during the week—big deal. He was young, he could handle it. This wouldn't be a problem.

He didn't know that the dull and endless work would wear David Taylor down more fully than any track practice or fraternity pledge week ever had, or that the fun he had planned for the summer of 1996 would be eradicated by his utter weariness. He didn't know that on Monday he wouldn't even imagine there being such a thing as Friday, and when Friday finally arrived, it would seem unreal that Monday had ever existed—it would seem so far in the past. And on Saturdays it would seem even more unreal that another Monday was starting two days later, and he'd have to ride the 6 train to Grand Central and then navigate the hot, crowded platforms to transfer to the Times Square shuttle and then another subway car downtown before climbing up into the chaos of the World Trade Center. And that would be before the workday even began. David didn't expect any of this, but this was how it happened.

The internship lasted ten weeks. There were no weekends in the Hamptons (there was almost one, but it lasted only six hours because Samona had said she was coming and then didn't show, which freaked David out enough to take an empty jitney back into Manhattan on a Friday night in July—a total disaster). The first three days of each week David could only concentrate on just getting through them and nothing else, and then he would go out with Samona and their friends on Thursday night, before spending a long and torturous Friday hungover in the office. The weekends were only about air-conditioning, dry cleaning, catching up on sleep.

But since it was only ten weeks, there was always that light at the end of the tunnel, and the internship would be painfully endured and happily forgotten. What David couldn't have predicted was that Ian Connor, the ex-runner who interviewed David at the beginning of that summer, would not believe that David Taylor had been honest about the track times listed on his résumé. David didn't seem athletic enough to have that kind of speed, and this pissed Ian off all summer. On top of that, there was something in David Taylor's easygoing smugness that pissed Ian Connor off even more. And since Ian Connor was trader as stereotype—aggressive, competitive, brash, crude—near the end of the summer of 1996 he challenged David to a 150-yard race in Central Park. Ian was shorter than David and a little stocky but he was basically still in shape—he lifted weights in the office gym each afternoon and took spin classes at Synergy in the evenings. David hadn't run much that summer and wasn't really all that interested (it was against NCAA training rules, too) but once word of the race leaked out, office wagers spiraled into the thousands, and since all of those wagering were his superiors, David felt he had no choice but to humor them. Before the race, James Leonard—the floor leader who had been at Merrill Lynch for twenty-seven years—told David Taylor that he had put $15,000 on David and he would "greatly appreciate it" if David won.

Twenty traders in two lines formed a straightaway across Sheep Meadow one Saturday afternoon in August. Ian used a crouching start. David was standing. Someone had come up with a real starter's pistol, and all the commands were given—*Runners take your marks, Get set,* and then the gun. David slipped at the start of the race and faced a choice: either throw his hands in the air and forget the whole thing since there was only one more week left in the internship or else play catch-up and try to win.

Something inside David Taylor—that fire which, as a freshman, had sent him around the track faster than anyone else in the Ivy League, amplified by the fact that this race was an opportunity to show these assholes who'd been torturing him all summer that he was in fact stronger than any of them—pushed him a half yard ahead of Ian Connor's choppy strides just before the finish line, where Samona Ashley was standing. David had told her to be at the finish line so he could use her as a mark to keep him running a straight line.

That half yard—David was sure of this ever since—was the sole reason he received one of only two offers from Merrill Lynch that year. It was a bear market, and a lot of salesmen and traders were losing their jobs, and though this wasn't where the dream was supposed to flow, David Taylor—to the astonishment and horror of Samona, who'd spent much of the summer enduring his complaints—accepted the offer.

Surprisingly, the choice was simple: while most of the guys in his class at Yale were going back to their final year of college wondering what they would do when they graduated (and tens of thousands of dollars in debt) David Taylor would have a job waiting for him. He would return to Yale in the fall of 1996 for his senior year and take it easy and focus on track and Samona and having fun. Plus, when he stopped to think about it, David could amuse himself at how he had neither worked very hard that summer nor been particularly good at the work he did. If he looked past the actual time spent and hours lost, it wasn't such a bad gig after all. So when James Leonard invited him into his office to offer David the job—along with his congratulations and thanks for the $15,000 Leonard earned in two-to-one odds—David Taylor convinced himself that he had outsmarted them all. He shook James Leonard's hand and gave two years of his life away. A half yard of flattened grass defined the beginning of David Taylor's adulthood.

The new plan: David would work hard and save up his money—a windfall for someone who had never been ambitious about anything other than running, and who had never expected to have a savings account worth more than a few nights out drinking—and then he would go back to school for his master's in education and he'd be able to do it without student loans. Because of the state of the market at the time, he was placed in the much-maligned international group, but he had prepared himself for that. (It would only be two years, remember?) Besides, it wouldn't hurt to live a little bit in the harsh light of the real world for a short while—it would make his dream all the more fulfilling.

That was, in effect, the end of David Taylor's dream—though he didn't know that yet.

There was a vital distraction that prevented him from realizing what he'd done.

In the summer of 1997, just after college graduation, as David Taylor was moving into the apartment in Battery Park City with the fellow athlete from Yale, Samona Ashley was helping her parents adjust to the move from Connecticut to Minneapolis, where her father had been transferred, before she would decide what to do with her BA in art history and where to do it. She tried to spend the majority of her days browsing the Internet for positions at Christie's and Sotheby's (there were none available for which she was even remotely qualified), but it was still a total nightmare: "Tana from Ghana" was acting more manic than usual, which ultimately amounted to Samona being unable to lift a box or drink a Diet Coke without initiating some tirade on how she could definitely stand to lose "at least eight" pounds from her "backside."

Samona—even though she probably should have been accustomed to this by the time she was twenty-two, especially with all the counseling she received at Yale's Mental Health Center—could never get used to being the focus of her mother's tirades. And her father was no help—he chose not to take sides—which pissed Samona off because he was the one who had asked her to come to Minneapolis in the first place. He'd said he "missed having his girl around" and that she should "take as much time as she needed to figure her life out," but each day that passed only cemented her belief that his reaching out had been just a ploy to divert Tana's "difficult nature" (he used that phrase because he somehow assumed it would soothe her) onto someone else.

The only saving grace was David Taylor calling her every night at eight o'clock from New York after *The Simpsons* reruns were over, before he went to bed. Samona never brought up how miserable she was in Minneapolis because David was so unhappy and still in shock that he was back to waking up every morning before 4 A.M. to get to an office he didn't want to go to and sit at a desk until 6 P.M., and how had he ended up at Merrill Lynch in the first place? Why hadn't Samona talked him out of it? How had he fooled himself into thinking he could take it for two years? What was he doing with his life? The nightly phone calls—even though they were all about David—provided exactly the kind of distraction Samona now craved, especially when he ended each conversation by telling Samona how beautiful she was and how much he missed her and that she was perfect—words she desperately needed to hear amid all the Tana-inspired self-loathing.

She assumed correctly that there were the intermittent "random girls" in his life while she was away, but from the sound of his voice—its desperate tone—she also assumed correctly that he wasn't excited by any of them the way other guys in his world were. The city was never a "playground" to David, which made him come off as more mature than the typical twenty-two-year-old. And since they hadn't made any kind of commitment to each other, she couldn't locate it in herself to fault him much for fooling around, and she never pried for details. In fact, Samona had a one-night stand of her own in Minneapolis one night in late June (a "friend of a friend"), but the faceless guy wasn't exhilarating in the least, and he was too "small" and into his own pleasure to be anywhere near the realm of giving her an orgasm, and the awkwardness and detachment of the whole encounter made her long for what she'd had with David even more.

She projected that he felt the same way about her. Ultimately, she was content simply to know that his days were filled with nothing, and she never had to admit to him how his unhappiness made her so much more at ease with her own.

Near the end of the summer of 1997, when they'd both reached crisis point, David asked Samona to visit him. He purchased her ticket from a consolidator Web site, splurged on a car service at the airport, and Samona Ashley left her parents in the approaching coldness of a Minnesota autumn and flew to New York for what was supposed to be a two-week visit. She had not seen David Taylor since graduation in May. They made love as soon as she arrived, but it was different than she remembered. He didn't have the energy he once had, and he didn't move the same way. He never found that place inside her that he had found so quickly their first time together.

Still, the simple presence of him within her took Samona so far from the bland condo in Minneapolis, her mother's voice, her father's unexpected apathy, and the growing awareness that her art-history degree was a useless sham and that she would never find a job she wanted. She didn't need intense pleasure from David so much as she needed a means to ignore certain realities.

She was lost and indecisive. She didn't want to go back to Minneapolis, but she didn't have the will to consider staying in New York—just seeing what the city had done to David in two months was enough to terrify her.

When David proudly set her up (through one of the account VPs on his floor) with an interview at the home of a private art dealer specializing in Spanish and Italian Renaissance masters (which had been part of her thesis at Yale) she bought a low-key dress and went to his house in Riverdale. She didn't have high hopes but at least it was something to do. Then the door opened and his saggy eyes lit up suggestively, causing her to recoil. For the next hour and a half, she endured the seventy-year-old man staring relentlessly at her legs while she murmured perfunctory answers to his pointless questions, repeatedly tugging her skirt down below her knees. She knew the whole time that, since she refused to acknowledge his interest, she'd never hear from him again.

"Please don't worry, baby," David pleaded with her over the phone while listening to her cry. "I'll find something else for you."

"There *is* nothing else," she sobbed back at him angrily, unable to decide what was more pathetic—how badly David wanted her to stay, or how badly she wanted to leave. "There's nothing here for me, and I just have to get out of here. Like, tomorrow."

Her impromptu "going-away party" was at a bar that night with David's "friends" from the office—people Samona found dully amusing. David was still trying desperately to cheer her up enough to make her stay a little longer. He was failing miserably—she kept having to go to the bathroom in order to hold back tears and, the last time, throw up—until he latched onto the story about Samona entering the model search at Yale—as a joke (he left out that she'd been prompted by him)—and how she had won anyway and her prize had been a set of free head shots and a meeting at the modeling agency that had sponsored the search (which she'd never set up), and this led to someone at the bar mentioning that as long as Samona was in town why not call the agency? Her face lit up slightly that night, and the following afternoon after David massaged her confidence over the phone ("The worst they can do is say no, which they won't") she did call them back. The agency had her come in for a set of head shots, and almost instantaneously she was contractually bound to a series of catalog photo shoots for two different cosmetics lines. Her look was "in" at that moment: "light-skinned island type" was how she often heard herself described. The half smile, the tentative expression, the way she was constantly looking away as if she was totally indifferent to the process (which she wanted to be but wasn't)—it all captured the camera "in a very millennial way," or so she was told.

And so Samona Ashley's two-week visit to see her boyfriend turned into two months. She started hitting the agency parties and charming all the right people in her own quiet, enigmatic way, and this led to an even more powerful agency wanting to represent her (maybe not one of the top five but definitely in the top ten), and she was also requested for the catwalk a few times, which paid extremely well even if they weren't exactly top-tier shows. David Taylor accompanied her to the first few parties—when Samona was still shy about throwing herself into the mix and needed someone beside her other than the specter of her mother ranting about everything wrong with her body—but he was too tired to enjoy them and he completely resented the male models from Omaha or L.A. or Queens who tried hard to discuss current events they didn't know anything about, and since all of the parties were during the week, David had a valid excuse to not accompany Samona anymore. His distaste turned out to be fine since, within three weeks of her first meeting, she had developed a base of acquaintances she hung with and suddenly she didn't mind going places without him.

They both knew that this logically should have been the end of their relationship. They were growing up. They were moving on. They weren't in college anymore. It wasn't a big deal as long as it happened painlessly (they told themselves independently of each other), right?

But something strange kept occurring: she still came back to Battery Park City every night, climbing into bed just a few minutes before he had to get up for work, even though she didn't have to—even though there were plenty of young guys (models, managers, agents, photographers) who would have been thrilled to take her home because, fortunately or unfortunately, Samona Ashley managed to exude sex without even trying.

Every time she came back, it would confuse him.

It confused him even more when she admitted to him that when she was being hit on, she would go so far as to attempt to make herself unattractive in some lame way—snorting when she laughed, acting like a ditz, telling them she was a dyke—before she figured out that acting moronic only seemed to heighten their interest.

It was all a mystery to him.

And it was too much for Samona to explain (not to mention that he wouldn't ask her to) that though being the object of so much energy might have been amusing and diverting and flattering at first, it became immediately apparent that none of these guys (or girls) would ever take care of her. Sure, it could be fun; it made her feel sexy; she'd always been intrigued at the thought of having a three-way; the freewheeling drug use could be liberating; her mother was finally proud of her. But none of these reasons accounted for the fact that Samona Ashley was the kind of girl who needed someone to go home to—specifically, someone who had his own life and his own dreams and was dependable, and who didn't think that nice suits, good looks, industry connections, and a shitload of money simply entitled him to some part of her she wasn't willing to give.

What made this man David Taylor and not anyone else she met who'd be more than happy to provide a spot for her in bed was Samona also finding that she couldn't shed the feeling of supremacy to which her Yale diploma entitled her—the BA might not have been enough to get her a decent job, but it was more than enough to make her feel superior to the group of people she was exposed to, most of whom hadn't gotten past high school. She found herself gravitating back toward David not out of loyalty or even pity but because David was on her level. He was able to challenge her, and he was able to do it with a gentle self-confidence that—having grown up as the object of Tana Ashley's ferocity—Samona was easily drawn to.

"Why are the office buildings in midtown so plain and ugly?" was a typical question.

"I guess they didn't teach you about cost-efficient architecture in art history," was a typical answer.

A lesser reason, of course, was that despite her relative financial stability, she'd been spending most of her earnings on clothes and drinks and didn't have enough yet for her own place. And David was saving his money—he'd been doing this religiously (though less so once it became apparent that Samona would be staying for "a while")—and he had his eye on the future.

But for now, in the present, they had their domestic routine: Samona crawled into bed late at night smelling of smoke and sweat and vodka, and around 3:45 A.M. when his internal clock woke him, David would reach over and place his hand on her stomach, and they would make love for five to seven minutes before David would shower and head to work.

If the odd overlapping of their schedules alarmed David Taylor—if Samona's apparently exciting nightlife cast any doubts in him—he never said anything. Samona attributed it simply to his fear of losing her. Because—and both of them knew this—Samona was the one thing he had in his new world of nothing.

She loved that about David.

She loved that about New York.

11

THE WEEKS after seeing Samona at Printing Divine brought rejection on all fronts. Silence from my editors (even the most insistent ones) forced me to swallow my rapidly dwindling pride and start making "outreach calls." Nothing was flying on the Gowanus Canal pitch, and the editor assigned to the Lower East Side piece I had written for *The Observer* had scrapped it entirely. The common response—from assistants whose voices sounded automated—was that there was a war going on, so magazines where I had connections ("Let's face it, we aren't exactly *TNR*") wanted to take their audience away from everything that was wrong with the world. People wanted distractions from pain and terrorist threats and the falling markets and airport delays and unemployment and all our brave young soldiers in Iraq. They wanted product sampling—reviews of skin creams and wristband cuffs from Italy and the latest line of Christian Louboutin shoes. They wanted to be reassured that Monday was the new Thursday, that pink was in and brown was out, that Schiller's Liquor Bar was the new Pastis, that Lisa Davies was the new Kate Moss, that Marc Jacobs was the new Armani, and that a little bit of color injected into your outfit could make—or break—a Saturday night. They wanted "smart fluff." The last thing anyone wanted, I was assured, were articles with a depressing edge. I would just have to wait for the world to cool down.

An added fact: I was broke.

And since there was nothing really going on with me that summer—except what was going on with three college friends—I spent my time conceiving and discarding roughly a dozen things I could do for a little money, including but not limited to bar-backing at Xunta or Doc Holliday's or Lucy's or some other dive bar nearby (not enough "service experience," I was told), walking dogs (fear of being bitten), bicycle messenger (didn't own a bike, couldn't afford one), selling my furniture at a flea market (Ethan's chairs were the only pieces worth more than five dollars), or the dreaded trip to a temp agency (didn't own a dark suit, couldn't afford one). And this was the state of being which compelled me during the third week of June ("Call if you're compelled," was how he'd left it) to return Ethan Hoevel's message from the day after the Randolph Torrance party, and since I was about to ask for advice on work, this meant the careful and indignant speech I had been preparing had to be tossed out.

(Even though I knew there was nothing I could say that might change his mind, I still wanted him to know that I disapproved of his relationship with Samona Taylor. Before the money crunch, I had been planning to ask him rhetorical questions like "What are you thinking?" and "Do you really want to destroy a marriage?" and "Is this just another fleeting experiment of yours that probably won't last through summer?" because it was obvious that there were so many things Ethan Hoevel and Samona Taylor didn't know about each other, and these things, I felt, mattered.)

Another reason for ditching the speech: I had a strong premonition that Ethan, of all people, would probably know the real reason I disapproved. And Ethan, of all people, wouldn't spare me the humiliation of it all.

Stanton Vaughn picked up the phone.

"Is Ethan there?" was all I asked. Suddenly Ethan's eyes—which I had always found hypnotic and beautiful—appeared in front of my line of vision, and I had to close my own to make the image go away.

"He's gone," Stanton said.

"Do you know what time he'll be back?"

"No. He's *gone* gone. You know. On one of his trips. He might be back in a week. He might be back in a year. He was incredibly vague about it. As usual."

"Where did he go?"

"What are you doing right now?" Stanton Vaughn said with what he deemed the appropriate measure of innuendo.

"So do you know where he went, Stanton, or not?"

Stanton sighed, giving up faster than he usually did. "He said Thailand, but I'm not sure I believe him. There was a message from his travel agent. Something about a Lufthansa flight. Does Lufthansa fly to Thailand? I don't think so."

"I think they connect in Germany somewhere."

"I told him not to go." I could hear Stanton lighting a cigarette and exhaling. "Thailand might as well be fucking Afghanistan. But he doesn't listen to me anymore. Kids trying to blow up planes with their fucking shoes? Who wants to go anywhere? Who wants to get out of bed?"

Suddenly my one mission in life was to get off the phone as quickly as possible.

"I mean I'm just the fucking boyfriend after all, right?"

"If you hear from Ethan, could you just tell him I called?"

"He isn't gonna call, man." There was a pause filled with Stanton's heavy breathing. "But hey, you wanna come over for a drink?"

"I'm very busy here."

"That's too bad." He paused. "Really just too bad."

Later that day I found myself at the corner ATM staring at the two-digit number on the receipt that signified the money I had left in my account. I was also aware of the rent notice on my windowsill, as well as the fact that I was now looking for meals in Manhattan that cost less than five dollars. Somewhere in the world Ethan Hoevel was lying on a beach, and David Taylor was in his office trading millions, and Stanton Vaughn had a show coming up for Fall Fashion Week. I dipped to the bottom of my pride and e-mailed my résumé to James Gutterson, and an hour later followed up with a phone call to ask him if The Leonard Company job might still be available.

The security desk stretched across the entire back wall of the lobby manned by four guards in navy-blue suits. I passed through the revolving door and noticed a number of construction workers walking through the metal detectors under a large banner announcing that The Leonard Company was renovating its floor: USHERING IN A NEW ERA WITH THE NEW CENTURY.

The elevator moved so fast my ears popped moments before I was deposited on the twenty-first floor. After showing a suspicious receptionist the pass one of the security guards had given me, I moved through a huge open space where executive offices lined one wall, and the conference rooms along the other wall were covered by tarps and ladders under which a stream of construction workers disappeared, and between these two walls was a vast wasteland of open desks inhabited by men my age hatefully barking into phones while striking their computer keyboards. After a lap, I finally tagged James Gutterson at one of these desks in the far corner on the twenty-first floor. Gutterson seemed bigger than I remembered, but this was mostly because the space he inhabited was barely large enough for his chair to swivel around in. There were stacks of paper everywhere—most of them printouts of graphs sloping downward. Gutterson's face was about three inches away from a computer screen, and he did not look up until I finally knocked on the plastic surface and murmured, "Hey."

"Have a seat, buddy." Gutterson returned to staring at the computer.

The desk was so small and cluttered that there was no room for another chair, so I moved one stack of paper onto another and simply sat against the desk.

"Try not to move anything, okay?" he asked, his face immobile. "I have things just the way I need them."

The computer screen was a Yahoo! Sports page: MAPLE LEAFS TRADE JASMOVICH IN OFF-SEASON POWERPLAY. His eyes were scanning horizontally across the screen. After about five minutes he closed the window and shifted his weight in the chair until he was comfortable. He didn't say anything.

"Busy?" I asked.

"You know it." He rubbed his temples with his fingertips. His stomach was actually resting on those monster thighs, remnants of afternoons gliding across the ice trying to shatter anyone in the way. With his feet tucked back under the chair and his hands resting in his lap, James Gutterson resembled, for a moment, the Buddha in a rumpled Hugo Boss suit.

"I really appreciate you seeing me, James."

He dug through the piles on his desk and a huge stack of graphs fell to the floor, spilling out into the walkway. James winced and then went to his bottom drawer as I started picking up the pages and then he sat up with another stack of paper and a few reference books along with the last three years of The Leonard Company annual reports.

"Here's all you need," James said, smiling as he dropped everything into my arms, the weight of it all causing me to lose my balance. "There's an outline somewhere in there that'll tell you how we want this thing laid out."

"Thanks."

There was a moment of silence during which I became aware of how heavily and somberly James was breathing. He slapped his big thighs and they trembled. "So."

"Yeah, well . . ."

"Have fun. Let me know if you need anything else."

"I don't think that would be possible," I said, gesturing at the stack I was holding.

"Aw, come on, it won't be so bad." He smiled good-naturedly.

I doubted that but nodded like everything was cool. "Is David around?"

The smile turned into a forced grin. "Mr. Taylor has his own office." He glanced to the opposite corner of the floor. "And that door is closed, sooo this means Mr. Taylor must be quite busy."

"Oh, of course, right."

James wasn't even grinning anymore. "It would be great to see some kind of draft done by the end of this week." He saw my brow furrow with concern. "Well," he relented. "Early next week at the latest. This whole thing has been on the table way too long."

He was already turning away. As I rearranged the material to make it easier to carry, he opened a new window: MIGHTY DUCKS OUTLOOK NOT SO MIGHTY FOR OCTOBER.

I walked over a mat of tarp and under a ladder to get to David Taylor's office, where his secretary stopped me and—after picking up the phone and reading the name on my pass, eyeing me warily as if I were intruding—said, "He wasn't expecting you but go on in."

David Taylor's desk was about fifteen times the size of James Gutterson's, and the office was color-coordinated in conservative bleached whites and faded browns with a graceful wood molding along its corners where the walls met the ceiling. David was framed at his desk between a new iMac computer and an old Bloomberg screen, and behind him floor-to-ceiling windows faced west across town where the Hudson River was barely visible between skyscrapers.

"This is a surprise," David said with a half smile. "What are you doing here?"

I deposited the stack on the leather couch and mentioned the meeting with James Gutterson.

"Right. Right," David said, leaning back and stretching his arms high over his head. The cracking of his back snapped throughout the office. "Yeah, I knew that. James told me you e-mailed him. Right. Just very busy today. Things just keep slipping my mind." I noted the deep circles under his eyes.

"So how goes it?" I asked.

"Fair to middling, as the older generation likes to say." He slumped forward against the desk.

A bookshelf had been built into the wall on the right side of the room, its bottom shelf packed with thick binders marked by year, and the shelf above it held all the corporate lit for the same period. A full set of the *Encyclopædia Britannica* took up the third shelf, and in the top three shelves were books I recognized from college organized alphabetically by author, starting with Aristotle's *Poetics* and ending with a Yeats collection and between them were the Brontë sisters and Dostoyevsky and Ralph Ellison and Faulkner and Hemingway and Melville, Plato and Shakespeare, Sophocles and Tolstoy. I imagined that David Taylor had never read any of these books and that they only existed as a reminder of the days when the definition of responsibility was reading the books you were assigned. I wished I had bypassed David's office and just taken the elevator down to the lobby.

The left side of the office was mostly empty space, halfheartedly filled with a black leather couch, and above it a framed poster with a woman's lithe body walking down a runway outlined above the words PRINTING DIVINE in large script. I scanned his track-and-field certificates surrounding the poster and an antique wall clock ticking loudly above them. On the left side of the clock I stopped on a photograph of David and Samona slow-dancing at their wedding. I turned away.

David was rubbing his hands down his face, smiling sadly, as if he was about to tell me a tragic joke.

"I lost fourteen million dollars yesterday. Just me. By myself. Fourteen million dollars. How does that sound to you?"

"Pretty much unfathomable."

"Actually, it's not as bad as it sounds." David paused. "It just means I have to . . . get with the program, I guess." He rubbed his face again. "Risks." He sighed. The smile was gone. "I fashioned a nice little career by taking risks and hitting them. It was sort of like a fairy tale for a bit. It was good while it lasted, you know? But now . . . desperate times . . ."

"Desperate measures." He let me complete the sentence.

"Actually, just conservative measures. I know what to do. Which just makes the days longer."

Suddenly he seemed confused as to the reason for my presence.

I was reminded of the way David Taylor used to run track—how he was not the kind of runner to hold back and explode in the last hundred meters, how at the beginning of his career, once or twice, he ran himself out too early and died at the end while the other runners overtook him, and how he learned from that mistake and started running more conservatively, measuring his pace to wear the other runners down.

I was staring out the window behind David's desk as I pictured this.

"Admiring the view?" I heard him ask.

"I was just thinking about track," I said. "About school."

"Aww, be careful or you're gonna get me very, very depressed," he muttered. "I definitely do not need to be reminded of our glory days."

"For some more than others."

"Oh, come on, you were really good."

"But you were really great."

He didn't disagree. He straightened the pages in a folder, then closed it.

I motioned to the Printing Divine poster.

"So, how is this new business of Samona's doing?"

He laughed but was forcing it. It became apparent that she hadn't told him I'd seen her. I wondered what that meant.

"I can't believe it, but she's actually doing really well. Like, in the last two weeks enough business has come in so that she's getting near the profit margin, which is totally unbelievable. And unexpected."

"That's amazing," I said, not sure if David Taylor was lying to me.

"Is it?" He sighed. "I barely see her anymore. She's so busy she's never there when I get home. She's planning for all these shows in September, I guess, and get this—"

"What?" He was looking at me, wide-eyed.

"Well, on Thursday she tells me she has to go away on business and explained something way too boring and complicated for me to pay attention to and then she left the next day and I'm still, like, shell-shocked that my wife is traveling on business. She's in Milan at a fashion show or something." He looked at his hands and splayed his fingers, studying them. "I was pretty worried about the security on Alitalia, but I guess she got there all right."

The phone rang.

In the wedding picture their faces were nearly touching as they danced.

His hand rested on the ringing phone. "I probably will have to take this, but you know what? I spent a hell of a lotta money so my wife could have a little hobby that would amuse her and all of a sudden right now it's like: What the hell did I do that for?"

Our eyes met briefly before he picked up the phone, and after saying "What's up?" gestured that it was an important call, and I held up a hand, nodding. I lifted my stack off the couch and let myself out of the office. On the street there were only two things I was thinking of as I blindly made my way down Broadway.

There are no shows in Milan during this time of year.

And the security on Alitalia was "reliable" according to *The New York Times.*

But, by then, I had already made the other connection.

The security on Alitalia didn't matter since they had taken Lufthansa.

The bank material—which I spent the next three days perusing—was a thousand pages of dry text accompanied by simple graphs trying to put a positive spin on a stagnant economy (think: "increasing potential" instead of "decreasing return"; think: "excess output" instead of "consumer drop"; think: "more efficient workforce" instead of "lay-offs"). The graphs simply switched the x and y axes so that the lines sloped up instead of down. All this job would succeed in doing was make me feel ashamed and embarrassed since it was the kind of work I had spent the last five years struggling to avoid. I told myself that the reason I couldn't concentrate on any of it was that I was holed up in an apartment on Tenth Street that I was about to be kicked out of, but I knew that the real reason—the distracting mystery of why I couldn't focus—had to do with the fact that I wanted to know where exactly Ethan Hoevel and Samona Taylor had traveled.

That opportunity arose a little over a week later, when Ethan Hoevel—back from wherever it was he'd taken her—called out of the blue on July 3.

"Hey."

"Ethan. Where've you been?"

"I've been away but that's not why I'm calling." He sounded rushed. "I forgot to tell you that my mom and older brother are both visiting for the holiday weekend—long story—and I'm hoping you can help me out."

"Um, maybe. I'm kind of busy. What do you need?"

"You remember my family, right?"

12

AIDAN HOEVEL JR.—Ethan's older brother by eleven months—held a particular stature in my memory as one of the few individuals about whom Ethan would talk at length with any kind of weightiness. I'd only seen Aidan once, at our graduation in New Haven in the spring of 1997. From a distance I'd watched as Ethan and Aidan and their mother, Angela Hoevel, posed for a photograph—Ethan standing tall in a black gown while Angela beamed at his side, bulging proudly out of her flowered sundress. But behind them, and with a noticeable separation, Aidan Hoevel had cast a mean shadow over their uncertain pride. Aidan Hoevel—a shorter, less handsome version of Ethan—was clenching his teeth through a fierce smile, which showed clearly that he couldn't ever be happy for his brother. And the reason he couldn't be happy had to do with a promise Ethan had made once, a promise that even then, on graduation day, Aidan knew would be broken.

That was the same Aidan Hoevel—teeth clenched, bitterness underlying every word and facial expression—whom I found ranting at the intimate group composed of Ethan, Stanton, Angela Hoevel, and Aidan's new girlfriend, Suzanne, in the living room of Ethan's loft when I walked in on the afternoon of July 4. The old elevator's cage slapped and clanked when it opened, but no one seemed to notice me entering the room except Ethan, who was sitting in one of his streamlined red velvet chairs in the far corner, between the bay window and gold-leafed banana tree. Ethan lifted his head and nodded slightly, both hands clasped under his chin, and I noticed his deep tan. And then Ethan turned back to glare at his brother.

Aidan Hoevel was going on about how "as soon as you walk outta the airport it's the only thing you hear: people blaring their horns for nothing and it was like what the fuck?" These people were—in order of offending Aidan—taxi drivers, Wall Street traders doing well enough to buy a goddamn Lexus, and rich mommies with kids packed in the back of their $80,000 SUVs—and what's up with that? According to Aidan Hoevel, it was simply a warped understanding between everyone: "I won't look you in the eye or smile while you're visiting the Big Apple, but I *will* honk my horn at you because I am an enraged New Yorker—I am enraged at goddamn tourists like yourself."

Stanton Vaughn interrupted Aidan, and even though this was the first time he had met Ethan's brother, he was not compelled to hold back.

"What in the hell are you talking about?"

Aidan feigned surprise. "What do you mean?"

"You've never heard people blaring their horns on the 405?"

Stanton was sitting between Ethan and Suzanne, directly across from Aidan and Angela Hoevel, who shared a space on a small sofa Ethan had designed.

(I did not know the specifics of the conversation that had taken place before Aidan and Angela and Suzanne arrived at Warren Street. All I knew was that Suzanne worked for a medical supplies company in Mission Viejo that was about to open offices in Boston and New York, and she was coming to the city to oversee the staffing. So Ethan had offered to fly Angela and Aidan to New York at the same time—not expecting them to take him up on it, of course. He'd ended up purchasing two business-class tickets for his mother and his brother—as well as upgrading Aidan's girlfriend from the coach seats her company had booked—and putting them up in two luxurious suites at the St. Regis, an offer that Aidan had refused at first, and then, after Angela demanded that he accept his brother's generosity, relented and came along. I also knew that Stanton had been introduced to the group as only a "friend" and that now Aidan Hoevel was regarding him—this *designer* who was obviously balling his little brother—with a barely controlled hostility that he was keeping in check only for the sake of Angela.)

"Well, in L.A. we do it because we're frustrated with traffic, Stanton," Aidan pointed out with a harsh and condescending emphasis. "We want to get home. It's not because we're pissed off at the world. That's the difference."

"Maybe that's what traffic is," Suzanne said in her feathery voice. "A little microcosm of each city."

Aidan shot Suzanne a glance that said: *you are not helping me.*

"So are you saying that L.A. isn't an angry place?" Stanton pointed this question directly at Aidan.

"Not like New York, my man."

"So I guess the rage that caused your city to burn in 1991 was predicated on just wanting to get home for dinner?"

"I don't get it," Aidan said.

"Car horns in New York? It's just noise. You supplied a meaning for something that doesn't exist. It's kind of like a lie and I'm just pointing out that I don't think it's true."

Aidan Hoevel replied, "You are so off base, dude, that I can't even respond to that."

"Boys, boys." This was Angela Hoevel, distant and meek.

I meet Mrs. Hoevel (she kept her married name after the divorce) when she visits Yale halfway through our junior year, and the three of us go out to lunch at an upscale Mexican place near campus. She is a portly woman with pale skin and long blond hair fading into gray. When Ethan introduces me outside his dorm Angela Hoevel shakes my hand as she laughs, "And I'm Ethan's mother, Mrs. How-evil," and I giggle politely even though I don't understand what she's getting at. As we walk across Elm Street to the restaurant, and as we sit in a corner booth in the back, and while Ethan and I dig into the chips and salsa, Angela Hoevel keeps laughing.

Her laughter is marked by a lack of infectiousness that—I know from Ethan—is rooted in the moment forty-three years earlier when Angela McGinniss is born in Ireland to a frightened and poor

Catholic couple, and she carries their fear with her when she escapes Dublin and sails across the Atlantic to New York City. She loses it momentarily when she lets a man named Aidan Hoevel hit on her at a bar in Hell's Kitchen, where she has gone with a few friends after a grueling day at her temp job. (By coincidence that bar—which would close a few years later—actually existed on the block that The Riverview Tower would later be erected on.) After a brief courtship she eventually marries the small-minded, mean-spirited Aidan Hoevel (not a big stretch, since this is really the only kind of man Angela McGinniss has ever known) and then moves with him to Los Angeles, where, through a friend's generosity, he starts selling real estate and where they have two sons, Aidan Jr. and Ethan—"Irish twins" born less than a year apart. A few years after Ethan is born, Aidan Hoevel Sr. predictably decides that, with his real estate properties thriving in Long Beach, he likes drinking and having sex with other women besides his wife (who hasn't lost her pregnancy weight, he keeps chiding), and so he abandons his family after agreeing to give Angela one of his town houses located a few miles south of Long Beach, because it is the fastest way to get out of their lives. He then inhabits another town house of his across town (living suddenly with a young secretary in his booming business), making it absolutely clear that he never loved Angela and that he does not want any part in the lives of their sons.

And Angela Hoevel, instead of going back home to Ireland, stays there in Long Beach without any family or money for help, and she devotes her life to her sons. She does this because the weather there is gorgeous, their home is spacious and has a backyard for the boys to run around in, and also because Angela Hoevel is something akin to agoraphobic.

Ethan becomes the one who loves his mother and wants to protect her and do everything in his power to please her, the one who performs well in school, who never breaks curfews, who only brings quiet, well-behaved friends (boys like himself) to the house on Fourth Avenue.

Aidan Jr., on the other hand, is the one who toilet-papers the house across town that his father inhabits, the one who on Halloween tosses a brick through the bay window of that house with the words *fuck you* carved into it six times, once on each face, the one who vows to embarrass his mother by losing his virginity at fourteen, the one who focuses his rage through a reckless philosophy: do whatever you want to do and make sure to let as many people down as you're able to while doing it.

After a semester of community college, Aidan drops out and signs on as a ship hand on a three-year-long expedition tracking the "state of the world's natural resources" (whatever that means) and Angela Hoevel is actually happy to be free of him until Aidan calls to borrow money for a plane ticket home just two weeks into that three-year-long expedition—during the summer and fall that Ethan heads east to Yale on a scholarship—having been kicked off the freighter for "disruptive behavior" (which Aidan never defines to her).

While Ethan is taking his first engineering class and making sure to call his mother once a week, Aidan is—in no particular order of importance—living at Angela's, working part-time gigs as a mechanic, occasionally bartending, and screwing half the female population of Redondo Beach.

So it is infinitely surprising to both brothers when Aidan Hoevel (who's just been kicked out of an older divorcée's condo and is now back at Angela's, freeloading, stoned, deciding his next move) is the second person to whom Ethan comes out.

"Should I tell her?" Ethan wonders out loud before the words *I'm gay* have even registered with Aidan. "Don't I *have* to tell her?"

"You tell her," Aidan says icily as he stomps around the town house with the cordless phone pressed hard to his ear while his mother watches *Judge Judy* upstairs in the enclosed solitude of her bedroom, crying behind the closed doors (as she tends to do nightly), "and I swear to God I will never speak to you again. I will no longer have a brother. Are you listening to me? Do you understand? If you wreck Mom with this, I will never forgive you."

Aidan's reaction shocks Ethan into silence, and the silence leads them to a mutual conclusion: they'll keep it as it has always been (Ethan the model son, Aidan the fuckup).

With this promise, Aidan relents enough to tell Ethan (under the presumption that Aidan is the more worldly of the two), "Maybe you need some time away from that fucking liberal place—maybe you need to go abroad" (even though the farthest Aidan ever sailed from California was Mexico City) "and get your head screwed on straight." His unfamiliar gentility belies the true motivation: Aidan wants his fag brother as far away from home as possible.

So Ethan Hoevel goes dutifully to Peru. He never tells his mother he's gay and begins to believe that maybe Aidan is right. After all, Angela is Catholic, and even though she never instilled the fear into her boys, she never lost the faith—the only day she risks the world outside is Sunday—and having a son who "lies with men" might send her straight into the hell of her nightmares.

Of course what happens then is completely unexpected and, to Aidan Hoevel, horrifying: Ethan comes back to New York and his face starts appearing in magazines his mother has never heard of, and some of Angela's friends start sending her photographs (taken by Bruce Weber or Terry Richardson or Ryan McGinley) which she then pins on the refrigerator in the kitchen while giggling with pride. Meanwhile, Aidan Hoevel is faced with these articles whenever he visits his mother, and between the lines—a place that Angela doesn't know exists—starts to see the secret slowly emerging from its hiding place. With Ethan's fame, Aidan Hoevel must confront the fact that the truth can be delayed but it cannot be stopped.

And since Aidan Hoevel fears change—he fears it immensely—his revelation makes him start hating his brother in the same way he will always hate his father, and nausea washes over him every time he sees the framed photo of the five-year-old Irish twins in matching red soccer jerseys on the mantelpiece above the fireplace.

Since Ethan had refused to engage his brother in any conversation whatsoever, the Fourth of July afternoon was revolving around Aidan and Stanton, and their asinine digressions were tiring everybody except Angela Hoevel, who giggled as Ethan poured her another glass of Riesling. She took a long sip (downing half of it) and said again, "Boys, boys." The more Angela Hoevel laughed, the more it revealed that her terrible life had been saved by her son Ethan's success (for instance, the pseudo agoraphobia that had practically made her a prisoner in the house south of Long Beach vanished when she was near him).

She noticed me standing shyly by the elevator and struggled to her feet. She was heavier than I remembered but she moved fast and suddenly I was receiving the hard hug of the inebriated Angela Hoevel, who was nearly lifting me off the floor as she cried out, "Oh, you look just the same as you did—when was it?—seven, eight years ago?"

"Eight," Ethan said, studying me with a blank expression. "Mom— could you let go of the guest, please?"

"Well, *you* look eight years younger, Mrs. Hoevel," I said as courteously as possible.

Angela introduced me to Aidan, who did not remember me, and Suzanne, who was very pretty in that So-Cal way: dirty-blond hair, tan, a thin body made for the beach. Aidan shook my hand hard and said, "Hey, man."

"How's your tooth?" Stanton smiled at me but didn't get up.

Before I could answer, Ethan stood. "We're all here now. Let's go up to the roof."

Ethan ushered us toward the kitchen and stairs. Everyone except our host and me walked up the spiral staircase that led to the roof. When Ethan handed me two bottles of Domaines Ott to carry up along with a tray of burgers and hot dogs, our eyes met and he smiled nervously, and all the questions I had about receiving an invitation to this lunch were answered.

I was the buffer between his old life and the new one he had created.

I was the buffer between the family and the boyfriend.

"Question, Ethan." He looked up. "Did you ever fantasize about inviting Samona to this lunch? I mean, couldn't she have made things easier here than I'm capable of making them?"

He just smiled and shook his head. "Yeah, but I couldn't get rid of Stanton. He knew they were coming."

As I climbed the stairs, I reasoned that Ethan was using me and I somehow deserved it; I would owe Ethan for the rest of my life because of how I'd failed him.

"L.A. sucks," Stanton was saying on that beautiful July day as we arranged ourselves around a massive tree trunk that had been transformed into a dining table, and it sat in the middle of the roof deck surrounded by six chairs Ethan had designed. "All people do there is make terrible movies and bad fashion statements."

"That's why we have you hip New Yorkers to tell us what's cool then, right?" Aidan was taking charge of Ethan's grill. As he squirted a steady stream of charcoal lighter with one hand and used the other to alternately smoke a cigarette and drink a beer, he made a face. "What's a 'good' fashion statement anyway? I don't even know what that means."

"Well, first of all, volcano red does not work for anybody, okay?" Stanton scanned Aidan's T-shirt while Suzanne and Angela giggled pleasantly.

Aidan took a drag off his Marlboro and winked menacingly at Stanton.

I heard a deep sigh from Ethan before he asked me, "So—how's life been treating you the last few weeks?"

I was surprised. "The usual—a constant struggle." I shrugged. "But I guess I get by."

Aidan threw his cigarette into the grill, waited a moment, and shook his head with disgust. "It didn't catch." He lit another cigarette and threw the match in, this time igniting the charcoal, which sent a fireball puffing up toward Aidan's face. He stepped back and then settled into one of the chairs that circled the table, trying to shift into a comfortable position. Immediately: "How do you sell these things? They make my ass hurt."

"Actually"—I breathed in, ignoring him—"I just got a job with this hedge fund."

Ethan was watching me, waiting. "Which one?"

"The Leonard Company," I said casually.

Ethan sat forward, shocked. "What?"

"Don't freak. I'm just working part-time on their Web site."

"How did this happen?" Ethan leaned forward, animated in a way I didn't expect.

"David Taylor helped me pin it down," I said. "Do you remember David Taylor?"

"No. Who is David Taylor?" Ethan said, slowly shutting himself off again.

"He went to school with us," I said, savoring this. "He married Samona—Samona Ashley."

"Samona. Is that a black chick's name?" Aidan asked.

Ethan smiled and regained his cool. My lame little joke was over.

"I think it's wonderful that you all can stay in touch with your college friends," Angela Hoevel said. "That's wonderful. Yale was just as wonderful as I imagined it would be."

"Well, Mom, it's a very liberal institution." Aidan pushed himself off the chair and was now standing at the grill again, turning over the briquettes with a tong. "There are a lot of liberal activities going on there that bring people together."

Silence hung over us once Aidan stopped talking. No one knew what to say.

"So you're at this Leonard Company?" Aidan turned to me. "How could you take a job like that?"

"Well, it's just freelance, Aidan. I'm working from home."

"Hedge fund?" he went on, not listening. "You work your ass off. You never see the sun. Jeez—is that what four years at a liberal arts school gets you? A crummy freelance job in an office with no light?" Aidan tilted his face toward the bright afternoon sky. "I like the *sun*."

"Aidan Junior is working very hard these days, too, aren't you, honey?" Angela Hoevel leaned boozily toward her eldest son.

"Ethan, will you stop pouring her wine?" Aidan asked, before telling his mother, "Mom, I told you never to call me Junior, and frankly I don't think anyone in this crowd would care."

"Oh, please tell us, Aidan." This was Stanton.

Aidan Hoevel had gotten a new job in the sales department of an "energy trading firm" where supposedly the "free energy market" had caused a demand for people like Aidan to help "expedite" the sale of "energy parts." The way Aidan explained this made no sense to any of us, but he went on. "Do you understand? It happens over the phone. It's like trading a couple of apples for an orange."

The burgers were hissing on the high flames now. Ethan excused himself to get the coleslaw and potato salad from downstairs.

Stanton piped up, "So you're in . . . telesales?" He snickered.

Angela Hoevel cut off Aidan's angry retort with a laugh, and then she waved her hand around and we all stared at her, incredulous, until Aidan said, "Look, it's a pretty good job." His needy gaze fell on me. "I mean, it's not up there with being a *writer*" (Aidan gestured at me) "or designing *clothes*" (Aidan gestured at Stanton) "but I do okay for now."

"Wait a minute." Stanton's eyes were closed as if he were hearing but not processing what Aidan was saying. "I don't get it. And you've got something in your stubble."

Aidan wiped his face. "Look, my brother makes furniture for a living and this guy's a writer for a hedge fund or something and you make clothes—jeez, what's so fucking impressive about any of it?"

His semiarticulateness astounded me. I glanced at Ethan as he returned with the two bowls. He set them on the table, and then he stared out over the river, sipping a glass of wine. The Hoboken ferry was chugging along, filled with people coming into Manhattan to enjoy the pretty holiday.

"Do any of you guys ever think there's someone out there with a bomb in his backpack?" This was Suzanne, staring at the skyline, spacing out. "Do you think there's someone with a bomb in his backpack boarding a subway as we speak?"

"All the time," I said. "Because there probably *is* someone out there with a bomb in his backpack and he's waiting."

"Oh, do you really think that?" Angela Hoevel asked this as if she were disappointed in me.

"Don't worry, Mom," Aidan said, turning away from her to grab another beer. He popped open the can and started slapping slices of cheese on the burgers. "It's not gonna happen to you."

Before they left, Angela asked Ethan whether he had kept his senior project. She wanted to see it. Suzanne and I followed Ethan and his mother into the design studio while Aidan used the bathroom and Stanton cleared the table.

Through the thin fiberglass wall, we heard the low murmur of Stanton confronting Aidan at the bathroom door. "I know what you're doing and I don't really like you."

We also heard Aidan's far less muted reply: "Dude, do you really want me to kick your flaming little ass?"

Ethan shook his head, exasperated, but Angela didn't appear to notice. She was gazing intently at Ethan's senior project, which was perched on a high shelf over his desk. She asked me to bring it down, but I couldn't look at it because, even though the wing still seemed sleek and futuristic, it would always be haunted by our past.

Ethan ended up pulling out a chair to reach it. As he wiped the dust from the glass, Angela leaned forward until her face was almost pressing against it.

"Can you make it move?" she whispered.

"I have to plug it in, Mom," Ethan complained.

I finally focused on the thing and the failure it represented.

"But who knows when I'll get back here again?" Angela murmured.

"That's really cool," Suzanne said. Aidan was suddenly in the room and rolling his eyes at Suzanne.

Ethan plugged the small machine into a socket and air whispered through the vacuum. Angela gazed at the moving form with a distant smile. I had forgotten how severely beautiful it was even though, to Ethan, it was just the representation of the physics that made things beautiful—a bird, a swaying tree branch, a passing cloud—and not the thing itself.

"Make it go faster," his mother whispered.

"Mom," Aidan said. "It's time to go."

Ethan unplugged the machine and placed it back on the shelf.

Aidan shook my hand extra firmly and Angela Hoevel delivered another hug and Suzanne gave me a peck on the cheek. The three of them were off to see the Brooklyn Bridge, a trek Ethan, Stanton, and I opted out of, citing work reasons (plus everyone was doubtful that Angela would make it without falling asleep). Ethan rattled off the necessary plans for them to be reunited at eight o'clock that night for a reservation at Nobu. The car would pick them up from the St. Regis. Afterward they would watch the fireworks from the roof deck. Then Angela was calling out "I love you" to Ethan as the elevator door clattered shut, and they were gone.

Stanton went to a window, opened it, and leaned out with an arm propped on each side of the frame, like he desperately needed air and wanted to scream. Then he did, piercingly.

Ethan ignored him and cleared a plate of crackers and cheese.

I was standing by the elevator since they hadn't asked me to leave.

Stanton drew himself back in. "Tell me something, Ethan. There's something I'm really curious about."

"Tell you what?" Ethan sighed. "What do you want to hear?"

"Tell me why you have to be such a faggot. I mean, I guess we're both fags, but you are a *fag-got*."

"I don't know what you're still doing here," Ethan said tiredly.

"I'm here because you invited me, Ethan—"

"That's not what I meant—"

Stanton cut him off. "I mean, I can handle you not telling your mom. I guess I kind of get it and I understand that's about her and not you, but the problem is I'm not gonna sit around in front of your family and lie. About us. I'm not gonna do it."

Ethan wiped a paper towel over the shiny chrome surface of the coffee table.

"You're so off base, Stanton, and you don't even know it."

"Today was pathetic." Stanton paused to take a deep breath. "You were pathetic." He took another breath. "I think I still have the right to tell you that."

"You sound like that terrible screenplay you wrote." Ethan turned to watch as Stanton marched toward the elevator. "Oh, look at Stanton. It's the dramatic exit. See Stanton storming to the elevator."

In fact, there would be no dramatic exit because the elevator was probably just now hitting the ground floor depositing Angela and Aidan and Suzanne into the lobby and would not make it back up to nine for at least two minutes, during which Stanton stood next to me without even glancing my way until we could hear the cage rising up and its door finally opened. He mumbled under his breath and was facing away from us when the door closed.

There was a moment when it seemed as if Ethan had forgotten that I was still standing in the loft until he said, "If you've recovered from that outburst and you feel like staying, you can—I don't know—check your e-mail. How's that?" He was smiling but his voice sounded exhausted. He was about to move toward the kitchen when he suddenly stopped and looked at me. "Are you really going to take that job at Leonard?"

I shrugged. "It's a job. It pays well . . ."

But Ethan didn't care about the job.

He wanted to know about something else.

"So how is David—how's David Taylor doing?"

It was such a strange question, and at the time I chose to interpret it as Ethan being evasive (which was the most obvious conclusion), and yet I didn't want to let him escape me. I felt like this was a rare opportunity to get back at him somehow—get back at Ethan for all the small manipulations I'd allowed him.

(Of course, I didn't stop to ask myself if this was, in fact, one of them.)

"Shouldn't the real question be how's Samona, Ethan? I mean, you two must have had fun in Thailand."

He started to reply evenly, "Samona . . ." but something caught on the last long vowel of her name, and he crumpled up the paper towel and sat down, rubbing his temples, grimacing as if he were under some massive weight.

I softened. "Or maybe not."

He looked up at me. "Do I need to ask how you found out?" Then quickly: "Forget it. It doesn't matter."

He motioned me to sit, and I did.

13

SOMETHING I'D learned through the hundreds of interviews I'd given over the years (even though most were less than thirty seconds long) was that, more often than not, it's the way a person tells a story that actually tells the story—it's the changes in tone, the inflections, the sighs, the glances to the floor and ceiling, past your shoulder, and, sometimes, directly into your blinking, watering eyes that provide the details words omit.

That was how I listened to Ethan tell me about Thailand. As had occurred over a month earlier when I saw Samona at Printing Divine, his words and gestures and expressions—some chosen carefully, some not—entered me, throwing relentless images onto the glass of my mind, and I had no choice but to sit there in the loft on Warren Street, gazing at the shifting, interlacing reflections of Ethan's story.

Having sex with men is a fight. Having sex with Samona Taylor makes Ethan Hoevel realize this. Every time Ethan has sex with a man it's always a reminder of the pain he wants to forget: the anguish of the locker room, the struggle to stay hard while losing his virginity to that first girl rocking against him, the horrible months that followed after the one guy he had ever loved told Ethan that he was, in fact, straight. Nothing compares to that pain; that pain is something so particular and so crippling that in some ways it has always defined Ethan and made him into the man he now is. This is the torment

Samona Taylor responds to in Ethan Hoevel's eyes that night she first meets him at the gallery, even though she doesn't know what it means yet. And when Ethan has sex with Samona he forgets about the roughness of men and their strength and selfishness and feels that it is possible to move toward someplace new. When he comes inside her, Stanton Vaughn and all those other demanding people he's ever been involved with don't matter. Because all he really wants is Samona: she's new and relenting and vulnerable and she craves him and the muffled whimpers she emits while being fucked—which contrast so sharply with her sultry voice—instill in him the urge to make her feel cared for. In the midst of this, Samona Taylor becomes the only person who can make Ethan move on from everything he once desired.

So it comes about naturally that, near the end of June, Ethan Hoevel asks Samona to go to Thailand with him—not on business, just to escape.

Samona accepts Ethan's invitation without even thinking, then goes home and tells David (per Ethan's instructions) something about going to Milan for a few fashion shows and that he can reach her—if he needs to—by leaving a message on her cell phone since it's all been arranged last-minute by Betsey Johnson's people and she doesn't have the details. This is at four in the morning, when he's half-asleep. The town car that Ethan orders picks Samona up and then makes its way to Tribeca, where Ethan is standing outside his building, wearing a Ramones T-shirt and wraparound sunglasses, holding a backpack and a small garment bag, and when she first sees him Samona squeezes her legs together tightly because she has gotten wet, instantly, effort-lessly, just from the sight of him (and that is what she whispers in Ethan's ear on their way to the airport).

Most flights out of JFK that morning are—as usual—delayed, but the Lufthansa Flight 407 to Frankfurt leaves on schedule, and she rests her head on his shoulder in the plane. The ocean is visible thirty-five thousand feet below through breaks in the clouds, and when Ethan closes his eyes to doze off he knows she's watching him, and he knows what she's thinking: *this is what I'm supposed to be doing—this isn't wrong and there's nothing to regret; I'm no longer running around with nowhere to go.* Because Ethan knows exactly what he's giving her when he puts his arms around her in the Frankfurt terminal while waiting for the connecting flight to Duong Mang: Ethan is giving her purpose. And he knows she's feeling that purpose after they ride in an open-roofed car that shuttles them from the chaos of the airport to the private resort at Pomtien Beach in Pattaya where Ethan has booked a private bungalow for the week—and again when they're lying in the sun next to a cabana on a beach where the sand is smooth and the color of peach ice cream. She feels it when they run across that sand and plunge into the warm, clear water where they swim together near the coral reefs, diving deep into the crystalline water, and each time they surface a shimmering school of silver minnows twirls around them; she feels it later when they stand naked together under a hot shower attached to their cabana while he tongues her. This sense of purpose flows on as they spend their first night together and continues as they wake up and—without speaking—make love, and when they finish, and when he lays his head next to hers, panting, and when she runs her fingers through his thick dark hair until his breathing returns to normal, and when they have breakfast on the terrace overlooking the ocean, drinking mimosas before walking lazily toward the waves foaming across the shore. Ethan gives all this to Samona, and they let each day go by without consequence on a deserted beach on the other side of the world.

And on the last night in Pattaya, Samona starts asking questions.

They're sitting on the sand, sharing a joint, and she's admiring the fire Ethan built.

"I haven't smoked a joint since college," she says, breaking the silence. "Do you believe me?"

By only nodding his head, Ethan tries to indicate that he prefers the cracking of the fire and the sounds of distant waves to anything either of them might say.

"There are a lot of things I haven't done since college," she says.

"Like what?" He asks this as he inhales off the joint.

"I don't know. It was simple back then. It was all very simple." She sighs. "Everything just happened the way it was supposed to happen. Don't you think?"

Ethan's silence, and the way his face glows dimly outside the fringe of firelight, is unfamiliar to her.

"No," he says grimly. "I don't."

"Why?" She tries to sit up a little but the pot weighs her down, even though she feels as if she's floating.

"You have to love a place and time for it to be that simple," Ethan says.

"So . . . you didn't like college?"

"No," he says. "I did not."

Samona laughs and aims for playfulness. "Maybe that's because you didn't know me then?"

More silence from Ethan. He tilts his head slightly and sucks in on the joint again, and then he studies the spliff and blows on its tip. She reaches for his wrist, but she will have to shift her weight and isn't capable of completing that action unless Ethan meets her halfway, which he doesn't.

"I don't think that was it—" he starts.

"Hey, I wasn't being serious," she says over him, slightly stung.

"There was just a lot of other stuff going on . . ."

"What kind of stuff?" She tries to hide the edge in her voice.

He leans forward again until his face comes into the direct light of the flames, his eyes gently on fire. "Just stuff. The usual."

He says this to end the conversation—to make sure Samona Taylor understands that they have an unspoken agreement about the things they don't know about each other, and that if they knew these things they couldn't be here together right now.

And she seems to get it as she leans back, nodding to herself.

"What about you?" he asks, much more formally.

"What do I miss?" She reaches for the joint and leans back on one arm, arching her spine, hoping he'll notice the way her breasts push upward. "I don't know. Sunday brunch in the cafeteria. Being able to walk two blocks to see your best friend."

"Or boyfriend."

Is this a statement or a question—Samona can't tell.

"Or . . . girlfriend?" she says tentatively.

A pause, and then, "Yeah."

"And all the dancing, and all the parties, and how even then you thought none of this really matters. Those were the simple things.

Those were the things I loved." She tries to blow a smoke ring and fails. "Come on, Ethan, you must have loved something."

He doesn't hesitate. "I never really loved my life or anything in it."

They're quiet for a long time. He has never said anything like this before with such harsh practicality. She stares at the silhouette of Ethan's face, and he loosens his jaw and smiles, playing it off as though it's just marijuana talking.

"What do you imagine love to be like, then?" she asks.

"Something that exists outside of circumstance."

She's watching him, confused. "What are you talking about?"

"I mean, life moves along according to certain circumstances—"

"That's not true, Ethan—"

"Wait, let me finish, okay?"

She doesn't want him to.

He continues. "I'm saying that everything is circumstance. Who your parents are, whether they stay married or get divorced, what you look like, where you go to school, who you meet there, what kind of job you land when it's all over, where you live, who you live with—all that shit. That's all circumstance, Samona. And what's any of that got to do with love?" Ethan waits for her to respond, but he's lost her. He shrugs. "Love only happens when you can step out of—all that."

She can't come up with anything to say. This is not a conversation she's interested in having anymore. A shadow comes over her face and she looks down and Ethan can tell she's flashing on her husband.

"That's not very romantic," she says. "That way of looking at things."

"There are a lot of different ways to define romance." He pauses. "But in the way you're thinking about it, no, I guess it's not."

"So let me get this straight: what you're saying is . . . you've never loved someone?" He looks at her for a long time, and then he shakes his head. She reaches out toward his thigh teasingly, intimately, then stops. "Can I ask you something?"

"I don't know if you want to."

"How do you know what it is?"

"I'm sitting here. I see you. I pay attention."

"And why don't you think I should ask it?"

"Because you're afraid of what the answer will be."

After a moment of indecision she decides not to ask (the question being something like: "What is Ethan Hoevel doing on a deserted beach in Thailand with a married woman who really doesn't have a lot to say?") and instead continues reaching for him. "I just . . . hope we have stepped out of circumstance, like you said."

"You want what we're sharing to be called love, Samona? Do you want that, really?"

"Maybe," she says, needing a moment to convince herself of this.

Ethan adjusts the burning logs—the fire is dying—and suddenly one of the logs collapses and a glowing ember flies into Samona's face, where she feels it sear the corner of her left eye. She isn't aware that she has cried out until Ethan is holding her, stroking her cheek, making sure she's okay, and she says she is and he tells her with a smile, "That's what you get for asking questions you shouldn't be asking." She is so wasted on the weird Indonesian grass that she just nods.

"But don't do that anymore," she says.

"Don't do what?"

"Don't feel things and not say them. You do that all the time. Don't."

Ethan sits there, serene, brushing his fingertips along her skin, her head cradled in his lap, and she squeezes his hand.

I hung there a moment, still attuned to his signals and the way they were saturated with a particular kind of mournfulness. Over the span of time it had taken him to tell me about Thailand, I'd become certain that Ethan Hoevel didn't know what he longed for anymore.

He lit a cigarette and was about to take a drag. Then his movement stopped. He was focused on me, genuinely interested, inviting a response.

"I guess I'm just . . . not sure if you really like her," I began hesitantly, "or if it's some kind of experiment to you."

He nodded—he'd expected this, somehow—and then everything inside him lashed out. "Like your experiment? Like that experiment you tested out all those years ago back in school?" He stood up, glaring at me. "Is that the kind of experiment you're talking about?"

"It's not the same," was all I could come up with in a weak voice. He was moving closer to me. "Ethan . . . we were just a bunch of kids then . . . and the consequences were different . . . and things matter more now—they matter . . ."

"No, you're wrong about that one," Ethan said. "They don't. They actually matter less to me." And then he stopped walking forward, disgusted with everything. "Oh Jesus, what in the hell do you know anyway?"

The last thing we said to each other that afternoon:

"Do you love her?"

(This was me.)

"I'd like to."

(This was Ethan.)

I took the same route home (up the river, east on Jane Street) that I'd taken the night Ethan first mentioned Samona's name.

Why had he wanted to see me after not returning any of my calls for four weeks? As I look back on it now, I realize that what Ethan truly wanted from me was sympathy. He wanted me to hear his story and to see that certain things he had set in motion were now feeling heavy and immense and involving. He wanted me to feel sorry for him, like I had back in college.

My reaction: I walked fast toward Tenth Street, vaguely giddy, because I couldn't stop thinking of how basely satisfying it would be to see Ethan coming down. After all, everyone struggled—it's why people lived here.

14

THE STORY OF DAVID AND SAMONA
Part 2: The Offer

THROUGH THE routine and logic of David Taylor's work, he quickly became more fundamentally sensible than he had ever been in college. By the winter of 1999, less than two years after graduation, the romance of the literature major had given way to the practicality of the trader. The trader knew better than to ask questions and demand answers from Samona as she—against all odds—kept coming back to him in the middle of the night, wearing revealing dresses gifted by retailers. Yes, he was as insecure about "the situation" as any guy would have been, but he was also aware of how much Samona needed him, and his ego reminded him that he was a good-looking guy who hadn't gained too much weight after college, and he was easygoing and well-read, and he kept his cool in a humorless, stressful, numbers-based universe. He could have gotten other girls. In fact, he was conscious of a solid group of women who fantasized around the watercooler about David Taylor. He wasn't above engaging in his share of flirting to make the days feel just a little bit shorter, either.

And so David Taylor allowed Samona to stay with him in the Battery Park City two-bedroom (his roommate had moved out over the previous Christmas—conquered by the city and driven back home to Wichita) without ever making the kinds of accusations, phrased as questions, that really ought to have doomed them after a year and a half of this routine. They made love in the middle of the night whenever he was up for it, and that single moment of obliteration rejuvenated David two or three times a week. And after the lovemaking, during his morning walk to Vesey Street, he pictured the two of them in their New England Victorian, just off the Exeter campus, eating dinner after a peaceful day of teaching, drinking red wine on the veranda facing down the grassy hill that led into a valley before rising again into the red-and-yellow mountain slopes and the dorm buildings and the sports complex and the fields and a church in the center of a wide green.

And because of his surprising behavior—because of his easy constancy, his new air of dignity—David became the one sure thing in Samona's world of crazy people and hectic schedules and shallow conversations, half of which were swallowed up by thumping techno music and double cosmopolitans. She couldn't help being charmed by the fact that David still watched two episodes of *The Simpsons* every night before turning in at eight. Wherever she was at that hour—usually at some cocktail function before dinner—she would think of him and often wish she could be there, because the simple fact that he was sleeping so early meant that he didn't buy into any of the guest-list bullshit she had to deal with on a nightly basis. David Taylor was somehow above all that—he worked hard and remained quiet and didn't seem to feel much need to impress. David Taylor was exactly the person he seemed to be, and being with him made Samona feel more real.

The only times he truly grated on her were when he'd launch into the increasingly frequent rant at the guys from the office about having a model for a girlfriend and how stupid and superficial that world was (though, in ranting, he was also bragging that his girlfriend was a model, and at the same time, privately, he knew her world was no more stupid or superficial than the world he was in), and though she never argued—she agreed, of course—Samona didn't understand why he even needed to lower himself.

His go-to complaint was that no one she worked with had ever read a book. He would cross his arms and grin as if that explained everything.

One night (which Samona had free because she'd been inexplicably "disinvited" from a function at the M·A·C cosmetics store), fueled by her sudden uncertainty about the extent to which she was still wanted in her world, Samona decided to challenge him: "When was the last time *you* actually read a novel, David?" This happened at a birthday party at an apartment on East Fifty-fifth Street. They were standing with a group in the corner, and the party was lame and Samona was bored. And though she'd said it only to amuse herself—she didn't actually care about his reading list—he looked stunned, glaring at her with bloodshot eyes. So she finished her thought convincingly: "I mean, if that observation is your attempt to explain what's wrong with my industry, then I'd just like to point out that I haven't seen a single book anywhere in your apartment since I've been there."

David, once he sobered up, took her claim seriously and considered it progress.

The next day, he bought a cherry-oak bookshelf and had all his old college books shipped from his parents' house to be displayed in his office. He did this without telling Samona. *She's coming into her own,* David thought proudly every time he glanced at his bookshelf (though he never picked up any of those books to actually read them). Samona Ashley was becoming a woman in New York City, picking up all the sass and arrogance and swagger that went along with that station while leaving behind all the hissy-fit whiny bullshit that her doting father and vicious mother had tagged her with at Yale.

It was all happening under David Taylor's watch. It made him forget that she was a model. It made him not care that she was still freeloading off him after almost a year. It made him believe more firmly that he might still be in love.

Still, there were the usual kinks along the way.

On one of the rare nights when Samona did not get home before David left for work, his mind wandered all morning. By the time his day was half over he had called the apartment three times and no one answered. He had tried her cell phone but it was turned off. When he was about to use his lunch break to head back to the apartment, something came in from a trader in Germany—sell eight thousand shares of Readycom. David's job required him to check the sell box in the bot-

tom right-hand corner of the spreadsheet, and forward it to the international trader. But David was so lost that morning that he checked
the buy box in the bottom left-hand corner instead. When he called
his apartment for the fourth time that morning, Samona answered. *A
girlfriend of mine . . . extreme heartbreak . . . needed to be calmed down . . . her head
exploding from too much cocaine . . . didn't want to call and wake you . . . must have gotten home just a few minutes after you left . . . so exhausted I turned off the phone . . . slept
through the morning . . . I'm sorry, sweetheart,* she whispered. David Taylor's
relief was so immense that he choked back a sob.

The moment he hung up the phone, Leonard called David into his
office to inform him that a careless mistake David had just made cost
the company $150,000. "More than two years of your salary,"
Leonard was quick to add, and then, "This happens, but it only happens once." David, of course, blamed Samona for turning off the
phone when she must have known he would call. But he swallowed
hard and accepted responsibility (for everything) and reminded himself that he was lucky to have Samona. When he came home that
evening he took her out for an early dinner at the Oyster Bar in
Grand Central before sending her off with a kiss to the round of parties she was attending that night.

But David Taylor never forgot about that day.

It was the fall of 1999—two years out of college—when Samona's
modeling career began its inevitable downturn. She only made it into
one runway show in September Fashion Week. When she asked her
agent what was up, he replied coolly that her "unique" look was going
rapidly out of style. Her face didn't fit into the new ad campaigns,
which—as it was explained to her over and over by various agency reps—
were becoming all about "good old-fashioned Americana as the end of
the millennium looms." People were looking for the Girl Next Door,
and not the Forbidden Goddess (Samona had never thought of herself
in that category). It was going to be miniskirts and retro-wear and
ridiculous perfumes with names like Twilight's Last Gleaming, and
that's just how the business went—in waves. ("Sometimes *tsunamis*,"
someone at an agency told her, wide-eyed.) If Samona was really
inspired to keep at it, she could still get gigs but they would eventually
become smaller and less prestigious, and let's face it, Samona Ashley

never seemed like she really cared and she was never going to make it into the big shows—not quite tall enough. She pressed them for answers and was finally told flat out by a frustrated intern that "there was a limit for the overeducated Yale girl with too much attitude."

She cut the career off right there, before it could keep fizzling out.

When Samona walked out of the agency for the last time, she hailed a cab on Madison and went back to David's apartment, where he was smugly (at least that was how she interpreted it) reading *The Economist* while snacking on a microwave quesadilla, cheese pasted to the side of his mouth as he barely looked up at her. It all became instantaneously clear—he had wanted her to fail. He wanted her to stay in the apartment all day and be there whenever he needed her. He would be happy about what she had to tell him.

"I'm done," she said. "I'm through with it all."

She would never forget David's surprising reaction: he put the magazine down, stood up, kissed her so gently on her forehead that her whole body tingled, and fixed her a Corona Extra.

He said while squeezing the lime: "You're so above them all anyway."

She thought: *he's right.* Then she became immensely ashamed of herself, because here was a guy who never cared that she was a model, who only wanted her to enjoy what she did, who provided a home and a bed and nice dinners for her, who was always waiting for her when she stumbled wasted through the front door, who never, for over a year of her bullshit, descended to the petty levels of waist sizes and raw vegetable diets and standing on the scale eight to ten times a day, who only wanted to love her and be happy for her—no matter what.

She savored that Corona and kept the empty bottle in a side-table drawer with old love letters and sentimental birthday cards from her girlfriends.

What Samona didn't know: David Taylor was not only happy that she decided to abandon modeling (or more accurately: that modeling decided to abandon her)—he was elated.

At that point, David Taylor's two-year program at Merrill Lynch was rapidly approaching its end, and with the market still down he knew he would be cut if there was even the slightest hint of a doubt in

Leonard's mind that David was going to re-sign. In fact, David Taylor was filling out grad school applications—which two years since leaving Yale and a year and a half since reading his last novel (*The Horse Whisperer*, by Nicholas Sparks) was slow going and uninspiring. The only reason he was pushing through them at all was the memory of a dream and the threat of unemployment. And he knew that Samona— as long as she was a model—would never settle into the life of a teacher in the hills of New England and live for the summers off and think about having children and being slightly poor. Her being a model had precluded even the thought of leaving the city.

But now the unpredictability of the consumer dictated that she was fully dependent on him. And since there was no way she was going back to Minnesota—not after the year and a half she'd just experienced—this gave David, in his mind, some room to mold her into the woman he knew she could be. He would become giddy when he thought of being not only the cool teacher of Shakespeare and Dickens (both of whose works were gathering dust on the shelf in his office), but also the cool teacher with the smokin'-hot wife. It would be like when he first started dating her junior year, and his fraternity brothers scanned her, openmouthed with envy, whenever she was with him.

So he let her sulk in the apartment, where her insecurities festered and her level of sobriety plunged until he was all she had anymore.

In the meantime, he had to fulfill his Merrill Lynch contract, and there was that essay question on the teachers' college program applications—*Describe a moment in your life that has defined you*—which had him totally stumped.

Then something unexpected happened:

The computers on his floor were shuffled around, and he found *Intertrade96*. It was just an icon on the screen of his new PC that looked like an antique cash register with two miniature white men in suits standing on top of it shaking hands. While dragging it to the trash, he accidentally double-clicked and opened a spreadsheet saturated with formulas too complicated for him to even try deciphering. For fun, he plugged a few stock-exchange numbers from that afternoon into the appropriate boxes, and he came out of that day 250 percent in the black. When he walked out of the office after the market closed and James Leonard came forward to shake his hand, David Taylor felt an ecstasy that surpassed any triumph on the track. In the space of fourteen hours just weeks before his contract was up, it all came together: the persistence in getting the job done well, and walking to work each morning, and staying until he had finished everything, and getting along with virtually everyone from the mail boy to James Leonard—it was all about that handshake at the end of the day, and it all became, somehow, right.

He took Samona out to Nobu that night, and he relished the sensation of not feeling guilty that the $35 salmon tartare appetizer he prodded her to order wasn't cheating them out of savings they'd need for car payments and dental insurance. He studied her face as he ordered a $115 bottle of sake—the amazement in her eyes—and took pride that this wasn't an illusion. It was sexy. It was happening. It was almost heroic.

When they got home from dinner—buzzed from the sake but not wasted—he fucked her so hard she screamed.

The next night it was Balthazar, followed by Blue Ribbon and even a venture out to Peter Lugers in Williamsburg (where she declined the steak and ate only a salad).

And like one of those signs you're not allowed to ignore, this windfall was accompanied a week later by another unexpected opportunity. After twenty-nine years at Merrill Lynch, James Leonard decided to start his own hedge fund and asked David Taylor to come with him. The hours would be much more comfortable (David would never have to wake up at 3:45 A.M. again) and he would have his own office on the twenty-first floor of a building on Seventh Avenue at Fifty-first Street and he would get to work in sales as well as trading, since that's "what you were meant for," as James Leonard told him. "It's about building relationships, and I've rarely seen someone so young with as much talent for it as you have." Where James Leonard got that idea, David Taylor couldn't even begin to fathom. But deep within, David couldn't help suspecting that this potential windfall was as much related to a footrace in Central Park three years ago on a hot, clear day in late August as it was to *Intertrade96*.

David looked at this choice the way a trader would: if he dropped out of finance, there was the chance he wouldn't get into the grad school program he wanted. He also wouldn't have much money because he hadn't saved like he had meant to (he had for a while, but after Samona moved in full-time the money had seeped away even though he'd been so careful) which dictated that he would have to get a job while attending grad school, and worse than that: Samona would have to work, too; Samona might not want to deal with the hardship and uncertainty of it all; she might leave him; he'd be alone; he didn't like to go out much; he didn't want to have to go through the hassle of finding another girl to be with; there were simply no guarantees—of anything.

His dream now appeared risky, and his job had unexpectedly become a sure thing.

This all happened within the space of three weeks.

David Taylor went with Jim Leonard and became one of the first associates at The Leonard Company. It was a decision he made more quickly than he would have liked to admit.

A few months after David received his signing bonus in the fall of 1999—more or less a gift from James Leonard to his protégé—David and Samona signed the lease on a new apartment. It was on the twenty-eighth floor of a Hell's Kitchen luxury high-rise on Forty-third Street and Eleventh Avenue, called The Riverview (though their particular apartment faced east toward Queens). David had pushed for The Riverview because it was a closer walk to his new office than any of the other places they looked at (but once they moved into the spacious one-bedroom with the stainless-steel kitchen and two bathrooms, David started taking cabs to Fifty-first and Seventh because he was tired from all the moving and unused to his new schedule and didn't want to walk anymore and four avenues was farther than it sounded—he simply didn't have the time).

Samona couldn't find a job (and never really looked that hard). David paid the $2,800 rent. He told her to take all the time she needed. He understood that the last year had been a strain on her and it was okay to wait for the perfect opportunity, and that in the meantime she should consider their new apartment a job—she should make it into her dream home.

"My dream home is in Tribeca," she said meekly. "It's much cooler downtown."

"Just you wait," was his strong and comforting reply. "Just wait."

The perfect career opportunity for Samona never managed to materialize—the nineties were almost over and the job market was competitive. But this didn't bother David Taylor. After the substantial raise from his Merrill Lynch salary and his new contract (which included commissions from the investors he brought into The Leonard Company) he began making his own sales (with the aid of the ever-reliable *Intertrade96,* of course) and quickly became the Midas of the new hedge fund. Everyone kept asking David Taylor for his secret. (There was even a small and quiet investigation to make sure no insider trading was going down, but it was all clean—the formulas locked in his computer were honest.) David told them the truth: he had a spreadsheet program and the figures were solid. It was all simple binary code. By the end of that first year at The Leonard Company— exactly twelve months after they moved into The Riverview—David Taylor was making $250,000 plus commissions plus bonus, which was more than enough for Samona Ashley's "extended job search" to fade away. And so she filled her days with shopping sprees, and visiting art galleries (thinking: *I could run a gallery better than any of these twenty-year-old socialite hacks if I only had the time*), Bikram yoga, talking to her dad, decorating and redecorating and redecorating the Riverview apartment (essentially treating it as her own gallery space), and having lunch with Olivia or Nikki or Sara, which inevitably led to the New York benefit circuit and the requisite cocktail parties. Samona Ashley became bored.

But David didn't notice Samona's boredom.

David had grown to love his job.

Dreams faded away. Dreams were secondhand.

Love was something entirely different.

Dreams didn't lead to love.

David Taylor began believing that success, in all its many ironic and erratic forms, led to love.

15

From: James.Gutterson@Leonardco.com
To: readyandwaiting@hotmail.com
Sent: Thursday, July 22, 4:59 PM
Subject: Re: working draft

Buddy—looking over the work—need to talk about
it—when can you come in? Gut.
p.s. Not today or tomorrow—Edmonton's screwing
themselves—again—in a SERIOUSLY bad mood about
it.

It had been two weeks since I submitted my draft to James
Gutterson—six days late. It was a much harder job than I ever imagined, and I was completely the wrong person for it. But financial
woes—the second most powerful motivator behind sex—paired with
the need for distraction after my last encounter with Ethan and his
family had driven me to endure the composition of 137 paragraphs
and 13,642 words, every one of them lifeless, dry, and uninteresting.
(And 87 totally recycled graphs were embedded in there as well.)
There was a part of me that could write at length on what the latest
fashion trends represented about our national psyche, and even if it
wasn't particularly satisfying, it also wasn't painful, and I could be, at
times, amused by my own masochism—which never lasted long
enough because the pieces were churned out so quickly. But it took

me over two hours to assemble a single paragraph about what The Leonard Company could do for you, and with every minute that passed it seemed as if my brain were shrinking into itself. It wasn't encouraging, either, when I realized—quite often during the writing of this thing—that I was composing it for someone who sat on the twenty-first floor and read ice-hockey scores all day.

Meanwhile, my phone didn't ring all week, and as soon as the Leonard business was over with it would be back to making calls and drafting proposals about the comeback of trench coats and a new line of celebrity face cream and who was the next Colin Farrell. I would have to reenter that universe again—I had no choice, really.

The upside happened halfway through the interminable process when—after plunging my face into a sink full of cold water to revive myself—it hit me that I'd lost the strange urge to find out what was going on with Ethan and Samona, et al., and I had lost track of them for most of July. This realization (I told myself that I was growing up; that I didn't need them anymore; that I could move on from their world) enabled me to accept what I'd been actively avoiding: that David Taylor and James Gutterson and The Leonard Company were doing me a favor, and the least I could attempt was a halfway decent job and maybe even try to learn something. (In the end, what I learned was that—factoring in my age and current income—I would be lucky to have a single dollar to invest by the time I was fifty.)

Yet the draft moved faster after that revelation, and early the following week I was happy enough with the document to e-mail it to James. It had been about forty hours of work (maybe half of that spent staring at the cruel blinking cursor) and after I sent it off it felt as if I had just escaped the one economics class I had taken at Yale—it all disappeared: the assigned reading, the working half-assed just to meet a due date, the pleading for more time, and all that was left was for James Gutterson to put my work to rest and then pay me and then I could save myself for maybe two more months in the apartment on Tenth Street—at least till the end of summer—before wandering off to something else.

At the time, it seemed that simple.

Late one afternoon—two days had passed since Edmonton's string of moronic off-season trades—I once again pushed through the revolving doors at 800 Seventh Avenue and went through the same steps of calling up Gutterson's office and being issued a giant visitor's pass with my name on it. Gutterson's face was set just inches away from the computer screen again, but there was now a spreadsheet where the articles about ice hockey had been. James was typing numbers from a sheet of paper into the computer.

"Be right with you," he said without looking up. "I messed up the fucking decimal points and I have to change each fucking one of them. Only forty-two more. So hold tight." His two index fingers hovered over the keyboard in a childlike hunt-and-peck method of typing. "You know, someone should really devise a way to do this automatically."

"Hey, maybe I'll go say hello to David while you're working," I suggested, after standing there realizing this could take James another thirty minutes. "Is that cool?"

"I think he's with a consultant right now. Someone's redesigning the conference rooms." James said this without looking away from the screen, a nod of the head toward a closed door to our right which was surrounded by electric tape. "Plus you and I are having drinks with him in about an hour so"—he squinted at the screen—"hold tight."

I waited while James typed in his agonizingly slow fashion, and as I glanced around his desk I noticed something that hadn't been there before—the Richard Yates novel *Revolutionary Road*.

"Are you reading this?" I asked, trying to mask my surprise.

"Hold on a sec. I'm . . . all . . . most . . . done. There!"

With a final strike of the return key, he closed the window.

A long moment passed as he stared at the screen.

His jaw slowly dropped. "Oh . . . fuck . . ."

"What is it?" I asked.

Very softly, he said, "I . . . forgot . . . to . . . save . . . it . . ." And then his voice rose to a shriek: "Fuck!"

All across the twenty-first floor curious faces peeked over the tops of computers, but they disappeared quickly because apparently this happened to James Gutterson all the time.

He shot a hard look my way as if my question was what had distracted him from hitting *Control S,* and so the calamity was directly attributable to me.

Then I watched with an odd fascination as James slowly accepted the fact that he had forgotten to save the work. It had been done and there was no undoing it. Anger faded to simple regret.

"Well, fuck it. It's not like I get paid by the hour." He switched on the screen saver before turning to me. "You know what this means?"

"What?"

"Might have to get really drunk tonight."

"I'm sorry about that."

"Getting drunk, my friend, is nothing to be sorry about."

I picked up *Revolutionary Road.* "Have you read this?"

"No. A girl told me to read it," he said. "Figure it'll help me get her into bed."

James took the book from me and flipped through it. He checked out the back cover and grimaced, shaking his head.

All the while I was thinking how I would love to meet a girl who had read *Revolutionary Road* and liked it enough to push it on me. I would pretend I hadn't read it (twice already) and thank her for making me read such a great novel and then we could have long discussions about it and—

The thought cut off and changed into something else, and suddenly—in my mind—I was giving the book to Samona in her print shop, and she was returning it to me a few days later, telling me how much the story meant to her, how she'd forgotten how utterly *"delightful"* reading could be, touching my arm intimately while asking me about my own writing, wanting to read my own stories . . .

And just like that—the act of picking up a novel James Gutterson was reading in order to get laid—the distraction of the last three weeks was obliterated, and it was hitting me all over again that the one woman I was truly interested in was not only married, but was also having an affair with a gay man who'd once had feelings for me. Or something like that. I almost had to laugh at the absurdity—except the laughter would inevitably cause James to ask "What's so funny?" and I wasn't sure if I'd be able to answer that without tears.

James was looking up at me, holding the book. "Did you read this?"

"Yeah."

"Want to tell me what it's about?"

"I think it'll help your cause more, James, if you read it yourself."

"I don't have time to read this shit." He nodded toward the computer screen.

The screen saver was a fluorescent orange line of text reading the time of day, ticking off the seconds as it bounced around the black screen.

. . . 5:23:42 . . . 5:23:43 . . . 5:23:44 . . . 5:23:45 . . .

"Come on, man. Just give me an *idea* of what it's about. Just enough to bullshit with her for five or ten minutes."

"Will that really be long enough to get her into bed?"

"Well, it all depends on the number of cosmos she's had," he said. "I'm thinking by the time we get to the book, it'll be three or four. Just e-mail me a summary and some, I don't know, plot points or whatever. It'll take you two seconds."

"Sure."

And then I reminded him of why I was there. I held up a copy of the booklet I had printed out.

James nodded solemnly and started lifting stacks of paper off his desk but he couldn't find it. It wasn't in any of his drawers. "I know I printed it out somewhere," he muttered, hunched over his desktop. He came up empty-handed, and then looked—again, regretfully—at his computer screen.

. . . 5:25:13 . . . 5:25:14 . . . 5:25:15 . . .

"Listen," James started. "I read the draft—most of it—and you're a good writer, but it's way too . . . poetic or something. You just have to tone it down . . ." He made a lowering motion with his hands, palms facing the floor. And then he shrugged. "That's all, really. Other than that, it's fine . . . Just, y'know: KISS."

"What?"

"Keep It Simple, Stupid."

"Oh, right, right . . ."

"Don't forget who you're writing for."

"Well, it *is* called corporate *literature.*"

James looked at me blankly until something connected and he forced out a labored chuckle. "Just take a quick pass and simple it up, eh?"

I sighed. "Sure."

He leaned back, stretched his arms over his head, and groaned. Then he looked at me in a very thoughtful way. "Why are people always trying to dress everything up? Making it look fancier than it really is? Things are pretty simple. Why make it more complicated? Don't you think so?"

"Are you still talking about . . . my work?"

"I'm talking about the big picture, dawg. And I don't talk about the big picture that much, so listen carefully."

I couldn't help but be amused.

"If people could just keep it simple, then the world we live in would be a much less fucked-up place."

"That's so . . . Zen."

"That's my story and I'm sticking to it."

"You might have something there, James."

"Straight up. Let's get drunk." James was putting on a wrinkled jacket, and after straightening his tie, he pulled out his cell phone.

"I'll leave a message for Taylor to hook up with us after his"—James suddenly bulged his eyes and mimicked the mincing stereotype of a gay man—"*consultation!*"

. . . *5:26:39* . . . *5:26:40* . . . *5:26:41* . . .

I was finishing my first beer and James had downed his second. We were in a dimly lit cocktail lounge called China Club on Forty-seventh Street off Broadway (the kind of place where martinis cost fourteen dollars) and it was beginning to fill up with young men like ourselves getting out of work and we were waiting for David Taylor while James talked about ice hockey.

"It's just so intense and you can't understand it from playing another sport like track or football. You can't understand hockey until you *play* hockey."

I raised my hands in mock surrender. "I don't presume to." (It occurred to me that this was a phrase I'd once used too often in college until Ethan had become annoyed.)

I focused in on James and what he was saying about the guys who could bench-press four plates on each side and how they came at you twenty miles per hour while you went after a puck you could barely see that's probably going fifty. How players nowadays looked at everything through a damn face mask because of pussy NCAA rules commissions and James was a purist because he grew up playing on Thunder Bay in Alberta and do you think *they* ever wore masks? Shit, Gretzky played until he was thirty-eight and do you think *he* ever wore a mask?

I thought it was a rhetorical question but he waited expectantly until I shook my head, and then he was talking about how his old man laced up his first pair of skates for him on his second birthday (we were regressing, I realized idly) and how he would skate across a frozen bay all afternoon and then it was the junior league, high school, PG year, Cornell, a year in Russia (was I listening correctly?) and all he wanted to do was *kill* people and then *score*.

"Did you ever try to go pro?" It was the only thing to ask him.

"Yeah, that year in Russia." James drained his beer. "But they play dirty hockey over there. Plus all you can drink is vodka, so your face gets all fat and the girls are way too pale. Personally, I like dark skin." He nudged me. "You know what I mean?"

"Like David's wife?" I asked, regretting it.

"You tell me how a scrawny stiff like David Taylor landed a piece like that," Gutterson said, with a mixture of bitterness and awe. "Tell me how he not only *landed* her but got her to *marry* him, and I'll buy you another beer. Unbelievable."

"I think it was kind of complicated."

I suddenly became more interesting to James Gutterson.

"Yeah? How?"

"Forget it. I don't know." I was shaking my head even though my own answer to that exact question had been consuming me to the point where I'd been writing it down. For me the whole point of writing was, in the end, to finish the story—to shut it away and hopefully get paid and then move on to the next one. It was a livelihood, and it had never been a problem to maintain that separation. But why was I finding this so impossible? Why did they have to be everywhere? Faced with James Gutterson's ripe, anticipating gaze, all I could do was keep shaking my head and mutter, "I don't know why I said that. It was all very simple."

"I'll tell you the simple part." He rubbed his index finger and thumb together, and I leaned away from him. "Cash: Taylor made it, she wanted it. Nothing simpler than that. You have cash, you can do whatever and *who*ever the hell you want." He paused—flashing on something—and his face darkened with a crooked smirk. "And trust me, Taylor *does*."

"Does what?" I blurted, intrigued and a little uneasy.

"Huh?" James was zoning out. He was watching the waitress behind the bar as she washed a set of highballs.

"He doesn't, like, *cheat* on her. Not David Taylor." I said this firmly, because I was pretty sure that—except for one time I'd heard about before they got married—David had never strayed. James laughed with the particular guffaw of someone who knows things you don't, which caused me to tack on, "It just seems like he's too busy to mess around. Right?"

He kept laughing and shook his head slowly. "Look, okay, you're a *writer*. I can tell you like to listen in and you notice things. And I'm sure there's plenty of shit you've heard about our friend David Taylor. But trust me, buddy"—he paused, as if the story had grown more suspenseful for me, and he wanted to prolong my interest—"there's plenty of shit you haven't. And I'll just leave it at that."

He took a deep sip from his beer.

"James," I urged him on, "will you just tell me what we're talking about?"

"Nope." James said this quietly, with no emphasis.

"Why not?"

"Because one: he's walking toward us right now, and two"—he raised an eyebrow ominously—"I'm sure you'll hear about it sometime from a more reliable source than me. Ha!"

He pounded his Kirin Light down on the table, where David Taylor was now pulling up a chair.

"Do I want to know?" he asked me, gesturing at James.

"No, you really don't," I said.

David shook both our hands—a mock formality that always eased everyone.

"Taylor, this is the first time I think I've seen you in daylight," James said, eyeing me.

"It's starting to ease up."

The bags were gone from under David's eyes and his hair looked freshly cut and neatly tousled with styling gel. He was wearing a very chic four-button gray Prada suit that he was a little too old for but still managed to pull off; in fact it made him look trimmer and more youthful than I had seen him in ages. But the strange thing was that this metamorphosis hadn't made him any less nervous. David Taylor was not a calm man that night (later I would find out why) and he ordered a double Grey Goose on the rocks. It arrived quickly. In response to our stares he informed us, "I'm a little wound up."

"So what's happening up there behind all the closed doors?" James was asking. "Besides all the renovating."

"I've been sorting some things out," David said. "Those fucking autolights are ruining my universe."

"Wait—are you gonna get a bigger office after the renovation?" James eyed me again to the point where I had to glance away.

"No," David said, his eyes darting around the lounge. "I was just consulting with someone about decorating. Giving it a little bit of *bam!*" He did an Emeril Lagasse impersonation that took a moment to register.

"I'm sure you were, buddy." James grinned. "I'm sure."

David did a quick double take at James and blinked. "They're still working on the conference rooms," he said drily. "That's all."

James seemed relieved to hear this and he was smiling again.

"What about the lights?" I asked David.

David sighed and crossed his legs. "Leonard had every office installed with these motion detectors, so the lights turn off automatically if there's no movement for five minutes or something like that."

James scoffed and shook his head like he understood what David was talking about even though Gutterson didn't have an office of his own.

"Except the sensors aren't that good, so the lights go out every five minutes when I'm sitting there and I have to, like, wave my arms around to get them back on. It happens five hundred times a day and it's ridiculous." David uncrossed his legs and started fidgeting with a napkin.

"So it's all on track again?" James asked.

"Margins up a little. Not like before but . . ." David shrugged.

"What's your secret, David?" This was asked by James with a wink in my direction.

Suddenly David stopped fidgeting. "Secret? What do you mean?"

"I mean"—James was leaning into him—"wanna give an old friend some tips?"

David breathed in, relieved. "The three bars of gold, James: hard work, patience, confidence."

"You taking notes?" James winked at me. "I think that would go pretty well in your intro. Those three bars of gold."

He pounded his open palm on the table.

"You told me nothing too poetic," I said.

"You know why?" And now James Gutterson was leaning into me. "Because that's not poetry, buddy. That's *bull-shit*. And you need to use as much bullshit as you can lay your hands on."

"Well, I knew there was a reason bankers were rich and writers were broke." I don't know what led me to extend this any further.

David stared impassively at both of us.

"Hell, yeah," James said. "You guys don't bullshit enough. We, on the other hand, bullshit *all the time*. Right, Dave-o? Right?" James was elbowing David hard in the ribs before he raised his bottle, which was empty, for a toast. "Bullshitting! And to eight-point-four billion in offshore accounts!"

"Eight-point-six," David Taylor corrected, then flinched as he finished his drink in a single gulp.

A few minutes later—after a few Leonard workers had wandered into the lounge and James became distracted drinking with them—David Taylor asked me to join him and Samona for dinner. He was about to pick her up from Printing Divine and then walk over to Woo Lae Oak on Mercer. I politely declined, but David insisted.

"Why can't it just be you and Samona?" I finally had to ask.

"Because I don't want to have dinner with my wife alone," he said, standing up. "How's that for an answer?"

He saw the startled expression on my face and then, as I stood up, he put his hand on my shoulder like he used to do before our relay runs, a comforting gesture that had always made me feel like we were going to win. "I meant just not at the end of a long week," he said, smiling sadly. "That's all." I had no idea why he was prodding me like this. "It's a free dinner."

In the cab heading toward SoHo, he stared intensely at the city passing by as if he had never seen it before. For some reason the cab we were in seemed darker than most. I kept glancing awkwardly at David while he sighed in the blackness of the cab.

Finally he said something when we hit traffic in Union Square.

"My wife's having an affair."

I froze.

"Pardon?" I leaned toward him. "I'm sorry, I didn't hear you."

I was hoping the cab would start rolling and we could pretend he hadn't said anything, but the night was already wrecked. David repeated the sentence louder.

"I said that my wife is having an affair." There was no inflection in his voice. "Samona." He glanced over at me. "I thought it was obvious."

"Um, no . . . I mean, is it? I don't know."

"You hadn't heard anything?" David Taylor asked me.

"Why would I?"

"I guess you wouldn't." He was studying me in the darkness of the cab. "It's just lately you seem more involved in our lives than you actually are. Maybe it's just the work you've been doing at Leonard."

"Yeah. That must be it." He looked away and seemed to lose interest in me. I leaned toward him. "Does she know you know this?"

"No. Maybe. I don't know."

"Are you sure you want me to come to dinner?" I asked.

"Don't ask me that anymore."

"David—"

"Don't. Forget I said anything."

16

THE STORY OF DAVID AND SAMONA
Part 3: The Ailment

EIGHTEEN MONTHS after Samona Ashley and David Taylor moved into their one-bedroom apartment in The Riverview, David contracted chlamydia.

The surprise (that neither one of them wanted to admit) was that it was David, and not Samona, who had strayed.

Samona Ashley was becoming disoriented as she floated through galleries in Chelsea and waited around fashionable restaurants for friends to show up and noticed the bell-shaped pattern of flab on older women's bodies during yoga. She found herself sighing all the time. She was sighing when David would get out of bed at six in the morning and accidentally awaken her, and sighing in the evenings when, after telling David she didn't feel like going out, he would return to the apartment with a cardboard box of pasta and some randomly chosen vegetables for her to prepare, and sighing sometimes during sex when David was working hard toward an orgasm (that might or might not happen) and Samona would have to close the eyes she had once kept open. She'd focus on David's pleasure in order to increase her own, but even this stopped helping since she couldn't tell whether David was having any fun. She sighed because he was gone all the time and because he was always so tired. She sighed because he was transferring his fatigue onto her.

Samona was twenty-five and her life had already become perfunctory.

(It somehow escaped her that she was the one who couldn't find a job.)

Meanwhile, the increasing frequency of her sighs was not lost on David Taylor. He was particularly attuned to the way she read the Sunday Styles section of the *Times* every weekend—her eyes glazed with a kind of mournfulness for something she'd let slip away. At first he tried to console her. "Sweetheart, that world wasn't *it* for you. You don't need any of *that*. You can and *will* do *better*." She barely responded to him, even with all the overemphasis, and he shut himself up before he became too bitter or resentful. The bottom line was he was the one taking care of her; David was giving her a life far easier than that of most other girls her age—it was the year 2001, after all, and everyone in his or her twenties needed a job; he never pushed her; he never tried to make her feel guilty or beholden; he never begrudged depositing money into her bank account; he'd been faithful ever since she'd officially moved in with him.

David Taylor knew that he was a good boyfriend. More than good, actually. And if she wanted his sympathy, she'd have to fucking earn it or else pull away. And then it hit David Taylor during one of those Sunday mornings: somehow, he'd become the catch in this relationship.

He was now the one who could do better.

This scared him into sending her away. He wanted to preempt the moment when their fears and frustrations would escalate to a gruesome fight that would end it all. Because, ultimately, he didn't want that to happen—he liked taking care of Samona.

He made the suggestion during an unusually intense auditing period after a particularly bad quarter.

"Minneapolis?" she responded, incredulous. "You want me to visit my parents? Alone?"

He spoke with the calmness of someone who knew more than she. "Samona, you haven't been back there for almost three years. They're your parents."

"I see them twice a year in Darien. Is that not enough?"

"I just think it would probably mean a lot to them if—"

"Is that supposed to be some kind of convincing argument?"

"It would mean a lot to me, Samona, if you took a break." She sighed, waiting expectantly, and he tacked on, "From the city. The city's getting to be too much for you."

"Is it the city, or is it something else?"

He sighed. "We're twenty-five, Samona. Twenty-five, and we're having a conversation that people don't have till they're . . . at least thirty."

She nodded at the last part. She agreed, of course—and when he phrased it in terms of getting older, she quickly realized that this was going to be "for the best." They continued to discuss in a more civilized manner over take-out sushi and an expensive bottle of pinot grigio and both became mildly optimistic. This wasn't "a break"—it didn't need to be. It was just "time to think independently and make good decisions." He was lecturing, but she let him continue with only a small sigh that he didn't notice as he went on to explain, in his own polite and logical manner, how the "claustrophobia" of a situation like theirs (he wisely didn't use the word *dependence*) could lead to a particular kind of "closed-offness" in which "you might not notice the possibilities and *opportunities* other than the ones lying right directly ahead."

It was agreed: she could spend some quality time with her father (Samona still called Keith once a day) while David would clear everything off his desk, and when she came back he would have more time for her. She proposed that he should think about becoming a mentor to inner-city children during whatever free time he had ("Which isn't much," he reminded her) and that an activity like that would take him back to some of that youthful idealism he'd (and she phrased this carefully) "given up in order to maintain a certain standard of living" and now it was David nodding along as she convinced him that doing something community-oriented like that would mean that he could still have that old dream that she always loved hearing about (well, not always, but . . .) and that he could have it both ways. They could have it all.

She got him so revved up that the conversation ended with him saying, "Hell, if it works out we might even start looking at places in Tribeca!"

He didn't mean to say that—he just blurted it out.

At the end of August 2001, on the third day after Samona Ashley flew to Minneapolis, David Taylor finally gave up on work at a not-unreasonable 9:30. He planned to a buy a six-pack of Sierra Nevada Pale Ale at the deli on the corner of Forty-eighth and Eleventh and watch *ER* at ten, and then either a rerun of *Friends* or *The Drew Carey Show* and wait for an Ambien to take effect. But James Gutterson, one of the new analysts fresh out of Cornell, caught him in the lobby of Fifty-first and Seventh (they had exited from different elevators). He was with a few of the guys from The Leonard Company Corporate Ice Hockey Team (that, yes, James Gutterson had started) and since they had beaten HSBC's "pussy squad" the night before, they were going out to celebrate. When James Gutterson invited him to come along, David found himself agreeing. And on the third night of Samona Ashley's absence, David Taylor was not missing his girlfriend at all.

He felt like a normal, successful guy in his midtwenties.

The group went to a sports bar in the Flatiron district and David bought the first round for the squad. While David was toasting their victory he noticed a young intern from London sitting in the corner with a girlfriend, and the young intern was staring at him. Three pints of lager and two vodka tonics later, while the ice-hockey team was breaking into a spirit song, the intern was still staring, and Samona Ashley didn't exist, and the night was wide open.

It was the British accent that won David Taylor over. It made her seem elegant and intelligent even as she offered up the most banal interpretations of Dickens that David had ever heard. (David wanted to talk about novels, and because the young intern was from London, David made certain primitive associations and brought up the literary giant.)

David did not care who saw them leave the sports bar together.

Mattie had a serious boyfriend (who was still in the U.K.). She was four years younger than David (cool). She was interning in his department (not cool). But none of it really mattered to him because

Samona was gone and the way he remembered it they'd decided to "take a break" (he'd momentarily forgotten the rest) and he was imagining the expression on Mattie McFarlane's face during orgasm.

The only thing that mattered to David Taylor was that they fuck at her place and not The Riverview.

He followed Mattie into a small studio where she pushed him onto a couch strewn with shoes and cats and a pillow inscribed with her initials, and promptly sucked him off. David came loudly and fourteen minutes later he was hard again. This vitality had been missing from the sex he'd been having with Samona.

(There she was, in his mind, sighing.)

The day before Samona Ashley came home from Minneapolis, David Taylor woke up at 3 A.M. to take a piss. He almost screamed. It felt as if a branding iron had been pushed down his urethra and straight through to his anus. He stumbled back to bed and endured a severe anxiety attack with the help of two one-milligram Xanax.

David Taylor's internist diagnosed him with chlamydia eight hours before Samona's plane was scheduled to land. He bought the necessary treatments (both oral and anal) and was hiding them in a piece of Gucci luggage in their spacious walk-in closet when Samona entered the apartment, six hours ahead of schedule.

Her time away had been rejuvenating, exactly as David had predicted. Tana had been on her best behavior (it didn't matter to Samona that Keith had bribed her with a promised Christmas vacation to St. Croix) and said nothing when Samona helped herself to a second scoop of low-fat Häagen-Dazs. She'd gone to a Twins game with her father and eaten chicken fingers with French fries and Bud Light in sixteen-ounce cups and didn't feel guilty about it until the following morning (she fasted all the next day). They'd talked about David for three innings. She explained their "situation" (omitting the unsavory details) and Keith had wrapped his arm around her and said, "If he loves you enough to let you come home to us and take this time to think it over, on your own, and he's waiting for you in New York, then he must love you almost as much as I do. He also must be thinking about the future—you know, long term."

She didn't think he meant it, but she felt better.

Tana was asleep when they got home, but later in the night Samona heard her parents having sex through the thin walls of the duplex condominium. A rush of feeling coursed through her in response to Tana's low-pitched moans, and Samona Ashley regretted all the times she'd judged her mother. Her parents seemed happy, and this was something that she hadn't been at all prepared for.

The next morning, when Samona sifted through the fridge and took only a Diet Coke for breakfast, her mother smiled, gratified, and Samona warily reached out: she asked Tana from Ghana for advice.

Tana said simply, "If you're bored, it's your own damn fault."

And Samona thought to herself that she'd been a fool to get so bored with David Taylor and let that boredom cause her to overlook certain realities: David took care of her; he always answered her questions, even the stupidest ones; he handled her craziness (she viewed her fits as "crazy" now, in that moment, in the kitchen with her mother) in the same caressing way that Keith handled Tana's.

It hit her: that's all Samona had ever really needed or wanted in a man.

And David Taylor wasn't the type of guy who would ever change on her.

She flew back to New York a half day early, and found David staring at her, wide-eyed, from the bedroom door.

Samona kissed him lightly on the mouth and then, in a move that surprised both of them, kissed him harder. She thanked him for sending her away. She told him about the Twins game, and hiking a lake trail with her father, and eating her mother's light West African recipes that had made her so sick as a child but which now she'd grown up enough to enjoy.

It took every vestige of strength in David Taylor's body to stand still without scratching himself or shaking violently. He had forgotten what real pain felt like, even though he had spent four years at Yale running himself through various thresholds of it. So far in David Taylor's relatively young life there had been nothing to compare with this. And the worst part was that Samona wanted him. She had been away too long without him. She told him she was getting wet just standing there. She wanted to make love. Now.

She reached for him, but he backed away. Samona interpreted this as a game and playfully reached for him again. David stepped away even farther. And then Samona was chasing him around the apartment, and David was running away from her, terrified. His muscles were tight from the pain and his jaw was clenched in agony as his urinary tract grated with every movement. And Samona was laughing because she had never been so happy to see him, and she became aroused because, she assumed, they were actually playing a sex game. Her mother's words echoed gleefully in her head, and she realized that she never had to be bored again.

Finally, David Taylor couldn't run anymore. He collapsed on the couch. He didn't have the strength to fight her advances. Suddenly she was on him, eating his lips, and when she unzipped his pants and pulled them down, David Taylor began to cry, his underwear at his knees, entirely helpless. But Samona didn't notice because she was staring at the erection that was sticking straight up and she was asking, confused, chuckling uneasily, "What's that? Did you . . . come already?" Samona instinctively began sighing again when she noticed that her boyfriend was weeping.

He told her everything.

That night Samona left The Riverview and stayed with Olivia.

When David called her the next day from the office she informed him that he was "a dress I've bought but might return."

By the beginning of September, the burning went away.

Samona Ashley used this time to take stock. She went out to nightclubs and bars with Sara and Nikki and Olivia, where men stared at her (many of them better-looking than David Taylor) and her friends egged her on. She gave out her number a few times but usually changed one or two of the digits, because none of it made her feel anything. It was so fucking confusing: this was what she'd been missing out on in being loyal to David Taylor, and yet (and she credited this to her modeling days spoiling her) it was all so lame. She shared Olivia's bed at her apartment on the Upper West Side, where they talked about men and settling and Samona cried and Olivia held her, the two of them cuddling like they used to do in college (they had even hooked up once on a dare) and Samona ate peanut-butter coffee swirls at Tasti

D-Lite every morning and thought about what her mother would say (which would sicken her and make her throw up).

After two weeks David stopped leaving messages for her.

A week after that, the World Trade Center fell. Samona was reading *Marie Claire* at Olivia's when it happened, and she attempted to make three calls from her cell phone—first her father, then Olivia, then David—but the lines were already filled up and all she could get was that ferocious, incessant beeping.

But when, during the days and weeks that followed, David never contacted her—not even an e-mail—she began to worry severely. She flashed on her favorite painting from art-history classes: Edvard Munch's *The Scream*, which then turned gradually into: Where was David? What could have happened to him? What if he had a meeting downtown that morning? Why had she left him? Why hadn't he called? What kind of bastard wouldn't call her after what had happened? What kind of bitch was she to not have run toward him that day? What did one small misfire in judgment matter during times like these? How could she hold one night against him? Was she really so petty? Was she really so needy? Hadn't she driven him away to begin with?

On a Saturday evening near the end of September, she went to the Duane Reade near The Riverview, where all her prescriptions still had to be called in, to refill her birth control and get more Prevacid for her sensitive stomach. She found herself looking up at the tower repeatedly, to the window on the southeast side of the twenty-eighth floor, and then, after circling the block six times in her high heels, she went inside. She still had the keys. In the elevator, going up, she decided: *If I catch him with someone, or if I see any signs, it's over.*

Otherwise, we'll talk.

He was sitting on a stool at the window when she stepped into the room. He had a bottle of Belvedere on the windowsill, out of which he was drinking the vodka straight. He was staring downtown toward where he once worked on Vesey Street. Most of Tribeca was still cordoned, the floodlights glowing brightly in the dusk. He was alone.

She went to the window and stood beside him.

"What have you . . . been doing?" she asked uneasily.

He gestured toward the bottle and shrugged.

"I've been worried," she said. "How come you never—"

"I tried to call. There was no way to get through. I just figured you were at Olivia's or somewhere."

"What about the day after? You could have gotten through the day after, or any day since then."

He stopped and looked up at her.

"You could have, too."

He slipped his arm around her waist.

Then he told her how he'd been at his desk that day, and he'd walked down the twenty-one flights of stairs with everyone else and come straight to The Riverview, and he'd never been in danger.

They drank vodka in silence and smoked a pack of cigarettes.

Later, she guided him into the bedroom.

They lay there together and held each other. And when he finally brushed a few strands of hair from over her eyes and just looked at her, it was the gaze with which she responded that—for the first time since he'd hurried out of his office building on September 11— allowed David Taylor to feel something close to heroic. Amid all the news articles about the firemen and policemen who'd performed extraordinary acts of valor, the simple acts of holding Samona and comforting her made David Taylor feel like a throwback—someone who would have been happy in less vicious times, when people found their life partner young and settled down into a moderately pleasant routine together and took care of each other unquestioningly and didn't have to go through all the bullshit of "finding yourself" and "figuring out what makes *you* happy first" (bullshit that in his mind was typified by the whole Mattie McFarlane "situation") that, frankly, David was too tired for.

It suddenly dawned on him, as they lay in their one-bedroom: *I can be that guy, the one who knows exactly what he wants; it would be easy.*

At the same time, Samona was seeing clearly that she didn't want to have to find anybody ever again. She didn't want to be alone.

She kissed him. They made love.

They married eight months later.

17

WHEN THE CAB rolled up over the cobblestones outside Printing Divine, David tipped the driver. The lights inside had been dimmed, and the Closed sign was hanging in the window, antique driftwood carved in an elaborate script.

"God, how I loathe this place." David laughed grimly as he unlocked the door with his own key.

The bell rang as we walked in and Samona—on cue—materialized above us, leaning over the loft's railing, wearing a tight strapless white dress that contrasted beautifully with her skin.

"Hey," David called up. "You ready? I brought a friend. You mind?"

Samona smiled at me and said softly, "Well, if I'd known, I would have invited a friend myself."

"I don't get it," David said. "What do you mean?"

"Just that there are a lot of gorgeous girls who would love to meet *your* friend, that's all." Samona turned her smile to David.

"Oh," was all David Taylor said.

I tried to ignore her, along with the whiny hum of awareness that I'd built a life in which I'd never be alluring enough to have her. I closed down and tried hard to concentrate on the moment that the three of us (or if I really wanted to be the poet James Gutterson accused me of being, was it the four of us?) were in.

"That's very thoughtful." I coughed.

We walked to Mercer Street and up two blocks—past the gallery where Samona and Ethan had met (and where I caught her glancing in the window)—and sat downstairs at Woo Lae Oak, a Korean restaurant with stone tables and orchids everywhere.

And for a moment, as they spread their napkins on their laps, Samona and David Taylor were simply another married couple that I was sitting across from, except that Samona was cheating on David—and so what? People cheated all the time. I'd seen it happening everywhere. I looked at David and smiled and decided that if they wanted to move forward through this elaborate, disorienting scenario, then I didn't have to read into it beyond the meal we were about to have.

And then I turned to Samona and there it was in the corner of her left eyelid—that seemingly extraneous detail Ethan had mentioned to me, that tiny circle of skin that had been seared by an ember on a beach in Thailand three weeks ago. It was flickering in the light of the candle, so glaringly obvious if you wanted to search for it as badly as I did. Lust brought me to it. Lust wouldn't let me avoid it. Lust rendered sitting at the table with Samona and her husband a petrifying place to be—because there was no other distraction for the two of them except me.

She caught me gazing, and she smiled but I couldn't tell what the smile meant.

"Thanks so much for having me, you guys," I murmured.

"Hey, it's a real pleasure. Seriously, pal." This was David.

At first we talked about nothing—old vignettes from college, which was so far in the past that it seemed like exactly that: nothing. And David resorted to telling the same stories he told whenever I saw him: he joked about how he won the league championship the first chance he got, and then never again; he joked about how that race so many summers ago in Central Park against Ian Connor was what had gotten him the job at The Leonard Company; he joked about the magic spreadsheet he had found—the thing that had caused their life to end up in the place it now was; he joked about Samona's modeling.

It occurred to me that amid all the stories he told before the waiter came, there wasn't a single one that—no matter how artfully David Taylor spun it—didn't involve some form of shortcoming.

Samona was gazing out the window onto Mercer Street, trying not to make a production of not listening, but she had heard it all before and she was moved to order another bottle of sake (since we had finished the first bottle in an alarmingly short period of time). Then David ran out of things to say and excused himself to use the men's room, and though I wasn't aware of it until David tossed his napkin on the table, I was drunk and sitting alone across from Samona Taylor in a restaurant at a candlelit table, and I had dreamed of this so many times that now, when it was actually happening, it seemed unreal. I didn't know what to say. I couldn't even remember whether we had ordered dinner yet.

And then she spoke.

"Do you remember when you tried to kiss me?"

I didn't respond.

The distance between one kiss in college and the end of an eight-year relationship—all told encompassing almost three years of marriage and a thousand conversations and two apartments and an affair—seemed vast to me, and I couldn't believe she remembered.

"Weird thing to say, huh?" she went on. I shook my head blankly and focused on the scar in order to keep from spinning backward. "But it's just that since Ethan—ever since Ethan, I've been remembering all these small things that I'd pretty much forgotten about . . . those days."

"What—what is it about Ethan?" I asked, glancing toward the bathroom, praying for David to come out and end this torture.

"Don't you already know?" She sounded suggestive. "He says you do."

"What—what do you mean?" I tried not to sound alarmed.

I was relieved when she replied, "Ethan—he has this way of taking you back to that place where all you had to worry about was the person at the party you might have kissed." She sighed and looked past me.

"No, I don't remember," I finally said, comforted by the fact that Samona still didn't know—that she didn't have the capacity to draw the necessary connections between the present and the past.

"Really?" she asked, pouting her lips in a way that made my heart pound harder—because it seemed like she wanted me to remember, to join in on her giddiness, and my noninterest had wounded her somehow. "You don't remember kissing the drunk girl at the SAE party?"

I tossed back another shot of sake. "No. I guess not."

"Well," she said, her eyes drifting toward the back of the restaurant where the restrooms were. "You did."

"Don't tell Ethan or David," I said wryly. "Because then things might actually get complicated."

She stopped pouting and lingered on me, the solidity of her stare accentuating the scar. She looked to the restrooms again, waiting for David to come back.

"You went to Milan, I hear." She pursed her lips, and nodded. "How are the beaches in Milan?" I asked.

"There aren't any beaches in Milan," she said.

"You know what I meant, Samona."

"I suppose we all take risks."

"Not me."

"Yeah. Maybe not you.."

As if in a dream David was sitting at the table again and he easily managed to move the conversation back to The Leonard Company and the renovations being done on the conference rooms. David's smile faded into a steely expression—even when he chuckled—and after absently draining the second bottle of sake, he announced, "I've got some interesting news, speaking of old college friends—"

"I wasn't aware that we had been," Samona interrupted.

"We contracted Ethan Hoevel to design the new conference rooms," David finished, undeterred.

There was the long silence that David Taylor had anticipated.

I assumed that Samona was already aware of this fact.

"It's a funny story actually—how this all happened." David was staring at Samona. "Remember when he showed up at Randolph Torrance's party? And I couldn't remember him?"

And then David Taylor turned and looked at me.

"I flashed on our friend here"—David gripped my shoulder and gave it the familiar squeeze—"and then I remembered very clearly who

Ethan Hoevel was." David looked at us with that practiced, professional ease that revealed nothing.

I was thinking about a night in college:

David comes by my dorm room to borrow a book, but he doesn't call first, and when he comes in I'm sitting on one end of my couch and Ethan's lying down on the other, his legs resting on my lap while we watch an Aerosmith video on MTV, and it's so conspicuous how rapidly I untangle myself when David walks in, and the hurt in Ethan's eyes is raw and unmistakable.

Finally Samona cleared her throat, rattling me back to the present. "Why is that a funny story?" she asked.

"Yeah. I don't get the punch line." This was me.

David ignored us and went on. "Well, we started getting reacquainted and he was telling me what he was doing and I mentioned to him how that week there'd been a meeting about the renovations to the conference rooms that had been initially planned and how they really weren't reflecting that modern edge we were looking for—that indefinable thing we wanted to make us seem more appealing to young investors—and so a week later Ethan Hoevel came by and talked to a couple of us and had some great ideas and he was hired." David drank deeply from his glass of sake and chased it with beer.

"That's very thoughtful of you."

Samona said this, and suddenly three things became clear to me.

David knew about my junior-year relationship with Ethan Hoevel.

Samona didn't know that Ethan was gay.

And Samona—amazingly—could not realize in Woo Lae Oak that David knew about her affair; she still thought it belonged to her only.

Food began arriving, and while plates were being arranged on the table, Samona looked loosely in my direction, as if her gaze had been wandering all over the place and had suddenly, accidentally, fallen on me.

"I'm sorry we haven't seen each other since you stopped by that day," she said.

David barely looked up from the food he was eating. But why should he care? I was gay. I was no threat to him or his wife.

"Things just got very busy," Samona was saying, and then she looked out the window behind me, focusing on something, following it across her line of vision with a curious look, and then coming back to David, and then coming back to me.

I turned around and saw the back of a dark jacket disappear at the edge of the window.

And then there was silence and David and I ate quickly and Samona didn't eat anything and David paid the check while the two of us shared a small dessert.

Outside, I waited while David hailed a cab on Houston.

"I hope to see you soon." Samona said this very softly into my ear after she kissed my cheek. Her whisper was warm against my skin, and I couldn't help what stirred inside of me. "Take care."

And then she climbed through the cab door David was holding open for her.

David took an extra moment to look at me, but it was impossible to discern what he was thinking.

The cab pulled away from the curb and I walked north, straight through NYU, her last words lingering forcefully.

Hope was not the right word.

Desire was so much stronger than hope.

Hope cares too much about the forces working against it.

Desire doesn't give a shit about anything.

Mercer ended on Eighth Street. That was when my cell phone rang.

I pulled it out of my jacket. I recognized the number and answered just before the call went to voice mail.

"What is it?" I asked.

"Where are you?"

"I'm on my way home. Why?"

"Do you want to get a drink?"

I sighed. "Not really, Stanton."

"I really need to talk to you. If you don't want to get a drink, then come over."

"Let me guess: this is about Ethan, right?" I said with heavy sarcasm. "Look, Stanton, you're a really nice guy but—"

"I'm serious. It's not about just Ethan anymore. It's about someone else you know."

"Who?" I asked, something tightening in my chest.

Stanton breathed in. "It's about the person Ethan is having an affair with."

I found myself turning toward the West Village.

18

STANTON VAUGHN kept an apartment on Twelfth Street and Seventh Avenue—a chic address but a dingy brownstone—even though he spent most of his time at Ethan's. But that night he was not in the loft on Warren Street, and he let me wait a long time after I hit the buzzer. I was deciding whether to hit it again or just leave

(but you wanted to hear about Samona and all the things you still didn't know and you were hoping that Stanton would clarify it all)

when the shrill sound of the door unlocking made the decision for me. Lightbulbs were flickering along the narrow hallways where paint peeled off the walls in large, random patches. The door to 4C was adorned with an old Christmas wreath, brown and covered with bells and candy canes and little doves. Stanton opened the door before I could knock and just stood there for a moment in an open bathrobe, a gray wife-beater and a pair of boxer briefs beneath it. Dark circles sagged under his eyes, and his hair—usually so stylishly groomed—tufted up sharply over each ear, and his characteristic four-day stubble looked closer to ten days.

He ushered me in and then shut the door, double-locking it.

Inside 4C, the narrow studio reeked of cigarette smoke. Stanton sat at a makeshift desk in front of a laptop and a printer and a thick stack of paper and a mirror where half a pile of white powder had been arranged into lines. He offered up the coke, which I refused because I knew it wouldn't take me anywhere I wanted to go.

On one wall was a huge poster for Stanton's "Boi-Wear" line featuring a darkly handsome teenage model with disheveled hair slouching down a runway. There was a long couch with an evergreen slipcover draped over it, and where a canvas bag filled with clothes had been tossed. At the far end of the studio sat an expensive futon above which hung another poster, this one for Banana Republic—a model standing sullenly on a beach whom I placed as a much younger Stanton Vaughn. The only other furniture was a steel armoire, designed by Ethan, which held a plasma TV and a DVD player (on top of which was a bright red disc entitled *Straight College Men IV*). A thick layer of dust covered every surface except the table where Stanton now sat, snorting another line off the mirror. The studio was somewhere between exactly what I would have imagined Stanton's apartment to be like and nothing I could have imagined at all.

"I know, I know," he muttered. "I should get a maid."

"I haven't seen you since that lunch with all the Hoevels," I said, staying calm with the help of the sake still coursing through me, highly aware of my own presence in the room.

"Fuck—don't remind me of that fucking nightmare."

Before he could start another tirade—and lose track of the real reason I was there—I changed the focus onto Stanton. "Is that your screenplay?" I gestured at the Final Draft window glowing in the darkness of the studio. Next to the laptop was a large ashtray overflowing with half-smoked Marlboros.

"Yeah, I'm working on it." He sniffed deeply as if to clear his nose, and then decided to use a Kleenex.

"How's it going?"

"It's all fucked up." He was staring at me, as if he were deciding whether he wanted to tell me things about this person we both knew, or if he had changed his mind and wanted to kick me out.

He made a motion for me to sit in a chair next to the sofa, but I declined.

"Stanton, I just want to know what's going on."

He shrugged. "You sure you don't want any?"

"It's late." I checked my watch—a hint for him to get moving.

"Ethan's having an affair."

This admission caused Stanton to do another line.

Neither of us spoke for a long time. He pulled out a pack of cigarettes and offered me one. I shook my head.

He turned back to the desk for matches but there were none left.

"You got a light?" he asked.

I struck a match (I had grabbed a book by the door of Woo Lae Oak, because after the trauma of that dinner I was dying for a cigarette, but when Samona had kissed me on Houston and whispered into my ear, I suddenly didn't want one anymore). Stanton took two deep drags and closed his eyes, exhaling. The smoke floated toward the ceiling.

"He wasn't even trying to hide it from me."

"But don't you guys have an understanding?"

"Yeah. You're right. We did have an understanding."

Stanton was starting to breathe hard—his back was pushing up and down, straining against the tightness of the robe.

"When did this happen?" I asked.

Stanton spoke in a drug rush: "A few days ago. Ethan didn't know I was coming over but when I was coming over never seemed to matter before until just a few weeks ago when he told me to start calling the loft before I came over to make sure he was there and I knew something was wrong. 'Get into the habit of calling' was the exact phrase."

"Stanton, I mean—"

"And listen here, I don't sneak up on people or follow people. I'm not like that. I go where I want to go. Ethan knew that about me. But that's not the point. The point is: he shouldn't be so shifty about his actions. We promised each other that. We promised that if either one of us ever had a problem, if either one of us wasn't feeling good about the whole thing—whatever the hell we had—we'd be totally up-front about it. We'd talk. We'd work it out or not work it out, and we wouldn't be shifty. *That* was our understanding."

"What happened, Stanton?"

"I showed up. The doorman was there. I said, 'Hey, Tommy,' and hung around outside to smoke a cigarette before going upstairs. I heard Ethan coming out of the elevator and talking on his cell phone all hush-hush like, 'I can't wait to see you. I'll see you in a minute.' And he came outside and didn't see me."

"You were hiding from him?"

He took a deep breath. "What have I been telling you? What's the point of all this? I'm. Not. Sneaky. I wasn't *hiding*—Ethan simply failed to *notice* me there. And then he got in a cab and I got in another cab behind him and we took a little trip to Hell's Kitchen."

He stopped to let it sink in. I blinked a few times.

I was picturing the scene: Ethan getting out at The Riverview. Stanton somehow following him upstairs, watching from around the corner or something as Samona let Ethan inside. He probably even put his ear up to the door, tuning in to their moans between his own sobs. I almost felt bad for him despite the freakishness of what he'd done as well as his failure to acknowledge his actions as abnormal in any way.

"I'm sorry, Stanton." I sighed.

"Hey, I'm not *sorry*. I'm pissed. There's a difference." He wiped something off his face and did another line. "I gave Ethan everything, and I know he gave me a lot, too, but when he goes to some midtown high-rise to get banged in the ass by that little rich boy . . ." He paused to sigh out another thick cloud of smoke. "I saw it. I could see through the window at the end of the hallway from outside and I saw it. So fucking sordid!"

I was relieved. It wasn't her. It was someone else—some lark Ethan had slept with and forgotten about an hour later.

I could leave now and head back to Tenth Street. I felt liberated.

"You know something? It took me months before Ethan would let me get behind him for sex. It was this whole power thing. It was a 'control issue,' he kept saying. Months. It took me months to finally get him to do it. And then he lets this little faggot do it the first time they hook up?"

He took out the last cigarette from the box and motioned for the matches.

I had trouble lighting it—I was drained from the night—and he snatched them away from me. By then I'd realized tiredly that this was just another one of Stanton Vaughn's ploys—to get me alone, to get me high, and eventually naked. I was ready to leave.

"Stanton, I'm sorry, but I don't know the guy."

Stanton looked at me. "I think you do know him."

I racked my mind but couldn't come up with anyone. I really didn't have any friends, and of the acquaintances I did have, few, if any, were gay.

"Well, did *you* know the guy?" I asked, hoping he didn't.

Stanton calmed down, centered himself, and looked at me hard.

And then Stanton Vaughn said the following.

I remember it so well that I am quoting it verbatim:

"I've been doing a little research of my own. He works at an office in midtown. He's a fucking banker, for God's sake. And—get this—he's *married*. To. A. Woman. How do I know this? Because she runs this print studio in SoHo and Ethan asked me to give her my business as a favor—can you believe it? Well, you can, because you already know. And I give this woman—this *slut hack*—work during the most important time of my career, and this is how I get repaid: her husband fucks my boyfriend. I mean, tell me, please, what kind of sick, twisted, fucking game is that?" He inhaled, then exhaled again, then did a line. "And yes, you do know him. His name is David Taylor. And you just had dinner with the fucker."

I flashed on Samona's face drifting toward the window.

I flashed on the black jacket disappearing, which was exactly the same black jacket that was now draped over the chair where Stanton was sitting.

There was a small cracking sound in the apartment. A leg supporting the desk had shifted, and the laptop slid dangerously close to the edge. Papers scattered across the floor, carpeting the dark wood. Stanton put his cigarette out and made a save for the mirror, laying it gently on the table in front of the sofa.

I wasn't aware that I was whispering to myself until Stanton pointed it out.

19

BY THE TIME I left Stanton Vaughn's apartment an hour later on that night near the end of July (after turning down seven more offers of cocaine and deflecting four more come-ons—though there had probably been others that I hadn't picked up on), Stanton—with varying combinations of bitterness and disbelief mixed in with his rage—had told me basically all that he knew or had heard.

Which was how the journalist in me constructed the events of the last month and a half. And though the journalist was striving to ask the right questions (the journalist wanted to account and to verify and to figure everything out), there was another part of me that kept interrupting these questions in order to wander.

And I surrendered to the wanderer, because this was the part that dreamed of these people and their dark hearts—the place where people loved.

During the Randolph Torrance cocktail party at the end of May celebrating the acquisition of *Fifteen Monkeys*, Samona Taylor introduces Ethan Hoevel to David as her "benefactor" before explaining how they had "come across each other" at an art gallery in SoHo a month earlier and how he has been sending her clients on an almost weekly basis. This is a business element neither of them considered while writing the proposal and, David realizes, the element that is altering his prediction of utter failure for Printing Divine.

David finally places Ethan Hoevel, whose brooding, pensive gaze makes David feel drunker than he is. The first thing that strikes him: Ethan Hoevel's face is more handsome than his own, which is starting to show the first signs of bloat from too much vodka and sitting at a desk all day. He asks Ethan about Peru and receives a tired response vaguely related to teaching. "That must have been pretty amazing," David Taylor says. Ethan's nod and subsequent silence make David feel ashamed to be offering such a meaningless compliment to someone he doesn't know. He sees himself through Ethan Hoevel's eyes and sobers up. Samona sighs again.

Ethan doesn't stay long at the Randolph Torrance cocktail party but makes enough of an impression on David to linger in his mind. He finds the guy intriguing if for no other reason than he's so different from the men David works with every day who are shaking it out to old Van Morrison songs while rubbing coke into their receding gums. David Taylor has never really known a gay man before (Randolph Torrance doesn't count) and he starts to feel narrow-minded. He feels he lacks some basic awareness that there are other worlds, and other lives, that are much more complicated than his own. The following day at the office, David Taylor Googles *Ethan Hoevel* and—impressed by the hundreds of thousands of hits, mostly magazine archives—visits ethanhoeveldesigns.com. Five minutes turn into an hour. Browsing through Ethan Hoevel's portfolio and gazing at all the beautiful things he's designed make David forget about Samona, who is so over her head in the business he bought for her (until he remembers forty minutes in that it's Ethan Hoevel who's turning Printing Divine into a success, and so really it's Ethan who's creating this hell for him).

Meanwhile, David has been tanking at work. Every move he makes is wrong. The war has apparently made *Intertrade96* obsolete. That $150,000 he lost six years ago by checking the wrong box was just a knock-knock joke compared to the $25 million that has come through his screen and vanished into thin air this quarter alone. And since he isn't making up for those losses by bringing in new clients, he is constantly waiting for Leonard to ask, "Could you come to my office for a moment, David?" And he never wants to go back to The Riverview, where Samona—if she isn't out partying (which she has been doing a lot lately)—will be talking to her father on the phone while playing her New Age music and proudly showing him the dye stains on her fingertips. And as he reaches into the freezer for that bottle of Grey Goose he'll notice the posting on the door of her long list of clients (the important ones triple underlined and highlighted in yellow). So instead, late at night, David Taylor moves away from his desk in his office at The Leonard Company and lies down on the black leather couch he bought at Jennifer Convertibles with Samona—their first joint purchase when they moved into The Riverview almost five years ago—for a few hours of half sleep until dawn.

One night Samona calls to say she's leaving work early since she'll be flying to Milan the next day. David softens enough to stop at Bangkok Four—a Thai place he knows she likes—and brings dinner home. As David tries to concentrate on the questions being asked as answers on *Jeopardy!* Samona goes on and on about a world he cares so little about even though it is her world, and this realization saddens him and he cuts the talking with a kiss. They move into the bedroom and undress and try to make love for the first time in over a month, but David can't get an erection. She works on him for twenty minutes (in a very perfunctory manner) and nothing happens. She says it's okay, that he's been stressed out, that maybe this is a sign to cool it for a while, but in the darkness of their bedroom he can hear her sighing again. He remains silent with his arm draped over his eyes.

"Maybe you should turn around?" He starts rotating onto his knees.

She sighs for a second time. "It makes my back hurt. Let's just go to sleep."

"You're leaving in the morning."

He's on his knees now, working on himself. She's lying on her back pulling the sheets up over her chest while David tugs them away. Then he stops stroking his penis (still flaccid) and stares down at Samona's exposed body.

"When did you stop waxing?" he asks.

"What are you talking about?" She pulls the sheet back over herself. "Jesus, David. Please."

What hurts David more than his own embarrassment (and why should any man be embarrassed about this in front of his own wife—isn't that what a marriage is all about?) is that the glaring fact that they will not be fucking tonight or any night for at least a week does not seem to bother her.

While Samona is in Milan there's a meeting at The Leonard Company regarding the conference rooms. Two of them will remain the same: elegant, polished mahogany, cozy, antique-laden. But there is a new movement to contemporize the other two, as junior data analysts are showing that The Leonard Company has been losing a large portion of the "young-investor demographic" and it's time to meet the "trends of the age."

David flashes on the interiors from Ethan Hoevel's Web site and blurts Ethan's name, and the bored associates at the meeting perk up—James Leonard's wife, in fact, had recently almost persuaded her husband to buy an Ethan Hoevel living-room set for their Hamptons home.

David calls Ethan's studio and listens to Ethan's outgoing message that he's out of town for a week. He clears his throat.

"Hey there, this is David Taylor . . . from Yale? . . . We hung out a little at Randolph Torrance's cocktail party a month or so ago . . . um, well, listen, Ethan, I'm up here at the office—The Leonard Company, our little hedge fund—did I tell you that before?—and we're actually remodeling our conference rooms, looking to change things around here, you know? So . . . ah . . . I was hoping you'd consider maybe coming up for a look-see? It would be interesting to hear what you think, okay? Okay . . . um, ciao."

A few minutes later, while waiting for a lunch delivery from Prêt à Manger to arrive, David asks himself, cringing: *Did you actually say "look-see"? Did you actually end that message with "ciao"?* And then he wonders why he never mentioned Samona in the message.

During the five lonely nights that follow, David Taylor sits at his desk or lies on his black leather couch or in the empty bedroom high above the city in The Riverview, wondering about all the wrong decisions he's made during his life. On one of those nights, around 4 A.M., he goes back to ethanhoeveldesigns.com and orders a love seat—a sister model to the most popular chair, silver and paper-thin and curving. He has no idea where it will fit—unless he gets rid of the couch—but it is something new, and that's what he likes most about it. After clicking the purchase button for the love seat, David checks Samona's flights on the Alitalia Web site. The fact that the flight numbers and departure/arrival times she'd given him don't match up seems alarming at first, but after thinking about it, he decides that Samona has always been flaky like that. This is the kind of mistake she's prone to make.

A very jealous Ethan Hoevel takes a cab back to Warren Street from Randolph Torrance's party. The image of David Taylor placing his hand on Samona's lower back forced him to leave.

(But isn't that why he went to the party in the first place? To see how this would make him feel?)

At the light on Thirty-fourth and Park Ethan, filled with longing, almost tells the cabdriver to turn around but Stanton is waiting for him while working on his screenplay. Later that night, while fucking Stanton, Ethan sees only the mole below Stanton's waist and the coarse hairs on his shoulders that Stanton waxes every month but that always grow back in a few days. He's thinking about the expression on Stanton's face that Ethan never looks at anyway because he only likes taking Stanton from behind and when did having sex with Stanton start making Ethan feel so angry? Stanton is always straining to change the position so that they can face each other or so that Stanton can fuck Ethan. It has become such a battle.

Meanwhile, sex with Samona is a calm and serene experience and she surrenders totally when she's with him. Ethan never takes his eyes off her face when they're having sex. She rides him and his hands glance over her full breasts, his fingers flicking the black, erect nipples, and even when he goes down on her (she stopped waxing the black mat of pubic hair after he told her he liked plunging into it) he props up her torso so his eyes can always be pinned to her face and he watches as she bites her lower lip and the intense concentration that is creasing her expression, and then she's coming and her mouth is open and then she'll smile, and it isn't the elusive smile she gave the camera when she was a model—the one that hides any feelings she may or may not have—but a smile that says: *yes, I want to come again.*

In Thailand they swim naked in the clear water along the labyrinth of orange- and purple- and green-colored coral and walk along a pearly beach collecting seashells. They drink mai tais at sunset while listening to an old Bob Marley CD, and he considers how undeniable she is. Not necessarily as a person (he doesn't really know her yet) but as a form, a thing of beauty. And that final night on the beach, before the ember burns her eye, Ethan's drifting into the past, wondering if the one real choice he ever had to make—abandoning someone he loved—the choice that has defined him ever since—was the wrong one. Samona has forced him to reassess so much about his life.

They return to Manhattan, where Ethan listens to David Taylor's request on his answering machine.

It's a message which—a week earlier—Ethan Hoevel would never have even considered returning.

Yet Ethan Hoevel returns David Taylor's call. He does this just a few minutes before Angela and Aidan and Suzanne and Stanton come through the door for lunch on the Fourth of July.

Because his curiosity about the man to whom Samona Taylor is married needs to be shut down and locked away.

(Or is it because Samona has taken a different kind of grip over Ethan after he saw her together with her husband at the party—she's become more desirable? He considers this idea and quickly dismisses it.)

"I just got back from Thailand and I'm totally beat—I've got way too much work on the table and, you know, that's not really what I do anyway."

"Well, do you want to have lunch and let me make the pitch?"

And Ethan, maybe in response to the desperate quality of David's voice, surprises both of them by saying, "Sure."

They meet at Corotta on July 7. David is waiting at a small corner table in the back when his cell phone rings. Ethan's running late (not because he's busy but because he likes the idea of Samona's husband waiting for him), but David assures him that it's okay because he's only been at the restaurant for five minutes. He orders a glass of wine and tries to convince himself that he isn't feeling tense. The morning was long and cutbacks have started again and all of them come through his desk for approval—essentially, he's been firing people—and the construction noises are getting louder. But the wine eases him. He orders another glass and drinks half of it and then three guys David recognizes from The Leonard Company sit at the table next to his and everyone nods at one another. David starts daydreaming while waiting for Ethan Hoevel to show up.

"David?" Ethan says.

David looks up, startled, and his thighs knock against the table as he stands, his napkin falling off his lap to the floor. There's an awkward moment during which David can't decide whether he should pick up the napkin first or shake Ethan's hand. He tries to do both at the same time. Ethan laughs and as they sit down David says, "I'm glad you could make it." Ethan's wearing a white Prada shirt—the top three buttons open—and faded jeans and a pair of three-hundred-dollar Nikes that David once thought about buying for himself.

David has trouble fitting both elbows on the table. He finishes the second glass of wine in one gulp. Ethan notices.

"Are we having a stressful day?" Ethan asks, gesturing at the empty glass.

"Yes. No. Just busy. The war is mucking everything up and . . . I don't know."

"Is it really like a war? The *Post* says it's more like diplomacy."

"Or the lack thereof. But it's a war. People are dying. It's a war." The wine David Taylor drank alleviates the pressure to perform. "And over here, a lot of talented young people are losing their jobs. Cutbacks. It all sucks."

"I kind of tuned out the war," Ethan says as a waiter hands him a menu. He notes that David doesn't have one, and it occurs to him that David Taylor knows the menu by heart. "I've always wanted to try this place," Ethan says.

"I come here a lot." David gives up on his elbows. He puts his hands in his lap.

Ethan opens the menu and asks, "What do you recommend?"

"The beet salad is pretty good." David reaches over and points out a few items. "The vegetable lasagna. The sea bass."

The heat David feels from his two glasses of wine prompts him to take off his jacket and drape it over his chair as he considers ordering a vodka.

"A nicer suit might fit you better," Ethan says offhand, scanning David before turning to the wine list. "Will you have some wine if I order a bottle?"

David hunches forward to hide whatever Ethan is looking at. "Definitely."

Ethan orders duck confit and a pinot grigio that David likes. David orders the beet salad.

"Where did you get that suit?" Ethan asks. "Barneys?"

David tries to locate the smugness in Ethan's tone—but it isn't there. He's genuinely interested. "Yeah. How'd you guess?"

"You should try Prada next time." Ethan unfolds his napkin. "I know some people there. I can put you in touch with them if you want."

"What's so great about Prada?" David asks.

"It'll fit you better. You have those skinny shoulders." David doesn't know what Ethan means by that. Ethan sees this. "You'll look good."

The wine comes and they each drink a glass quickly.

"So," Ethan says. "Why am I here? What is it exactly you guys need?"

"Well, as I mentioned before we're looking to contemporize a couple of conference rooms. You know, sort of make the office look hipper, younger, whatever." David pauses to pour himself another glass. "We're sort of thinking as we go."

"Even though all the young people are losing their jobs?"

David smiles. He likes playfulness. He responds to it.

"It's more for the investors. There are a lot of young investors. And the problem is that they perceive Leonard as a firm for old money—even though it's not—and our job right now is to make it appealing to them. To that particular . . . money."

"And I fit in . . . because?"

"Because I just . . . think you'd be good. I've . . . seen your Web site." David almost mentions that he bought a love seat at four in the morning last week, which is in a storage room in the basement of his office building and which he hasn't yet gone down to see because first he has to figure out what to do with the leather sofa.

Ethan frowns. "For a conference room?"

"Yeah. For renovating a conference room." David pauses. "Actually two of them."

"I have to tell you, I really don't do things like that."

"There's a very generous budget allocated to this project and I think we would make it very much worth your time and effort." David hates how that comes out. He sounds like a corporate hack.

Ethan doesn't say anything.

"Look, you should at least come by the offices before you say no."

David notices that Ethan Hoevel seems to be studying him with curiosity.

Finally, Ethan says, "I'll take a look."

For some reason relief floods through David Taylor. "You want to do it today? After lunch?"

"I can't do it today. How's tomorrow?"

David rolls through his schedule. "I can do it after six. Does that work?"

"My class gets out at five-thirty." Ethan tilts his head slightly, still studying him. "So, yeah. Sure."

"Great." A pause. "What kind of class are you taking?"

Because David Taylor expects an answer like "Pilates," he's surprised to hear: "I teach, actually."

David's eyes widen with interest as he picks up his wineglass. "What do you teach?" He can't help noticing Ethan's smile.

"Design classes at Parsons. Like, products design."

"Wow," is all David can say before he takes another sip of his wine.

"Yeah." Ethan leans back slightly because David is now leaning forward.

David's voice sounds far away when he asks, "What's it like, teaching?"

"It's fun, you know? I mean the kids are mostly whiny idealists, but I guess we all were."

A forced chuckle from David. "Yeah."

"I don't know," Ethan says. "I like it."

"Yeah . . ." and then David's voice trails off and it seems as if he's talking to someone else when he says, "It's just really impressive that you can do that."

"Well, you must do your share of"—Ethan turns his fingers into quotations—"'teaching' to the young guys in the office, right? The ones losing their jobs?"

David chuckles again but it sounds like he is drugged. "Right. I guess I do."

After their food comes they talk about college.

David Taylor brings up the Amber Blues playing at one of his frat parties, and he even hums a few bars of their amputee love song, though he can't remember any of the lyrics.

Ethan Hoevel praises the stellar track career.

They both recall the performance of *Love's Labour's Lost* on the quad, though they disagree on which quad it was.

They joke about the one class they had taken together.

During their conversation—even after all the wine and feeling loose—David processes his words before they come out, measuring them, and he's speaking quietly, with emphasis, but David Taylor is also thinking about his marriage and how it isn't moving anywhere—why don't they have a child? Why are they still living in Manhattan? What happened to the house in Connecticut? Why is their sex life not happening?

And that is when he flashes on the idea—for the first time, while talking to Ethan Hoevel—that his wife is having an affair.

What makes David Taylor suddenly suspect this?

While staring at Ethan's hands, David Taylor realizes that Samona never answered him when he asked her why she stopped waxing.

His mind suddenly becomes overloaded and he tries to stay calm and maintain the lightness of the conversation.

But Ethan Hoevel doesn't know any of this because now David Taylor is becoming a real person to him, and Ethan is finding it easy to smile at David, and that smile at first seems to cause David Taylor a certain level of discomfort for all the usual reasons—this guy is gay, right?—which is then transferred onto Ethan when he apprehends the fact that he's actually cruising David Taylor in a crowded restaurant in midtown during lunch hour, and then he knows he has to cut this thing short. Ethan finds himself attracted to David Taylor. And he does not want to be. This is the last thing he expected.

David does not mention any of his marital fears to Ethan at Corotta.

And later in the day, he can't process the reason why Ethan Hoevel's presence, of all people's, was what moved him to become conscious of Samona's infidelity.

After lunch Ethan goes back to his loft and has sex with David's wife for the rest of the afternoon.

And while Ethan is fucking Samona, she becomes David Taylor, and Ethan's thrusting into him as he comes.

At the same time, David is in his office staring at the wedding photo while listening to the ticking of the antique clock.

20

AUGUST IN New York weighs down on us; everything gets absorbed into the heat and humidity that envelops the city. The weather weakens us and inspires a deep longing for the spring months that preceded this hell and will not be around again for almost another year. Air conditioners conk out, sleepless nights are drenched in sweat, the murder rate spikes, and a latent, low-level panic creeps up on everyone. There is always a fear in August—a fear that the heat will never rise off. People do things in August that they would never do in any other month.

I was leaning against the railing of the Hudson Riverwalk at Canal Street. The Hoboken ferry was pulling in a few blocks south, its bumper slamming hard against the wooden pilings. A half mile beyond the ferry the Hudson River poured into the harbor. Kayaks paddled on the fringes of the channel, struggling to avoid the myriad sailboats that were gliding across the water. The Statue of Liberty was a muddied silhouette in the late-summer haze. The Liberty Island ferry steamed toward it.

Then Ethan Hoevel was beside me, following my gaze.

"They letting people up to the crown again?"

I pretended not to be startled by his presence. "No. Just to the gift shop at the base."

"You ever been up there?"

"Me? No."

"I haven't either."

Ethan had been jogging along the riverwalk when he spotted me. He was wearing blue shorts and a white tank top and his hair was matted with sweat.

"There are about two thousand people just a few blocks away from my place circling ground zero. Looking for what, I do not know."

"Remnants of hope amidst monstrous destruction." It was a line from a piece I had written a few months after the attack that had never been published.

"Bulldozers and garbage trucks clearing the way for yet another tall building that hasn't even been designed yet three years after the things fell, while tourists wander around stupidly, should not inspire hope." He was still panting, and his eyes scanned the river and the haze suspended above it.

When I only shrugged, he assumed an expression of mock hurt. "You're not happy to see me?"

The key to Ethan Hoevel was that he didn't give a fuck. A terrorist kills a loved one. You hurt a friend. Someone causes you unhappiness. Ethan understood that if you just didn't care, then you didn't need to search for signs of hope in the wreckage of it all. You could just travel on.

"I guess not. You've been doing a pretty good job of not talking to me lately," he said when he finally caught his breath. "But why don't you come over right now and have dinner with us?"

"Who's 'us'?" I asked, getting ready to cringe at the answer.

"Aidan and me." He smiled at my surprise. "Yeah, my brother. Surprise, surprise—he got fired from his job at the energy trading company and then that girl Suzanne dumped him and got transferred here, so now he's coming here to" —he stopped to put his fingers into quotation marks—" 'hang out for a while.' Draw your own conclusions. He's moving some stuff in right now, actually."

"You must be over the moon with excitement," I said playfully.

"I just hope he's not here for long," he replied, deadpan. "I don't know how much I can take." He paused, considering something. "But anyway, you should come over. Come help me ease the burden that is Aidan Hoevel. I'm ordering good food." He looked around. "And it doesn't seem like you're doing anything else. Are you?"

I tried to ignore his presumption and turned to the water.

I hadn't seen Ethan since the Fourth of July lunch and I wasn't sure that our friendship was a possibility anymore. But he leaned closer to me in order to meet my eyes, and I had to stare at him for a moment—to admire the beauty of Ethan Hoevel. He smiled unthreateningly and touched my elbow and then I moved along the river with him back toward Warren Street. I was hungry and at least his offer would stave off a serious dent in my meager account at Chase. I'd eat, I'd split, maybe I'd cry. My life had come down to this: an opportunity to satiate any lingering curiosities became a free meal.

"So, what are you doing?" I asked in an obvious way that caused Ethan to roll his eyes.

He laughed and wiped sweat off his face with his shirt. "What do you want to know? I suppose you want me to get something off my chest." He laughed again. "I mean, don't you?"

"What I don't want is to fight with you, Ethan."

I stopped for effect, and he turned around and glared at me. Those piercing eyes struck their target once again—the gleam in his eye, the smirk on his mouth—and I took it all in. "Things are never simple," he said. "Not for me. And you know that."

I started walking with him again, weaving around groups of children and dodging Rollerbladers and cyclists until we were in a clearing, where I asked, "Don't you think they could have been?" and shrugged.

"No." He smiled, but there was something more behind it—something he was hiding from me. And since I assumed this involved what I already knew about David Taylor, I felt like I had the upper hand as he added, "Someday you might understand why."

"It's not like you're the only guy in the world with a fucked-up family," I pressed. "It's not like you're the only guy who's ever had an affair. Jesus, it's not like you're the only gay person."

Ethan smiled and lifted his head. "What if I'm not?"

"Not what?"

"Gay."

"I don't want to get into that with you, Ethan. It's not what this is about anyway."

"Oh, look, you're so cute when you're hurt."

"As cute as David Taylor?"

Ethan shot me a look.

I could see him trying to figure it out.

A biker drinking from a water bottle, head upturned, flew between us in a rush as Ethan paused and slowed his pace, thinking, letting me walk a half step ahead.

"Stanton. That's how you know. He called you. Right?"

"Whatever," I muttered.

"I broke up with Stanton."

"Is that right?"

"But he hangs around outside my building. I've seen him ducking behind corners, trailing me up to the Village. Sometimes late at night when I'm looking down from the roof I can see him. It's sad."

"Aren't you a little worried?"

"He'd never do anything." A pause filled with dark thoughts. "Not to me, at least."

We were walking past the trapeze near Battery Park. A little boy was on the high platform strapped in a harness, and a teenage instructor stood behind him with her hands on his waist. The little boy didn't want to swing even though a huge mesh safety net hung only eight feet beneath him, and the instructor was whispering words of encouragement into his ear. Ethan and I both watched as the instructor gave him a gentle push and the little boy fell. He swung forward and back again. He swung until all his momentum was gone and he was just hanging a foot above the net. On the ground his mother was clapping. She yelled for him to let go. And he did, bouncing lightly on the net, lying there for a moment as he stared up at the sky. He scampered off and smiled as his mother hugged him.

"He fucked around, too, you know," Ethan said as we began walking again.

"It's a shitty thing you're doing."

"Oh, fuck you. You're so tired. Don't you get exhausted from worrying too much?"

"What do you want? My approval?"

"Oh yeah, I so want that from you. In fact if you gave it to me everyone would be saved." He was walking faster now, back in stride with me. "Thank you for opening my eyes to all the horror that is me."

"You know I'm right. But, of course, that never mattered to you."

He stopped and grabbed my shoulder—I'd gotten to him. He was stronger than he looked and there was real power in those long, delicately muscled arms. "You think I'm just holding a gun up to everyone's head? That I'm the sole reason why people do the things they do?"

"You're certainly not discouraging anyone."

"Okay. Let's start with you, then. Between my loft, Samona's studio, and David's office, you seem to be turning up everywhere this summer."

"Funny how that happens, huh?" I tried to match the mincing quality of his voice.

"Does this happen because, A: You care about our friendship, if you can call it that? B: You're trying to save a marriage that shouldn't even exist? Or is it C: Because you're obsessed with a girl who's barely even glanced your way since college, when you used to follow her around like some rare breed of toy dog?"

"Let go of me," I said, pulling away.

I stood a few yards away from him, embarrassed by how hard I was breathing. Then Ethan, still perfectly calm, seemed to soften. "Hey, you're still coming over for dinner, right?"

In the lobby of Ethan's building the doorman was stacking boxes into the elevator with Aidan Hoevel.

"Yo, bro," Aidan said to Ethan, glancing at me uncertainly as he tried to remember my name (of course, I had made that large of an impression, as usual). "Hey there . . . dude."

The three of us stepped into the packed elevator. I noticed Aidan had shaved the stubble from his face since the last time I had seen him, and it made him look more like Ethan than I had ever noticed before.

"How long are you staying here?" I asked him.

"Don't know really. Depends on how it goes."

"How what goes?"

He just shrugged and stared through the bars of the cage as we rose to the ninth floor.

In one corner of the loft were Aidan's things: a laundry sack filled with rumpled clothes, an ancient pair of torn-up Air Jordans, a bathroom kit, the Mötley Crüe autobiography, and a PlayStation 2.

In another corner were all the things that Ethan had moved out of his studio: cardboard tubes containing sketches, plastic molds for new designs, various tools, the black wing (recently polished) from his senior project. Ethan had rearranged a number of adjustable walls to build a separate bedroom for Aidan.

"I'm gonna hop in the shower," Ethan said, stopping on the way to screw two more bolts into the partition. When he left the room, I stood there awkwardly with Aidan while the sound of water running filled the background. He picked up his laundry bag and then dropped it again in the same place.

I tried to reach out. "So I'm . . . sorry about your job . . . and your girlfriend."

He shrugged and muttered, "Fuck it."

We were again silent until the intercom rang. Aidan picked it up and said, "Yo, food or girl?" He paused, then nodded. "Sweet." Then, as if I weren't there, he went into Ethan's bedroom and came out with Ethan's wallet.

"Girl?" I asked tentatively.

"I know. It's crazy," Aidan replied, removing four twenties.

I let it go. I had not eaten anything all day. I was so hungry that I thought I could identify the various aromas drifting in from the elevator before it opened: curried beef, potatoes, cooked vegetables.

Aidan paid the delivery guy three twenties and put the change along with the fourth twenty into his own pocket before taking Ethan's wallet back into the bedroom. When he came out, the bag of food was open and he was pulling out chunks of corn bread.

"I don't know who the hell eats Peruvian food, but it smells all right," he said, not necessarily to me.

Ethan came out of the bathroom draped in a towel, his pale, wiry frame still dripping. He caught me staring at his chest and smiled as he turned on the stereo and the Clash started playing "London Calling" in surround sound all across the loft.

"I hope you guys like the food," he said, still smiling at me. "My next trip I'm going back to Peru."

I scanned his body again before forcing myself to look away.

Ethan had ordered generously from Lima Taste in the East Village—three different kinds of meat, heavy starches, all of it still hot. It was the kind of heavy, intimate dinner I didn't feel I deserved or belonged at but, being broke, I was so grateful to be fed that I ate silently while the brothers talked.

They made gentle fun of their mother, they spoke good-naturedly about the future, they joked about the way they used to be. These were not the same brothers sitting on the roof a month ago who had not exchanged a single word during that excruciating lunch. A new vibe had developed between them, and I couldn't tell who was generating it or why.

"This is a really great place, Ethan," Aidan Hoevel was saying.

"You can stay as long as you'd like." Ethan said this in a tone of voice I didn't recognize.

"You've done really well for yourself." Aidan paused. "I'm proud of you."

"Hey, none of that bogus Irish sentimentality allowed."

Aidan nodded gratefully while—as inconspicuously as possible—I helped myself to seconds. And as I was setting my plate down on the bamboo place mat in front of me, the intercom buzzer rang again. I looked up at both of them—Aidan first, then Ethan—as Aidan said, "That the chick?"

Ethan was grinning at me as he answered, "Yes, that's gonna be Samona."

"Sweet," Aidan said again, wiping his mouth. "This'll be like one of those sitcoms Mom's always watching."

"Yeah—three people share a loft in New York and calamity reigns."

I didn't flinch.

I stared at all the food I had heaped onto the massive white plate.

I knew that I was not going to eat any of it as everything came together in a rush. I sat still and rode out a small wave of nausea while Ethan went to the front to tell the doorman to let Samona up.

"Hey . . . hey . . ." Somewhere from far off, Aidan Hoevel was trying to get my attention. When I finally looked at him, he grinned and said, "You know what I told Ethan when he asked me what to do when you're having an affair with a woman who wants to leave her husband for you? You know what I told him when he asked that?"

"What?" I could barely hear my own voice.

He paused to give his answer authority and weight. "She gives." Pause. "You take." Another pause. "You forget."

"Dude," Ethan added, returning to the room. "But that was only after he'd asked, 'Are you sure she's a woman?,' 'Is she hot?,' and 'When did you figure out you're not gay?' "

I could only glare at him. "So . . . what? She's coming for dinner?"

"Better," Aidan said through a full mouth. "She's moving in."

"I'll tell you about it later," Ethan said coolly. "But I thought you'd enjoy the surprise."

"Hey, you guys are creeping me out," Aidan said. And then to me, lowering his voice, wide-eyed, "And remember, dude, we're not allowed to tell her my bro sleeps with dudes."

Samona came out of the elevator. She was pulling a suitcase on wheels and carrying a six-layer black-and-white cake from Dean & DeLuca. The beaming expression on her face seemed false to me.

"Hey," was all she said to me as our eyes met, and I could only nod at her and then look down at my plate again. "This food smells amazing. I wish my stomach weren't bothering me so much."

She sat down, and I still wasn't able to say anything, not even to murmur a greeting.

The particular moment taught me that I wasn't capable of hating Samona, that the most I could ever hope for was to become numb to her.

She sighed exhaustedly and I managed a glance during which I studied her face distantly—the blush that had been rapidly applied and was already crumbling; the hair pulled back so tightly I could see the tautness in her forehead; the scar near her eye that she would pick at from time to time; the way she looked to Ethan as if waiting to be told it was okay to speak.

Ethan introduced her to his brother. Aidan grinned at her like he knew a secret and said, "Samona's a beautiful name. Where's it from?"

"My mother was born in Ghana."

"That's, like, on the east coast of Africa, right?" Aidan asked.

"West coast."

"Right, right. I was on an expedition once. We were gonna stop there."

Ethan Hoevel watched his brother scanning Samona and cut in: "Weren't you, shall we say, *extradited* from the boat before you made it into international waters?"

Aidan flicked his wrist and rattled off: "I was cooped up with a bunch of environmentalists." He paused. "They didn't like to have any fun."

"Aidan got drunk and shot a dolphin with a speargun," Ethan clarified.

"Oh God."

Samona brought a hand to her mouth while Aidan scoffed at his brother. "What the hell do you know about it, dude? Weren't you busy already, doing your *thing* at *Yale*?" He turned to Samona. "Mellow out— I thought it was a shark. Plus I drank too much Jack." When that failed to soothe her, he added, "I cried for like a day afterward."

On the edge of the table, Samona's hands crept toward Ethan's arm. She rested her fingers lightly over his wrist as her eyes searched for a comforting glance. Ethan gave it to her—the kind of look that assured her everything was working out exactly the way it should be, that nothing was out of place, that she was fine.

It was not the kind of look that told her Ethan was screwing her husband, I noted.

"How about some of that cake?" Aidan said, wiping his lips. And then he stopped. "Or should I have some more green beans? I've got to start eating healthy now that I'm in New York. Right?"

Samona placed the cake carefully in the middle of the table. Ethan served small portions to Samona and then Aidan before cutting nearly a quarter of the cake for me.

"Why do they call it that?" Aidan asked no one. "Black-and-white?

Chocolate isn't black. Vanilla isn't white. It should be called a brown-and-yellow cake." He was shoveling creamy slabs of it into his mouth, chewing furiously, when he noticed the long silence and all of us staring at him.

Ethan turned away from Aidan, and then—smiling tightly, gripping Samona's hand—he said, "It's okay—we'll get used to it."

Samona sighed tiredly and rubbed her eyes. She and Ethan had one of those brief aside conversations—soft, intimate tones that no one else could hear, coupled with the requisite subtle gestures—and then he stroked her hair and nodded and murmured, "Yeah, let's get you to bed."

They stood up. Samona said, "It's really cool to meet you, Aidan," and then to me, "Sorry I'm such a drag but it's been . . . a long week."

I replied nonchalantly, "I'm sure."

"But come by the shop this week and we'll really catch up."

"Sure," I said. "Sure."

"Night, sweets," Aidan chimed in.

She let Ethan lead her to the bedroom while Aidan devoured his cake and then made a pot of rocket-fuel coffee, shaking his hips grossly to the music. When Ethan came back fifteen minutes later, Aidan said, "So we gonna roll?"

"Yeah," Ethan said. "Let's go."

"We're going out?" This was me.

The three of us took a cab to Lot 61, where Ethan had reserved a table with bottle service. The bouncer wasn't going to let Aidan in—"no T-shirts, no sneakers"—but all Ethan had to do was tell the bouncer his name and the velvet rope dropped. Once we were seated, Aidan Hoevel scanned the lithe bodies in the small black dresses that filled the room as he poured three glasses half full with chilled Grey Goose and added a little tonic. Since I couldn't stomach the vodka (and didn't know what I was doing there anymore) I pushed it over to Aidan, who started double-fisting. The big room was now packed and Aidan had an excited grin on his face while Ethan leaned back and sipped his vodka.

I yelled into Ethan's ear over the din of the music so that only he could hear. "She's moving in with you guys?"

"She wants a divorce."

"You're an asshole," I said. "Is that why you invited me to dinner? So you could screw with me over this shit?" My voice was muffled by the sounds of lasers backed up with the moans of a female echoing across the dance floor.

"Listen, let's get out of here," Ethan said.

"What about Aidan?"

He nodded at his brother, who was walking toward the dance floor, starting to flail his arms, then pushing his way between two college-age girls who were too wasted on Ecstasy to care.

Ethan paid for the bottle service and I followed him outside, where we got into a cab. I didn't hear what address he gave the driver.

"Look," he started as we turned down Ninth Avenue. "I don't know what you've got going on inside your head, but—"

"What is this? Your little revenge on me?" I asked. "Did I hurt you that much?"

Ethan surrendered his head to the torn leather seat. "You've got to wrap your head around a very simple fact."

"Which is?"

"This isn't about you."

"I don't think that's true, Ethan," I said. "It sometimes feels like it's very much about me. Because otherwise why would I be in this fucking cab with you?"

"Well, you're the writer. So I guess you have to answer that your-self."

I ignored his mocking tone and caught the driver's glance in the rearview mirror. "I mean, Jesus, has she really not figured out that you're gay yet?" I was looking out the window at the delis, hardware stores, and service stations passing on Ninth Avenue.

"*Gay*'s just a word. You know that as well as anyone."

Then we rode in silence until the cab pulled up outside Arthur's Tavern in the West Village. "This jazz quartet's playing here tonight," Ethan tried to reconcile. "And I just want to talk to you alone for a minute."

I calmed down as we found an empty table so close to the stage that when the trumpet player swayed back and forth Ethan and I had to lean away in order to avoid contact. I just sat there, numb, watching the bassist as he pulled strings rapidly with his thumb and forefinger. During a break in their set I turned to him. "She's really moving in with you?"

He sighed and caught a passing waitress lightly by the arm: a glass of cabernet for him and a Budweiser for me.

"I wish we could still smoke in bars," Ethan murmured. He raised his head and looked away.

The next set began as soon as he finished uttering that sentence: the singer pointed to the saxophonist sitting against the wall offstage right and howled a summoning. The saxophonist was an old man, but the skin on his face was smooth and tight, and he had a full head of thick black hair crawling under the rim of his fedora. He held a drink in one hand and the neck of his instrument in the other. I thought he had passed out but as soon as he heard the singer's call he sat up and began playing.

I didn't touch my beer during the entire set.

When the saxophonist finished and collapsed again, Ethan's cell phone rang and he took it out.

"Should I answer it?" he asked.

"Well, you did leave her alone in your loft. It would be the polite thing to do."

"It's not Samona," he said, putting the phone on the bar where I could see the caller ID read *David Taylor*.

We waited for the phone to stop ringing.

"She found something," Ethan said. "There were stains. On his pants. Very particular stains that she recognized. And that's what set everything in motion." He made a face as he sipped the glass of red wine. "This tastes like vinegar."

"What did she find exactly?"

"He threw a pair of pants into the hamper that Samona goes through when the guy from the dry cleaners stops by each Tuesday morning. And as she was sorting through his clothes she came across the pants." Ethan thought about something—the way he had ended the last sentence—and smiled weakly. "She assumed that he was fucking a young summer intern that—surprise, surprise—he'd fucked before, and she assumed from the pattern of the stains that he had fucked her standing up and pulled out before he came. She has this whole scenario blocked out in her mind." Ethan waited a beat. "It's not far from the truth. But obviously there was no intern."

"Shouldn't you guys be more careful?" was all I could ask, weakly sarcastic.

Ethan finished the glass of wine and made a face again. "What I cannot wrap my head around is that David did not take the pants to the cleaners himself. I cannot wrap my head around the fact that David just tossed them into the hamper without inspecting them first."

I did not know whether I believed the scenario Ethan was playing out for me. The outrageousness of it made the world a different place and yet he spoke in a tone bordering on utter indifference.

"Why is she staying with you? Why don't you get a hotel? Why doesn't she stay with one of her friends?"

"She wants to live with me. That's what she said yesterday when she called: 'I'm leaving him and I want to be with you.'"

"You're inviting her to live with you and your brother while you're fucking her husband." Ethan seemed amused at the urgency in my voice, and I raised my hands defensively. "Just so I'm clear on what you're doing."

"What I'm doing is giving a girl who hasn't felt comfortable or beautiful in years a place where she feels comfortable and beautiful. I'm giving Aidan—who, as I'm sure you've seen, is borderline schizo— a bed to crash in while he calms down and moves on. And David . . ." he trailed off and took out a cigarette, then looked at me, those green eyes piercing the dim yellow light. "I'm just giving people what they want."

"And what do you want?"

Ethan lit the cigarette and scanned the bar disinterestedly. A waitress noticed the cigarette and started to say something, but Ethan smiled at her, and she let it go. And then he said the following as if it made sense, as if it was the simplest thing in the world: "I want to know that people can change."

21

THAT NIGHT IN Arthur's Tavern, Ethan Hoevel told me another story.

When he reaches the twenty-first floor of 800 Seventh Avenue on July 8—the day after the lunch at Corotta—Ethan Hoevel compliments the receptionist's lime-green Versace blouse. It's six o'clock and the office is beginning to drain away on that Friday night. Ethan Hoevel is walking against its tide, down a narrow aisle, moving deeper into the building toward David Taylor's office, his eyes falling on the young men in cheap to moderately expensive suits as they drift by.

He reaches David Taylor's office just as the automatic light inside switches off. He listens to David sigh in the darkness and then watches the shadow of him wave an arm, and when the light clicks on, Ethan materializes in the doorway. David smiles sheepishly as Ethan quietly absorbs the office with his eyes, which scan the black leather couch, the Printing Divine poster, David Taylor, the view behind David's desk—the river, the southwest corner of Central Park, even The Riverview—the antique clock, and then stop and lock onto something.

They're dancing with their foreheads pressed together, her long dark fingers clasping his pale hand just below their faces. Ethan keeps staring at the photograph of Samona and David at their wedding in Darien and he's thinking, *Why would he hang it next to the clock?* The very first moment of their marriage, immortalized, is hanging next to an antique clock whose ceaseless ticking must be nothing less than a steady reminder of how long David Taylor's days are.

Ethan quickly looks away from the photograph as David starts picking up a stack of papers and sliding them into a file, and then he places the file into a drawer and stands.

This is my office. This is where I work. This is me. Thanks for coming. He's just mumbling jittery and meaningless phrases until he finally meets Ethan's eyes and seems to calm down. He takes a breath and says, "How was your class?"

"What?" Ethan surfaces from his reverie.

"The class you just got out of. How was it?"

"Oh." Ethan shrugs. "You know. The usual."

"I'd like to hear about it sometime. I always wanted to teach."

Their eyes meet again. "That wouldn't be a problem." Ethan pauses and looks away. "Even if you want to sit in on a class—it's no problem."

"I just think it's really impressive."

Ethan Hoevel realizes strangely that David's fawning over him, and he waits for David to glance away before he looks back and quickly studies his face: cleanly shaven, pale, skin unblemished, hair gently tussled, mouth and chin almost graceful. It's all very harried and worn but at the same time still—in a way very specific to David Taylor—kind of gorgeous.

A mild distraction comes in the form of a beeping from his computer, where a graph and trading chart begin flashing that fifteen thousand shares of an energy company in Tulsa called Duke (actually, one of Randolph Torrance's subsidiary companies) have hit their peak and the value is dropping. David explains how his computer program, *Intertrade96,* has been set to warn him whenever this happens, and how it's time to sell.

Ethan says, "Cool," but he seems uninterested, so David clicks his mouse quickly on the bottom left side of the screen before leading Ethan into Conference Room Three, where a canvas mat covers the floor scattered with sawdust and white flecks of paint and other remnants of removal. David gestures with his arm. Ethan walks into the middle of the room. He takes in the molded seams between the walls and ceiling. He stands in three different places and studies the room as if he's channeling a certain vision. His eyes keep circling the room for a few minutes, and when they fall on David they stop circling.

Outside the half-open door, the last of the construction crew along with a few junior analysts are leaving, glancing curiously at the two men standing motionless, watching each other, not saying anything. Friday night: men returning home for a weekend, a few of them catching the jitney to the Hamptons.

Ethan says, "Well, yeah. I guess."

David, anxious, asks, "What?"

"I'll do it."

Ethan is aware that he's staring at David.

Ethan is also aware that because of this, David's staring back.

"What do you see?" he asks Ethan.

He's thinking green walls—jade—and chrome swivel chairs and a fiberglass table with monitors built into it and four large plasma screens on each wall and he's thinking a silver chandelier but something low-key, complex, modern, and not garish and disco. David is barely listening.

"Well," he starts. "I'm not the one making the final decisions but I like it." And then, genuinely intrigued, he asks Ethan, "How do you do that? See all that in an empty white room? That's what I don't get."

Ethan shrugs. "It's just what I do." He pauses, staring at David again. "I mean, how do you see a profitable trade in a bunch of numbers flowing across a screen?"

"It's . . ." David doesn't know how to begin explaining. "I guess it's just what *I* do." David is still meeting Ethan's eyes, and Ethan knows he's thinking, *Is this how it happens between men? Is it this simple?* "What made you decide to take on the job?" Ethan looks away, and then moves closer to David. "I mean, if it's not something you normally do?"

Ethan shrugs again. "It's a cool opportunity to do something different."

This remark seems to move David Taylor considerably: that someone would need to come to The Leonard Company to find something different. Ethan senses this sadness and moves closer, but David is looking at the floor. Ethan startles him again. He asks David, "Do people have sex in these rooms? I mean, I've never worked in an office but you see the movies, you hear the rumors, all those Playboy cartoons . . . I mean, is that something that goes on?"

David deflects the tension in the room by laughing. "What—you want to take this into account?"

But Ethan's serious.

David clears his throat.

"Sure. It happens. There's a lock on the door. It's private." He pauses. "Christmas parties. Kind of innocent. Like college kids having sex in the library. Whatever."

"Did you ever do that?" Ethan asks.

"In the library or here?"

"Library."

"Um, me and Samona, yeah, one time."

David shifts and puts his hands in his pockets to adjust his pants casually, which is when Ethan becomes aware that David's penis is starting to stiffen.

David asks, "Did you?"

"Remember Amanda Callahan? Played lacrosse?"

David is suddenly a frat boy again and he can't hide his giddiness. "Wait a minute. *You* had sex with Amanda Callahan? She was gorgeous." And then David laughs to himself before admitting, "I hooked up with her once."

Ethan is nearing David again. "Where did you guys do it?"

"In my room at SAE."

Right now, in this moment, the two of them do not seem that different to each other.

"How did you know you were gay?" he asks Ethan.

"I didn't know I was gay until I just felt that I was. I know that's not an answer. But it's hard to explain."

"No, I know, I'm sorry, I shouldn't have asked." David looks away nervously.

"Don't be. The thing I hated the most was how hard it was to admit it to others." Ethan stops. "I don't feel uncomfortable talking about it."

"So when could you admit it? I mean, when could you admit that you were gay?"

"To myself? Or to everyone else?"

"Both."

Ethan counters with, "When could you admit that you were straight?" He asks this very gently. He isn't accusing David of anything.

"What do you mean?"

"When could you admit to yourself that you liked girls? When could you admit that you were straight to everyone else?"

"That's . . . something I guess I never had to do."

From Ethan Hoevel's vantage point David Taylor is a little boy listening to a man in the center of an empty conference room, trying to make sense of him. David Taylor is waiting to be told what to do.

Ethan takes another step toward him, but David abruptly turns away and walks to the half-open door and stands there breathing heavily.

Ethan sighs. He knows he pushed too hard. He's overstepped a boundary. He's being a fool. Just because he's succeeded in seducing straight guys in the past

(after a lot of alcohol and drugs and promises of introductions and besides they had all been boys and not married men for God's sake)

what makes Ethan Hoevel think he's capable of seducing David Taylor?

It's never going to happen. The meeting is over. He looks at David standing in the door frame.

David stays there for a long time. The aisles are empty. Computers are humming. The offices that line the central wall are dark now, and locked. In David's office—the only one still lit—the light clicks off automatically.

David Taylor closes the door to Conference Room Three, locking it in the same movement. He turns back into the room. The fluorescent lights flicker above them.

Ethan's eyes are still fixed on David.

And because David is just standing there, lingering in the doorway, Ethan is able ask, "Does this feel complicated to you?"

"I don't know."

"Do you want to do it?" Ethan asks. "Are you curious?"

"I don't know," and then, barely audible, "Maybe."

And then as something tall and pale and beautiful moves toward David, he answers, "Yeah, I am."

22

THE STORY OF DAVID AND SAMONA
Part 4: The Gift

A LONG TIME ago, even before she left for college, Samona Ashley assured herself that she could sustain anything, live anywhere, be with anyone, as long as she wasn't bored.

Standing on the tiny balcony in The Riverview Tower one cool October evening, gazing out over midtown and beyond it, Samona Taylor was drinking a gimlet and thinking about how bored she was.

At the same time, David Taylor was buying shares of a company in Lebanon. He had been home earlier to shower and Samona had told him blatantly that—since her period was coming in a day or two— maybe they should have sex. But David had been too tired and he was in a hurry anyway since the international conference call had been bumped up thirty minutes.

All of her friends were drifting away. No one was available that night in October. Sara was at home with a new child and an unfaithful husband. Olivia was at Palm on a blind date with a corporate attorney who, she recognized midway through appetizers, had no interest in her whatsoever (and whom she would marry six months later). Nikki was in rehab.

Regret. It was everywhere. Samona finished the gimlet.

"Wouldn't it be fun to look at apartments this weekend?" Samona asked David that night when he came back from the office at 11:15.

He blinked at her. "You mean Tribeca?" he finally asked.

(Hadn't this been shut and closed a million years ago?)

"Maybe."

"My long day has made me invulnerable to impressionability."

David Taylor knew how badly Samona wanted to move downtown but he didn't really care. He was tired. He hadn't worked out in months. His life was so regimented that he was afraid any change was only going to make things more complicated and exhausting. There were too many obligations already. (This is also what David Taylor began to consider his marriage.)

Later that night he softened to the point where they attempted to have sex—thinking maybe it would cheer them both up—but the only thing that seemed to get David hard was if Samona performed fellatio.

Samona Taylor decided to redecorate the apartment on the twenty-eighth floor of The Riverview Tower. It was the third time she'd undertaken this task since they'd moved in four years ago, and she began by getting rid of all the crap they had bought the last time at Pottery Barn and replacing it with modern Dutch (the teakettle, the wine rack, high-ball glasses) from a chic store in Nolita. She bought a Persian rug on a whim from a merchant on Lafayette. Samona began cruising auctions and soon David Taylor would come home at night to find that she had bought three watercolors that afternoon from an obscure French painter. He endured this for a while because at least she wasn't complaining anymore.

When he sensed that she was getting antsy again a few weeks later, he decided to cut her off at the pass before Tribeca came up again. "Why don't we have a dinner party?" He'd surprised her on purpose, and she could only look at him and blink. "I know, I know. But the place looks so amazing after all the work you've done, we might as well show it off, no?"

She thought about it, and—amazingly—she liked the idea.

The outcome of this suggestion consisted of planning exactly three dinner parties.

Complications: David Taylor could not stand any of Samona Taylor's friends (the ones who were drifting away) but they didn't like David, either (Olivia had noticed that David had developed a "smug chuckle"), but since David had no friends at the office the first party consisted of Olivia, Sara, and Nikki.

Since Samona Taylor didn't cook (rebellion against her mother), she ordered in prepared foods from Citarella. This caused the setting to seem vaguely impersonal while showing up how desperate Samona Taylor was becoming.

David coasted through the dinner stylishly, thinking at one point, *Who would have thought ten years ago that I would be the host of a dinner party with girls I didn't like in an apartment I rented in Manhattan after a long day at the bank?*

Ultimately, the forced giggling and boring reminiscing about "college shenanigans" moved him to excuse himself to the bedroom, where he organized his desk before figuring out he was drunk. Then he went to sleep.

The second dinner party was canceled at the last minute after a particularly acrimonious fight between Samona and David.

The third party consisted of only Samona and Martha, an old friend from the year Samona had been a model—the year Samona thought she was going to make it.

That dinner with Martha—and David's absence from it, for which he cited work reasons—was the genesis of Printing Divine.

Being with Martha offered up intense associations with that year of modeling that Samona thought she had forgotten. But it all came back to her: Lot 61, The Apartment, Lotus, cameras flashing at her, the makeup sessions, the free clothes, the elation at being selected for a show—even a small one. Samona Taylor convinced herself that though this period might not have been great or even very productive, where she existed now was definitely not an improvement. She convinced herself that the year after college was the last time that she had felt alive.

After getting over this initial nostalgia, Samona and Martha talked.

According to Martha, there was a burgeoning market for fashion printing, and Martha felt old and was tired of being a stylist, and of course the stars were in line—Samona was a Virgo (adaptable) and Martha was a Taurus (persistent)—so: Why not?

Samona Taylor listened, wide-eyed, nodding her head exces-

sively, and kept refilling her red wine. Then she envisioned a future
without Martha and the fashion print business. She shuddered.

David Taylor would ask Samona to stop using the pill.

And then David would tell her one Sunday morning about this
great house in Summit or Chatham or fucking Englewood, and that
they might as well just do it since the mortgage rates were so low.

Because somewhere along the line—either while she had been
walking a runway or bidding on a $3,000 Impressionist imitation at
Sotheby's or drinking a glass of wine by herself in front of a *7th Heaven*
rerun—Samona Taylor had decided that she did not want children and
she did not want a house in Darien or Greenwich or Englewood.

Because Samona knew that silence—the quiet that David Taylor
craved—was the deadening end of everything. The "quaint" streets
named Cherry Hill and Orchard Avenue and Devonshire Way, the
ostentatious mailboxes, the pudgy kids missing layups in the hoop that
hung above the three-car garage, the endless hours of children wasting
their lives in a basement playing Doom—Samona Taylor knew that the
semblance of normalcy that was so strenuously maintained only fed the
particular darkness that hung unseen over each day.

Samona knew that David only wanted this move to happen because
he was still giddy about being "a throwback" and getting married at a
young age and his wife not having to work because he could support
her. He bragged about these things constantly at bars and parties
before he got too drunk to articulate them. Sometimes he'd be subtle
about it, but usually not. He formed his own expressions like, "What
can I say? I knew what I wanted to do. I did it!" and "It was crazy that
after the nineties happened, people thought you didn't have to settle
down and get married till your late thirties. Well, I said fuck that!" and
"I just figured that if someone needs a lot of time to find himself, then
there can't be too much to find" and "I don't want Samona to work. It
wouldn't be good for her."

Very soon it stopped bothering her that he never used the word *we*
because she'd be too busy sighing to herself to listen very closely. What
made his boasting all the more painful for Samona was her knowledge
that between the lines, all it meant was that her husband didn't have a
life: he ate; he slept; he worked; sometimes he had sex with his wife

but mostly he was too tired; sometimes there was a dinner at a pretty good restaurant but he would always get too drunk before the food arrived; maybe he would catch part of a movie on HBO that amused him but he could only watch half of it before drifting off into a heavy, dreamless sleep. David Taylor's life had been stripped to its basics in order for him to become a success, and the only way he knew how to separate himself from everyone else—in David Taylor's mind—was that he'd been "man" enough to get married.

And now that two years had passed since their wedding, and it was 2003 and he was coming up on thirty and he'd committed himself to a life in which the only sign of progress was leaving the energy and noise and bustle of the city for quiet Sunday mornings with nothing to do, David Taylor had made certain adjustments to his dreams.

What was even more sad to Samona—and what made her feel enough sympathy to forgive him over and over—was that this re-adjusted dream was a minor variation on the life his father, Patrick Taylor, had lived. Waking up each morning to a wife who kissed his cheek, pretending it was someone else's cheek, as she handed him a thermal coffee mug that he would drink on his way to the hardware store; the shitty little time share on Lake Michigan where they spent long weekends during the summer doing nothing; the beers shared with men his father trained himself to like at the bar two blocks from his store where he watched Cubs games before heading back home to read to his little boy in bed; on Saturdays he would take his son to the movies or teach him how to throw a baseball.

But David Taylor had promised Samona that he was going to make sure the dream ended differently than his father's. There would be no other women. He was not going to get drunk in front of his kids. There would be no separate checking accounts. There would be no screaming fights followed by separations followed by begging for-giveness followed by two months of being polite and outgoing to his wife followed by the inevitable regression into anger and resent-ment. His son was not going to walk in on David Taylor while he was performing cunnilingus on the nanny in the room next to the pantry.

Samona was sympathetic to her husband's sadness and undercur-rents of self-loathing (for which he compensated by pledging to take care of her and direct-depositing $3,500 into her HSBC checking account on the first and fifteenth of each month), but she didn't want to be his redeemer anymore. She didn't want to be his charity or his mirror or the object of his frustration anymore, and yet she was too accustomed to being with him and too afraid of the alternative to allow their already moderately unstable marriage to dematerialize any further. And it hit her while brewing a skim-milk latte with Splenda that the only way to save them had nothing to do with redecorating and dinner parties and other minor distractions.

It had everything to do with not being dependent on him anymore.

Except this required her to be dependent on him one more time.

After Martha went home from the final dinner party, David Taylor walked in to find Samona watching a cable-on-demand movie about a woman who dresses like a man in the conservative South and the girlfriend of the abusive town hick who falls in love with her (or something like that), which he vaguely recognizes because Hilary Swank won an Oscar for embracing what David considered the movie's hard-core liberal humanism.

"What are you watching?"

"A movie."

"Any good?"

"It's okay."

In the kitchen David poured himself a tumbler of Grey Goose and noticed the dishes left over from the "dinner party" his wife had thrown that night. Pathetic. When he was placing the bottle of vodka back into the freezer he saw that there were two packs of Marlboro Lights on the top shelf. He decided not to ask about the cigarettes because he was tired. And then he sat down next to her and tried to absorb the movie that was flashing across the flat-screen TV.

"It started an hour ago," Samona informed him. "You're not going to get it."

"I wasn't going to ask any questions."

This exasperated her. "What's the point of watching something if you don't know what's happening?"

"I can figure it out."

"You missed all the backstory. It's not going to make any sense."

"Then I'll just sit here with you."

She switched the movie off with the remote.

He stared at the TV screen, confused. "Don't you wanna watch it?"

"Jesus Christ, David. It's not even that good."

He sipped the vodka, and then thought what the hell and drank it very fast. She stared at him. He was aware of this and also that he wanted another drink. He sighed heavily to make a point.

"Oh, I know—they're *all* long days, right, David?"

She sat back on the couch and didn't know why she was shaking.

David put his hand on her shoulder and massaged her neck.

Samona pulled away.

"So." He sighed. "What is it tonight?"

"I feel like smoking," she said.

He could only half argue—that's all he was up for. "Since when have you been buying cigarettes?"

"Stop it."

She walked into the kitchen and pulled a pack from the freezer and then David followed Samona out onto the tiny balcony. It was so small they could barely fit on it together.

(Had the balcony held the promise of being a romantic notion when they first moved in?)

Cigarettes were so expensive now, David was thinking. Something like ten dollars a pack. He did the arithmetic of being a pack-per-day smoker and felt dizzy.

David heard Samona say, "It's too cramped out here."

"Do you want me to go inside?"

"Go inside if you want to go inside."

"I want to stand here with you."

She shrugged.

"May I have a drag?"

She shrugged again as he took the cigarette from her.

He exhaled and started coughing.

She thought she was going to scream.

"I know," David Taylor was saying. "I'm dull. I'm limited. I can't help it." Samona turned to him. "Do you think that? About me?" David asked.

"No. I don't think that about you." She paused before turning away. "I think that about us."

And then Samona told David about Martha's idea.

He quickly understood how serious she was.

"But—" he started, buzzed by the cigarette.

"I'm supposed to be moving forward," she pleaded. "Don't you understand that?" Then she said three things very slowly.

"I want to do this.

"I need to do this.

"Let me do this."

David spoke. "How are you going to finance this . . ." What did she say it was? A printing fashion house? What?

"Martha's looking into getting a loan. Or maybe equity from an investment."

"But Martha can't get that kind of money. And she doesn't have the collateral."

"But . . ."

He waited for the inevitable. It only took a moment.

"You do."

The cigarette buzz quickly faded. David Taylor scanned the building tops that surrounded them. They were still on the balcony. He was looking toward Queens and he was thinking about a house he had seen on a Web site that was in a New Jersey suburb. David Taylor could give his wife her career. He could take the money that he had been putting away for a house along with the bonus he would be receiving in December and he could give it to Samona and she could rent a space and start a business.

David Taylor thought: *This development would push my plans back two years. Maybe three.*

David Taylor thought: *That should be more than enough time for her to fail.*

The inevitable failure of Samona Taylor's dream would become the beginning of David's dream.

"I can move on this," he said. "But there's something I need from you."

She was taking a deep breath. She was looking at him, wide-eyed. She was clasping her hands together tightly.

"What do you need?" she said. "Anything."

"I want you to write a business proposal."

"But I just told you what the business is."

David sighed. He sighed the same way Samona had sighed so many thousands of times. He enjoyed the serenity the sigh gave him. He stood a little straighter and became a quarter of an inch taller.

"But if I'm going to invest in this—and that's what it is: an investment, pure and simple—then I want to see the figures, I want to see the designs, I want to see a budget, I want to see a client list. I want a trajectory. I want to know what you two are capable of before I commit anything."

He punctuated this by sighing again.

Samona nodded as if she understood what he was talking about.

"It's very standard," he assured her.

"I'll call Martha tomorrow. We'll get something together fast."

"Just make sure it's completely thorough. You should learn as much as you can before plunging in. That's something I can tell you from experience."

The next morning, Samona met Martha at Così with a laptop and they wrote their Printing Divine business plan for David Taylor.

At the same time, David Taylor made the call to his accountant asking him to transfer his savings into an active assets account.

It was a very easy thing to do.

23

_____

From: James.Gutterson@Leonardco.com
To: readyandwaiting@hotmail.com
Sent: Tuesday, August 24, 4:20 PM
Subject: (no subject)

Lost my fucking job. Cutbacks. Have check for
you. I think.

PS Don't know if you'll get this. Leonard—
fucking—Company sometimes screens emails with
the word fuck and this one has it twice. No,
three times.

New email: THE_GUT@yahoo.com

I received the same message from the Yahoo! address.

A few days later I went to James Gutterson's apartment in the void of Murray Hill—nondescript apartment buildings that looked as if they were designed by not very imaginative children. A Starbucks or Così punctuated every corner. Laundromats surrounded the Morgan Library & Museum.

It was two in the afternoon. I rang the buzzer before static screamed over the intercom and the door clicked open. I was starving. I was so broke that I could barely afford a bagel at the corner deli. I was going to collect the Leonard Company check from him and immediately deposit it into my near empty Chase account.

James was wearing sweatpants with MH (Men's Hockey) stenciled on the left thigh, and he was pulling on a sky-blue T-shirt with the number 32 emblazoned on it as he opened the door.

"My happy home," he said wryly, ushering me in.

As we passed through the kitchen I noticed a number of items scattered across a small Formica table: a few cartons of Post-it notes, pens, a plastic paperweight in the shape of a hand flipping its middle finger, various manila envelopes, and a mouse pad with the Edmonton Oilers logo on it.

We headed toward the living room where Outkast's "Hey Ya" poured from two six-foot-high Dunwood speakers that framed a huge entertainment center (TV, VCR, DVD player, CD player, Xbox). A long red sofa was packed into the room directly across from it. A bright red-and-yellow poster of Che Guevara covered one entire wall over a bookshelf that was crammed with pictures of various hockey teams to which James Gutterson had belonged as well as the trophies and varsity letters James Gutterson had accumulated. There was also a dartboard hanging near a cluster of framed photographs of a family composed entirely of men except for a tiny, robust woman. They all had the same wide face and wore hockey jerseys.

"You don't have any pot, do you?" James asked me, falling onto the sofa with a grunt. "Or some blow, maybe?" His eyes widened with the thought of it. "I know it's early but *fuck.*"

"Sorry."

He sighed before assuring me, "Don't worry. I know someone."

I motioned to the Che Guevara poster and said playfully, "What's this, James? Are you a closet communist?"

"No." he replied, deadpan. "I'm Canadian. I just picked that up for eight bucks in Times Square and thought it looked cool." His face turned forlorn. "That was back when I had eight bucks to spare. Back when I was all excited to move to this fucking pisshole."

The ache was palpable. It was in the stale air that smelled like marijuana, and it was in the family photos and the molding dishes piled in the kitchen sink, and it was in James Gutterson's bloated face and thin, unwashed hair. The bouncy Outkast tune only intensified the ache.

Since sitting down would only be an invitation to engage James Gutterson in a conversation, I decided instead to feign interest in his vast collection of DVDs (*Slap Shot, Youngblood, Bull Durham, North Dallas Forty, Remember the Titans*) but when I got to the porn titles I pulled back from the shelf. "Hey Ya" looped around for a second time. I turned toward James. My stomach made an audible growl.

"Fuck it," Gutterson moaned with a wave of his hand. He leaned back into the cushions and draped his forearm across his face. "Fuck it, fuck them, fuck you, fuck me, fuck all. Just . . . *fuck.*" His chest rose and fell as he glared at me and said, "I wish you'd at least brought some pot."

All I wanted was the check. "I didn't know about the cutbacks until I got your e-mail." And then I suddenly flashed on David. "What about Taylor? Did he survive?"

James Gutterson's face curled up into a grotesque, fleshy mask. "You would have thought that David Taylor would have stood up for me."

"How do you know he didn't?" I asked.

"Because David Taylor was making a lot of the decisions," James said. "Let's just say he was very instrumental in weeding out the twenty-first floor."

I didn't say anything—I knew better than to interrupt as he leaned forward severely.

"And it doesn't even bother me that I got fired. I mean, it does, but it doesn't. No, what bothers me—what *really* bothers the *shit* out of me—is that he knew who was getting fired and he never warned me. I had to get the news *in an e-mail*. Now that's fucked up. That, my friend, is the punishable offense." I breathed in at those words and the thought of James Gutterson doling out punishment. "And then they locked my computer, took all my files, and wouldn't even let me keep a fucking stapler." He sighed and continued to stare at me. "You think I got a call or a note or anything from David Taylor?" An extended pause, and then, "No, because David Taylor was too busy doing his thing in the conference room."

"What?" I blurted out.

James just replied, "You think I look like someone who would steal a stapler?"

"I don't know what you want me to say."

He paused, sizing me up, then broke into a smile. "I think you're a good guy," James said. "If you weren't you wouldn't be here right now. But David Taylor. You want to know the problem with David?"

"You know what, James? There are probably a lot but—"

"No, I'm talking about something that you can't fix." His smile became a grimace. "He can't laugh at himself."

James was right. This was a key component in the makeup of David Taylor. He didn't have the necessary faculties. Yes and?

He moaned again. "Aw, fuck it. What am I whining about? Millions of guys—Americans—are out of work. But at least I'm a *Canadian!*" He looked up and seemed to see me for the first time. "You want to sit down?"

"I've been sitting all day."

"You know what? The last time I took off my skates—after a real game and not that corporate-bonding shit—but that last time I took off my skates I knew that something was wrong. It was like alarm bells in my head."

"Alarming you of . . . what, James?"

"Life!" He seemed offended that we weren't connecting. "And how it's never gonna get any better than a hockey game!"

James Gutterson started droning on about Thunder Bay and the thickness of the lake's ice and how sometimes it broke and you fell through but one of your friends would extend their stick and pull you back onto the ice and the game kept on going and how simple it was to skirt around the holes and the deep black water, and how that's all he'd been thinking about: childhood games on the ice. You knocked people down and they got up. You fell and someone reached for you. You shot, you scored. By the end of winter the sheet of ice covering the lake was a collage of brown bloodstains.

"What have I learned since coming to New York?" he asked. "No one is ever gonna reach out their stick to help you. You are on your own, my man. And the David Taylors of this world will let you sink and drown and freeze without blinking an eye. And if you're lucky? Maybe you'll float back up in the spring."

That was James Gutterson's story and he was sticking to it.

As soon as his lease was up on the apartment in Murray Hill, James was heading back to Thunder Bay, back to his roots, back to his brothers. One of them ran a small tech firm servicing lower Ontario. Another one owned a landscaping business and lived down the street from his parents. And at the end of the day James Gutterson—the only son who had escaped Thunder Bay and gone to school in the States (all the way to Cornell) and made good on the promise—was now going to recross the border, where he would probably coach a junior league ice-hockey team in Alberta while starting (what James Gutterson euphemistically called) a "financial service" company.

I asked what that meant.

"Like, tracking down debtors for credit-card companies and making them pay up—with interest," he explained.

"Sort of like . . . a bail bondsman?" I asked innocently.

"No," he deadpanned back. "Financial services."

"Hey Ya" started again.

"What are you going to do until your lease ends?" I asked.

"You're looking at it. I don't know. Try and enjoy this fucking city for once? And then haul ass outta here. I guess I'll try and fuck the hell out of every girl I can. Isn't that what I should have been doing all along?"

There was a silence, and he was about to add something else but I spoke first. "Do you have my check?"

He rubbed his forehead with the palm of his left hand. "Yeah. I was actually looking for that. It ought to be around here somewhere." He shrugged evasively and then was lost in thought. He didn't get up from the couch. "Um, can I mail it to you?" he asked meekly.

My voice hardened. "It would be great if I could get it, like, today. Really great, actually."

"I know it would. But what does that matter if I can't find it?" He finally lifted himself to his feet. "Look, buddy, I'm either gonna have to mail it to you or you're gonna have to find it yourself. Because I'm beat and frankly, I'm in a generally pissed-the-fuck-off mood."

He picked up six darts from his bookshelf and hurled them at the dartboard, sidearmed, from six feet away, repeating "fuck, fuck, fuck, fuck" with each hard, dull thud of metal on foam, his aim deteriorating rapidly. As I backed against the wall, he flung the last dart with all his strength. It plunged into the plaster wall above the board.

He gave me a sidelong glance, gesturing toward the darts. "A little help, please?"

I moved toward the door discreetly. "I really have to go."

I entered the kitchen and heard, "Hey, do you want to see something even better than your check?" James left the darts and came forward menacingly. I was now eyeing the door, which was almost within reach. "Just something really quick. I think you'd appreciate it."

"I'm actually in kind of a hurry. Maybe next time?"

"Just one second. Stay here."

James Gutterson opened a drawer on a side table under the Che Guevara poster and pulled out an envelope.

"Look inside. C'mon, c'mon." He thrust it into my hand, giddy. "It's why Dave Taylor was so busy in the office while I was getting fired."

As I opened the envelope, and as I unfolded the grainy black-and-white photograph that was inside—a video-camera still frame from an odd corner angle, dated in large Helvetica font on the lower right-hand corner to July 8, just past 7 P.M.—and as I stared at the image of two men I recognized engaged in a sex act on the table in a room they both thought had been locked, a room they assumed was theirs only, James went on, "You can keep that if you want—I made extras."

I could see David Taylor's face clearly. He was leaning against a table, his neck bent to the side, his mouth open, his head facing upward.

Ethan Hoevel's shadow below him was not as clear, but if you knew Ethan like I did, his profile was undeniable.

"How did you . . . get this, James?" I stuttered.

He shrugged. "Pretty crazy what kinds of things happen in the office after hours, eh? It was back around cutback time, and I was taking a shit and then I went looking for Taylor to make sure I was okay. Heard some weird noises in one of the new conference rooms, peeked in, and . . . *what the fuck?*" He stared at me with bulging eyes and exaggerated awe. "I mean, have you ever . . . *seen* what those guys do, like, up close?" I shook my head, studying David Taylor's face in the photo, marveling at the rawness of his expression. "Crazy, crazy. I could barely watch for more than a minute. And hey, you want to know the first thing I did when that fucker Taylor let me get sacked?"

I had an ominous feeling that I already did.

"Paid the security guys fifty bucks each for copies—totally worth it, of course—and sent one to Taylor's bitch wife. A little going-away present—just to fuck with him." He then added, "Suckaah!"

He waited a moment to let it all sink in, and he seemed disappointed that I wasn't more shocked, that the image he'd provided didn't blow my mind and instead I could just stare at it distantly. "Buddy, what's your problem?" he asked. "Doesn't anything ever get to you?"

I looked up. "Sometimes."

That same afternoon I walked in silence through the weekend crowds of SoHo and turned onto Greene Street.

I pushed open the door to Printing Divine and the bell rang. Martha looked up from the front desk. It took her a moment to place me.

"She's in her office" was all she said before turning back to her work.

Through the glass partition behind the counter, Samona was swiveling in her chair as she talked on a cell phone. Even from my vantage point through the glass, I could tell from the expression on her face that she hadn't received the "present" from James. I almost turned to leave before Samona saw me and waved me in.

I sighed—not quite ready for this—and leaned forward on the front desk, peering playfully at the notebook Martha was studying. She moved the notebook away from me. "Samona is in her office," she said again with more emphasis, and went back to the notebook as if it was something very urgent and important. It struck me how much Martha must have resented that the success of Printing Divine could be entirely attributed not to her flawless and faithful interpretations of the cosmos, but rather to Samona's husband's seed capital and, more recently, to Samona's affair with Ethan Hoevel, and that the latter was a secret she had to keep in order for the business to prosper.

This moved me back to Samona, who waved me in again, and I slid into her office, where the first thing I noticed as she clicked off the cell was the Diet Coke she sipped and how she just stared at me without saying anything. The second thing I noticed was the credit-card-sized bowl designed by Ethan Hoevel—like the one from the gallery show where I had reconnected with him so many years ago. It lay next to a Baggie half-filled with marijuana and the office reeked of it. The third thing I noticed was one of Stanton's Boi-Wear outfits—a brown shirt with a big collar and the logo printed on the back, black bell-bottoms with rips just below the seat—laid out on the other side of the table. The fourth thing I noticed was the bag of ice wrapped around Samona's ankle.

And as I scanned the floor in an imaginary line extending from her bare toes, the last thing I noticed was the wedding photo on the bottom bookshelf. It was the same photo that hung on a wall at The Leonard Company in a corner office on the twenty-first floor. The shelves held other pictures: Olivia wasted at the Yale-Harvard football game; Mr. and Mrs. Ashley posing, stiff and distant, a sprawling lake behind them; Samona and Martha standing in front of the shop at the party celebrating Printing Divine's opening. But the wedding picture—luminous with the promise of a future and romance—was what I was staring at.

What are you going to do? What are you hoping for? Why are you hoping at all?

I shook myself out of it as Samona broke the silence. "I was just leaving a message for . . . Ethan."

"Sorry about stopping in during working hours," I murmured.

"It's a Saturday." She shrugged. Her bare shoulders flexed rigidly as she packed the small concavity with weed. She brought a lighter up to it and took a big hit. She closed her eyes and exhaled as she handed the pipe to me. She looked aimless and mellow and lost.

"I don't think so, Samona."

She shrugged again and leaned over to open a small refrigerator and pull out an open bottle of white wine. "Have a drink, then."

"No, thanks."

She set the wine on top of the refrigerator next to a stack of mail. Near the top of the stack was a small white envelope, its corners wrinkled and torn, the address—just visible—scrawled in writing I remembered from my visits to James's office.

(There, in that envelope, was the reason I'd come.)

(I would bear witness as Samona opened it.)

(I would look on as the photograph wrenched her from the belief—ingrained in her by all the years of being mind-fucked by guys like her father and any half-decent-looking stud in high school and college, and then David, and then Ethan—that she was the singular force who had changed people this summer.)

(I would watch her face turn ashen as it hit her that she hadn't been beautiful or strong or attentive enough to prevent what was now happening.)

(And then—finally—I would be waiting there across the table from Samona, in the position where I could show her how the steady adoration of a guy who didn't matter could make all her hurt vanish, how maybe it wasn't too late to alter certain decisions and eliminate certain regrets, how we could escape them together.)

"Are you in pain?" I asked, motioning toward her iced ankle.

"No. that's nothing. Heels." She held the pipe out. "Take it. Come on."

I sucked through the pin-sized hole that was in the center of the card, my lips tasting the lipstick traces she had left.

I was already high when I handed the pipe back to her, watching her through swaying eyes.

She blinked at me a few times, then put the pipe down and asked harshly, "Why are you staring at me like that?"

"Like . . . what?" I stammered.

"Like you're judging me." She studied my face, then softened again. "Though I guess you can't help it, being a writer."

"I'm not judging you, and I'm not really a writer . . ." I drifted off—she was taking another hit.

"Whatever. As long as you're aware that everything you think about me is wrong." I was trying to identify the conversation we were having. "As long as you're aware there are things you don't know."

"Samona, I didn't come here to—"

"You didn't?" she asked spitefully. "You didn't come to tell me I'm a bad person? That I'm just another one of those fucked-up ex—fashion models you like to write about?"

I glanced at the envelope on the shelf. "Actually, no."

"Then why did you come? What are you doing here?"

"I just . . . wanted to see you and—"

"Look." She sighed. "I'm being paranoid. But I can explain it to you. I can tell you a story that will prove you're all wrong about me."

Her shifting tone was dizzying.

"What kind of story?"

"I'd call it a romance."

"Oh? Does the romance end in marriage?"

"No. This one starts when the marriage is already over." She looked away and smiled. "More than half of all marriages end in divorce, you know."

"Does it really matter what I think?" I asked.

"Yeah," she replied thoughtfully. "Because I know I'm not the person I used to be—people change, you know—but that doesn't make me this evil human being. So yeah, it does matter—it matters to me."

I tried to let the words stand alone without projecting the meaning I longed for.

She didn't include many details in what she told me next, nor did she speak for very long. It was really just an outline, as if she was trying to straighten out certain hazy developments in her own head—trying to tell herself that she wasn't confused anymore. Meanwhile, I followed along dutifully, painting in the corners of the canvas she was laying out.

On the night of August 23, a week after she moves into the Warren Street loft, Samona undresses and lies in Ethan's bed and waits for him to fuck her, and when he does, she relishes his low murmurs informing her not how beautiful she is (which was always David Taylor's fallback) but how sexy she is. He tells her where to put her

tongue and how to rotate her hips in small circles to increase the
intensity of her orgasm—things most people feel awkward saying, but
Ethan does not. When he asks her to turn around so he can take her
from behind, she's excited. And when he tongues her and then
enters, she finds it painful and thrilling. She doesn't think to ask
questions.

This goes on for about fifteen minutes before Ethan loses his erection and pulls out softly. He blames it on the creaking in the lower
left-hand corner of the bed.

Ethan's phone—in his jeans on the floor—rings. He reaches down,
looks at the ID, and turns the ringer off.

Samona Taylor is still awake, her eyes locked open as Ethan lies
zonked out beside her, when Aidan comes back to the loft on Warren
Street at 3 A.M. after a night of binge drinking. Her irritation—at
Aidan for being the man he is, and at Ethan for not being able to fin-
ish earlier—makes her brave, and she checks the incoming calls list on
Ethan's cell phone and sees David Taylor at the top.

That stupid conference room, is all she thinks.

The next morning—the third Monday in August—while Ethan
Hoevel is trying to finish a few sketches on a makeshift desk he set up
outside the pod, Samona Taylor pours herself coffee and is
delighted to find soy milk in the fridge. She sits in a chair he
designed a long time ago, a translucent bowl, and asks Ethan non-
sensical questions—about the weather, the terrorists, the industry—
which he stifles with vague rhetorical responses like: "What makes
you think I know anything?" "What makes you think I haven't been
extraordinarily lucky in what I do?" "Are you sure?" "There's a little bit of circumstance in everything" and "Isn't that what you just
said?"

She finally pulls away when they hear Aidan Hoevel groaning just
before noon.

She walks through Tribeca to Printing Divine and is calm again,
deciding that she should start keeping a lower profile at social events
and acclimate herself to the sweeping change in her life. She will
ignore the nightly invitations and spend as much time as she can in
the loft on Warren Street. She buys a Diet Coke from a vendor on

Greene Street and sings to herself—Dave Matthews, "Crash"—until she arrives at Printing Divine and finds a saggy-eyed Martha upstairs. Martha has been in the shop all weekend because she works more efficiently alone listening to her favorite Patsy Cline CDs instead of the New Age music Samona insists on during business days (and she probably doesn't want to hear about Samona's disastrous love life anymore).

Martha has gotten everything done except the last Stanton Vaughn cycle, which still needs retouching because the purple dye ran out. Samona says she'll take care of that while Martha takes the rest of the day off. Martha accepts the offer, and Samona turns out the best-looking set of fabric she ever produced for Stanton Vaughn. Looking over them at the end of the day, extremely self-satisfied, she attributes the perfect bleed and the overall fine look of them to the loft on Warren Street and the new place she's found in life.

Samona closes the shop at ten o'clock that night and after walking through Tribeca she approaches the loft on Warren Street. She notices a shadow across the street and the yellow ember of a cigarette tip. When she realizes the shadow is watching her she starts walking faster.

The click of her heels on the concrete suddenly sounds like a roar.

When she looks over her shoulder and watches as the shadow throws the cigarette away and moves quickly toward her, Samona is thinking three things:

She wrote her senior thesis at Yale on *The Scream*.

Why in the hell is she wearing heels?

David.

Then one of the heels turns sideways, and she falls. Pain shoots up her tendons but she isn't injured. Samona tries to remember the safety class from college orientation. Is she supposed to scream in this situation? Or does screaming make it worse? She can't remember. Suddenly Stanton Vaughn is beside her, helping Samona up, but seeing Stanton's familiar face doesn't make Samona feel any safer because Stanton Vaughn has always given her the creeps.

Samona Taylor says, "Oh, it's you."

Stanton replies, "And I scared you, didn't I?"

"No. You didn't."

Stanton says, "I'm sorry" at the same time she's saying, "I just get easily freaked."

From where she's standing Samona sees Jamie, the new doorman, leaning out of the lobby for a cigarette and she feels a little safer. Her one goal in life is to get upstairs as quickly as possible without bringing up Ethan Hoevel or the fashion prints or anything that might extend this encounter. Stanton doesn't seem to be listening to her anyway—he's staring up at Ethan's roof deck.

Finally, he brings his gaze back down. "So, how do you like living here?"

"I'm not living here."

"Just stopping by after a long day at the office, then?" he says, making a suggestion she doesn't want to interpret.

"It's not really your concern, Stanton." She starts moving past him.

"Right. Of course it isn't." And then he says the oddest thing: "Don't tell him I was down here."

She hurries upstairs, passing Aidan as he watches the Hilary Swank movie about the woman who pretends to be a man somewhere in Texas, and she hears Aidan saying, "Hey, gorgeous, you've *got* to watch this. It's the most hilarious thing I've ever seen."

The first thing Samona Taylor does when she finds Ethan Hoevel on the roof is tell him about Stanton Vaughn.

Having located Ethan and told him how afraid she is, Samona is expecting him to soothe her, to comfort her, to acknowledge the situation, to say the right thing.

Ethan puts his glass of wine on a piece of slate and continues to stare out over the river, where two army helicopters are circling the sky, reminding him of another threat.

Ethan's silence frightens Samona in a new way as he stands up and walks by her.

She limps behind him down the stairs and into the living room, where Ethan waits for the elevator.

"I'll go talk to Stanton," he explains.

And they're all now watching the TV: Hilary Swank is shot and left dead on the floor while Chloë Sevigny weeps uncontrollably. Aidan Hoevel is rolling with laughter.

Samona lets Ethan get into the elevator. She doesn't stop him.

And when Ethan does not come back to the loft on Warren Street that night, Samona Taylor will not be able to prevent herself from looking back on that moment and knowing she made a mistake in letting him go. And yet the uncertainty that is Ethan Hoevel does not bother her in the way she expects it to.

Certainty is something Samona has known her entire adult life—in the form of David's plans—and she's become tired of it.

With Ethan she's basking in the mystery of it all.

She hasn't experienced this mystery since she was twenty-two and walking down a runway with cameras flashing around her.

She hasn't experienced this mystery since that time in her life when she was too young and too stupid to understand the pure and utter ridiculousness of certainty.

And, as Samona goes to sleep—and she sleeps well—she marvels at the way the mystery that is Ethan Hoevel can make the memory of this night a romance, and not something more sinister.

The marijuana she'd been smoking all afternoon had let her cross boundaries with me that I was sure, under different circumstances, she wouldn't have, and that she would most likely regret.

"So? What do you think? Honestly."

"I think—" I cut myself off from saying anything she didn't want to hear as she started packing the bowl again. I could only stare at the envelope from James Gutterson. "Did Ethan tell you where he was that night?"

"I didn't even ask. Because with Ethan it's not about those kinds of questions, don't you see?"

"What's it about, Samona?"

"It's about me not being so needy that I have to ask them. It's about me getting over all that. It's about me . . . changing. Growing."

I watched her replay what she'd just said slowly in her mind and nod, convincing herself that it was true.

"And that's why this is romantic to you?" There was a long silence while she smoked, pursing her lips and looking at me, as if posing.

Because she had no reply—and she didn't want to dwell on the meaning of this long enough to invent one—she looked me gently in the eyes and said, "Listen, I really just want to thank you. For keeping your promise. I know it would have been easy to say something."

"Don't worry about that."

"And for listening," she added. "You're a good listener. That's pretty uncommon nowadays."

I was remembering the metallic guitar riffs of "Sweet Child o' Mine."

I was remembering our kiss and then all the sadness that flowed from that kiss.

I marveled at how many times a person could tell himself a kiss means nothing and still not be able to eliminate the sadness.

"Have you heard anything from David?" I finally asked.

"I'm sure David's at work," she said, but this led her mind to another thought, and she muttered, "But what kind of freaking idiot doesn't clean stains off his pants before putting them in the hamper?" She leaned forward and massaged her eyes.

I couldn't tell if she was crying or laughing or angry.

Instead of reaching out to her, afraid of her reaction, I grabbed the envelope out of her stack of mail. I put it in my pocket just before she lifted her head and rubbed her hands together, accidentally knocking the pipe off the table and spilling ash on the floor. She left it there and peered up at me as if I had caught her in a lie.

"David cheated on me with his British whore at the worst possible time." She sounded almost defensive.

"British whore? Is that what he told you?"

"No. That's what I just know."

"Why was it the worst time?"

"At the risk of sounding like a total bitch: it happened when I was cheating on him." She said this as if it should have been obvious.

Clutching the envelope in my pocket, my thoughts mellowed

from the weed, I wondered what exactly—besides boredom—would drive James Gutterson to send Samona Taylor a photograph of her husband screwing another man. And then I glanced at her face—the sculpted quality that enabled you to see only what you wanted to see, obscuring anything beyond that—and it struck me that when James Gutterson looked at her the way I was right now, he saw the fashion model, the girl he could never obtain, the girl who was too sophisticated for him.

And embedded in the black-and-white image inside the envelope in my pocket was James's cold, hard proof that Samona Taylor was just as broken as the rest of us.

"Samona," I finally said, my high suddenly fading, "does David know where you're staying?"

"No. He thinks I'm staying with one of my girlfriends."

"Before I go, can I just suggest that—in this situation—a small measure of restraint would be the smart thing."

She put her hand on mine and leaned forward. "I'm through with restraint. Restraint's such a fucking bore." She lowered her head. When she looked back up at me her eyes were completely glazed. "Ethan's a lovely person," she said. "A complicated person. Don't you know that?"

There was no reply from me.

My hand was clenched around the envelope in my pocket.

Stealing it was the only chance I would ever have to feel like I was the one taking care of Samona.

"But the one part of all this I don't understand?" she asked.

I still didn't say anything.

"The one part I keep coming back to . . . the thing I don't understand is"—and she paused now for emphasis—"why does this matter so much to you that you need to keep hearing it?"

"I—didn't ask you to tell me anything. I never asked."

Her face darkened with an anger that I didn't feel I deserved. It was time for everything to end.

"You know what I think the real answer is?"

I was aware that I was looking at her, and then I looked away.

"I think you *do* know he's a lovely person," she said softly. "At least, I think you did." She paused again. "Once."

I walked quickly away from Printing Divine late that afternoon on August 31, stopping only to toss the crumpled envelope into a Dumpster outside Kelly & Ping.

III

24

ETHAN CALLED a week after I saw James and Samona, and I found myself walking from my studio to his loft again—down Second Avenue past Houston, the din of live music in the bars lending an ominous, seedy quality to the Lower East Side, then all the way west on Broome until Watts Street branched off to the left, and then I took Greenwich south to Warren Street, my eyes wandering toward Ethan's roof when it came into view. I took the elevator upstairs, grabbed a beer in the kitchen, and sat on the front end of the lounge chair beside Ethan Hoevel.

"I have a small proposition for you," he said almost immediately. "I've been thinking about it a lot."

"Dare I ask?"

"But first, you need to know why."

"Does this involve another story?"

He nodded, and I settled back in the lounge, resetting the white screen in my mind while waiting for him to start the projector.

On the night of August 24—the night that Samona twists her ankle—Ethan Hoevel leaves the loft on Warren Street and doesn't see Stanton Vaughn outside. But Ethan only gives the street a cursory scan before he hails a cab on Church Street, which travels up the West Side Highway to Hell's Kitchen and comes to a stop outside The Riverview.

He doesn't say anything when David Taylor opens the door. He just stares into David's hazel eyes and then reaches out to touch the hair that's still wet from a recent shower, and Ethan feels a screaming, raking need because he is about to relive a moment that has been haunting his fantasies.

And though Ethan Hoevel has come to The Riverview this night to end whatever is happening between them, he changes his mind now.

He's looking at the man in front of him, and he knows that David Taylor is standing in the middle of what might be the first minute of his life that hasn't involved some form of strategy or planning. Ethan knows how the man's wife has left him; how his future is now uncertain; how all the many variations on the dream he once had are now obsolete. What Ethan also knows is that he erased all the anxieties which should have been coupled with these changes the first time he came into this man; David's old habit of constantly sizing everything up (girth of his cock, level of his salary, quality of his suits), a habit cultivated by four years in a fraternity and eight years in finance and three years of marriage, seems muted. With Ethan standing in front of him, it doesn't matter that Samona has stormed out of his life, or that he'd had to fire a bunch of young upstarts in order to save his own job, or that Ethan is better-looking than him, and has a longer dick and cooler clothes and those piercing eyes.

Because it's really just the pure physical pleasure of it all that astounds them both, and right now they can give in to the way they've lost control of themselves.

They have sex in the bedroom that night, and Ethan is tender with him—much more so than David would have ever considered possible between men—and afterward, they're lying next to each other, staring at the ceiling. Ethan lights a cigarette. David turns on his side to face him and then reaches across the gap between them and takes the cigarette but doesn't smoke it—he simply holds it to Ethan's mouth while asking him, "Would you call this a situation?"

Ethan replies, "I wouldn't call it anything."

"How did it—how did it happen?"

"You called me." Ethan props himself up on the pillow. "Why—why did you call?"

David sighs and tells him about the night before—the night he called Ethan late and left a message—when he was walking from The Riverview to Atomic Wings on Tenth Avenue and Forty-fourth Street for dinner, and the intersections were buzzing with cars and trucks angling for the Lincoln Tunnel but the sidewalk along Forty-third Street seemed emptier than usual, which was the reason David Taylor took note when he bumped arms with a passing man. The man was a little younger, tall with big shoulders and very good-looking. He was wearing a leather jacket with yellow racing stripes. David Taylor couldn't help noticing how extraordinarily handsome the man was, and as he glanced back over his shoulder to look again he saw that the man was just standing in the middle of the empty street staring at him with a vague aura of cold menace, and his face was grinning predato-rily. David didn't know that men did things like this in the streets of the city—he was being scanned. A surge of panic almost caused him to start running, and he turned right on Tenth Avenue and then walked quickly back to The Riverview, glancing over his shoulder every few steps, and he didn't realize how unreasonably he was acting until he was back in the safety of his apartment drinking a glass of white Bur-gundy to calm his nerves. And then, bored and alone in the apart-ment, David got on the Internet and went to www.newschool.edu, which forwarded him to www.parsons.edu, where he looked up Ethan Hoevel on the "Meet Our Faculty" page and skimmed the résumé—
. . . *spent two years living in Peru, where he established his creative roots while helping third-world children raise their quality of life . . . work has been featured extensively in the periodicals* Town & Country, Elle Decor, Martha Stewart Living, House Beautiful, Dwell . . . *as well as the books* A Roadmap for Product Develop-ment *and* The Art of Innovation: Lessons in Creativity . . . *unmatched in his field . . . a pioneer in combining classical artistic form with modern methodol-ogy* . . .—and then David Taylor stared for a full minute at the thumb-nail picture of Ethan smiling in front of a blackboard diagram, and all David could think about was how it seemed so much more impressive than managing a hedge fund in an office at 800 Seventh Avenue. That was when he called Ethan and left the message: "Ethan, hi, it's me, David . . . and I was . . . I guess, going through my closet and thinking maybe I could use a new suit . . . sooooo, this got me thinking about

those guys you said you knew at, ah, Prada? If you could call me back, that would be, uh, cool. Okay, bye."

He explains all of this sheepishly to Ethan, who's gently running his fingers along David's stomach, and then down farther—testing him, seeing how far he'll let them go before hesitating—and Ethan says, "We'll get you a nice suit."

"Am I crazy?" David asks.

Ethan's hand reaches the tip of his penis, and he circles it with his index finger. David begins to stiffen, and Ethan pulls away.

He flashes on something: a gift he'd given Stanton once, a vintage black leather jacket with yellow racing stripes down the arms.

He pushes Stanton from his mind.

"A weird guy comes on to you on the street and this makes you want to buy a new suit." Ethan smiles. "No, I wouldn't call that crazy."

Neither of them says anything for a long time.

"But do you want to hear something crazy?" Ethan finally says, rolling over.

David doesn't know what he's referring to. He begins reaching for a sheet that's been pushed to the bottom of the bed. "What?"

"I'm leaving for Lima in two weeks," Ethan says flatly. "I bought two tickets."

It takes a few seconds for David to understand. "Ethan, there's no way."

The pause doesn't change Ethan's eagerness, because manipulation is what Ethan knows how to do, and he's been planning this since Samona moved in.

"It's just . . . it's not possible," David stammers.

"Of course it's possible," Ethan says. "Just think about it."

"You want me to go to Peru with you? I have work." David pauses and sits up enough to pull the sheet over him up to his waist. Ethan can see him looking around for his shirt. "This is all getting so . . . so . . ."

"So what?"

David won't look him in the eye. "I don't know. It's so . . ."

Ethan stares straight into David and lets him trail off into silence before using a comment Samona had made (offhand, somewhat scornfully): that David has marked two weeks' vacation in October for a trip to Minnesota to see her parents.

"You told me you had two weeks' vacation coming up."

"When did I tell you that?" David looks up from the bed, surprised.

"I don't know. You guys were going to Minneapolis, right? Maybe Samona told me?"

"When did Samona tell you that?"

"When I was in the shop or something." Ethan sighs. "Look, so were you going or not?"

David considers. "We were going to. Yeah."

The word *we* bothers Ethan, and he pushes a little harder.

"I want you to come with me," Ethan says. "It'll be cool for you to get away." (He almost uses the word *us,* but decides in the end that it's too much.)

David rubs his eyes. Ethan reaches for his shoulder and begins to rub it gently, but David pulls away farther.

He is aware of Ethan's unwavering gaze.

David Taylor says, "I can't."

There's an awkward pause before Ethan accepts this and nods but makes no move to get out of bed—he waits for David to ask him to leave.

David's eyes shift around the room as he looks for an anchor—the skiing pictures from Jackson Hole, the closet filled with navy-blue suits, the vanity with most of Samona's jewelry, the iPod and Bose speakers—but fails to connect with any of it.

"Okay . . . well . . . um . . ."

Ethan nods casually and gets out of bed and begins dressing, wondering how it went wrong. Did he push too hard or not hard enough?

Regardless, with his refusal, David Taylor has become much more interesting.

The only question for Ethan now is: How long will it take for David to say yes?

He takes a cab home, still planning the trip in his head, unwilling to relinquish the thought of it.

Because it's almost September, and Ethan Hoevel has to leave New York.

He has to leave because he cannot handle Aidan any longer. Everything about Aidan has quickly become grating: his laugh, his insomnia, his PlayStation. It's been two weeks since Aidan Hoevel came to stay in the loft on Warren Street, and Aidan has shown no signs of moving on or even looking for a job—a job that will be difficult to find with Aidan's thin résumé (a résumé he has never written). Instead Aidan Hoevel watches TV and DVDs and plays video games while eating cheeseburgers, and drinks beer or whatever else is lying around. He will not stop complaining about how expensive everything is in this city even though Ethan is footing the bill. After the first few all-nighters, the situation has become worse. Aidan becomes immobile, and he spends most of the day talking to Ethan (and Samona when she's there) about absolutely nothing ("Why are manhole covers round?" "These chairs hurt my ass") and Ethan will sit there and think about different methods of erasing a human being from this world. Ethan Hoevel has learned a lot about his brother and he cannot endure any of it.

He has to leave because Stanton Vaughn isn't hanging out on Warren Street after dark anymore, and Ethan has learned (with a chill) that he prefers Stanton watching and waiting (for what? Ethan doesn't know for sure). He's grown to like the reliability of Stanton's presence and what scares him is not knowing where Stanton is anymore. This has become a troubling thing for Ethan. Yes, Stanton is and always has been ridiculous and confused, but now he is also *out there,* and a threat because of all the things he knows. (Samona Taylor has not heard from Stanton since her run-in with him at the end of summer, and Printing Divine is dealing exclusively with one of Stanton's assistants, a hot young kid Stanton started keeping around after Ethan broke it off.) The threatening allure of Stanton Vaughn is what Ethan Hoevel was first attracted to (Stanton has punched Ethan several times during sex; Stanton made scenes at Cipriani's on West Broadway just for the sake of having people stare at him; Stanton stole cars when he was young; Stanton carries a switchblade) but now Ethan worries about what he brought out in Stanton—how maybe Ethan's actions escalated the imbalance.

But mostly, Ethan Hoevel has to leave because when he comes back to Samona Taylor from The Riverview in the early hours of that Tuesday morning near the end of August, he finds her lying naked in his bed with a bag of ice on her ankle and she's awake but she keeps her eyes closed. She doesn't say anything. Ethan pretends she's asleep.

It is the first time Ethan cannot look at her face.

It is also the first time he does not want to have sex with her.

Their relationship is beginning to resemble a marriage. And being accounted for (even though she knows better than to say it out loud, she's still wondering) is something Ethan has never wanted to deal with.

It is an awakening.

Ethan gets out of bed the next morning, makes coffee, and finishes up a few project outlines before heading to Parsons to teach a class.

Meanwhile, he knows that David, dazed, would be drifting back to his office, where he'd stare at the wedding photo. And then he'd be studying the Printing Divine poster. He'd be resting on the couch. He'd gaze out the window.

Ethan predicts that, a little later in the morning, David would start cruising the Internet looking at Web sites for hotels in Peru—since he'd be curious—and this would lead to minor fantasies about being with Ethan.

David would then flash through the Minnesota vacation he'd been planning to take with Samona (and that won't be happening anyway since she'd left him two weeks ago) in bullet points: share a Greek salad at the airport, maybe a Xanax for the plane, get picked up by Samona's father, talk to Samona's father about the fraternity days, gently discard her mother's remarks about Samona's figure and how much nonexistent weight she has gained, comfort Samona in their guest bedroom that night while she cries.

Ethan sees the automatic lights above him clicking off. He sees David not moving. He imagines the office remaining dark.

Later that afternoon, Ethan is finishing up his class at Parsons. An undergraduate design competition is being held this weekend and Ethan moves from desk to desk giving final advice on the various entries.

He watches as a twenty-two-year-old girl named Lauren, overweight with a very warm face, demonstrates a tomato slicer for him. It looks like a large pair of scissors, but the bottom lever ends in a small spoon which holds the tomato, while the top lever forks into two separate blades which fit into the spoon and, in theory, slice down to cut the tomato into thirds. The problem Lauren has is that unless the tomato's very ripe, it tends to collapse under the pressure of the blades.

"You need to seriously sharpen it for now, and after the competition maybe think about spending the money on a finer metal or maybe something synthetic."

"But you think it's okay? I mean, the idea?" Lauren gazes up at Ethan, her eyes wide with attraction.

Ethan smiles and is flattered that Lauren is scanning him.

"I really think you've got a chance next weekend." He's referring to the competition, which is in Philadelphia. "And after that, we might start thinking about a patent."

"Really?" she asks. "Will you be there this weekend?"

Ethan doesn't know the answer. All he knows is that he has to get out of the Warren Street loft.

But when he looks up, David Taylor is standing at the door.

"No," Ethan tells Lauren. "I'll be out of the country, unfortunately."

Ethan put out his cigarette and flicked it over the railing. I sat there, silent, as usual, and listened to the dreary Coldplay album that was playing in the background.

"So we're leaving tomorrow," he said.

"And I care because?" It was just a futile pretense, and Ethan's laughter called me out on it.

"Because I'd like you to do something for me while I'm gone."

"Oh, sure, great, anything," I blurted out harshly. "Whatever you want, Ethan. I'm here for you, man."

"Calm down and listen. Your mission, should you choose to accept it: stay in my loft."

"Why would I do that, Ethan?"

"To distract her." He squinted at me, sizing up my response. "Plus, you could use a little distraction yourself."

"Jesus, Ethan, I have work—"

"You don't have that much work," he countered, and then went on suggestively, "And who the hell knows what might happen if you do certain things right?"

"I don't even get what you mean. Nor do I want to."

"It's not that difficult to grasp."

"You're suggesting I live here and maybe get some action from the girl whose head you've been messing with. And in the meantime, you'll be fucking her husband in South America? Am I close?" I rubbed my forehead.

"Calm down. All I'm suggesting is you hang around here, sublet your studio for a thousand bucks—which I'm under the impression that you need—and keep her occupied. I thought I'd be doing you a favor."

"So what? I'm like your little charity case? I'm going to just accept this oh-so-generous offer from you?"

"You always have before," he said quietly. "Except it never used to torture you this much."

"What about Aidan?" I asked, trying to ignore him and his cruelty.

"I'd be surprised if Aidan survives another week here. And let's face it: the guy'll probably end up in Iraq or something by the end of the year. Iraq, or else choking to death on his own vomit in a gutter near some happy hour in the Village."

I crossed my arms and leaned back into the chair. I tried to sound heavy and foreboding. "Didn't you say just a few weeks ago that maybe you weren't gay?"

He leaned forward, his elbows on his knees. "Recent events have led me to reconsider a few things," he said with a shrug, and then: "Kind of like you did, once upon a time."

We heard Samona's footsteps on the stairs, and I started to get up.

"No," Ethan said, grabbing my arm. "Stay for this."

Without speaking she came up behind him and rubbed his shoulders until Ethan shrugged her off.

"Ooh, frigid," Samona tried to say lightly as she took the empty seat on the other side of him. "Hello again," she murmured to me.

Her embarrassment surrounding our last encounter sounded clearly in her voice.

Sadly, she had no idea how much embarrassment I'd spared her.

When Ethan didn't say anything, Samona crossed a leg over her knee and inspected her ankle.

"Still hurts?" he asked.

She chose to interpret this as being sincere concern. "Yes."

"Have you been icing it?"

"On and off, I guess. It feels all right."

Ethan lit a cigarette.

"Got one for me?" she asked, trying not to sound pathetic, which, she realized, Ethan was pretty much forcing her to do. The fact that I was sitting on the other side of him observing this only intensified her stiffness. He gave her the cigarette he'd just lit and took out two more—one for me, one for him—but a light breeze kept blowing out the flame from the lighter.

"We can all share." She took a drag and handed the cigarette across to me. There was lipstick on the end of it where her lips had been. She turned to Ethan. "I couldn't help noticing your suitcase is out."

I silently passed him the cigarette. He looked at her and nodded. "Yeah."

The practiced nonchalance irritated her. Her face wrinkled in a scowl.

"You're going somewhere?"

"Yeah. I am."

"And you were going to tell me this . . ."

He shrugged with a sidelong glance at me. "Now, I guess." He handed the cigarette back to her. "There's some pot downstairs. If you want to smoke."

"Are you in the mood?"

"I could get there."

"Do you want to get something to eat first?"

(I knew that Ethan had actually shared an early dinner with David at Bar Six before they'd each gone home to pack. But I also knew that he'd only eaten a salad—he could still eat more if she made him.)

"Nice job," Samona said. "Changing the subject."

"What's the subject?"

"Not telling me you were leaving . . ." She turned to me. "I'm sure you knew all about this?"

"Not . . . really." I tried to meet her eyes, but she was staring at Ethan. What surprised me the most—and Ethan, too, I assumed—was that she wasn't asking him where he was going. He'd already come up with the story—a movie set in Vancouver, which was close enough not to sound shocking and far enough away that she wouldn't ask to come with him. He'd concocted the details in such a way that she would have to go along with it, and it would be easy for me to uphold the lie.

Ethan played it mellow and laughed and reached for the cigarette, but she didn't give it to him. She took another drag and decided to start playing his game.

"I guess I could be in the mood to eat," Ethan finally said.

"What are you hungry for? Thai, Indian—" She blinked at me. "Are you eating with us?"

"I . . . can't take Indian—my stomach."

She gave the cigarette back to me. But she'd smoked most of it—all I had was the lipstick, which I flicked away.

"Doesn't have to be Indian. We could all go to Balthazar?"

"I think I'm . . . not really hungry after all," I murmured, standing.

"Me neither, actually." This was Ethan. "I'm not really in the mood." He turned to her. "But you two can eat at Balthazar all you want while I'm away. Our old college friend's going to crash here."

She leaned back, startled, and I was carefully attuned to her confusion. It hurt a lot when she blurted out, "But don't you have an apartment?"

"Relax," Ethan replied for me. "I just want him around to supervise my brother." He added, "This should make you happy."

"Where—where are you going to sleep?"

"There's plenty of room," Ethan said. "It's a big loft."

Neither of them moved and Ethan was following a helicopter that seemed to be flying low across the water. Samona just sat there alternating between him and me.

"What's the problem?" he asked, laughing out loud. "I don't know what it is but you're so hot when you're disappointed."

"I'm not," she blurted out before realizing how defensive she must have sounded. She lowered her voice, now sensitive to me listening. "I mean, I'm not."

"You're not what?" Ethan asked. "Hot? Or disappointed?"

"Don't be mean like that." She turned to me, on the verge of tears. The look she gave me—and which I'll never forget—pleaded with me to leave.

A warm breeze—but cooler than the humid air that had been hovering all month—passed over us as I nodded good-byes and tried to ignore Ethan saying, "I'll leave keys for you with the doorman." I walked slowly across the roof, and behind me Ethan glared at Samona. In a condescending tone Samona didn't know existed, I heard him add, "I'm pretty sure that's not mean. But let me extend my deepest apologies if you choose to see it that way."

"Shut up." She sighed. "Just shut up. You've been acting so distant and now you're going away and leaving me here with your brother and . . . *him*?" (She didn't realize in her anger that I hadn't reached the stairs yet—that I could still hear.) "How do you expect me to see things?"

"I'll be back in less than two weeks. We'll figure it out from there."

"Figure what out?" she asked urgently, ashamed.

Ethan lit another cigarette while Samona limped away.

While I waited for the elevator downstairs, I heard her rustling halfheartedly in the kitchen.

I knew I would take Ethan up on his offer. And it wasn't just because spending a week in the same space with Samona was his twisted gift to me.

And it wasn't just because I decided (while riding the elevator downstairs, flashing back on the way Ethan was wrecking her) that I was through with being afraid, and that I could still save her.

There was another reason, almost as powerful.

Ethan was right: I needed the thousand bucks.

25

THE FOLLOWING night, I left my keys in the mailbox for the subletter I'd found online (who was in town from Oregon for a week with her cat) and took my computer and a small duffel bag of clothes to Warren Street. Samona was already asleep, and I stood just outside the closed door, listening to her deep breathing. And after spending most of the night trying unsuccessfully to work (Ethan had been right: there wasn't much anymore, and I felt forgotten by that world which I'd once been so eager to enter) and ignoring Aidan's constant badgering after he stumbled in from a night of binge drinking, his eyes bloodshot, I went upstairs and walked around the empty roof deck, scuffing my sandals on the slate, cleaning up old cigarette butts and putting them in empty wine bottles, gazing at the river, and wondering what had been leading me up there all summer—what was the craving that made me so attuned to these stories even though they pained me?

In the end I supposed that it had a lot to do with the secret we shared.

Then I went downstairs and drank a bottle of wine in order to fall asleep on one of Ethan's couches, which was difficult to do amid Aidan's snoring and my gaze wandering constantly to Samona's door.

I woke and smelled strong coffee brewing. I put on jeans and a T-shirt and heard rustling in Samona's room. And since the door was ajar, I peeked in to see her standing in front of his senior project, and before she noticed me there (I had that much presence, as usual) she took it down—almost dropping it since it was heavier than it looked—and she sat and held it in her lap, running her fingers over the glass, plugging it in and turning it on, and then watching the thick, polished black wing begin to glide up and down. She looked curious and innocent—*how does the damn thing work?* she seemed to be wondering—and this was when I knocked lightly on the door and stepped into the room.

"Pretty cool, isn't it?"

She stood up, startled, and unplugged the box. "All I did for my senior thesis was a stupid paper on Munch that I finished the night before it was due. And he had to go and make . . . this."

"Dude, are you fucking my brother's girlfriend in there?" Aidan called from the living room. Out the door, I could see him in his underwear setting up a game of Madden NFL on his PlayStation.

"I wonder why he keeps it around?" she asked out loud. "I mean, it takes up so much space."

"It's a reminder," I replied without thinking.

(Of course it occurred to me that all I had to do was tell her about the project—really tell her about it—and I'd simply be telling an interesting story, and it would put an end to everything.)

(Of course Ethan had known that I would never tell—not because I was too ashamed, or even because I'd promised not to—but because I was still afraid to risk myself that way.)

What I said was, "I hope I'm not intruding here. I hope I'm not bothering you."

What she said was, "No, I'm actually glad you're here. Because I couldn't be alone with—" She gestured into the living room and grimaced.

Later that afternoon, Samona Taylor asked me to go with her to The Riverview—knowing David would be at work—because she was getting ready for Fashion Week and wanted to remove the rest of her clothes from the walk-in closet she and David once shared, but she didn't want to "go in that place alone." We took a cab together, mostly in mildly awkward silence as she locked onto different clusters of people we passed—street vendors, tourists, businessmen on their lunch break.

"Do you think anyone's really happy in this city? I mean, truly happy?" she finally asked as we passed Thirty-fourth Street.

"I think people are as happy as they let themselves be," I murmured. It was just a bland reply and I didn't really know what it meant.

Then we were walking across the grandiose driveway and through the gold-tinted rotating doors of The Riverview. She said "Hi, Gerald" to the doorman and then we passed into the deep and ornate lobby with mosaic floors, and I noticed the way Gerald looked after her with barely masked pity—apparently he knew things, too.

We went upstairs, and she thanked me once again before letting us in. It was the only time I ever saw the apartment. It was the kind of habitat that reeked of commitments and promises: the solid eggshell walls, the oak desk spilling over with the work David brought home, the armoire packed with satellite cable boxes, stereo equipment, two separate CD collections (they each obviously kept their own, his headlined by Tom Petty, hers by Sarah McLachlan), the balcony that must have been David Taylor's own sad version of Ethan Hoevel's roof. Aside from the glaringly out-of-place framed prints (Renoir, Monet, Munch, van Gogh) that Samona had hung all over, and despite all the many attempts to redecorate, the space could have been taken out of the Crate & Barrel catalog.

Seeing the apartment gave a certain clarity to what I knew about them.

It made me not blame them—either of them—for the decisions they'd made.

It seemed to justify—or at least explain—their ignorance and cruelty to each other.

Samona hurried past the fact that this was where she'd lived for four years (and had been a wife during most of that time), and she assured me, "The only touches of myself in this hellhole are the paintings."

"They add a lot to the place," I replied dully. "I mean, you must know a lot about art."

"I don't know that much about art. What I do know is that I will never live in this room again."

Then we moved through the apartment in earnest—her first, then me—at which point she noticed a few key details:

The number 13 was flashing on the answering machine. "That seems above average," she murmured. "No one really calls David here." Her finger hovered over the play button, tempted to listen to the messages until something else caught her attention.

The power strip behind the armoire had been unplugged.

In fact, all the power strips in the apartment had been unplugged.

This led her to the bedroom, where the bed was cleanly made—"He never fucking makes the bed. What the fuck?"—and she started scurrying around, leafing through notepads, opening drawers with the urgency of the heroine in a B-level psychological thriller. A Post-it on the bedside table listed LAN Chile flight numbers and departure times. She opened the closet and saw that David's suitcases were gone.

I was standing close behind her between the bed and the closet. Her scent was everywhere.

"You think he just wanted to get away after you moved out?" I asked. "A spontaneous little vacation to clear his head?"

"No," she declared. "David doesn't do things like that."

"Then maybe . . . a work trip? Doesn't he fly to London sometimes?" I didn't know why I was defending him, except that this kind of mystery—this distraction—would only pull Samona farther away.

"Not on LAN Chile he doesn't."

I could see her noting a particular coincidence in her head.

I could see an image pass in front of her and block everything else out as she glanced at the neatly made bed.

I could see her forcefully push the image from her mind because it could not possibly be true.

As we left The Riverview (without the clothes or shoes we'd come to pick up) she took a step back in the elevator, looked up at the mirrored ceiling, sighed, and then shook it off.

"You okay?" I asked.

She barely nodded. I couldn't tell if she even heard me.

"I have to get to work," she murmured.

And I knew that—at least for a few minutes—Samona missed her husband.

*　　*　　*

"See, when we first got together, she was making me breakfast all week. Two pancakes and two eggs over easy, shit like that. By the end, she was just getting up at six and running off to work every morning and it just got to feeling so demeaning."

"What felt so demeaning?"

"No action."

"What do you mean?"

"We stopped having sex when we woke up."

"I see."

"I mean I was feeling like the bitch and that was seriously fucked—that was reason enough to end it."

This was Aidan Hoevel, and we were eating brunch at the Moondance Diner on Sixth Avenue.

Samona hadn't come back to the loft in two days, and neither of us had heard from her.

I'd been in the kitchen refining a few pitches to distract myself—for instance, I'd put off Gowanus but not forgotten it—while Aidan rifled through the fridge and, finding nothing of interest, had said, "Let's you and me roll for some food—I'll buy."

So now we were sitting in a booth at the Moondance because Bubby's was too expensive and I was listening to Aidan Hoevel complain about the lack of sex that had ended his brief relationship with Suzanne. What surprised me about being alone with Aidan Hoevel was that he didn't seem like a bad guy. He was just angry—and considering what I knew of his past, I didn't blame him.

"Plus she got a puppy. She was walking from the bus stop to her office in Mission Viejo and she saw one in a window. She bought it. Now that was right before I got let go—I still had a job—and even then you know who was walking that thing at midnight? You know who was standing there waiting for it to crap on the street? You know who was picking up that crap?" Aidan paused to thrust his fork toward his chest. "Me. So I ended it. I mean, it was a cocker. Those thing yap, dude, like you have never heard before."

"And then you . . . lost your job? Was she cool with that?"

Aidan Hoevel moaned. "Don't get me started on that nightmare. Seriously, it was better arguing about the dog."

I thought about the expedition Aidan had been on. "You could have killed it accidentally."

Aidan pointed his fork at me. "Why doesn't anyone believe that I thought it was a *shark*?" He shook his head and concentrated on his double stack of pancakes, spearing the fork into it so hard that it moved through four flapjacks and made a clinking sound on the plate, and then, frustrated by the pancakes, he poured half a bottle of syrup over them. "Anyway, then she skipped town for this fucking city."

"Is that why you came?"

"No, no, no," he said a little too defensively. "I'm just screwing around here for a little while. It's got nothing to do with *Suzanne*." He winced while eating another bite.

"But it must have occurred to you, right? That you might bump into her?"

"What am I, a stalker? Like that ex–boy toy of my brother's who hangs out across the street all the time? No, dude—you got me all wrong. I'm just . . . trying to figure everything out."

"Did you love her?" I asked, since I couldn't think of anything else to say. "I mean, if you took care of her dog . . ."

"You think I believe in love?" he asked incredulously. "I mean, that a girl can hold my interest for any amount of time? Whoa, dude—my heart's not that big. And I don't make bones about it." And then Aidan Hoevel stopped and looked at me, studying my reaction, and I could tell I was suddenly interesting to him. "You know what, dude? I've been watching you a little bit this week, and I think you're too nice."

I just stared at him.

"You look too softly upon this world." Aidan lowered his fork. "You really have to keep an eye on how shitty people are." He was studying my face. "I mean, people are fucked up." He paused again. "Take Ethan."

I settled in for whatever was coming.

Aidan continued. "Okay, he's crazy. He's gay." Aidan stopped. "I mean, you knew that, right?"

I nodded.

"He's got some cash flow. He's got this little world of his where he's kind of a superstar, I guess. And he's got this weird girl"—I sighed, and

Aidan noticed the sigh but kept going—"and now he's got me. And my question is this." He speared another wedge of pancake and seemed to contemplate the beer he had ordered. He was getting the words straight in his head before he said them. "Why does he take me so seriously?" He then swigged the beer. "Why does a guy like Ethan take a guy like me so seriously that he's actually, like, parading this girl Samona around? I mean—what? Just so I won't think he's a fag anymore? And if that's what he wants, then why does he bring you into the mix?"

"He was really just doing me a favor. I needed a little money and—"

"Don't you fucking know yet that Ethan doesn't *do* favors?" Aidan turned and stared out the window at the traffic heading up Sixth. "That poor girl. What a mind fuck!"

I shrugged. "Maybe you've got it wrong."

(Of course I knew that Aidan was right, and I was completely blown away by the fact that he'd been paying this much attention.)

Aidan laughed harshly. "Dude, you just proved my point."

"How's that?"

"You're too nice."

After he paid out of Ethan's billfold—though I offered to leave the tip and Aidan Hoevel didn't insist otherwise, which left me with $89.69 in my Chase account plus the $850 check from my subletter that I'd just deposited and still had to clear—we walked to Warren Street, where the beer and cigarettes Aidan pulled out seemed a more attractive prospect than going back to my computer.

Aidan was strangely likable, and now he was also interesting—I'd learned during brunch that Aidan Hoevel possessed a much keener awareness of the world he inhabited than I ever would have assumed.

(He knew even more than I could have imagined, as it would turn out.)

As he poured drinks and lit two smokes in his mouth at the same time, passing me one, I felt bonded to him.

"New York, dude," Aidan Hoevel rasped a little while later, after we were already drunk, as if this was an epiphany. "It's like this big, this big, like, irrigation system, you know? And like the streets are like canals and like the people are water like—" I didn't listen to anything else until Aidan said, "That's the last beer, dude—there are no more."

He disappeared into the kitchen and returned with a bottle of Domaines Ott and two coffee mugs.

"Ethan won't care—he only buys this pink crap so he can make flower vases out of the bottles." Aidan wrestled with the cork. "Christ, what a completely faggy thing."

I was thinking dazedly that rosé was a beautiful wine, pink like a faded seashell.

"Sorry, dude. I know you're friends with him and all." He inflected the word *friends* with a particular emphasis. Then, suddenly, Aidan thought about something else. "Beer then wine, never fine? Is that the saying?"

"It might be the other way around." I sighed.

"Screw it." He poured almost half a bottle in each of the two mugs and then flopped down on the couch next to me. "What do you know about Samona?" he asked.

"Not much." I shrugged. "I don't want to talk about her."

This caught his attention but only for a moment.

"I don't think I've seen her in a couple days—"

I immediately cut in. "She's in a weird state."

"Aren't we all, dude?" he said, shaking his head. "Aren't we all?"

We sat in silence, drinking the wine.

Then Aidan said, "Do you think my brother's actually screwing her? I'm wondering about that."

I paused. "It seems that way."

"Don't you think my brother likes to mess with people?"

I sighed.

"I was saying it before," Aidan went on. "Like—I don't know—with their heads and shit?"

We had emptied our mugs in less than two minutes.

"Doesn't everybody?" I asked.

Aidan raised his eyebrows and considered this. "You don't."

"I don't think I'm following you anymore. I don't know."

"What I'm asking is, how in the hell did my brother score that girl?" He didn't wait for me to answer before he sat up straight. "Want to hear something? A few nights ago—right after you got here, actually—I was bored out of my mind and watching *Groundhog Day* and you were on your fucking laptop on the roof and I could hear Samona shuffling around Ethan's room and so I went in to talk and I just asked her if she knew where Ethan was—even though I could tell she didn't. And that's why she was in this big state about it and that's why she wasn't talking and I just got the idea that there was no way Ethan was really into her, because he's into guys. I mean, don't get me wrong, dude, I would be *thrilled* if he was with her. She's gorgeous, right? But he's not into her and I think she's just now finding this out."

"Did she say anything?"

"When I pressed her on where my brother was she just told me that he had business to take care of and I asked her if Ethan went by himself to take care of this so-called business and she said yeah and I asked her if she was absolutely sure and she said yeah she was and then I said she was a lucky girl to have my little brother and she asked why and I said, well, you know he's a real *man's* man if you get my drift and I was just fucking with her, you know, just seeing how she'd react and then she looked at me hard and said something."

"What did she say?"

In a deliberate tone, enunciating each word clearly, Aidan Hoevel said, "'I. Think. You. Need. To. Get. A. Job.'"

I took this in and nodded gravely as if it meant something. "Is that all?"

"Pretty much." Aidan seemed unfazed. "I wanted to keep talking because, well, I'll talk to pretty much anyone. I mean I'm talking to you, right? Just kidding." He finished his wine. "I think she's just a very weird girl. Fucking *beautiful* but weird." He turned the mug over and raised his eyes. "I hope there's more."

"Why did you say that to her?" My voice sounded urgent and strained enough to get his attention again.

"I was bored. Wanted to see what she knew about my brother and his—ooh—secret past."

"I think you need to know that these people are all in a serious—"

"These people? Who? You mean my brother and the black chick?" I nodded and realized I was drunker than I thought. "Look, I don't know anything, dude—I'm just a guy sitting around trying to figure out what to do with my life. Want to see what's on TV?"

"Not really."

Aidan turned on the television and surfed so fast through the channels that they became a blur. He kept saying in the same toneless voice, "No, no, no, no, no," until he finally landed on *Scarface* and settled back into his chair. Still looking at the TV, he smiled and asked nonchalantly, "So you were the guy sitting next to my brother at your graduation, right?"

Aidan must have known I was staring at him, but he didn't look up.

"From college?" I asked.

"No, from kindergarten." He rolled his eyes and groaned. "Yes, from college."

"I guess I was. Yeah. Why?"

"So you must have known then. Right?"

"Must have known about what?"

Aidan looked up, though he was still switching channels. "Secret past."

"Are you talking about him being gay?" I asked. "What's the secret? Besides Samona."

"I guess there's a lot I don't know."

"Don't you think Ethan prefers it that way?"

The smile left Aidan's face. The channels stopped flipping. He stared at me, his finger making slow circles around the rim of his empty mug. "Look, do you think I'd be hanging around here if I gave a shit about what Ethan *prefers*?"

"Then why are you staying here, Aidan?"

He gazed around the cluttered room. "You wouldn't even get it. All I'm saying, *dude*, is that the way I remember it, you and my brother were sitting pretty damn close that day." He sat back again and mimed a drumroll. "And it looked to me like you were holding hands."

It didn't matter anymore. "So?"

He lost interest when I said this and took a cell phone off the table my feet were resting on and dialed. "So? Whatever. You used to fuck Ethan, too. I don't give a shit, dude. It doesn't matter. You're a cool dude. Kind of."

"Who are you calling?" I asked.

"I'm calling that freak—the other one who used to fuck my brother. You know him. The one who was mouthing off to me at lunch? I found his number in Ethan's room. I do it all the time. The guy gets very, very pissed—it's hilarious."

"That really isn't a smart thing to do."

"Why would you think I ever do the smart thing?"

Aidan dialed and immediately yelled into the phone in a lousy Latino accent going for Tony Montana in *Scarface*, which was still playing on TV—the scene where he kills his best friend who's just married his sister.

"What up, main? Yeah, I talkin' to you. All I got in this world is my word and my balls. And I ain't break them for no man and not for no faggot like you. Main. You standin' under my window all night. Waiting to get fucked by my brother again? You wanna go to war? Then I take you to war! Say hello to my little friend!"

This was followed by a weak attempt at the sounds of a machine gun, and then, hanging up: "Oh, that's going to piss him off really bad."

I collapsed onto the couch and he seemed to soften, pouring me another mug of wine and consoling me very sincerely. "I know what's on your mind, and it's not worth it, dude. Trust me—Ethan, Samona—they aren't worth it."

I took the wine and choked it down. He was putting his sneakers on and heading for the elevator, looking at his watch.

"Where are you going?" I asked.

"Out, dude. Your stupid depression is boring me."

When the elevator finally clanked open, Aidan disappeared. It was three o'clock. I opened another bottle of wine and watched the end of *Scarface*. When the movie ended, I sat on one of Ethan's chairs—the R-shaped one—in front of the window and peered down on Warren Street for a while, drinking and trying not to think at all. I felt unemployed. I felt ineffectual. I felt, ultimately, alone.

It was dark gray outside when I finished the bottle of wine and opened the door to Ethan's room. I stood underneath the shelf holding his senior project. The woozy wine drunkenness reduced my ambition down to a single objective: I wanted to see the wing move inside the glass case. Because it occurred to me that after Ethan got home, I might never be in his loft again. I also felt like I'd been a component in the thing's creation, and I was entitled to see it whenever I wanted.

I reached up to the shelf and placed a hand on each end of the glass. Maybe it was the wine, or maybe it was my shaken state of mind, or maybe it was just clumsiness and sweaty palms, but as I was lowering it down the glass slipped through my hands. The machine hit the floor and seemed to bounce once before rolling onto its side, where I could already see the crack in the glass. Then I heard the elevator and hurriedly lifted the machine onto its shelf just as Aidan came back into the loft.

He walked in slow motion across the living room and then back into the kitchen, staring at his feet, and didn't seem to notice me watching him from the bedroom door. When he reappeared, he was opening a new bottle of Grey Goose. He sat on the R-shaped chair (the one he hated the most) in front of the window and stared down at the street in the same way I'd been doing an hour earlier. The sound he emitted was halfway between a groan and a whimper.

"Aidan?" I said quietly.

"What, dude?" His voice was seething and dark.

"Where'd . . . you go?"

"Nowhere."

I tentatively sat on the couch as he swigged straight from the bottle. "You want your mug?"

He shook his head. "I just saw her."

"Who? Samona?"

"No, you twat. Suzanne."

"Oh? Where'd you see her?"

His eyes were narrow and his right hand was clenching the neck of the bottle tightly while he rubbed his forehead with the palm of his left hand. "Outside her office."

"What were you doing there?"

"Hanging out!" His voice rose sharply before he took a deep breath to calm down. "What's with all your fucking questions, anyway?"

"Sorry. I was just—I know how it feels, Aidan—"

"You don't actually. You don't know how it feels to see your girl smoking a cigarette outside her fancy new office with some fucking dude who then starts sucking her face while laying his hand on her ass before they go back inside. You don't know how that feels. Nope." He collapsed back in the chair and sighed and drank more vodka. "But whatever. Fuck it—whatever."

As a peace offering, I held my mug out to him. He poured me about three shots—the bottle trembling in his fist—and massaged his temples as his eyes fluttered.

It was almost 11 P.M. when I woke from an alcohol-induced nap, already severely hungover, and through the haze I was trying to figure out where to go from here, what I could do that would erase the summer from my memory.

I saw Aidan Hoevel passed out in the same chair in front of the window, snoring next to the empty bottle of Grey Goose, his breath thick with vodka even across the room.

Otherwise, it was silent and dim—the kind of silence that shouldn't exist in New York City.

A strange feeling came over me, as if I hadn't woken up on my own.

There was another presence in the loft on Warren Street, and I looked up.

Samona Taylor was standing in front of the elevator.

I tried to present myself in a way that didn't appear slovenly and disgusting.

Samona stood there in the dark. She had changed, even in the few days since we'd gone to The Riverview. There was a weariness draped all over her: circles under her eyes; her dress sagging; her hair in a frizz; her shoulders slumped.

She was still beautiful—of course she was—but not as beautiful as she'd been before falling in love with Ethan Hoevel.

What I had to accept—the real reason I was trying so hard to put myself together and failing so miserably—was that Ethan Hoevel affected her in a way that I never could.

And it became clear to me now, as I squirmed and averted my gaze, that this was exactly why Ethan had lured me into staying at his loft while he was away (and also why it had been so easy for him): he was showing me in no uncertain terms that the world we all lived in now had been designed by him.

I hadn't moved since noticing Samona in the room.

Strangely, neither had she. Finally, she whispered, "He's out there."

"Um . . . what? Who?" I was slurring.

"Stanton Vaughn. He's standing downstairs in the alley. He's smoking and looking up here."

I went to the window, careful to stay out of eyeline with the street, and saw Stanton in his black jacket, just out of the lamplight in the loading alley beside an empty office building.

I would later blame it on the beer and wine I'd been drinking all afternoon, as well as on my sadness, but faced with the specter of Stanton—alone, in the dark, watching this room—a pure unease gripped me.

"What do we do?" Samona whispered urgently.

"I guess we should . . . stay up here?" I suggested.

"No, I'm calling 911." She hurried to the cordless phone holder, but it was empty. "Where's the phone?"

I stopped her, taking her wrists in mine, gripping them close to my chest. "Samona." I tried to comfort her. "It's just Stanton. I don't think—I mean, what's Stanton going to do?"

"Spend the night in jail, hopefully," she replied, locking onto the phone that was jammed between Aidan's thigh and the chair he was sleeping in. She wrenched her hands away from me. "He's a freak."

She moved warily toward Aidan, gripping the phone gently and attempting to slide it out from under him.

"I wouldn't wake him right now—"

He snorted twice, then sat up.

"What is it, babe?" Aidan hacked up some phlegm, eyes still closed, and reached out to kiss her but stopped when he opened his eyes and almost fell off the chair. "Oh shit," he blurted out. "I'm sorry—I'm so drunk—"

"Go back to sleep," she whispered. "I just need the phone."

"You look all freaked," he observed, then turned to me accusingly. "What's going on? What did you do, dude?"

"Nothing, Aidan. You probably should go back to sleep."

"Hell no. I'm awake now."

"Oh God." Samona sighed.

Aidan hopped to his feet but fell down as the blood rushed to his head. He grabbed the chair for support but it was top-heavy and didn't hold his weight, sending him down to the floor again. He used the windowsill to pull himself up, which was when he looked down and saw Stanton, the tip of his cigarette glowing, then fading, then glowing again, almost rhythmically.

"Aw, it's that little fag—" Aidan cut off in order to lean out the window and scream, "What, bitch? You want a *piece*? Because I'll come down there and beat your ass!"

Stanton didn't move. He just stood there.

"Aidan, he carries a switchblade!" was all I could think to say.

"And he also used to fuck my brother. I don't give a shit." Then to himself, Aidan muttered, "Wait, I've got a sweet idea."

His words hung in the air, and I turned toward Samona.

"Samona—" I cut myself off because I didn't know what would come out.

She walked quickly into Ethan's bedroom and locked the door.

I stumbled across the room as it closed, pressing myself up against the opaque fiberglass.

"Samona," I cried.

"You know what?" she said. "It doesn't matter."

I couldn't say anything. I could hear her packing her things.

"Why are you out there?" she asked. "What are you doing out there?"

I didn't know. I couldn't protect her anymore.

I took a deep breath and managed to say, "Ask me what you want to know, and I'll tell you."

"Goddammit, leave me alone," I heard. That her voice was breaking didn't lessen the pain it inflicted. "You think it's not too late for that? You think I didn't already know anyway? You think I'm that stupid? God, we're not having this conversation. So just go away." She pounded her fist abruptly against the inside of the door. "Why are you here? Why are you always around?"

This was the moment when I heard footsteps and muffled screaming coming from the roof.

And since I couldn't be this close to her anymore—or ever again—I rushed through the kitchen and tripped up the stairs toward the roof, where Aidan Hoevel held the empty Grey Goose bottle, scanning the darkness of Warren Street until he locked onto the tip of a cigarette lighting up again, deeper in the alley.

"Say hello to my . . . little . . . friend!" Aidan screamed.

And then Aidan Hoevel heaved the bottle.

I was coming out of the stairwell when the momentum of the throw sent Aidan's body over the railing.

I was halfway across the roof as his hand flailed for something to grab—but nothing was there.

The bottle hurled end over end across Warren Street.

His feet left the slate rooftop completely and, in what seemed like slow motion, began floating through the space where his head had been and then he was falling to the sidewalk.

The bottle shattered against a wall just a few feet over Stanton's head.

The sound of glass raining down on his face and the concrete around him was clear, even across the street and nine stories above, where I'd reached the rail in time to see Aidan hit the ground feetfirst, just left of the front door.

But it wasn't as clear as the shattering of ankles, the rending of kneecaps, the dislocation of hips, the compression of vertebrae, and the fierce, high-pitched roar that was quickly snuffed out as Aidan Hoevel came to rest on his back and experienced the presumably welcome release of oblivion.

And then the only sound left was that of Stanton's footsteps running down the alley.

26

THE THIRD WEEK in September began with a voice-mail message from David Taylor early on a Saturday afternoon: "Call me—I'm at the office."

This was two days after Aidan had fallen, and even after all the police reports I'd filled out (the shattered glass, traces of blood, cigarette butts across the street, witnesses who'd heard the screaming, Aidan Hoevel's history of violence paired with his .18 blood alcohol level—all the evidence had corroborated my story), he still hadn't woken up.

During that time, I'd largely assumed Ethan's role as Aidan's brother, which had entailed gathering a suitcase for him (I even did his laundry), figuring out his Social Security number (I found his wallet in a Ziploc bag with two nip bottles of Jack Daniel's, a half-full Vicodin prescription, and a plastic bag of marijuana), and notifying Angela Hoevel in Long Beach of his "condition." After reminding her who I was—which wasn't easy—my biggest challenge was reducing the facts into a story that wouldn't make her heart stop beating and also wouldn't cause her to think either of her boys was anyone other than who she thought he was.

The journalist in me was still adept at such modifications.

"He'd been calling someone from the roof, Mrs. Hoevel."

"He'd had a few drinks, Mrs. Hoevel, since it was Wednesday night."

"He slipped, Mrs. Hoevel—there was a bad spot near the railing. The railing was too low."

(She'd started whining softly to herself by this time.)

"It was a horrible, horrible accident, Mrs. Hoevel. It was just a horrible accident."

"And you were there?" This was her—curious, not accusatory.

"Uh-huh. We were just hanging out, Aidan and I."

"But where was Ethan?" The question seemed to baffle her, like she couldn't imagine why he wouldn't have been with Aidan—she couldn't fathom why he would have wanted to be anywhere else.

"He's . . . traveling . . . it's kind of . . . complicated . . . but I'm trying to reach him. I'll reach him as soon as it's possible."

"But where was Ethan? Why wasn't he there to stop it? Nothing like that *happens* when Ethan's there!"

Of course, I'd been wondering the same thing myself.

And since David's message meant that Ethan was also home from Peru, I called him first. He came directly to the hospital, where his uninsured brother lay in a coma, and where he received a $10,000-plus hospital bill. I was careful to keep a few steps between us while he cursed under his breath for a while before asking the requisite questions with varying degrees of frustration: "He's okay?"; "Have you heard from Stanton?"; "How did he fall exactly?"; "He was imitating Al Pacino?"; and then with genuine concern, "Does my mom know?"

"She's at home in Long Beach. She's waiting for more news."

"What about Samona? Was she there?"

"She was in the loft," I answered after a brief pause. "She didn't see anything—and I don't know what happened to her after. She just left."

He looked at me with pity, as if I'd failed once again.

An hour later, after all the paperwork and credit-card info were finished, it was just the two of us (and an old black woman with frizzy gray hair whose husband had suffered a mild stroke, and the parents of a boy who'd broken his arm, who were sitting one seat apart from each other) in the bright, claustrophobic waiting room at Beth Israel. This was when Ethan told me what had happened in Peru. I hadn't asked him to tell me—in fact, I'd actively avoided the subject—and he was careful to leave space between the details, as if he knew I was filling them in on my own.

On September 7, the LAN Chile flight to Lima is delayed. The terminal at JFK has been locked down because a janitor found a crude homemade blade in a stall in the men's room near Gate 4 (which means that somehow the blade went undetected through security). And even after the terminal is reopened, Ethan knows that the blade makes David Taylor nervous—that it becomes a symbol in his head. Maybe the trip is a mistake. Maybe the silence in the terminal is an omen. Maybe he's being impulsive. David waits nervously in the first-class lounge—shifting in his seat incessantly, tapping his foot against the chair leg—while Ethan talks evasively about the strange vibe of airports these days and about the blade and to whom it might have belonged before landing in the stall.

Ethan gives David two Ambiens as the 777 accelerates up the runway and lifts, swaying, into the sky.

They drift in and out of half sleep as dusk becomes night and then dawn again, and when David is conscious he gazes out the window at the dark sky while focusing on the flashing light on the wing's tip, occasionally glancing at Ethan, who is either resting with his eyes half-open or reading, and then they're walking through the Jorge Chávez Aeropuerto, and David fixates on the oppressively low-raftered ceiling. He's looking mildly concerned before Ethan taps his shoulder, breaking the spell, and takes his hand to lead him through a throbbing crowd of people holding signs with Peruvian names like Zavaleta, Ponce, Callirgos. It's loud and confusing until they get to the Sheraton high-rise in Miraflores—a suburb that Ethan chose because he knew its resemblance to a typical American suburb would comfort David.

Mildly relaxed, he stands at the window, gazing in wonder at the sprawl of city concentrated a few miles away, while Ethan sits up in the bed reading. (Ethan finished two books on the plane; contemporary fiction—stuff David's never heard of.) From time to time Ethan looks up but never says anything, opting to let David take in the newness of their surroundings on his own, and then he orders room service: steaks, French fries, comfort food—another small effort to ease David into their foreign surroundings. When they finish, David settles on the opposite side of the bed.

On the shuttle flight from Lima to Cuzco the next morning, David watches the unreal mountains pass below and seems to tense up again, and then he looks up at the overhead TVs showing a British comedy show called *Just for Laughs:* actors pretending they're blind and walking into people whose reactions are recorded via hidden cameras. When the plane banks sharply between two mountain peaks toward the short runway, he clutches the armrests—white-knuckled—and doesn't let go until after the Fasten Seat Belt sign blinks off. He remains tense as Ethan rents them a car at Hertz, and he grips the dashboard while they drive through the shantytowns and then down into the basin of the city, through old cathedral plazas and impossibly narrow streets. On the radio Eminem is singing "Stan" while the sidewalk vendors press themselves against the walls to let them pass, and David won't let go of the dashboard. There's snow on the highest peaks. David shivers against the cold.

"Are you okay?" Ethan asks casually.

"Yeah, yeah. I just have a headache. Also, you could have told me it was winter here."

Ethan smiles and keeps driving. "Stan" is still playing when they pull into Cuzco's only four-star hotel—the José Antonio—which has hot water and cable TV and two restaurants. David fails to find the luxury of it calming.

Ethan says, "The air's really thin up here—we should maybe rest. You need to get acclimated."

In response, David points to a huge white Christ statue on the southernmost hilltop overlooking the city, which doesn't seem far away. "Is there a path that goes up?"

Ethan is fully aware that David suggests this because as long as they keep moving and don't stop to think, they're only tourists here.

Five minutes into the walk David begins hacking from the exertion.

"Do you want to rest for a minute?" Ethan asks gently. "It's okay if you do."

David just walks faster and says over his shoulder, "I used to run a four-oh-nine mile without even thinking about it. I can get to the top of this hill."

Three minutes later, as Ethan comes up behind him, David coughs again and can't stop. He gives up and sits on the side of the path muttering, "I can't fucking believe this," while Ethan buys him a large bottle of Fiji water, then takes him back to the hotel. David heads upstairs to lie down while Ethan leaves to visit some of the old schools where he worked—but not a single kid he knew is there anymore, a reminder that it has been six years now. The sadness he feels moves him to walk around the Plaza del Armas until nightfall and sit on the cathedral steps in the pale street light and think about the past, which is coming back to him in the blurred images of the kids he taught and the stray dogs that wandered the streets and the roughly cut Peruvian cocaine and the narrowness of the sidewalks and all the *battatis* he drank at a restaurant called the Witch's Brew. Ethan goes to this restaurant on a whim and finds that the manager is still there—a Brazilian named Alejandro whom Ethan knew back when he lived in Cuzco (they hooked up occasionally during that time). Alejandro and Ethan sit talking mostly about the restaurants Alejandro has since opened in Rio while Ethan gets buzzed off three *battatis* and the thin air.

When he gets back to the room—after declining Alejandro's invitation home and wandering around for another hour in amazement—David is deeply asleep, already in the throes of full-fledged altitude sickness. Ethan settles into the bed, careful not to wake him, trying to shut out the constant moaning in order to sleep (he can't), and in the morning David is so messed up he can't open his eyes or move his head without dry-heaving.

Ethan orders cocaine tea. He puts the mug to David's lips, but David quickly takes it away from him and drinks, murmuring, "Is there cocaine in this? Because my firm gives random drug tests." The tea stimulates him enough to sit up.

"Let's take a drive," Ethan says gently.

David puts his face in his hands and gives an exaggerated groan. "Eh. I don't know if I'm up for anything right now."

"Come on. It'll be good for you and you don't have to walk—or exert yourself at all." His voice is slightly accusing.

"I'm fine, I'm okay," David replies defensively. "Just . . . a little weak."

Ethan sits on the bed beside him. He reaches for David's arm, then pulls back. "Don't you want to see some of the country?"

David shifts a few inches away and forces a painful grin. "It's mostly dirt, right?" He laughs at his joke before understanding how humorless it was.

Ethan glances at his own reflection in the mirror across from the bed, and he sees that he's grimacing—and that the pain in his face is sincere. He wishes it weren't this way before turning back to David, who is looking at him, picking up on his hurt. David Taylor softens, and then nods his head.

In the car, David's hands rap out some nameless radio music. He watches the hills pass and says, "This was a good idea. I feel a lot better."

Ethan consciously looks away and doesn't talk and in his mind comes up with a list of things he has enabled David Taylor to do:

Have sex with a man.

Let his wife leave him without an argument.

Take time off work to fly to Peru.

Face the possibilities that exist outside the plan David Taylor laid out so carefully for himself a long time ago.

He's wondering what compelled him to create this list when the front tire blows out.

"What do we do now?" David asks in a state of mild panic, looking around them, scanning all the empty space and the few dilapidated farms farther up in the hills. "Do you have a cell phone? Or what?"

"You've never changed a flat tire before?" Ethan asks, amused.

David sheepishly shakes his head, and Ethan finally lets himself smile as he teaches this man—who's afraid to go underneath the car because the jack that came with it is brown with rust, trembling under the weight—how to change the tire.

Ethan adds "change a flat tire" to his mental list as they start moving again.

"What should we do when we get back?" Ethan asks suggestively, hoping that maybe the flat has erased the tension between them.

"I don't know. I'm still really tired."

"It's just the altitude."

"I know. You're right." He hears Ethan's sigh and adds, "It's really beautiful here."

A few miles pass. The hills are a muddy green. David reads out loud the words *Viva Peru*, which are scorched in gigantic letters into the grass near one of the taller peaks.

This is when Ethan says casually, "Are you worried about your wife?" David gives a forced shrug and shakes his head resignedly, and Ethan trains his eyes on the road. "Sorry. I didn't mean to bring that up."

"You didn't?" The words come out too fast.

"Relax. I'm sorry I said anything."

David sits up. "I am relaxed. I'm relaxed and I'm fucking sick. And no, I'm not worried about her. Would I be here if I were?"

"I don't know. I guess that's why I asked."

They move through a mountain pass and Cuzco spreads out before them again. David pans across the red-roofed houses crawling up the slopes on every side of the city until his gaze falls on the Christ statue towering above them.

"It's called the Cristo Blanco," Ethan says. "I didn't tell you that before."

A moment passes, and then David asks quietly, "Are *you* worried about my wife?" He opens his mouth to say something more, but Ethan's hard silence stifles him for the rest of the drive.

David goes to bed early again while Ethan goes back to Alejandro's restaurant, and they talk easily, sometimes reaching out to tap the other's forearm, rehashing hazy memories—the three-day coke binges in Ethan's apartment, the hikes in the mountains, the crazy trip to Rio, the simplicity of it all, and then the way Ethan left so abruptly to go back to New York—and, after the restaurant has cleared, Alejandro ends the conversation by asking Ethan to come home with him again, and Ethan shakes his head—even though he really does want to—and walks back through the Plaza del Armas to sleep next to David, even though he knows that nothing will happen, that this trip is basically a failure.

(*Failure of what?* he asks himself, but doesn't answer.)

He gets back to the hotel and stands over David, watching him sleep, thinking about the times they've been together, and the times Ethan has been together with his wife, and the moment eight years ago when he saw them sitting together at *Love's Labour's Lost*, and how that vision on the quad lawn cemented Ethan's desire never to be as naive as David Taylor and Samona Ashley were.

Then Ethan shakes himself out of it—it's painful for him to dwell there—and settles in on the other side of the bed.

He thinks: *fuck all this; fuck David Taylor; fuck the illusions.*

The next morning he wakes to the sound of David slipping out the door quietly.

Ethan, after brief consideration, follows him outside into the city.

He watches David Taylor have lunch at an empty pizzeria, where his presence only makes the room seem more empty.

He drifts thirty, forty, sometimes fifty yards behind as David wanders aimlessly along the stone walkways, carefully avoiding the stray dogs everywhere, carting an intense loneliness on his shoulders, still trying hard to pretend that he is just traveling with an old college friend.

Ethan stares from behind a corner as David stops at a street vendor's cart and picks up a pair of earrings—dangly, jade green.

He watches David take out his wallet and realize he hasn't changed any money, and then Ethan keeps following while David gets lost looking for a bank on the narrow winding streets.

Then David looks up again at the *Cristo Blanco*—backlit by blue lights—and he seems to forget about the earrings and instead he starts climbing up to the statue.

Trailing behind David Taylor, Ethan senses how the pure physicality of climbing inspires a deep and unfamiliar nostalgia in the former runner, and he senses the feeling of supreme accomplishment David experiences when, an hour later, he collapses on a bench at the foot of the *Cristo Blanco*.

Everything's quiet there. David takes heavy breaths and begins to absorb the small details around him—the bleached, chipped marble;

the flowers and prayer beads spread around its base; the vendors selling jewelry and keepsakes and water; the chilled, clean air; the muffled
echo of traffic rising from the streets—and then, on a bench eight
hundred feet above the city, David Taylor smiles.

As Ethan turns around and hurries down the steep hillside, he
understands that David Taylor has experienced a revelation, and that
he's shed the feeling of guilt that, for David, comes naturally with not
working, and being in a foreign country, and having his wife leave
him, and traveling to this place with a person like Ethan Hoevel.

This is when Ethan comes up with a plan for the night ahead.

When David comes back to the room, Ethan is leaning over the
antique table at the foot of the bed with Alejandro, snorting lines
together.

"Hey," is all David says. He awkwardly comes forward to shake Alejandro's hand.

"Where've you been?" Ethan asks.

"A little exploring, just walking around."

After introducing them, Ethan then makes sure that David picks
up on the knowing smiles and the shared laughter between him and
his old friend.

When the jealousy he's been trying to invoke finally starts to grip
David—it flashes over his face—Ethan glances up at him between
lines, and the glance is a suggestion.

As Ethan expected, David Taylor sits down and does two lines himself, and Alejandro says, "I should take you guys out tonight."

While walking to the club, David trails two steps behind, tuning in
to their laughter and the way their shoulders are touching with every
other step, and then he moves forward between them and—blasted by
the cocaine he's not accustomed to—starts giddily asking Alejandro
questions about the risks involved in the restaurant business in South
America, nodding his head like he understands.

Ethan isn't surprised when, at the club, David stays close.

Ethan isn't surprised when David puts his arm around Ethan's
shoulders.

This gesture—and Ethan's gratified response—makes Alejandro
disappear into the crowd.

A few hours seem like a few minutes while the drinks and drugs ease David's stiffness until he doesn't have to force himself anymore. Ethan asks David if he's okay and David is fine, great actually, awesome, and then Ethan leads David into a bathroom where they share more of the cocaine while David asks, referring to Alejandro, "Who was that guy?" and Ethan silences David by kissing him on the mouth, positioning him against the mirror of the locked stall, then turning him around, and David keeps letting him do these things—David's in another place right now—and then Ethan kneels behind him, using his tongue and forefinger, first gently, then harder, and then David lets him push inside him, and he slides in so easily and, breathing hard, David pushes back against Ethan and quickly comes and then they're both focusing on the small green tiles on the floor beneath them until Ethan starts coming a few seconds later and David tenses with a sharp intake of breath.

"Are you okay?" Ethan asks a few moments later, over the din of techno music outside the door.

David just nods, sweating. He doesn't meet Ethan's gaze, or react at all when Ethan rubs his hand along the back of David's neck. He keeps breathing hard, looking away.

"Come on—I'll get you another drink."

Ethan heads to the bar, and when he turns around again, David is gone.

He's lying on his stomach when Ethan walks into the hotel room and stands next to the bed, peering down on the body and gently asking, with anger and longing, "Are you still awake?" and David Taylor doesn't say anything and closes his eyes tightly while Ethan undresses.

And the next afternoon turns out to be their last in Cuzco, because a dense fog rolls in over the mountains and Ethan Hoevel knows that fog in Cuzco can ground every plane for a week, so they go to the airport three days early and change their tickets and then stare out the departure gate windows toward the snowcapped mountains beyond the end of the runway. They don't exchange a genuine word until after the plane takes off, when David says, "I'm glad we won't be stuck there," and then realizes how that sounded and adds, "I had a really good time."

Ethan nods. "I don't know why I came back. It was all just so long ago that—I don't know—it doesn't mean that much anymore." He turns to David. "I probably should have come alone."

And then David is suddenly saying, "I told you I didn't mean to leave you at that club—I was just messed up. Everything got so crazy."

"You might find this hard to believe, David, but what we did happens all the time. It's not that crazy."

David pretends that he doesn't know what Ethan is talking about. "Well, I'm sorry if I've never been in a club full of Peruvians while high on cocaine. I'm sorry I don't have sex in bathroom stalls."

Ethan laughs spitefully.

David's eyes follow a stewardess gliding up the aisle. "Jesus, I couldn't breathe. And that guy was there and . . . anyway."

Ethan winces.

"Ethan . . ." David is obviously not comfortable voicing the name. "What can I say?" He tries to laugh at himself. "I was tired."

David turns away then to stare down at the mountains they've already flown over, which are strewn with pockets of fog.

27

"WE DIDN'T TALK much on the plane coming back." Ethan finished the story in a low murmur that was tinged with the sadness of knowing he couldn't exist back in that place with David Taylor anymore. Then a nurse walked tentatively into the room, scanning for us in the corner.

"He's awake," she said softly. "He can see you now." And with a firm look at me: "Family members only."

I started to sit—I didn't want to go in anyway—but Ethan took my hand. "I want him to come." He looked at the nurse and because of the force of that look she nodded and then I was following Ethan down the long white hospital corridors until we walked into Aidan's room, where one leg was raised in traction, a thick black brace wrapped around the other, and a plaster cast encircled his entire abdomen from his hips to his underarms. An assortment of tubes ran into various orifices, his neck was immobilized, and the sheets were stained with small drops of blood. Aidan Hoevel was also strapped to the bed.

Ethan stood over his brother for a long moment. "Hey," he finally said.

"Can you get me some more drugs?" Aidan's voice was soaked from the intravenous drip and he was peering through glazed eyes. A thin rivulet of drool clung to his chin. "I tried but I'm no good at stuff like that. Maybe if you asked . . ."

"They told me you've had plenty." Ethan sat down in the chair adjacent to the bed while I stood back against the wall, glancing every once in a while at the football game on the overhead TV that was mostly static. It was easier than looking at Aidan.

Aidan grimaced with a bolt of pain. The wires elevating his leg trembled. We were all silent for a moment, and then Aidan started fading into sleep.

"It's what I was always afraid of." This was Aidan. His eyes were now closed but his voice was uncharacteristically steady. "Something like this . . . look at me."

"You fell off a roof, Aidan. You're lucky to be alive."

"How many times do you think I heard that today?"

"You should stop talking."

Aidan's lips located a smile. "Ever since you told me . . . this is the exact thing. This is what I feared."

"Aidan, cut it out."

"Mom's home right now in Long Beach. She's afraid to go outside. She's in her room watching *Ellen* or something. And she doesn't even know about any of this . . ."

Ethan gestured to me. "He called her. He told her what happened."

I considered this. "Well, I sort of told her," I murmured.

Aidan opened his eyes and gazed, unfaltering, at his brother. "You're way off, Ethan. You don't even know what I mean." Then his eyelids fluttered and closed again. "This is really all about you."

"You got drunk, Aidan," Ethan said, indignant. "You got drunk and you fell off a roof."

"No, no . . ." Aidan turned his head weakly from side to side, grimacing again. "This is about you . . . this is about you in your gradu-ation gown—"

Ethan stood up and turned toward the door and was about to call for a nurse.

"—and . . . and you were in your graduation gown and you were holding that guy's hand . . ." His eyes flickered toward me, in the cor-ner where I'd been slowly backing away. "Ethan . . . both of you . . . please—please don't get me wrong." Aidan breathed in and then exhaled, rasping. "You're my brother and I have to love you—even if I didn't . . . and you" (this was directed at me) ". . . I don't mind you, dude . . . and the way you're always hanging around looking at my bro with those . . . I-want-you-back eyes . . . it's kind of—I don't know . . . sweet or something." Aidan Hoevel paused and licked the spittle off his lower lip. Ethan Hoevel locked onto me, remembering certain moments and decisions and failures we'd experienced—there was no escaping any of them right now. "But ever since then . . . that morning I saw you two . . . ever since then I knew you were gonna hurt someone . . . I really did . . . I just never thought it was gonna be me . . ."

Ethan was reeling at this point. I could see him resisting everything he heard. I could see him becoming afraid. "Aidan. You got drunk. You fell off a roof."

But Aidan wasn't listening anymore; he was spent and his voice dropped as he struggled to continue. "And you know what I'm afraid of? You know what's gonna haunt me when I'm sleeping tonight and every night after this one? You know what that is, Ethan?"

"What? The feeling of falling nine stories onto a concrete sidewalk?"

"It's that—"

"Jesus! Not having a job? Not having insurance?"

"—I'm not the first person you've hurt before—"

"Killing a dolphin with a speargun?"

"—and I'm not going to . . . be the last—"

"That someday you'll die?"

"—and the ground you walk on will be littered with all the people . . . that you've hurt . . ."

And then Aidan Hoevel passed out again, his eyelids dreamlessly still.

Ethan watched his brother for a few minutes. Aidan's leg started twitching and pulling on the thin traction cables, and I couldn't help flashing on the nano-wires of Ethan's senior project.

"Should we . . . get him some drugs?" I murmured.

Ethan nodded grimly and sighed. "Yeah, I'll try." And that spark of mild amusement that usually clung to the pain in his eyes was gone when he said to me, "You should go home. I want you to not be here anymore."

I left the hospital without telling him how Samona had slipped out of the loft before any of the ambulances came, and that I hadn't heard from her since.

I also left the hospital without telling him about the note I'd found in his room, the note she'd left for him which he would find later, written on Ethan Hoevel Designs stationery: *You asked me once why it took so long for us to meet. Now I know the answer and the only question left is why it took so long for me to figure it out. Samona.*

Then I walked slowly back to my studio, where the subletter had left lumps of cat hair clinging to almost everything. The sheets were unwashed and stained all over with ominous brown flecks, and the toilet was clogged.

It occurred to me while plunging that the only reason I'd known Ethan had come home was that David had called that afternoon. When I finally returned David's call, it was out of the need for distraction as much as anything else. I didn't want to dwell on pain and sadness anymore.

"Did you send that letter?" he asked immediately.

"I'm sorry—what?"

"The letter to Leonard. Was it you?"

"I don't know what you're talking about. A lot's been going on, David, and—"

"And the picture. If you sent it, just tell me right now. I'll have you fucking arrested. You'll never work in this city—"

"David, the only mail I've sent in the last month was an overdue rent check to my landlord."

The harsh and unfamiliar tone in his voice grew more urgent. It sounded as if David Taylor was pressing the mouthpiece against his lips.

"So you didn't send it?"

"No. David, what's going on?"

He wasn't listening to me. "Because if it wasn't you . . ." There was a long pause and then there was a click. The conversation was over, and I went to sleep.

Of course I already knew what letter and photograph he was talking about.

*   *   *

There was no way to know then what had occurred in James Leonard's office on the afternoon David returned from Peru. It was only months later—when I began writing this story and found the journalist in me desperate for the few missing details—that I made the last-ditch decision to call Mr. Leonard under the guise of "a reporter working on a small piece for the *Times* focusing on the particular attributes that separated people in hedge funds who'd lost their jobs from those who'd been able to keep them." He didn't name names, but he did in fact allude to a certain executive who'd spent the previous summer under "the burden of a curious brand of personal duress." Then James Leonard told me that "as the CEO of a boutique investment fund such as The Leonard Company, it's my responsibility to take *everything* into account during the grueling decision-making process." After speaking with Mr. Leonard for twenty minutes and taking liberties with the facts I already knew, I was able to envision David Taylor's afternoon on the second Friday in September:

On his return from Peru, David checks his messages from his cell phone while waiting for his luggage in the terminal at JFK.

He's been flying for nine hours and is entering a dull state of depression when the first thing he hears is James Leonard's voice: "David. Please come to my office as soon as you get in. Thanks."

David embraces Ethan in a formalized way before getting into his own cab, since Ethan is going downtown and David is heading up to The Leonard Company.

When David walks into Leonard's office—after being told to wait five minutes in the chair next to his secretary's desk, a tactic he knows is designed to create anxiety—Leonard says, "Close the door please, David."

James Leonard's aged and handsome face is looking at David with a kind of calculated curiosity.

Then David sits down, and there's a silent stretch of pointed unease before James asks with a stern expression, "How was your vacation?"

David answers automatically. "It was pretty good. A little break always helps."

"Where did you go?"

"I was in Peru."

"Really?" James asked. He keeps studying David as if looking for an answer. "Did you go to Machu Picchu?"

"No. We mostly stayed in Cuzco. It was very pretty." The answer is well practiced and flawlessly executed.

"Was Samona with you?"

"Actually, no."

James leans back, surprised. "Oh?"

"She stayed in the city." David clarifies, "I mean she stayed home."

"How come?"

"She needed a break, too, James." David weakly attempts a chuckle.

James offers a sad smile. "But you've been spending all of your time at the office."

"Right. No, I know. We just—I mean, I just needed to get away . . . it hasn't been all that easy . . ."

"It's been a tough year for everyone," James concedes. "It's just the market. You can't blame yourself." He pauses. "You know that, don't you?"

David looks at his own feet and admires how the weaves in the carpet all flow in the same direction before nodding his head.

James sighs and swivels his computer screen toward David. On the screen is a spreadsheet for Duke Energy. "Does this ring a bell?"

"Yeah," David says, leaning toward the screen, relieved because he clearly remembers taking care of this. "Right, yeah—for Randolph Torrance. I put that trade through before I left."

"As sure a sell as I've ever seen."

David's recollection of the actual moment becomes more vague as a result of the accusatory tone of James's voice. "Is there—is there a problem?" But he now knows exactly what happened.

The sell box is on the right-hand corner of the computer screen. The buy box is on the left.

"The question concerning me is why did you *buy*?" James would usually be too dignified to let David Taylor scramble for an answer, but today he sits back in his chair and doesn't speak until David meets his stare. "Thirty-four years in the business. Twenty-nine at Merrill Lynch. Five more building this company. Trust me, David, I've seen my share of bear markets. What I'm saying is, you can't let it *affect* you more than it should. Otherwise, you don't belong in this business."

"Sure." David is still squinting into the screen, his eyes scanning the graphs.

"Insider trading. Depression. Divorce. Even suicide. Some real sad sacks. I've seen them all. Too many times."

"Yes. Right."

"And I also recall telling you years ago that this kind of fuckup—the kind that costs me money off a sure deal—only happens once in a career. Which is what brings us to this."

There's a pause during which David Taylor stares out the window behind James, at the view facing downtown toward SoHo, Tribeca, Wall Street.

James opens a drawer and brings out a sheet of plain white paper and a folded photograph. James hands them both to David. He watches David's eyes as he unfolds the picture. He raises his hand when David's face shoots up, shocked.

"Read it."

David reads the letter silently to himself.

(The second phone call I made after speaking with James Leonard was to James Gutterson, who by that time—remember, this was a few months after that summer ended—had settled in the attic apartment of a small house in Thunder Bay. After I pressed him about it over the phone, he recited the letter to me verbatim. When I thanked him, he responded, "What-the-fuck-ever. Not like any of that bullshit matters to me anymore.")

Mr. James E. Leonard, Managing Director
The Leonard Company
800 Seventh Avenue, 21st Floor
New York, NY 10038
September 10th, 2004

Dear Mr. Leonard,

On behalf of the respectability of The Leonard Company name, I would like to inform you of troubling developments that have taken shape of late. Mr. David Tay-

lor, one of your junior vice presidents and a respected member of the Leonard "team," has been conducting an illicit affair on the property of the most respected Leonard Company. He is engaged in an extramarital affair with the young man hired to redesign Conference Rooms 2 and 3 on the respected twenty-first floor. Now I of all people acknowledge that what a man does in his private life ought to remain private, but when he conducts himself in such a disrespectful manner within the respected halls of The Leonard Company, I feel it is my duty as an employee to bring said behavior to the attention of our respected managing director—you, sir.

Respectfully Concerned,
A Troubled Employee

David then studies the photograph. To him it seems like someone else, someone who isn't David Taylor—but that doesn't matter.

He's positive that he will momentarily be terminated from The Leonard Company.

He knows that, without Samona, this will leave him completely alone as he looks for a new job.

He flashes on teacher's college. Somehow, he remembers the dream he once had.

He has the money in his 401(k) to live comfortably—though not luxuriously—for most of his life, even at a teacher's salary.

Especially if he finds someplace more modest than the Riverview apartment.

And if Samona repays his investment with minor interest.

In his mind, he sees clearly that this is what the whole summer has been leading up to: David Taylor being fired the day he returns from Peru with Ethan Hoevel two weeks after his wife leaves him.

And, during the long minute James gives him to process the situation, David Taylor is slightly happier than he's been since the day he won the footrace in Central Park.

James says, "I don't presume to put much stock in anonymous letters or possibly doctored photos, especially during cutback time. And it's not my business, really, except in as far as whatever *might* have happened, *seems* to have happened in the office . . ."

David is breathing in and it's all he can do to pay attention. He turns the photograph over. He studies the date. He glances at his own, clearly illuminated face. He starts planning out the rest of his life, year by year in bullet points, and he feels rejuvenated:

Teacher's college.

Public school placement.

The satisfaction of giving back.

Gaining of respect; shedding of self-loathing.

The summers off.

The beach weekends.

Applying to private school positions.

Leaving New York behind.

The cozy house in New England.

He stops flashing forward at this point—the point at which he might think about starting a family.

He comes back to Samona.

And then he's planning out everything he'll have to say to get her back (*"It didn't mean anything, Samona," "We were happy once," "We can do it all again," "You cheated too, right?," "We'll forgive each other, right?"*) when James Leonard, through the haze, says something very unexpected.

"You've been with me down a hard road and—mostly—you've been a great asset. You've helped expand from a little five-billion-dollar hedge fund to—what is it now?—eight-point-nine? At any rate, how goddamned good you are at this job is something I'd be an idiot to ignore on principle."

"What are you—what do you mean?"

James Leonard interprets the whiny desperation in David's voice as the appropriate reaction of a man who wants—needs—his job. "What I mean is, now that you've had some time away, let's settle back in, okay? I'm behind you. We all are. That's what being part of a team means."

When David walks out of James Leonard's office, he still has a job.

The bright images of an alternate future fade just as quickly as they'd been illuminated, and then they disappear entirely while he brings the Duke Energy deal up on his computer to start the damage control with Randolph Torrance (who will formally void his contract with David the following Monday, citing "outrageous negligence to the basic tenets of finance") and then someone from the mailroom calls up concerning the package he'd ordered from Ethan Hoevel Designs (the guy reads this slowly off the shipping label and mispronounces *Hoevel* so that it comes out sounding like "how-evil") which has not been picked up and what does David want them to do?

Later, as David Taylor sits at his desk in front of his computer, the light in his office clicks off but he doesn't wave his arm to bring it back on. He's moved the wedding photo off the wall and placed it on his desk, where it's propped against the side of the Bloomberg screen. With the computer glow now the only light, David alternates between looking at the space where the photo was—a faint rectangular impression left in the thin film of dust (which automatically acts as a reminder to David Taylor to have his office cleaned)—and then back at the actual frame and the image inside it. David wants to throw it, just hurl the thing against the clock or else at the shelves with all the books whose contents he's forgotten and stopped caring about. The sound of it shattering keeps echoing through his mind. But David Taylor doesn't do this. David Taylor only stares until he doesn't want to throw it anymore.

And then he begins writing an e-mail to Ethan Hoevel, unaware that Ethan will forward the e-mail to me. Because right now, I am really the only person left in Ethan Hoevel's world.

To: readyandwaiting@hotmail.com
From: ethan@ethanhoeveldesigns.com
Sent: 10:49 AM, Sunday, September 12
Subject: Fwd: (no subject)

Thought you might be interested . . .

To: ethan@ethanhoeveldesigns.com
From: David.Taylor@Leonardco.com
Sent: 12:09 AM Saturday, September 11
Subject: (no subject)

sorry been busy. disaster zone over here. but i
have to tell you something—i don't think this is
me—who i am. i don't regret it. not really—i let
it happen right? and part of me wanted it to. but

```
so much else going on. just trying not to make a
big deal out of this. but what's going on with
you? i want to know. take care. d.
```

The coda to the message was the Leonard Company confidentiality disclaimer.

And as the journalist in me imagined David Taylor carefully writing and revising the words over and over (between conference calls with young analysts and follow-ups to Randolph Torrance and his lawyer) to make them seem gentle, sensitive, casual—just like I'd tried to do eight years earlier—and that other part of me imagined Ethan reading them, wondering why they didn't carry the same weight they once had, trying to decipher what had changed since junior year of college—to locate what in him had hardened so much, and why—I decided that there was only one more thing left for me to do.

The next day, I went by Printing Divine to see Samona.

I walked into the empty waiting area and heard Martha running the machines upstairs, getting ready for Fashion Week while muttering, "I might as well be self-employed." Ignoring her, I closed the door softly, so the bell wouldn't ring, and then I saw someone through the glass partition in Samona's office; it was her old college friend Olivia, collecting piles of mail and folders.

I knocked on the glass and Olivia's mild alarm signified that she didn't remember me, and it wasn't until after we made the vague Yale connection and I told her I'd seen Samona a few days ago and just wanted to make sure she was all right that Olivia started slipping me the disjointed fragments—the way college girls gossip, pushing secrets off her chest in a perky voice—of what had happened:

Samona Taylor had gone to Olivia's directly from Ethan's loft the night Aidan fell.

She'd been freaked out to the point of shaking, which Olivia just assumed had to do with the probable divorce that was looming.

They had a late dinner and talked about nothing important because Olivia's husband was there, too, and Tim "had had a rough day—he was kind of a bore."

In the kitchen Samona helped Olivia load the dishwasher and

said vacantly, "Thank you so much for having me. It really means a lot."

"Well, you know you're always welcome."

"I'll try not to be for too long. But can we not talk about it? Can we just laugh about all the things that happened? I left my husband because he cheated on me. Let's play a game and try to find the humor in that." She paused. "Maybe I'll just start dating women."

Olivia said, "Do you remember when we kissed?"

Samona shoved another plate in the rack. "We were so drunk. Wait—wasn't it a dare?"

"Yeah," Olivia said, trying to figure out how the dare was made.

"It was . . . but who made the dare?"

This was a sincere question. They both thought about it for a moment and the smile left Samona's face.

"It was David."

"That's right," Olivia said. "At SAE."

"It was four in the morning."

The game ended.

They leaned against the granite counter while Olivia split the last of the chardonnay into two glasses.

Samona raised her glass and then stopped, considering something.

"Do you remember a guy named Ethan Hoevel?"

"Isn't he helping out with your . . ."—Olivia didn't quite know what to call it—"business?"

"I mean, do you remember him from school?"

"I guess so. I don't know." There was a pause and then Olivia asked, "Why?"

Unease creased Samona's face, and now Olivia became curious, intrigued (though she was bashful about admitting this to me) that Samona Ashley Taylor—the princess with the best stories, the needy one—was now so lost.

Samona turned away. "Nothing."

"Come on," Olivia pressed. "What?"

"Do you remember if he was gay or not? Can you think of any reason why I'd assume that he wouldn't be gay?"

Olivia looked at Samona (who was anxiously waiting for an answer) while thinking: *I'm pretty sure Ethan Hoevel was gay.* But this was only based on a few hazy rumors Olivia could barely remember.

Olivia pressed her hand against her forehead like she was thinking deeply and then shook her head. "To be honest, I think I partied way too hard to remember much of anything."

After the kitchen was clean, she cuddled Samona Taylor in the guest bedroom the way they used to do in college (and also during her brief "break" from David) while Samona complained about having eaten what her mother Tana would have called an "indulgent" meal—sugar-glazed salmon, pasta with chopped bacon, a large Caesar salad, and chocolate cake with buttercream frosting—and then Olivia left her alone with the special Fashion Week preview insert in the *Post* entitled "One Week and Counting."

A few minutes later, while Olivia was going over testimonies for court the next day and her husband watched *SportsCenter*, they heard retching sounds coming from the bathroom, but neither of them wanted to deal with what they knew Samona was doing.

The next morning, Olivia found a spare toothbrush stained with flecks of the vomit it had induced—a problem Olivia thought had been taken care of back in college, when David had urged her to go to the Mental Health Center for counseling.

Olivia came back to me at this point and asked, "Do you know anything about . . . what was going on?"

I was already backing out of the office. "I guess it's . . . complicated."

"Well, at least it's not my problem anymore, thank *God*."

I stopped. And even though the reason I'd gone to the office that day was to figure out how to despise Samona Ashley Taylor—to lock her away and forget her—I knew in that moment that being in love with Samona was something I had to continue living with.

Off my look she added, "He came by here this morning, I guess. And talked to her. She was in such a rush to get her stuff out of my place that she forgot all her files for Fashion Week, and I have a meeting near their apartment later, so I'm just going to drop it off."

"She's moving back in with him?" I blurted out.

She nodded, grinning. "He must have been awfully smooth to get out of that one. I mean, right?"

I imagined: David Taylor getting out of a cab outside Printing Divine, and then walking around the block twice, glancing absently in store windows, and then standing outside the shop scuffing his $450 Prada loafers (the ones that go with his new suit) on the sidewalk.

I imagined: David Taylor taking deep breaths as a woman passes him being dragged by a huge golden retriever, and an old man pushes a stroller, and a young couple holds hands while they window-shop, and then David Taylor does everything in his power not to let these people take on more significance than they should, and then convinces himself that not only is this the right thing to do, but that this is also the heroic thing to do (in fact, he's already completed the cost/benefit analysis of his decision—has actually written it out on Leonard Company stationery before ripping it to shreds).

I imagined: David Taylor nodding to himself before walking into Printing Divine to reconcile with his wife.

Then I looked up and Olivia was gawking. "Hey, listen," she said while collecting the rest of Samona's mail. "Don't you think they deserve each other?"

The pity with which she offered this consolation was obviously a response to what I'd been trying to hide on my face.

Then I left Printing Divine and walked through the muggy grayness of NYU toward Tenth Street, and I splurged on a six-pack of Stella and cigarettes and the *Post* and I went up to the roof to read it back to front like I usually did, to forget about everything. The Yankees were looking strong and mean as the Red Sox loomed in the postseason; Gucci was coming out with a new line of beauty products for Fashion Week; the fire chief was (maybe) cheating on his wife; 32 percent of New York public school kids were failing the standardized tests. I finished the paper and downed four beers.

I also reread David's e-mail to Ethan.

I also recited Samona's note to Ethan.

I began revising the Gowanus Canal pitch.

I replied yes to an e-mail from an editor asking me to cover a lineup of Fashion Week shows.

I assumed the events of the summer were behind me—after all, there wasn't anything left to know.

28

WHICH WAS WHY it seemed unreal when, on the night of September 20, in a tent on one of the new Hudson Riverwalk promenades, a bright and very pale light enveloped all of us at Stanton Vaughn's fashion show. Since I was looking up when these lights ignited, I experienced a temporary blindness and by the time I cleared my eyes Samona and David Taylor were taking their seats on the other side of the runway while Ethan shifted on the catwalk directly above them (I'd been looking at him when the lights changed), and I found my way, dazed, to the press section, where the gift bag under the seat (a silver cigarette lighter, white chocolates with Kama Sutra positions imprinted in gold icing, a miniature bottle of cologne, four ounces of cognac) wasn't enough to distract me from the fact that we were all back at the beginning of the story together—college, a quad, *Love's Labour's Lost,* and Ethan Hoevel with his unsettling eyes on the new couple, which would lead to a basement in Trumbull College and Thailand and then to a conference room under construction on the twenty-first floor of a skyscraper on Fifty-first and Broadway.

The glaring white lights dimmed and a new light focused on the runway and generic alternative music pumped out of the speakers.

And when the show ended and the lights faded up once again there was not a single word written on my notepad.

Models were parading in a line and Stanton materialized behind them at the head of the runway grinning widely (which accentuated the jagged stitches over his left eye) and taking a bow even though most of the audience had already begun moving cattlelike toward the exit (passing James Gutterson on his way in) and the more important shows tonight at the SoHo House and the Maritime Hotel and Gotham.

Samona stood.

She turned to her husband and followed his gaze upward.

Her mouth hardened, and that evasive smile didn't exist anymore.

David Taylor had located Ethan Hoevel on the catwalk, and now Samona had located him, too.

And it was clear from the way they stood (side by side, gazing up at him independently of each other) that neither David nor Samona truly knew what the other had done—that whatever words they'd exchanged to "work things out" in Printing Divine a few days earlier had not included the name Ethan Hoevel, that they were both still very much lost in Ethan Hoevel's world, and that I remained the only one who knew any of this. The awareness drove me to the bar on the other side of the emptying tent where I drank three glasses of wine with an urgency that surprised even me, and where I marveled at all of us being here, in this place, on this night, together.

What I didn't know that night, and what I would figure out over the weeks that followed:

Very late on Monday, the thirteenth of September, a resident working an all-night shift at Beth Israel hears a coughing, gurgling sound in room 343. She rushes in to find Aidan Hoevel choking on his own vomit, unable to turn his head to the side because he is still immobilized, and by the time the resident discovers with horror what's happened—an acid reflux reaction caused by Aidan's anesthesia and aided by the traces of alcohol still lingering in his system has begun filling his stomach with bile—the acid is already leaking into his lungs, and before they can even intubate his stomach for pumping, his right lung collapses, followed shortly by his left. Aidan Hoevel drowns quickly and is pronounced dead at 10:36 P.M.

Two days later, Stanton Vaughn calls Ethan to tell him how sorry he is about Aidan, and that it isn't his fault—that Aidan Hoevel has been en route to disaster for the majority of his life (something Ethan already knows and agrees with) and it was just a huge fucking unpreventable accident—and that Stanton still wants to see him; all he's ever wanted is just to see Ethan. So Stanton suggests he comes to the fashion show on Monday. Ethan designed the set, after all, and the show will be a necessary distraction for the "at least minor grief" Ethan must be experiencing—and through all the begging forgiveness and pleading for more chances and the pronouncements of regret, Stanton Vaughn almost sounds sincere.

And then James Gutterson—who's leaving for Thunder Bay in a few days—sees a listing for Stanton Vaughn's show in the *Post* Fashion Week spread which includes Samona's name in very small print since she did the color work, and a little later—obliterated by seven martinis and an eight ball—he calls David Taylor to ask if he's going (and really to find out if his mailings have gotten him divorced and/or fired), and when David tells him that he is in fact going—that he and Samona "had talked" and decided to try "working things out"—James pleads to be put on the guest list, at least for the after-party, and David (who's so distracted by everything going on that he hasn't even connected the pink slip he approved for James Gutterson's termination a month ago with the letter and incriminating photograph James Leonard received from a "Troubled Employee") says he doesn't know about the show but, sure, he can probably get him into the after-party. He says this out of pity more than anything else: he can't help feeling responsible for the downturn of his old colleague's life into absolute wastedness even though James's history at The Leonard Company was marked by nothing but laziness and failure.

And somewhere in the midst of that week, Ethan Hoevel called a publicity contact to make sure I would be covering Stanton Vaughn's show—that I would be in that tent with them all on the night of September 20.

After I composed myself enough to turn and survey the crowd: Ethan was gone, David was squinting into the room with his hands in the pockets of the Prada suit Ethan had inspired him to buy, and

Samona—wearing a strapless black cocktail dress and her hair straight-ened—stood a few feet away, her back to David as she talked animatedly with a potential client. The remaining crowd made a push toward the bar as the after-party started, and I drank another glass of wine and watched her and began falling into that place again—the place where it was so impossible not to see the soft brown nape of her neck flowing into her shoulders, and how the makeup that had been painstakingly applied still couldn't hide the weariness in her face, and the way her skin turned pale, almost white, under the blue lights.

In that place it didn't matter that Ethan was somewhere close, hov-ering.

And it didn't matter that James Gutterson was at the other end of the bar, rubbing his gums, scanning the room hungrily.

And it didn't matter when David Taylor's voice sounded close to my ear, dulled by the vodka gimlets he'd been pounding before the show. "It's cool," he said.

I turned to him and blinked. "What is?"

"The way you're staring at my wife."

I was reduced to stammering out, "David—"

He raised his hand and smiled. "Hey, it's not like you'd try any-thing, right?"

What made me angry was how easygoing he sounded—how he didn't view me as a threat.

"So are you still, you know, tight with Ethan Hoevel?" he went on, gently mocking. I offered a blank stare, and he added, "I mean you guys were pretty close in college, right?"

"Not really."

"But I saw you guys together all the time."

"No, you didn't."

David scowled, exasperated, and shook his head. "I was just curious."

And this exchange moved me outside to smoke a cigarette on the promenade, where it was twilight and warm and breezy. The lights from Jersey and the buildings along the West Side Highway reflected off the wavelets of the river. Army helicopters hovered low, a reminder of where we all were now. But the world felt different there, away from everyone; it was casual and hazy and calm. The seasons were changing—it would be fall soon—and it didn't seem to matter anymore what I knew and felt; it seemed like none of it needed to push me back into all the regret hovering over that tent tonight, and instead I could just walk home and smoke and sleep and not be burdened with disappointment anymore.

Then I turned around and saw that Ethan had been standing behind me. He leaned close and took the last drag off my cigarette. Our shoulders touched.

He said, "There are moments—and you won't believe me when I say this—but there are actually moments when you are a much more interesting person than you think you are."

Our shoulders touched again, and his hand brushed my arm gently and then moved to the back of my neck and I was thinking about how I had followed him to the basement of Trumbull College and how I'd convinced myself so many different times that those moments didn't matter.

We were kids then. I'd been repeating this to myself for eight years. *Just fucking kids.*

I stopped and pushed his hand away.

He accepted this—my rejection—with a smile because it was an easy game for Ethan Hoevel, a game he could rely on in the midst of all the pain and uncertainty he'd caused.

Standing there against the rail with the glowing vein of water behind him, the sky a weak red fading into a harsh dark blue, Ethan Hoevel looked undeniably alone.

"How's Aidan?" I asked, and he shook his head and glanced across the river and didn't tell me that his brother had died five days ago.

(Later, after that night was over, I would decide that he'd refused to allow the realities to interfere with what he wanted to happen at Stanton Vaughn's party—he'd craved the distraction of it all for a few more hours before the summer ended.)

"How come you never said anything?" he asked. "How could the whole summer go by, and you had every chance and you never told anyone anything?"

"You knew I wouldn't."

"Yeah. But why?"

"Because—I wasn't involved. Because none of it mattered to me."

He squinted and his eyes became less piercing and he gave me that familiar, knowing smile. "Was that it or was it . . . something else?"

I didn't answer. I knew that Ethan was waiting for me to answer, and I refused. When he didn't hear what he so badly desired—the words that would take him back to a place and time when he was just a smart, young, interesting kid, when he was just distancing himself from Long Beach enough to start creating his own world, when his brother didn't hate him, when relationships had no consequences, when no one wanted anything from him, when no one knew anything about him, when the only thing that mattered to Ethan Hoevel was the two of us in a room alone together, when he didn't have to go seeking a consciousness that was different and novel in order to pursue a particular kind of happiness that was really only an illusion anyway—he just took a step back and looked at me and smiled.

That smile was the only time I ever saw desperation in Ethan Hoevel. I was suddenly afraid of him and his influence over me.

A moment later the velvet rope lifted.

He took my wrist. His face was reckless and inviting and beautiful and his eyes were suddenly scornful of all the threats waiting for us inside that door.

And then I went in with him—because I wanted to convince myself that my fear of Ethan Hoevel shouldn't exist anymore.

The after-party had officially started and long horizontal lights in the shape of inverted pyramids were flashing around the sides of the tent but failed to add the necessary excitement to the anonymous techno music and the empty dance floor.

I was already scanning the room for her when we heard, "Thanks for coming to my party," and Stanton pushed between Ethan and me, an arm around each of us, a bright red drink in a martini glass sloshing dangerously close to my face while his head turned to Ethan and I used that to slip out of his embrace. But Stanton didn't notice because Ethan was looking down the bar where David Taylor and James Gutterson were drinking vodka tonics.

Stanton was already drunk and oblivious and pulled at Ethan's arm to the point where Ethan winced and said, "Why do you keep wasting yourself over me?"

Stanton (who had presumably played this conversation a hundred times in his head but never with this beginning) let go in order to flail his arm toward a banker named David Taylor. "You think you can change him?" Stanton asked. "Is that what you think? Your brother's dead and I'm a wreck and you still think you can take that guy to Peru and fuck his brains out and he'll just change for you and everything will be okay?" And then he turned to me. "What are you staring at?"

"Stanton, calm down," Ethan consoled, and I took small steps away from them.

"I am calm!" Stanton raised his arms, wide-eyed. "I'm so fucking calm." People around the room turned.

I kept backing away until I reached the bar, where David saw me, winced, and muttered, "What did you think of the show?"

I was watching Stanton push Ethan away as James Gutterson spat out, "Two words: menswear."

I said, "I think that's one word," but he looked at me so contemptuously that I regretted saying anything. I turned back to David and, being as bland and polite as I could, asked, "Are you going to hang out awhile?"

And David, with a hardened, expressionless glare, replied, "As soon as Samona stops talking to people, we're leaving. Trust me." There it was again—that awful, patronizing self-assurance that, in the end, would come to define David Taylor.

He shrugged and took a big sip of his vodka tonic.

I scanned the room again before asking, "So where is Samona?"

He leaned back, a little bit startled by my brazenness. "I don't know—this is work for her."

James laughed. "You can't even make that sound halfway convincing."

"So you two just . . . figured everything out?" This was me, fueled enough by my encounter with Ethan to finally be able to say what I wanted. "And everything's fine now?"

"Yeah, I don't get that," James said. "How does that happen?"

"People fuck up, you know," David shot back without missing a beat—without even thinking about it. "Happens all the time, every minute. We fucked up and then we talked about it and we made promises to each other and that's just what people do when they fuck up. In the real world, that's how you make everything okay again." David nodded absently at his own answer before adding, "So, yeah—it's all fine."

There was a brief silence marked only by James's laughter, and then David glanced up at the balcony where Ethan was now standing alone. James—by following his eyes—located the guy who had redesigned Conference Room Three, and a cruel grin spread across his lips.

Ethan met David's gaze, and as David looked away—ashamed that he'd looked, that he'd been unable to stop himself from looking—Ethan Hoevel smiled.

David turned back to me.

"Must have made a lot of promises," I told him, trying to channel Ethan's elusiveness.

But I failed. He didn't get it, and he responded only by gesturing at James nonchalantly. It was a diversion from what had just occurred. "Oh, your prospectus is up on the Web site—and I reissued your check personally."

But I wasn't listening to his charitable, cringe-inducing voice because I'd spotted Samona as she walked toward us from the direction of the bathroom. She came straight to the bar, where David handed her a cosmo and James Gutterson was now talking about his 6 A.M. flight out of JFK to Ontario the next morning. "I always get stuck next to the fat guys with, like, pieces of their bodies spilling onto me—" He stopped talking in order to leer at Samona.

I hadn't eaten all day and the wine was already hitting me and I let my eyes linger on her. That she didn't even look back at me—didn't even think it—did nothing to subdue my yearning. It only made the yearning more powerful as she drained her glass and with an overhead glance to where Ethan Hoevel was still standing—still alone—grabbed David's hand and pulled him onto the empty dance floor.

James muttered to himself, the cruel, bitter grin still etched on his face.

Stanton was at the far end of the bar holding a drink, the stitches clearly making his forehead throb, appearing to find the whole party loud and confusing.

Ethan shifted against the rail.

And we were all watching the same thing: David Taylor moving his weight from one foot to the other, upper teeth clenched over his lower lip, shoulders rotating awkwardly from side to side while Samona moved around him gracefully, leading him, glancing up to the balcony every so often.

James pulled out a vial and—without even concealing it—did two massive bumps. "Taylor's such a fucking pussy. It's just so fucked up." He rubbed his nose and then started laughing. "Did you know that all the models were going to be dudes?"

I ordered another glass of merlot and then shuffled awkwardly down the bar away from him and didn't realize I had put myself within talking distance of Stanton until I heard him say, "It's over with me and Ethan—totally over." I nodded uninterestedly as I surrendered to the fact that I couldn't take my eyes off her.

Samona stopped dancing and whispered in David's ear. He nodded. She headed toward the bar and left David alone in the middle of the empty dance floor.

I polished off my glass in one sip and ordered another.

I glanced up and didn't see Ethan anymore, and this didn't scare me the way it should have.

Because Samona was leaning on the bar three stools away, gesturing for the bartender.

I took a deep breath, but before I could do anything James Gutterson came up from another bump and immediately locked on Samona Taylor's profile. He took a sip of his vodka and leaned toward her. His anger was seething and naked—because in an hour he'd be lying in bed, unable to sleep because of all the coke, trying to masturbate, and in ten hours he'd be on a plane drinking a Bloody Mary, and a year from now he'd be coaching preteen hockey players on a pond in Thunder Bay, and five years after that he'd probably marry a fat girl—and all these small depressions that would one day sum up James Gutterson's life were standing there now, mocking him in the form of Samona in a strapless dress.

He whistled and she looked up from her reflection in the surface of the bar. She regarded James warily and motioned the bartender to hurry.

"Will you answer one question?" This was James, grinning and breathing heavily through his nose. "How come you hate me so much?"

Samona sighed without emotion and said nothing.

James laughed and his eyes scanned her legs tucked under the bar as he reached into his pocket and pulled out a folded envelope. Slipping it casually into her purse, he said, "Did you know, beautiful, that your husband has been getting banged in the ass by the guy designing the conference rooms?"

Her face went from indifferent to disbelieving to ashen in the span of a few seconds.

I was invisible, three stools away, and it seemed as though I were watching a scene that I had witnessed before.

She grabbed her purse and left the bar and walked quickly to the bathrooms in the far left corner of the tent. She moved right past David, who was searching for his jacket behind the DJ booth.

And Stanton was saying, "You know the only thing I ever learned from Ethan was—" but he cut off as he traced Samona's path back to where David Taylor was now scanning the room anxiously from the edge of the dance floor.

Stanton stood up and approached him—this reminder of all his failures—and David immediately placed the face to a night almost a month ago along a deserted stretch of sidewalk on Forty-third Street. Before David could back away, Stanton grabbed his shoulder firmly and held him in place.

(And I know this to have occurred, because I saw what was coming and followed Stanton across the room in order to be near it.)

(I had lied to Ethan—it did matter to me.)

"Do you want to know the really fucked-up part?" Stanton asked, shocking David into paralysis. "The totally fucked portion of all this is that your wife has been fucking Ethan Hoevel at the same time that Ethan Hoevel was fucking you." Stanton stared at David and marveled. "You guys have quite the modern marriage."

I saw David Taylor's face tighten—this suggestion making perfect and gruesome sense inside his head—as I walked past them on my way to the bathroom.

But it was strangely just one of so many details (the music, the people, the past) and coursing through me now was a sense of liberation.

Because David and Samona now knew what I knew.

Because eight years was too long not to tell a girl that you loved her.

Because that place—outside the bathroom, waiting for Samona Taylor—was where I was supposed to be.

I leaned against the door frame, my heart pounding.

I didn't realize my eyes were closed until Ethan took my hand.

He whispered, "Are you finally going to go in? Do you need my help?"

And I was shaking as he used my hand to knock on the door.

We both heard a sobbing voice. "Just a second. I'll just be a minute."

"It's me," Ethan called softly.

We heard her footsteps, and the lock clicked open.

Then we went inside—Ethan first, then me. Samona stood with her back to the mirror and she looked at us. The photo was in her hand.

He let go of me and moved a step closer to her.

He said, "You're so sexy, Samona."

He said, "You know you're so sexy."

He said, "Don't you know that, Samona?"

I stood there watching their faces—hers in front of me, his in the mirror behind her. I didn't exist. Ethan and Samona inhabited this room alone.

"Why did you do this?" she murmured, holding up the photo.

Ethan flinched and asked, "Does it even matter anymore?"

He reached for her, but she pushed him away violently. Then she slapped his face.

"It matters, Ethan. Things fucking matter."

She was running to the door but I was standing in her way; I was in her way and she was looking at me now—listening and waiting.

I held my breath and leaned toward her. My gaze moved past her shoulder to Ethan. He was watching us in the mirror.

I closed my eyes, and then I breathed out—so close that her hair moved in my breath—and was able to whisper, "I do remember when we kissed, Samona. I remember that."

Then she was gone, and it was too late. It didn't matter anymore. It never really happened.

I heard the door close and lock.

I felt Ethan. His breath was warm on my neck.

"No," I said quietly.

Two hands reached around me and slid down my chest.

"No, Ethan."

A tongue trailed along the back of my neck and then it flicked my ear. "We're not any different right now," he whispered.

"Please. No." I was whimpering.

"I want to forget everything, just like you. I just want to pull away and forget and not be here anymore."

Fingers slid inside my mouth and stifled my voice and I wet them with my tongue as I bent my neck back, knowing that after this moment—because I had let him take this moment from me—I would never see Ethan Hoevel's face again.

That's when the summer ended.

And as I walked home in the middle of the night, I knew that James Gutterson would still be at the bar, looking at his watch and realizing distantly that his plane was leaving in five hours, and his teeth weren't numb anymore but his jaw was sore and there was no one left to talk to except for this trim, angry man in a leather jacket with a rancid scar across his forehead, lighting a cigarette two stools down—Stanton Vaughn, whose party was over as a distant voice faded into a techno version of "Besame Mucho" and men in blue jumpsuits dismantled the tent—and then James, the big guy in gray slacks and a black button-down, would stand and point a finger at him and say, "Hey, you can't smoke in here," and in response Stanton would then blow smoke in his face and turn away and hear "Listen, you little f—" before swinging his arm with all the rage built up through the last three sweltering months, sending them both to the floor as James, with the hand that wasn't being pinned behind his back, would strike a very carefully aimed blow at the line of stitches above Stanton Vaughn's eye, ripping them apart.

As I walked through Union Square, I knew that David Taylor would be feeling his own end of summer in the stillness of being near the river as he stared at a bus depot and drifted past a darkened art gallery and the white noise of the city grew muffled, and he'd inhale a deep breath and turn toward Tenth Avenue, pausing to take his jacket off, and then he'd stop walking when he saw—across the street and halfway down the block—Ethan Hoevel hailing a cab, and for David Taylor there'd be so many choices left to be made—millions of them actually, every day—and the thought would make his mind reel as he stepped back behind the corner until Ethan disappeared, and then he'd continue slowly north to Twenty-third Street and find a cab and rest his head on the back of the seat and roll down the window, closing his eyes and picturing the mist drifting over the mountains; Ethan's profile fading away, indifferent; the jade earrings he never bought Samona, and then he would be walking through the Riverview lobby and standing in the elevator rising up to his apartment and then the doors would open and he'd become aware that he left his jacket, the one he had bought to impress Ethan Hoevel, in the cab with his keys and wallet.

And when I stopped in a deli on Tenth Street for cigarettes that I didn't want, I knew that Samona would be sitting outside their door with her knees tucked up against her chest, a crumpled sheet of matte paper on the floor a few feet away, and she would watch her husband shuffle across the beige carpeting, beneath the bright lights and past the plastic floral arrangements, and she would catch his reflection in the gilded mirror that panels the length of the hallway—golden hues, slightly distorted—and she'd murmur, "I left my key ring . . ." and not finish because she had left it at Ethan's loft a week earlier, so instead she'd look up at David and not tell him where her keys were, and she'd say gently, "Do you mind getting them from the doorman?" and her husband would then hesitate a moment, about to speak until she would cut him off by raising her hand and whispering, "Tomorrow."

I got to my door, and I decided to linger on the stoop for a minute—not even to smoke, but just to sit there—and a slight breeze passed which carried downtown to Warren Street, where I knew Ethan would be stepping into his loft, and the loft's dimness and emptiness would intensify the dull ache that had been gripping him all the way home, and then he'd climbed to the roof and opened a bottle of wine to soothe this ache, and only then would it hit Ethan Hoevel, as he stood there watching the river, that he was alone.

IV

29

THE STORY OF DAVID AND SAMONA

Part 5: The Settlement

SAMONA WAS ANGRY and then the anger hardened into a pointed sadness. She cried for a few days and then flew to Minnesota because she couldn't stay in that awful apartment with David. She did not tell either of her parents what had happened because she could barely admit it to herself.

David went to The Leonard Company every day but didn't do anything. He just stared into his screens for twelve hours at a time. The blinking cursors had never seemed more useless. Every five minutes the light switched off and he would either wave an arm or sit in the dark. There were trades waiting to be put through and assets waiting to be transferred but David Taylor didn't care anymore.

Sitting in The Riverview with a tall glass of vodka, David called his lawyer and asked about the cost/benefit of filing for a divorce. This call was made after David Taylor found the photograph of him and Ethan Hoevel in Conference Room Three inside Samona's nightstand drawer.

David Taylor went to Minneapolis with the necessary papers to be signed, and it was not lost on him that they had been meaning to visit her parents in October anyway. Samona's father let him into the house. Samona was in her room, staring at a wall. All she said when she saw David was, "Did I miss anything?"

Tana cooked dinner and when they sat down to eat wondered aloud why everyone was silent. David looked so grim when she asked this that Samona's mother unhappily decided not to say anything else. Samona's father took David out for drinks since he had always been fond of David—they had both been SAE, after all, and they were brothers in a nostalgic sense—and he told him what a special girl Samona was, just like her mother, Tana, was special—"challenging but special" was how he phrased it—and that all marriages have their "highs and lows" and that somehow he knew David and Samona would find a way out of whatever it was they were lost in. David had no idea what to say to the man.

David and Samona walked around the rim of a lake near her parents' home and they told each other the things they already knew. The words took some of the horror away. David was carrying the papers with him. When they sat together on a rock at the far end of the water David placed the papers between them. They both stared down at all the small type and the bold lines where their signatures would be. This was when they stopped and considered their two options.

If they ended it, they would be erasing the last eight years of their lives together. David would have his job at The Leonard Company, and Samona would have a print shop on the outskirts of SoHo. David would forgive the investment in Printing Divine. Samona would leave the apartment. They would learn to live again, because that's what people did. They would do it with interest rates and fabric racks and updating magazine subscriptions—they would do it by busying themselves with the little things.

This prospect seemed utterly devoid of hope, and it led to the second option that neither had seriously considered. They could stay together. They wouldn't be able to forget everything that had happened but they could try to forgive. And if they found that they couldn't forgive, then they could pretend. And if they found they couldn't pretend anymore, the divorce papers weren't going any-where—that would always be an out. They agreed it would be so much easier living together. Maybe it was worth a try.

Before leaving the rock, Samona and David made a desperate vow.
They went back to New York.

David returned to work at The Leonard Company.

Samona spent fewer hours at Printing Divine. She took mornings
and evenings off and gave more responsibility to Martha and the
young (and drop-dead gorgeous, Samona couldn't help but notice)
assistant she had hired at the end of summer. The two of them soon
developed a bond that shut Samona out of every decision being
made. She became attuned to the sidelong glances, the muffled giggling, the bitter challenges to everything Samona said, no matter how
inconsequential, and she believed that the two of them were ganging
up on her to make her feel useless and—worse than that—incompetent.
When she mentioned this to David between sobs, he told her gently
that she "didn't need to be involved in that world anymore."

David laid a down payment on a house in Short Hills, New Jersey.
He had found it during the winter and put everything in motion right
away. Samona did not object. The adjustments—glassing in the porch,
laying a brick patio, installing an island in the kitchen—were completed by the end of April, and they left The Riverview during the first
week of May.

It was a nice house on Knollwood Road. A two-story, pale yellow
neo-Colonial with black shutters on a one-acre plot of land. Downstairs: a kitchen, a dining room, living room, a porch. Upstairs: two
bedrooms and a study with an angled ceiling. There was a stone-lined
pond in back. There were brick pillars at the driveway's entrance. There
was a mailbox with the silhouette of a bird flying in front of the sun.

David Taylor bought a new oak desk for his home office and
placed it in the study next to the black leather couch, which had been
moved from his office at The Leonard Company (he gave the Ethan
Hoevel Designs love seat to James Leonard's wife as a birthday gift).
Other items for the house included a $30,000 dining-room table
that seated six with a leaflet extension to accommodate four more, a
piano, a Sony home-entertainment system with a forty-two-inch
flat-screen TV, DVD player, surround sound, and a three-thousand-
disc hi-fi CD changer that worked like a jukebox, a John Deere
2004 model lawn mower, a Krups espresso machine, and a king-size

antique "opium bed" from a gallery on Wooster Street. They woke to the sound of water being filtered through the fishpond.

They would walk to town for mediocre Italian food or ice cream or a movie.

They set their espresso machine on an automatic timer which had coffee brewing in the morning before they woke up. They drank it together before David drove his new Lexus seven miles to the train station. The train ride was then forty-six minutes to Penn Station. Since Short Hills was relatively far out on the morning commute (eleven stops) David always had his own seat while he ate a bagel and read the *Times* and stared absently at the satellite towns passing by.

Unless she was meeting a friend in the city or going to an auction at Christie's, Samona stayed home reading magazines while she drank coffee in her nightgown until noon, at which point she got dressed. Then she would drive the Passat David had bought her to the Short Hills Mall a mile away or else she'd stay home and sketch or research the interior design company she wanted to start. She filled small notebooks with arcane details about this phantom company that she knew was never going to happen. She went to yoga four times a week.

Each day at Penn Station David would take the subway uptown to Forty-ninth and Broadway, where he hoped to avoid the car displaying the dermatologist ad with pictures of a homely woman with repulsive acne. He would use the walk from Forty-ninth to Fifty-first to clear his head and get ready for another day. On his thirtieth birthday there was a banner in the office, and a cake was brought in and presented to him by James Leonard.

If Samona was in the city for the day, sometimes David would head to wherever she was for lunch. He never stepped into Woo Lae Oak again, and she stayed away from Balthazar. During meals, they talked mostly about movies they wanted to rent. Occasionally they would have a minor argument.

When they began having sex again, they didn't use condoms or any contraceptive for that matter because there was no chance for Samona to become pregnant—the chlamydia David Taylor had contracted from Mattie McFarlane had left him sterile. This development didn't bother them because they had both made the decision—independently of each other—that bringing a child into the world they now inhabited was not something they wanted to do.

David registered with a mentorship nonprofit to spend three hours each month with an eleven-year-old boy from sad circumstances in Newark. Samona had been halfheartedly urging him to do this for three years, and for David it was a motion toward a greater ideal that he'd lost track of. The boy's name was Leonard (David found this coincidence unsettling), and he was a little overweight but still wore T-shirts that hung down to his knees. Leonard's father was in prison for manslaughter, his mother had run off with a crane operator, and Leonard lived with his single aunt and three younger cousins. The thing David noticed most was his oppressive quietness, which at first David assumed was due to being lonely and shy, but he soon realized was a reaction to all the gaping holes that lay between them—social, educational, financial—which David knew would be impossible to overcome, even if he tried hard. David's hesitant questions like "How's school going?" and "Do you have any brothers?" and "Hey, aren't there any girls you like at school?" were answered with dull grunts and murmurs. After three get-togethers spread over four months, David decided that Leonard made him uncomfortable, and besides it was too much time spent getting to Newark and looking for parking near a baseball field to play catch, which gave him blisters anyway, and worrying about the Lexus being broken into or, worse, stolen. He resigned from the program. "Someone else will be a lot better at it," he told the director during the brief phone call. Hearing himself say this—and believing the words—justified the decision.

Instead, to take his mind off things, David started running again in June. He bought a pair of New Balance trainers, woke up a half hour early each morning, and jogged slowly through the silent suburban streets. He could only make it a half mile at first before he became nauseated. By the end of July he was up to a mile and a half and breathing easier. During each of these runs he concluded that there had to be millions of people unhappier than he was. There simply had to be.

Samona started joining him. It was a gesture. She wanted to show that she was trying as hard as he was; that she, too, wanted it to work.

David was polite and refrained from telling her how much she annoyed him—her steady, exaggerated breathing, the way she balled her hands into tight fists with the thumb sticking straight up, the constant stream of questions ("Don't you think that house is totally pretentious?"; "Do you have time to pick up my skin cream at the M·A·C store on Twenty-second Street?")—yet her presence also distracted him from the darkness of his thoughts. Soon David wasn't so regretful of the series of choices he made that had landed him in this particular course in life, and he stopped dwelling on all the what-ifs. They both considered this to represent progress.

30

From: Svaughndelite@boiwear.com
To: Undisclosed Recipients
Sent: Sunday, November 14, 2:17 AM
Subject: Sublet my studio!

Dear Y'all,

Yup, it's happened—I sold my script to an indie
and now I'm leaving this goddamn city behind
. . . for La-La Land! I promise you all I will
romp with those Hollywood flame-boys in ways
they've never imagined.

In the meantime, I want to sublet my studio.
Most of you have seen it. I'm leaving it half-
furnished. Taking my writing table, TV shit,
computer (of course), posters, and clothes.
Everything else is yours, including the bed
(I promise no stains) for 1600/month, plus
utilities. Think about it, boys.

Regards, SV.

Stanton Vaughn called me to follow up on the mass e-mail—
"C'mon, you have to get out of the East Vill if you can afford it,
y'know? I'll even give you a discount!"—and after forcefully declining,
I listened numbly as he told me he was just "moving on with this crazy
shit-show known as my life" and "leaving everything else behind—
which I should have done a long time ago, y'know" and he was "trying
to quit smoking but it just doesn't seem in the realm of possibility
right now" and he was writing another screenplay. When I asked what
it was about Stanton said, "How can you fall in love with someone if
you fall in love with everyone?"

"Have you heard from Ethan?" I couldn't help asking.

Stanton scoffed. "Ethan's gone. Ethan disappeared."

"Do you—do you know where?"

"No. And I don't exactly think I'll hear from him after what went
down. Guess he went home to bury his brother and whatever . . ." He
trailed off, and then: "What a fuckin' nightmare, y'know?"

I rarely thought of Stanton Vaughn after that conversation ended.

Meanwhile, the Gowanus Canal story had been picked up and
commissioned for a series in the Sunday *New York Post* focusing on
underdeveloped, decaying places all over the five boroughs—the river-
bank under the George Washington Bridge, the dark corners of
Prospect Park in Brooklyn and the east section of Van Cortland in the
Bronx, the old armory building in Harlem, the Lower East Side
between East Broadway and Henry Street. I figured being able to pay
the rent would help me move on.

But it didn't.

I needed more than relative stability.

And I thought I might find it at the track reunion that December.
We were at Spring Lounge in Nolita, and David Taylor sat across the
table from me. He would smile sadly at the bland conversation and I
noted the distance between us. When dinner ended (David paid for
us all, as usual) David Taylor looked directly at me while he signed for
the bill. People drifted away as David sat there drinking a beer, glancing up at me with a look that told me to stay there with him. And then
it was just the two of us awkwardly walking outside where a recent
snow had left mounds of dirt and ice on the curb. I scanned the

street hoping to see a cab. David put his hand on my shoulder and gave it a gentle squeeze.

"You used to do that before every race," I murmured.

"Where are you headed now?"

I was wondering why David had wanted this moment to occur—what he hoped to get out of it.

"Home."

"You know we plan on moving soon. Jersey."

I nodded at the "we" and buried my chin in the collar of my coat, marveling at the way David Taylor could act as if that summer had never existed, as if he had never pressed his body against Ethan Hoevel's, as if I'd never been in love with his wife. He had somehow put all that to bed, and I was—once again—envious of David Taylor.

A cab rolled up Lafayette.

"You take this one," he said.

"You can have it, David."

He nodded and shook my hand weakly. "Hope to see you around sometime."

"Maybe at the next reunion?"

And then he was gone.

Since it was just a few blocks away I walked over to Greene Street to see Samona that evening. I had no idea what I was going to say exactly and when I got there I stood around outside and scuffed my shoes on the icy sidewalk, looking in the windows from across the street, trying to steal a glance at her face, her profile, her shadow—just a glance was all I wanted anymore. But I couldn't see anything, and then I finally worked up the nerve to go inside only to be told by Martha that—as of two weeks ago—Samona wasn't a part of Printing Divine anymore.

I went home for Christmas.

The year ended.

I informed my list of editors that I would not be "participating" in Winter Fashion Week that February.

I hadn't seen Ethan since September, and no one I knew had any idea where he'd gone.

And still I couldn't free myself from that muted feeling of detachment I'd felt ever since leaving Ethan Hoevel's roof last May (and in some ways, ever since coming to New York): the feeling of being rooted in a particular moment that was gone; the feeling of existing in an opportunity that you've already missed; the feeling of knowing how a single moment can ensure you'll never get it back again.

And when a UPS man buzzed the apartment on Tenth Street near the beginning of spring, I went down the six flights of stairs and signed for a box the size of a small television set. It was heavy and I had to stop twice to rest on the way back to my apartment. Ethan Hoevel's name and the address of a Mail Boxes Etc. on Mercer were attached, along with a note taped under the top flap, which said: *What's more than "good friends"?*

Inside the box was the black wing encased in a glass vacuum.

When I plugged it in the air didn't flow through the way it had been intended—the current wasn't strong enough since the air was leaking out through the glass I had broken.

I put it up on my bureau in the top corner of the room and stared at it for a while. It grew dark outside, and I was alone amid the shadows cast by streetlights and the dull murmurs of city noise drifting up and the frigid air seeping through the windows, and then, in that place, I no longer needed to wonder where Ethan had disappeared to—whether it was home to Long Beach or off traveling by himself or somewhere else I probably couldn't imagine if I tried. Because what I was left with was this thing he'd made, which took me back to a particular moment in our lives: we hadn't spoken in almost two semesters and Ethan Hoevel invited me to his lab to see his senior project, and I didn't know where I was heading and had no idea what would happen to any of us and all I could really be certain of was that it was snowing and dark and I was trudging alone uphill. After I arrived outside the lab and stood in the cold too long, I finally went in. Ethan was waiting for me in his small cluttered office. We didn't touch. He simply motioned toward the glass case and, without explaining what it was, turned it on. As we both watched the wing oscillate in its vacuum he quietly said, "Do you like it?" and he moved around the table beside me and he was so close I could feel him breathing. The only other sound was the soft whisper of air flowing through the vacuum, and that

was when I understood how he'd created this thing out of the disen-
chantment that I'd caused.

That night, in my dream, I take the same route to his loft that I usually
do: down Lafayette, across Grand, down West Broadway, and I enter
the elevator (in the dream I know the code). The rug is rolled up in
the living room. The furniture's gone. The bedroom/studio has
been disassembled. Most of the cookware from all over the world is
packed in boxes.

I open the refrigerator for a beer but it's empty. I hear U2's new
album playing softly as background music while I climb the spiral
staircase to the roof. Ethan is sitting in a chair drinking a glass of
wine and smoking a cigarette, watching the helicopters flying low over
the river. It's getting cold but he's only wearing a denim jacket. It fits
him well.

And since Ethan doesn't see me (it's a dream and he didn't know I
was coming) I just gaze at the back of his head. And even though he
must hear my heavy breathing and be aware that I'm standing there, he
doesn't turn around.

I leave silently and walk along the river smoking cigarettes for a
while before heading home along Jane Street.

I don't need to think about him.

People fade, people disappear—it's happening all the time.

I can move on.

These are the things I tell myself when I wake up.

Acknowledgments

David Halpern—a great agent and a great, great friend. Sarah Self, who was kind enough to read an unpublished, unagented wannabe "writer," and then make a tremendous phone call, for which I will always be grateful. Terra Chalberg for her many, many insights and unwavering intelligence in editing this book.

Mom and Dad for reading to me when I broke my leg at age three, and for being there always. Bryan, Lindsay, Andy, Grandma, and all my family, for love and support beyond my capacity to describe.

Kathy Robbins, Yaniv Soha, Kate Rizzo, and everyone at the Robbins Office. My teachers: Hugh Atkins, John Crowley, Nelson Donegan, Laurie Edinger, John MacKay, David Marshal, John Robinson. My friends and family: Thom Bishops, Carter Coleman, James, Martina, Jackson, and Louis Donahower, Josie Freedman, James Jordan, Mara Medoff, Seamus Moran, Alexia Paul, Marty Scott, Marion and Henry Silliman, Cara Silverman, Halsey and Gretchen Spruance, Jess and Andy Wuertele, David Yamner. The always-inspiring Learnard Girls: Emmie, Ruthie, Lainie, Annie, Pixie, and Batab. Martin and Sugar Goldstein for welcoming me to "The Family" in true Brooklyn style.

My best friend, Noah, who slept faithfully at my feet throughout the lengthy and quite boring (for him, since he's a dog) composition of these pages.

Lastly, Rebecca, for an infinity of reasons that have nothing to do with this or any book, and one that does: I will forever cherish *The Tourists* for the chance it gave to meet and fall in love with my wife.

About the Author

JEFF HOBBS graduated from Yale in 2002 with a BA in English language and literature. Hobbs spent three years in New York and Tanzania while working with the African Rainforest Conservancy. He now lives in Los Angeles with his wife, Rebecca, and their dog, Noah.